"I promise not to hit you again,"
she replied, forcing a light tone. "If you promise not to throw me to the ground and—"

"And?" One eyebrow shot up.

"Provoke me."

He laughed then, a full, rich sound that seemed to drop the tension from his face. He was more recognizable now, and Madeline felt her shoulders relax.

"I am sorry," she added. "My behavior that day was unforgivable. I do hope we can start over as friends, Lord Douglas."

She held out her hand, the small warning bell in her head quickly silenced.

"It would be my pleasure." He took the offered fingers, bending slightly to press them against his lips. Not a trace of impropriety, but a sigh caught in her throat all the same, and she held it there, no longer breathing.

In the back of her mind she knew this was not a good idea. She knew perfectly well she should invent some excuse, run straight back into the ballroom and discuss Lady Farris's flowers. She didn't move.

"And since we are already intimately acquainted, I must insist you call me Colin."

"Colin," she said, finally exhaling so the name rushed out in a breathless tone. She wildly searched her mind for something else to say but never managed a word.

Colin pulled her to him, the kiss as much a surprise as her own response to it. Madeline's body instantly betrayed her, melting against the strong arms that held her until she had lost all sense of her earlier outrage. The world fell away, leaving nothing but Colin's searing lips blistering her own—and the faint smell of lilacs.

Also by Jennifer Ann Coffeen...

LOVER'S GAMBLE

Sophie Hartlend likes to play with fire.

The reckless and beautiful Miss Sophie has spent her young life doing whatever she pleases without much consequence—except for that one night when passions went too far with the maddeningly handsome Lord Rayburn.

Months after their encounter, Sophie's newfound infatuation with gambling has landed her in trouble, threatening her precious independence. Lord Rayburn gallantly offers to help, but he insists the wild Miss Sophie do things his way. Once again they find themselves in a battle of wills, attracted but with opposing views.

Will Sophie relent when she discovers she must lay down all her cards in order to win Lord Rayburn's heart?

~published by The Wild Rose Press

Priceless Deception

by

Jennifer Ann Coffeen

Ryam,

So great getting to know you!

Hope you enjoy the regency romps!

Priceless Deception

COPYRIGHT © 2011 by Jennifer Ann Coffeen

Cover Art by *Tina Lynn Stout*

The Wild Rose Press
PO Box 706
Adams Basin, NY 14410-0706
Visit us at www.thewildrosepress.com

Publishing History
First English Tea Rose Edition, 2011
Print ISBN 1-60154-947-4

Published in the United States of America

Dedication

To my husband

Chapter One

London, England
April 1812

"Fresh rolls for a haypenny!" The burly man yelled from his stall, ignorant of the young boy snaking a small hand around the man's back to pinch an apple. "Fruit for a shilling! Hey, come back here, you little scamp, afore I tear your head off!" Lady Madeline Sinclair held her breath as the fruit seller swatted his massive hand, but the child was gone, instantly absorbed into the early morning crowd.

Unable to suppress a grin for the little thief, Madeline sat back against the plush velvet seat of Lady Milburg's new carriage, wondering again how her aunt could suddenly afford such a luxurious vehicle. After scarcely a week in London, Madeline had not failed to notice the strange custom of openly flaunting one's wealth, whether one actually possessed wealth or not.

Tense and restless, she batted away an errant lock of russet hair for the fourth time. Why could her hair never stay put when it needed to, she thought, shoving the heavy mass under her hood before turning back to the window. Her restless gaze roamed over the streets, the noisy shouts and chaotic hum of the city overwhelming her almost as much as the exotic unwashed scents wafting through the carriage window. It was exhilaration and disorder all at once, creating a small bubble of excitement around the grief she had carried since

1

her father died.

I buried the diamond in the cellar, under the floorboards, the eighth stone from the stairs. You must find it, Maddie, before it's too late.

It had been barely six months since Madeline found herself thrust from a peaceful though admittedly lonely home in the wilds of northern Scotland. It was the only home she could remember, though she had been born in England and still had relatives here, information her father told her only days before his death.

Lady Milburg is your mother's older sister, Maddie. You must go to her. Make your way to London and the house where we once lived, 52 Baker Street. There you will find it—the French Blue diamond.

Brimming with excitement and fear, Madeline could barely remain still. After spending the long winter months ensconced in her aunt's country home in Norfolk, she had finally arrived in London. At last! While Aunt Cecilia spent her first days in London buying dresses and procuring invitations to only the most fabulous of parties in the infamous Season, Madeline had quickly formulated a plan to fulfill her vow. If there truly was a diamond buried in the cellar of their old home, then she would find it, just as she had promised.

"I could murder him!" Lady Helena Weston, most beloved daughter to the Marchioness of Milburg, wailed for the tenth time, her voice twisting in self pity. "Horrible, despicable Lord Vickem! The man is determined to ruin me!"

Madeline tore her gaze away from the carriage window to cast a quick glance at her distraught cousin. The heart-shaped face surrounded by perfectly arranged blonde curls usually left Madeline with the impression of a highly excitable cherub. This morning, however, the bright cheeks were stained with tears as Helena crushed an unwanted love letter inside her small fist, as though wishing it was the neck of the man who penned it.

"This is the very thing he did last season, Madeline! Sending me awful letters every day, professing his love in public. No other man would come near me! Lord Vickem is determined that I am to be his wife, but why?"

"Perhaps he truly has feelings for you," Madeline offered. "Though I must admit his poetry is awful. Is he still attempting to rhyme your name with obscure French words?" Though a full three years older, Madeline didn't have the faintest idea how to counsel anyone's love affairs, but no one seemed aware of this shortcoming.

A snort of outrage bounced through the tiny carriage.

"A rapturous merlin could not do you justice, my love. You have flown overhead and sunk your talons in my heart."

Helena smacked the letter down. "There, do you see? He not only compares me to a bird but a horrible, ugly, brown, shrieking one!"

"It is rather humiliating," Madeline admitted, marveling over the man's strange obsession with Helena. Lord Vickem had yet to arrive in London, yet her cousin received love notes daily, ranging from outrageous to absurd. "What is he like in person?"

"Oh much worse, a horrible, whey-faced, little rat of a man—"

Helena's tirade was cut off as the carriage lurched drunkenly, causing both women to shriek.

"Slow down, Sam!" Madeline shouted at the groom as the carriage jolted back onto the road. She knew perfectly well he couldn't hear her, but she found a good shout to be a soothing balm to her mounting frustration. The morning was not going at

3

all as she planned. Sam had been recklessly driving them around the streets of London for nearly an hour, leaving Madeline with grave misgivings about his ability to handle a carriage.

This was taking much longer than she had anticipated; what if her Aunt Cecilia awoke early and found them gone? Madeline pushed aside her guilt, turning back toward the window in time to see the weak light of dawn stealing across the clouds.

What choice did she have? She knew perfectly well her dear aunt would strongly disapprove of her niece stealing her carriage and sneaking off before sunrise, but today could very well be her only chance to find the French Blue diamond! It had taken no small amount of planning and bribery to escape this morning; there was nothing else to be done. Her plan simply had to work.

"Mama even had the gall to say Lord Vickem should be considered a suitor this year. Isn't that awful?" Helena continued on, unable to think past her own woes. "I know exactly what her plan is. Mama is hoping I will soften toward that odious man, and then she can marry me right off," she scoffed. "Vickem must have heard of our regrettable situation, or he would have never dared to renew his advances. Well, if he believes I will marry him just because we are poor, he can think again! I don't care if he has all the riches in England. I find him horrid and dull as sticks. What do you think, Madeline?"

"I think at this speed we will surely break a wheel and end up floating in the Thames," Madeline muttered, cursing Sam and his horrible driving. She and Helena suddenly lurched forward, forcing Madeline to throw out a hand to steady herself as they made yet another aimless circle through the maze of London streets.

"You don't agree with Mama, do you? That I should be forced to marry someone so horrid?"

The pitch in Helena's voice was steadily rising, a clear warning that she was on the edge of tears. "Of course not," Madeline quickly replied, wondering how on earth her cousin could still be discussing suitors when they seemed mere moments away from crashing. "I was only pondering the problem, that's all. Perhaps you should tell him you are in love with another," she offered. "If Lord Vickem believes you are taken, surely he will cease his attentions. A man does have his pride." She held her breath while Helena's face brightened at the advice.

"Madeline, you are so very clever! That's just the thing to do."

She returned her cousin's smile. *Dealing with suitors isn't so very difficult,* Madeline told herself. *I wonder why everyone raises such a fuss about it.* Even her father had been stern in his warnings of men, but they all seemed like silly fops to her. Madeline gratefully turned her attention back to more important matters, nervously drumming her fingers together as she peered out into the murky grey light.

"We must be getting close," she whispered. "Any moment now."

Her cousin gave a loud yelp as the carriage hit an enormous bump in the road. "I feel this is a bad idea, Madeline. It's unnaturally early to pay a call, even a secret one." Helena suddenly leaned forward, grasping Madeline's arm. "Can you not see Sam is hopelessly lost? And Mama will never recover if she finds we went out alone. Perhaps we should go back."

Madeline bit back a shout of denial, forcing her expression into a reassuring smile. "Your Mama won't notice a thing. She is suffering from a terrible cold, remember? No doubt she will sleep until noon, and by then we shall have all your problems with Vickem sorted out."

"I guess that's true," Helena admitted, reluctantly leaning back in her seat, "and Brigette did give her a large dose of wine before bed. Mama does tend to sleep late after she's had a little wine."

She does indeed. Under most circumstances Aunt Cecilia took her duties as chaperone very seriously, scarcely letting her niece and daughter out of her sight, but one too many glasses of wine and Aunt Cecilia's sharp eyes began to glaze over with indifference.

"Everything will be fine," Madeline reassured her cousin with a bright smile. "I'm simply going to pop inside our old home and be back before you know it!"

Helena's brow flew up in alarm. "You're not planning to go inside the house, are you, Madeline? I thought we were only going to look at it!"

"A small change of plans," Madeline hastily replied. It had been the tiniest of lies; she had needed Helena's help to procure the carriage, and her skittish cousin never would have agreed if she knew Madeline's real reasons for visiting the house on Baker Street. "But I cannot come all this way and not look inside! I promise to be very quick. Now then, tell me again how Lord Vickem humiliated you last year?"

But Helena wasn't to be so easily distracted. She merely shrugged, nervously twisting her hands around her dainty pink parasol.

Desperate to reach her destination, Madeline began to feel slightly sick as Lady Milburg's carriage made its third circle past the immense homes of Mayfair. It was nearly light now, and there was little doubt Sam had been less than truthful when he claimed to know his way around London. *We are indeed hopelessly lost,* she despaired; *the sun will rise at any moment, and Aunt Cecilia will wake to find us gone...*

The carriage jolted to a stop.

Madeline glanced up as two sharp knocks were heard from the top of the carriage—a signal from Sam.

"Have we arrived?" Helena whispered. "Is this the house you are looking for?"

"52 Baker Street," Madeline slowly replied, sharing her cousin's look of apprehension. "There's no time to be afraid now."

The carriage door flew open on her declaration, revealing young Sam, his face flushed bright red with excitement under the oversized coachman's hat. Madeline had insisted he dress in the dark green livery of a proper groom, and he played the part rather well for a fifteen-year-old boy.

"I finally found it, my lady!" he announced, shooting her a rascal grin before remembering to fall into a low bow.

Madeline laughed at the sight of Sam's impish grin. *It seems everyone is rather swept into my intrigue today, although Sam should be smiling after what he's been paid.*

"Excellent, Sam. I had complete faith in you," she lied, accepting his hand to step out of the carriage.

"What should we do?" Helena asked. "Just knock on the door?"

"If I may suggest something, my lady? If you really wish to be sneakin' up on the house and such, goin' round through the servants' doors would be my choice." Sam tugged at the collar of the green velvet coat. "If you wait here a moment, I'll take a peek inside the kitchens and see if anyone's about."

"Wonderful idea, Sam!" Madeline knew she had bribed the right servant. "But do hurry. We mustn't waste any more time."

He stumbled into a quick bow and ran off, leaving Madeline and Helena alone beside the carriage.

"Do you really mean to go inside?" Helena asked as they stared up at the white stone townhouse Sam had pointed out to them. "Why, a madman could be living here, for all we know! Some sad soul gibbering away in his nightclothes like our poor King."

Madeline barely heard her. For all her trepidation, the house at 52 Baker Street looked quite normal. It stood tall and dignified along the rows of other stone townhouses; the only thing setting it apart from its neighbors was the black iron spires that surrounded each window, looming out at her like sharp claws. *This was our home.* Her parents had walked these very steps together many times, perhaps on their way out to dine with friends, or to find refuge inside and spend a quiet evening alone. *I should have grown up here.*

"Could we not just leave a note with one of the servants?" Helena pleaded. "Surely whoever lives here will respond with a gracious letter or an invitation to tea." Madeline barely heard her over the blood rushing in her ears.

I'm here, Papa. I've almost found it. She was so close now; she had to get inside, find her way to the cellar.

"Madeline, I think we should—"

"We're in!" Sam ran up to the carriage, his eyes flashing with excitement. "I spoke to Greta, the cook, and a pleasing one she is, too. Said she'd be more than happy to let you sneak in through the back door. Promises she won't even glance your way, if you're real quiet."

Madeline clapped her hands together. "Sam, what would I ever do without you? You certainly have earned your fee."

He shuffled his feet, pleased by the praise. "Just don't be tellin' Brigette about this, if you don't mind. I wouldn't want her to get the wrong idea."

"I see." She hid her smile, wondering how many kitchen maids young Sam was courting. "Your secret is safe with me. Come, Helena!"

"Madeline, I am beginning to fear this plan," her cousin pleaded as they approached the townhouse. "I know I promised to accompany you, but truly I am less courageous than I seem."

"Perhaps you should watch the door," Madeline interrupted, unable to wait a moment longer. Dawn was fast approaching, and she could not spare another moment to soothe Helena's fears. "I shall quickly dash inside, and then we can return home before your mother has begun to stir."

With a nod of relief, Helena pressed herself against the large white pillars, and Madeline took her chance. Moving quickly, she crept down the stairs leading to the basement, glancing back to see the hem of Helena's gown swishing nervously between the iron railings.

She slipped inside the door, finding it unlocked just as Sam had promised. As she made her way through the kitchens, Madeline could have sworn she saw a pair of eyes peeking out from behind a rack of pots. Greta? She didn't dare stop to investigate.

Moving out of the smoky kitchen, Madeline's gaze spotted the only other door in the cramped corridor, and she rushed toward it.

It was locked.

Even when she employed all of her strength, the half-rusted door didn't budge. To come all this way and find the cellar door locked? Madeline bit back a frustrated scream. It would not do. She had to find the diamond today; this was her only chance. Even if by some miracle Aunt Cecilia failed to notice her ward's sudden disappearance, Madeline would be hard pressed to manage such an escape again.

"Greta!" she whispered, praying the pair of eyes

did indeed belong to Sam's friend. She went back into the kitchen and found a round little woman, dark hair springing out from beneath her cap, peeping out from behind the pots.

"Can I help you, my lady?" She looked Madeline up and down, clearly bewildered by the sight of her in the kitchen.

"Please excuse my intrusion," Madeline began, deciding the only way out of this mess was extreme politeness. "I seem to have encountered a problem. The door next to this one, it leads to the cellar?"

"It does, my lady."

"Oh, marvelous." She smiled, hoping to put the woman at ease. "I know this is terribly inconvenient, but I must get in there right away, and the door is rather locked. Could you possibly give me the key?" Madeline tried her best to look harmless; she didn't want poor Greta to think she was some kind of thief, but the maid was shaking her head.

"I'm so sorry, my lady, but I haven't got that key, or any other, for that matter. Mr. Halbert keeps all of that sort of thing, and guards them something fierce, I should say." Over her fears, Greta stepped out from her hiding place, still talking. "Would never let one out of his sight for fear of someone sneakin' off with one of the master's fine possessions. No, you'll never get that key away from Mr. Halbert, that's for certain. Though I do believe Lord Douglas keeps a spare set in his study."

"Lord Douglas?" Madeline snapped to attention. "He owns this house?"

Greta nodded. "Yes, my lady, for several weeks now. I've only recently come to work here myself."

"And this Lord Douglas, does he usually sleep late?"

"Oh, yes, my lady, he stays out till all hours of the night. I believe he's drowning his sorrows after breaking that beautiful lady's heart. A true shame, that was."

"Of course," Madeline muttered absently, her mind quickly turning. Did she dare take such a risk? There was nothing to be done; she had come this far. She must have that key. "Tell me, Greta," she said, plucking up her courage with a charming smile, "which direction is Lord Douglas's study?"

Chapter Two

Madeline reached the ground floor, praying the rest of the servants had not yet begun their day. Thankfully, the entrance hall was empty—deserted, really; it stood silent as a tomb. The stark walls around her held no color or decoration, nothing to give her an idea of the man who now owned them.

She made her way past the first room, pausing to peek inside at the gold-splashed dining room, magnificently laid out as though guests would be seating themselves in the majestic red velvet chairs at any moment. It opened up into an equally splendid drawing room, decorated with a light blue wallpaper and matching curtains shielding full windows that, when opened, would spill sunlight throughout the enticing room. This was obviously where Lord Douglas entertained his guests, when he allowed them in, she recalled. Still, very odd to have these beautiful rooms hidden behind such a bare front hall; almost as if Lord Douglas only wished for those invited inside to be comfortable.

Shrugging off her strange thoughts, Madeline moved toward the last door. It was firmly shut, unlike the others, and with a pounding heart she pushed it open, her other hand clenched at her side.

The study stood empty, though it certainly had the look of a well-inhabited room. Stacks of books and papers were hurled about with little care, several lying precariously close to a dwindling fire. A fawn-colored coat and boots had been tossed recklessly on the desk, resting against a tray filled with smooth glass bottles of spirits, most of them empty. A rather unkempt man, she thought, marveling at the mess. Her meticulous father would be horrified. *Why, it looks as though Lord Douglas has been living in here!* Not even the dust stirred when she crept across the thick Persian carpet, and a strange feeling of foreboding prickling her skin.

Madeline moved toward the once beautiful mahogany desk, littered with Lord Douglas's correspondence, most of it invitations to various balls, breakfasts, garden parties: *Lord Eversham duly invites you to... The Countess and Earl of Maybury cordially invite Lord Douglas... Lord and Lady Farris request the pleasure of Lord Colin, Duke of Douglas's company...* She sifted through them, marveling over the amount. Despite all the rumors, Lord Douglas must be an immensely popular man. Far beneath the large pile, Madeline unearthed an intriguing letter, written with a firm and direct hand.

Colin,

Do be so kind as to answer my letter this time. I understand from your brother that although you are still recovering from your misfortunes, you are well enough to hold a pen. I shall return to London in one week's time and hope to find you in better spirits than when I left. The date for my dinner party has been set for the twenty-first. I have informed everyone that my sons will be in attendance. I fully expect an argument. You shall find me prepared when I arrive.

Much love,

Mother

Madeline refolded the letter, scolding herself for wasting valuable time. Helena was likely in a full panic. She opened the top drawer of the desk and, to her great delight, saw a large ring of keys sitting right on top, as though they had been waiting for her. Seizing them triumphantly, Madeline had turned to leave when out of the corner of her eye she noticed the sleeping man.

He was lying on a chair, sprawled out in complete abandon, his long legs spilling onto the rug. One hand had fallen to the floor, carelessly throwing wide the unbuttoned shirt that hung from his shoulders. Madeline stepped softly over to him, drawn by a strange fascination.

A beautiful man, she thought, staring down at him. He seemed born from the very earth, with his coal black hair, his skin smooth as bronzed marble. His chiseled features were hammered into a slight frown, reminding her of the many statues of Greek warriors she had seen throughout the city, and only the faint snore he emitted told her she was not gazing upon stone. Who was this man?

Her curious gaze drifted down to his chest, and she blushed, awed by the tanned muscles beneath. *He's an Adonis,* she thought wildly, remembering the story of the Greek god born from the bark of a myrrh tree.

His face was flushed red in the early morning chill, and Madeline reached out to smooth the frown beneath his dark locks. Her Adonis stirred restlessly against her hand, as though uncomfortable in his own skin, and it was then she saw the large jagged cut, red and angry with infection, above his left eye. How did he come by such an injury? It must have happened fairly recently, she thought, noting the dried blood crusted around the edges.

He moved then, making her jump as the white cloth of his shirt opened further, revealing a thick scar across his chest. Truly hypnotized now, Madeline reached out to him, wondering what mishap had befallen her Adonis. He wasn't invincible after all—

"Don't!" Something snaked out from below, clutching her arm, and Madeline tumbled in surprise as her fanciful statue turned to life.

She managed to catch only a blur as she fell, shrieking when her back hit the floor. Her next scream only made it to the edge of her throat before being cut off by Adonis's large hand on her mouth, the man's charming frown now replaced by the most ferocious glare she'd ever seen. He loomed over her, pinning her to the ground with only one arm.

"What are you doing in here?" The voice matched his threatening scowl, and Madeline fought the stranger, trying unsuccessfully to push him away. His tousled dark hair, black as the devil's soul, brushed against her cheek.

"Let go of me!" she whispered hoarsely, annoyed that the sound came out so weak. She repeated it again, this time in a shout.

"Who are you? What are you doing in my house?"

She shook her head and fought against the iron bands that held her prisoner as the brute increased the pressure on her arm until she feared the very bones might snap.

"My father sent me!" she finally screamed at him. "Now let me go!" He lessened his hold only the slightest, while Madeline struggled to sit up, desperately aware of his large hand only inches from her breast, his legs appallingly draped across hers.

She was bewildered; was this awful man Lord Douglas? She wrinkled her nose, suddenly aware of a strong scent of spirits, likely brandy. Why, the man was half drunk! She glared harder at him, instantly disgusted.

"Your father sent you to kill me?" The wicked man drew back in surprise.

He is mad, Madeline decided, as her ears rang from his bellows. Helena had informed her of those sad, unfortunate souls tucked away in the city, gentlemen whose minds were broken and raving, hidden away in the family's home, far from the prying eyes of society. She had obviously discovered Lord Douglas's secret, and he would soon lock her in his underground dungeon full of rat bones.

He gave her a small shake. "Answer me!"

Madeline's patience vanished, dissolved into the air like a puff of smoke. She'd had enough of this, madman or not.

"Unhand me!" she shouted back, freeing one arm from the steel trap of his grip, and before he could react she clenched her hand into a small fist and sent it flying, with all the strength she possessed, directly into his injured eye. Her estimations had been correct; the wound apparently felt as raw as it looked, for Adonis let out a shout of pain and fell backward, releasing her completely.

"Sir, I don't know who the bloody hell you are, but if anyone should fear for her life it would be me." Madeline stood up, snatching the precious keys back into her hand. "I came here simply to fulfill a small duty, nothing more, no nefarious murder plots of any kind." She ended her tirade with a fierce nod, watching Adonis's pale sweaty face as he cradled his eye.

His thunderous expression was slowly clouding over to one of confusion. "You haven't been sent to kill me?"

Madeline's mouth fell open. "Kill you?" she yelled at him. "What a preposterous thing to say! Perhaps if you worked a bit on your evil manners you wouldn't worry about such things." He was staring at her, a stunned look on his face, as though her head had popped off and rolled onto the floor. Madeline stared back, her anger fading a bit as she saw that his wound had begun bleeding again. Her Adonis was truly hurt, she realized, watching him struggle to his feet. Despite his terrible manners and obvious drunkenness she felt a twinge of guilt for inflicting more pain on the man.

"I believe your wound is infected," she added, keeping a fair distance. "You need to wash it in warm water and then apply a poultice of garlic and vinegar to draw out the infection."

"Garlic and vinegar?" he asked, his tone suggesting that she was the insane one, and Madeline took immediate offense.

"You certainly won't regain your health by wallowing about in this appalling mess," she informed him with a haughty sweep of her hand. "This room isn't fit to be seen by anyone decent!"

"That is precisely the reason," he replied testily, "that I did not offer you an invitation into my study. Who are you?" he demanded.

She took a step back. "My name is of no importance to you, sir, for I doubt we will ever meet again, though you are welcome to remember me as the innocent lady you assaulted for no reason."

To tell the truth, she hoped for a contrite word or two from him but was left empty; the chiseled face looked slightly amused, but not the least bit sorry.

"And why have you chosen to break into my study today, Lady Innocent?" he inquired, the question put so mildly it took her a moment to realize it was mocking her. Lord Douglas seemed more relaxed, now that he had decided she wasn't planning to slit his throat. He leaned casually against the door, not coincidentally her only means of escape, and nodded toward her hands. "And are those my keys that you are hiding behind your back like a jealous lover?"

She masked her embarrassment with a frown, her fingers tightening around the cool metal. "Is it possible, sir, that I could leave now? Or shall I have to endure a few more insults first? If so, please do hurry them along, for the day is passing quickly."

He opened his mouth, and, braced for another rude remark, she was surprised by his laughter, a loud booming sound that stripped all the hard lines from his face, making him look at once softer and rather handsome.

He finished the laugh with a shake of his head. "Whoever you are, you certainly say the most outrageous things. You must not be from London, with a mouth like that." He met her eyes when he said this, and she felt a sudden heat shoot directly into her, causing her next breath to vanish. Did all men in London speak this way?

"I beg your pardon?" she stammered.

"Your accent," he said, though she knew perfectly well that wasn't what he meant. "Northern Scotland?"

She nodded, wondering how he knew. No one else had been able to detect her slight accent at all, thanks to Aunt Cecilia's many hours of forced language lessons.

"You hide it very well," he said, the beginnings of a smile crinkling his eyes. "I can only hear it when you're shouting."

Madeline didn't trust herself to speak.

"Come, then." He took a step toward her; she shrieked, quickly covering her lips.

"The keys," he said impatiently. "For God's sake, woman, you don't think I'm going to let you walk off with them? Do I look as though I wish to be robbed this morning?"

She pressed them tightly against her chest. "You look like an asylum patient, sir, and I resent your continued suggestion that I am some sort of a thief. I have never stolen anything in my life."

"Do you dare to call me a liar? In my own home?"

She was convinced the windows would soon shatter from his roars.

"No woman has ever called me a liar!"

"Perhaps not to your face," she replied, "but with

a temper like yours, who knows what is said behind your back? I personally think I was being complimentary."

Closing his eyes, Lord Douglas laid one palm against the top of his forehead. *Serves him right,* she thought. *He has given himself a terrible headache.*

"Then perhaps you would care to tell me why you are here." His voice had turned dangerously mild, and Madeline found she much preferred the shouting.

"It's quite simple, really." Madeline raced through her mind for a plausible story, one that would get her away from the horrible Lord Douglas and back down to the cellar. "I am new to your city and not yet used to all the streets." She paused to offer an embarrassed laugh. "I'm afraid to say I've become hopelessly lost and..."

Madeline's words fell dead upon her lips. Somewhere in the far recesses of her mind she heard Lord Douglas speaking to her, but she made no sense of it. Her attention was riveted on a small portrait, about the size of a good novel, hanging just above the door. She didn't know how she could have missed it before, the proud beautiful woman gently posing in her best finery, with a subtle, playful smile upon her lips. The woman's face was beautifully drawn, likely bringing pleasure to many who had gazed upon it, but to Madeline that face brought only horror. It was her own.

"Please tell me," she whispered, forcing out one word after another, "who is the lady in that portrait?"

Lord Douglas looked behind him before answering. "Some Lady Caithness or other. My servants found it and it intrigued me, so I had it placed in here." A low churning noise began in her ears, and Madeline felt the small seed of panic take root in her stomach, beginning its slow journey through her limbs. She watched as Lord Douglas turned back to her, an eerie awareness forming in his eyes. "She looks exactly like you."

Her fear was confirmed. A small cry escaped her lips as the panic suddenly burst forth in full bloom, the weight of it nearly knocking her to the floor.

The look on her face must have alarmed him, for Lord Douglas was instantly at her side, concern furrowing his brow. He took her arm, his touch tender and undemanding now, and eased her into the chair. "Sit down." He spoke quietly. "You've had quite a shock."

A long minute passed before Madeline's breathing calmed. When she finally looked up, she found Lord Douglas kneeling in front of her, carefully taking her measure.

"You weren't simply taking a walk, were you?"

"A what?"

"It's not important." He rested his hands gently on her shoulders. "Did you come here looking for that portrait?"

"She's dead," Madeline replied, the wave of terror surfacing once again.

She feared the argument would go on until nightfall, but her infuriating companion called out, "Halbert!"

"Your Grace?" The door opened at once, leaving Madeline little doubt the ancient white-coated butler had been standing outside the room for some time.

"Shall I fetch salts to revive the lady?" Halbert asked, apparently finding nothing amiss about a strange lady in his employer's study.

"You're the one who won't let the keys out of your sight," Madeline said to the butler, finding solace in her memory of the kind Greta. "Everyone seems afraid of thieves in this house." She was babbling but couldn't seem to stop herself.

"Perhaps I should call Dr. Harwin," Halbert

said, eyeing her carefully, and Madeline flapped one hand at him, embarrassed by all the fuss.

"No, thank you, I promise not to faint." She pushed Lord Douglas's arms away and squeezed her eyes tight, trying to stop her shaking fingers. How had this happened? She had meant to be out of the house in only a few moments. And what was her dead mother's portrait still doing in this room?

"Thank you, Halbert." She heard Lord Douglas dismissing his servant. "One moment," he added.

"Yes, milord?" Halbert hesitated at the door, clearly anxious to stay.

"Have you ever seen this woman before?"

"No, Lord Douglas, though I do not doubt she is somehow connected to the young lady hiding in your rose bushes."

Madeline's head jerked up as the door closed. Helena! Good Lord, her cousin must be frantic.

"I must go." Madeline pulled herself to her feet, taking one last glance at her mother's portrait before opening the door.

"Please wait." Lord Douglas gently took her hand, and she marveled over the change in him.

"I cannot," she replied, stubbornly, unable to remain in this room a moment longer. She needed time to think, to place her emotions aside until she could decide what should be done. And Lord Douglas's nearness wasn't helping. He held her up as though she were a feeble old woman, and Madeline felt overwhelmed by him, her thoughts no longer her own.

"I must get back," she said, angry at the sudden tears that sparked her eyes. "I've made a terrible mistake. I'm sorry."

"I don't think it was a mistake." He tightened his hold on her hand, slowly pulling her toward him until she met his eyes. *Such an unusual color,* Madeline thought foolishly, *a mix of blue and grey*

21

like a stormy sea, and he's so very tall! Her forehead reached to just below his mouth, and Madeline shuddered slightly when he reached out to wipe the tears from her cheeks.

"I would like to help you," he said softly, bending closer, his hands cautiously making their way around her waist. "And I confess I am intrigued by a lady who would go to such lengths to steal my keys." He slipped them from her hand, but Madeline didn't move.

She had never been this close to a man before, and the effect was fascinating, the very nearness of him wrapping around her senses like a haze, his touch igniting the slow fire now burning in the very center of her abdomen. She knew perfectly well she should run out the door and find Helena, but somehow these thoughts faded into the background, and Madeline lifted her mouth ever so slightly toward his.

Lord Douglas reacted instantly: taking her chin in his hand, he brought his lips down to hers. Madeline moaned, sinking into the new sensation, marveling at the feel of his fingers sliding around the back of her neck, deepening the kiss, his tongue sweeping in to mingle with hers—

She bit him. Hard, on the lower lip, and before he could regain his senses Madeline snatched back the keys and ran. With the earthy, sweet taste of him still in her mouth, she darted out the door, very nearly falling over the stunned butler, who crouched outside. Madeline continued her retreat, ignoring the shouts from behind, making her way back through the kitchen door to where a white-faced Helena stood trembling in the sun.

"What happened?" she gasped, as Madeline grabbed onto her tightly, a solid surface in the crashing sea. "I heard a terrible scream and ran to get Sam, but then you screamed again and I ran back to help! Did I do the right thing? I think his butler saw me!"

Madeline couldn't bring herself to reply. She grabbed a firm hold on her cousin's arm, and they ran together, pulling one another along to the safety of the carriage.

Colin Andrews Montgomery, the sixth Duke of Douglas, stood at his front entrance, dumbfounded by the sight of two young ladies running in the weak morning sun. His mysterious vixen moved quickly, her unbound hair flying behind her—*the color of cinnamon,* he mused—as she dragged her smaller companion along.

"She escaped through the kitchens, sir," Halbert informed him, panting hard as he finally caught up with his lordship.

"Likely scaring the wits out of the staff." Colin watched her enticing figure vanish from sight. He couldn't help but grin at the memory of the woman's bite. She saw a vulnerable spot and took it; he would have done the same in such a situation.

"She claimed to be lost." Colin turned to his butler, a man he had known since infancy, whose calm, unflappable gaze witnessed all the secrets of his family.

"And did you believe her, sir?"

"Not in the least." Although completely drenched in sweat and all too aware of the many bruises he'd recently acquired, Colin felt human again. Something about that woman brought him back to his senses. He couldn't rationalize it, but for the first time in weeks his head was clear from the fog that had plagued him since Juliana's betrayal.

"Halbert, I do believe I'll have a bath. And a fresh change of clothes," he added. "It would seem I have become offensive to the eye." He laughed, remembering the beautiful woman's prim expression, and her obvious irritation with his living conditions.

"Do you wish for me to stop the ladies, sir?" Halbert wheezed the question, still breathing heavily from his run down the stairs.

"Let them go for now," Colin replied. "I'll find her again." Halbert's raised brows told him the butler was stunned over the sudden change in him. He was rather mystified himself. The sharp sting on his lower lip vividly recalled the ending to their kiss. He was certain he'd find her again. What might happen after that he couldn't begin to guess.

Halbert gave a small, diplomatic cough, pulling him from his thoughts. "Your eye, sir, looks to be bleeding again."

"A bit of a scuffle last night," Colin admitted, accepting one of Halbert's handkerchiefs to hold above his eye.

"You've had quite a time of it; perhaps Your Grace should take a bit more care of himself these days."

Colin laughed again. "Worried for me, Halbert? I was the winner, in case you had your doubts."

"I did not doubt that, sir. I only wish to see you settled once more."

There was a long silence while Colin thought over the past weeks since the abrupt end of his engagement. He hadn't handled it particularly well. Jealous and humiliated, he'd spent every night drinking himself into a stupor. Halbert was right. He'd let his anger carry him too far. His past with Juliana was over. It was time to move on with life.

"Shall I fetch a bandage, sir?"

"Yes," Colin said, and then suddenly remembered the vixen's other piece of advice. "And do we have any vinegar in the house?"

"Vinegar, sir?" Halbert asked, perplexed.

"And garlic, too. It would seem I am on the mend."

Chapter Three

The ride home became an eternity, each passing moment finding Madeline more terrified that the shadowy Lord Douglas would suddenly appear behind them. The power of his blue-grey gaze did indeed follow her, a swirling sea threatening to pull her down to its very depths.

"Madeline!" Helena's sharp squeal jolted her back, scattering the strange thoughts. "Have you heard nothing I've said? What happened?" She didn't wait for an answer but continued babbling. "I heard such awful yelling! And then you came running as if you'd seen a ghost. I didn't know what to do! What happened?"

She finally paused for breath, and Madeline answered slowly. "I met Lord Douglas, in his study." Hearing the words aloud brought a certain horrible finality to her plan; she had come so far, made it inside the house, but she had still failed to recover the French Blue diamond.

Helena gasped. "Lord Douglas! Was he the one shouting at you? Is he horribly cruel? Did he threaten you?"

"He kissed me."

She cut her cousin off, unable to relive the terrible humiliation again, and sank into her seat, her heart pounding faster with each turn of the carriage wheels.

Why had Papa asked this of her? For the first time since she'd arrived in London Madeline felt isolated and afraid, a lamb sent into the lion's den. How little she knew of her family's past. Even her aunt and cousin, the only relatives Madeline possessed, had been utterly unknown to her six months ago! Why had her father persisted in these endless secrets? And the painting—seeing it had been an overwhelming shock. Though Madeline had no memory of her mother, she had instinctively recognized her. *It was as if the painting was of me.*

As Madeline wrestled with her emotions, a relieved Helena sat back against the plush cushions, adjusting her lace gloves, mussed during their flight. "Well then, that's not so bad, is it? I had thought you were being thrashed by the servants or something awful. I'm glad that's all over. Tell me," she said, her mind already flitting back to her favorite subject, "do you think I should write a very stern letter to Vickem, or ignore him completely?"

The moment they were returned to her aunt's, Madeline leapt from her seat, and, determining they hadn't been followed, accosted Sam with questions.

"What can you tell me about Lord Douglas?"

"He lives in the house you just broke into," Helena helpfully chimed in.

"Yes, I'm sure we all remember," Madeline said impatiently, "but what else? Does he live alone? What is he like?"

"The Duke of Douglas is most definitely not married," Sam scrunched up his brows, "and I doubt he is the type of man you should be botherin' with, if you pardon my bein' so forward."

Helena looked perplexed. "Why? Is he very unpleasant?"

"You could say that. Though one can hardly blame the man, what with all the gossip over his scandal."

Madeline's heart plunged to her feet. "What scandal?"

"He jilted his poor fiancée three days before their wedding. A terrible thing to do. The lady is said

26

to have fled England with a broken heart." His voice lowered. "And I must tell you, Lord Douglas is known as a man not to be trifled with." Sam added a nod for good measure. "There are some who say Lady Juliana Reynolds won't be coming back to London at all."

"What does that mean?" Madeline asked, as Sam rubbed his jaw, his fingers brushing over the few hairs beginning to sprout.

"I'm not exactly sure myself, but it sounds bad, doesn't it?" He grinned at her. "If you won't be needin' anything else, my lady, I should get these horses back before Jarvis catches my hide."

Absolutely grand. Madeline marched into the house. *Not only is Lord Douglas a bully and a rake but perhaps a murderer, as well!* She felt utterly foolish; at least she had not told Lord Douglas her name! She shuddered to think what he would do with that information. Still, she couldn't forget how gentle his hands had been on her shoulders, or his soft mouth, a contradiction to the hard heat of his body...

Safely inside her room, Madeline fell onto the bed, burying her scalding face in the pillow. A jingle of metal followed her down onto the bed, and she immediately sat up again, fumbling through her cloak for the small pocket inside.

Lord Douglas's keys! In all the chaos she had forgotten about them, but what to do now? She had grave doubts about sneaking back inside his townhouse; Lord Douglas would certainly warn his staff about her.

Madeline sat running her fingers up and down the oddly-shaped brass keys, pondering over which was the one that fit the lock in the cellar door. She felt a stab of sadness for her father; Papa had been so firm in his instructions, but what to do if she failed? Madeline rubbed her shoulders to ward off the damp chill of the morning. She couldn't deny there was a strange, heavy feeling in the London air, thick and ominous, quite different from the innocent country breezes they had left in Norfolk. One thing was for certain: she must find this French Blue diamond and discover for herself what secrets it contained. *There is little time to waste. I must find a way back into Lord Douglas's house.*

"Helena? Madeline, dove, where is everyone? We have news to discuss, and ribbons!" Madeline jumped at the sound of her Aunt Cecilia's shrill voice and, like a skittish thief, stuffed the keys under her pillow before running to greet her.

****

"Don't stray too far, girls; I have the dressmaker coming at four." Lady Cecilia, the fashionably widowed Marchioness of Milburg, spoke with a great rolling enthusiasm from the head of the breakfast table, utterly ignored by her daughter and niece. "Honestly! You both are so dull, I feel as though I am talking with myself. What have the two of you been doing all morning?"

Madeline paid little attention to the question; her mind was spinning with various ways to get back to Lord Douglas's cellar door. *Preferably when Lord Douglas is absent from home,* she acknowledged, the memory of his kiss flushing her cheeks.

"Oh, this dreary silence is undoubtedly too much! Will no one answer?" her aunt cried.

Helena sighed and threw down her fork. "I was drawing in the garden, and Madeline was reading, but really, Mother, why is Mr. Banbury coming here? No one wishes to see the old toad."

Madeline couldn't help but smile at the description, impressed by Helena's speed at steering the subject away from the morning's deceitful activities. In the brief time she had spent under her

28

aunt's protection Madeline had learned two things: Aunt Cecilia abhorred improper behavior, and stealing her aunt's carriage to visit strange men before dawn would be considered highly improper.

"For ball gowns, my darling! Do you expect to wear last season's attire? It didn't do you much good then, did it?"

"Mama, have you forgotten our regrettable situation? We are poor now; we cannot afford more gowns."

"Yes, if I may agree, Aunt, have we not bought enough new clothes? I already have more than I know what to do with." Madeline did not exaggerate in the least; her wardrobe was nearly bursting with brightly colored silks and the many hats, ribbons, gloves, and shoes that accompanied them. In truth, she had become so overwhelmed by it all that she continued to wear her light grey half-mourning clothes, though it had been weeks since they were required. Nor did her attire go unnoticed by Aunt Cecilia, whose eyes narrowed at the drab dress the moment Madeline entered a room.

Aunt Cecilia set the cup of tea down with a sympathetic clink. "Oh, my dear, you really have been kept under lock and key, haven't you? This is precisely why we need the very best gowns, the very best of everything!" She waved her hand around at their lavishly furnished dining room. "Our very last shilling has gone into this season: your clothes, this lovely townhouse...though Brigette and I must make a few teensy improvements." She pointed a stern finger toward the plain blue wallpaper. "And Miss Lillian has lent us one of her fine carriages to use. No one will even know ours was sold off!"

"Miss Lillian?" Madeline asked, bewildered by the news that she had stolen a stranger's carriage that morning.

"Dearest Miss Lillian! She is my darling friend

and can well afford to help, my dear; her father was a viscount. A bit miserly with the family money and left her near a fortune." Aunt Cecilia sniffed her approval and patted the thick covering of lace at her throat before continuing. "There is no time to waste. We must present ourselves to the *ton* as though we are as wealthy and eligible as ever. It's the only way to procure a good marriage, and you both must marry well." Aunt Cecilia looked back and forth between them in ominous warning. "Marry well or be utterly destitute."

Madeline dropped the slice of toast in her hand.

"You cannot be serious, Aunt. You are spending the last of your money trying to get us husbands?"

"Darling, why do you think you're here?" She shook her head. "Your father sent you to me precisely because he knew I could obtain a good marriage for you. He left you practically penniless, you know."

Madeline bit back an angry retort. "My father did not send me to London for marriage," she insisted, Lord Douglas and his cellar door momentarily forgotten alongside the disturbing news. "Of that I am quite sure."

"Oh, darling, you mustn't say such things! I know you've had a wobbly start, but Mr. Banbury will make you look just as eligible as Helena." She smiled, oblivious to Madeline's look of horror, and turned to her daughter. "Brigette has informed me you've received another lovely letter from our Lord Vickem."

"Mama!" Helena's voice rattled the rented china. "I rejected Lord Vickem's hideous advances last season, and you agreed! You said no mother wishes to have a bleating goat for a son-in-law."

"Circumstances have changed, my darling," Aunt Cecelia sang out. "One must be prepared to go with the tide. Lord Vickem inherited his late father's

30

title of Viscount, and the family is quite flush, due to their dull ways. You could do much worse."

"Mama!"

"Now, darlings, please, we must be ready to meet with Mr. Banbury as soon as he arrives. He gets fussy as a princess if made to wait this time of year, and who can blame him? What with everyone clamoring at his door for the newest fashions. He is from Paris, you know." She swooped up a bite of cold ham, popping it into her mouth.

"Miss Lillian told me she kept him waiting over an hour last year while she finished her letter to the Colby widow, and he had the very gall to blister her the moment she arrived! On and on he went about wasting his time, and would she perhaps be better suited to another tailor with more hours to spare?"

Aunt Cecilia clicked her tongue. "Not to mention," she dropped her voice to an octave suitable for drama, "darling Miss Lillian swears her last three dresses have been made too small. Claims he did it on purpose to make her arms look like little sausages."

Helena snorted. "If her figure has grown, she should lay less blame on the dressmaker and more on the endless stream of seed cakes she finds in her mouth."

"This is precisely the kind of remark that has you attending your second season *sans* husband," Aunt Cecilia said, turning a censorious eye on her daughter. "Men do not enjoy a sharp tongue, and the sooner you realize that the better."

"Miss Lillian should find herself another tailor," Madeline spoke up, her temper flaring. "Perhaps someone who specializes in dressing young women who do not wish to marry."

Aunt Cecilia very deliberately set her napkin down, turning toward her niece with a seriousness that was a bit undermined by her large amounts of blusher.

"My dear girl," she spoke slowly, "one cannot be expected to allow just anyone to make her gowns; it isn't the thing." She very gently adjusted the pale purple muslin on her bodice as though to emphasize the quality. "We put up with Mr. Banbury because, frankly, Mr. Banbury is the best. His gowns have a certain mark about them; the cut of the skirt, a delicate hand that one can spot across the room and think to themselves, 'There! She is wearing such a lovely gown from the hand of our own Mr. Banbury, how elegant! She must come from real quality to be a customer of such a man, as Mr. Banbury only accepts the most refined families in London.'" She stopped to smile indulgently at her niece, who wasn't quite sure whether she should scream or cry. "Do you see, Madeline? The importance of these things?"

****

That afternoon, Madeline found herself agreeing with Helena's earlier remarks about the infamous Mr. Banbury. Indeed, she was beginning to wonder if she could get away with kicking him. The man was nothing less than a dressmaking tyrant. She had been poked, prodded, pinched, and berated since he walked in the door and declared her simple grey wool skirt to be "an assault upon the eyes!" before dramatically covering up the offended parts.

She held her temper while the odious man stuck her with needles and discussed dressing her as if she were a spoiled child's new doll, gritting her teeth while Helena looked on in sympathy. "Ah, these colors, like soot from a chimney! So dark and drab on her skin!" Mr. Banbury flicked at the grey folds, shaking his head.

"Oh, sir, I agree! I told my niece that her skin was much too pale, and putting such dark colors next to her, well, I don't have to tell you, but it does tend to give one an air of illness." Aunt Cecilia shook her head over the sad attire.

"Indeed, who will wish to speak to such a gloomy lady? Green is her color, I think; it will go with the dark hair. Or perhaps a light purple?"

"No purple." Madeline finally spoke for herself, and both Mr. Banbury and her aunt looked up, as though surprised she could talk. "Thank you for the suggestion, but could we not find another color?"

"Pardon my asking, but are you the expert, madam?" he said, nodding toward her dress with pinched nostrils.

"I was in mourning," she snapped, yanking her skirt out of his hand. "My dress was most appropriate."

"Ah, yes! The poor Earl of Caithness! My deepest condolences for such a fine man."

"You knew my father?" she asked, surprised.

"Of course, though it is your mother who burns in my memory; a truly exquisite creature, and such an eye for laces I could hardly keep up with her." Mr. Banbury's fat little fingers reclaimed the edge of Madeline's silk hem and forcibly pulled her back.

"She was beautiful, then?" Madeline asked, wincing a bit at the sad fluttering that awoke in her heart whenever she spoke of her mother.

"Indeed! Most beautiful, with such bright red hair, and a neck like a swan. Why, you only have to look in the glass to see; you are the exact image of her." The little man continued his work, oblivious to the emotions he was causing. "And always in green! It was truly her color. It suited her beauty perfectly."

Madeline couldn't help herself; her gaze sought out her aunt. "Is it true? Do I look very much like my mother?" The portrait in Lord Douglas's study burned in her memory, those grey-blue eyes staring at her with a dark, shivering intensity.

Finally, Cecilia spoke. "Yes you do," she said firmly, taking a long look at her niece. "The shape of your chin, the line of your cheeks..." She suddenly looked away. "It's uncanny."

Madeline remained silent, thousands of questions on her tongue.

"Though your hair is an ordinary brown. Thank heavens for that," her aunt continued quietly, as though speaking to herself. "Sarah's red hair brought her nothing but trouble." A look of fear slipped over Aunt Cecilia's face, vanishing as quickly as it came. "Just try and stay out of the sunlight, dear," she added. "It will keep the red strands from showing."

Madeline nodded obediently at the ridiculous advice, aware the moment had become too heavy, as though the air might shatter.

"I shall put her in a deep green silk, molded well to the body. Nothing to offend, but a dress to let the world know someone special has arrived!" Mr. Banbury exclaimed.

Nodding her approval, Aunt Cecilia moved on to scrutinize Helena, while Madeline stood staring at the little Frenchman. He was from Paris and would likely know something of the French Blue diamond. Did she dare to ask him? She glanced quickly at her aunt, busily lecturing Helena on her uncouth posture.

"Mr. Banbury," Madeline felt the words slide impulsively from her lips, "pardon the question, but you said you were from Paris?"

"Oui, mademoiselle! Such a beautiful city; tragic what it has become."

"Indeed." She further lowered her voice, as though relating a tragic tale. "May I ask, have you ever heard of the French Blue diamond?"

He looked at her curiously. "The French Blue? But of course! Who has not heard of this beautiful gem? It was stolen from the King's own treasury during the revolution and never seen again."

"And the curse?" she continued, trying to mask her excitement, but Mr. Banbury's lips instantly drew together.

"Madamoiselle, you do not believe such tales! A silly child's story, that's all." He shook his head. "Believe me when I tell you that all of Paris was cursed in those days." Mr. Banbury stood up, satisfied as much with himself as his work. "Everyone is intrigued by you, my lady. Lady Huntington can speak of nothing else, and the Duchess of Ravens is overcome with fears that you will outshine her daughter. And with the right dress," he shot another scornful look at the wool, "I have no doubt of it!"

****

It was hours later when the happy—and certainly richer—Mr. Banbury left, with strict orders to have the dresses finished by next week. Madeline finally returned to her room, numb from the day's events. Could it be true? Had her father really given Aunt Cecilia instructions to marry her off? What about the diamond? She was beginning to realize that though she had spent nearly every day of her life with her father, she didn't really know him at all. A sick feeling washed through her, bringing along tears, and she forcefully wiped her eyes as she pulled the grey mourning dress over her head, tossing it to the floor. Aunt Cecilia was right, her mourning days were over.

Utterly exhausted from the day, Madeline lay on the bed, and, forcing her mind to close, fell instantly asleep.

She was digging in the dirt.

Out of the earth she pulled a black velvet bag, the rotting cloth falling apart in her trembling hands. Eagerly she tore open the bundle, revealing a gleam of light from inside.

The French Blue diamond.

35

It was stunning, a deep color, nearly purple, that caught even the weak light of the candles, soaking in the light to create a glow, as though the very stone itself was on fire, lit from within. She held it, entranced by the power contained in those rich blue facets.

She heard a cry from below. It came from underground, and Madeline, unable to release the diamond from her grasp, now began to dig furiously with one hand. She dug deep, beads of her sweat mixing with the black dirt as she used all her strength to uncover the loud insistent cries.

"Papa!"

It was her father, barely recognizable after many months underground, his face now as rotted as the black velvet bag. She reached out a hand to his cheek, but found she no longer had the courage to touch him.

"Beware, Madeline," he rasped. He coughed then, dust spewing forth from his dead lips; Madeline couldn't help herself, she shrank back in horror, clutching the diamond against her heart.

"Papa, what has happened to you?" she screamed.

"The diamond is cursed!"

Madeline awoke with the scream trapped in her throat, her hair and gown soaked in sweat from the nightmare. She forced herself to breathe, slowly becoming aware of the faded light in the room, accompanied by a soft knocking sound.

" My lady, your aunt has requested you in the dining room with much haste." The housemaid's voice rang from outside her door.

"It's only Brigette," she whispered, wiping the strands of hair from her eyes. "Papa is gone and buried; there's nothing to fear."

"My lady, is something amiss?"

"Not at all, Brigette," she replied loudly, finding

reassurance in her own voice. "I shall be right down."

She carefully sat up in her bed, the images from her dream still vividly raw as sleep cleared from her mind.

Madeline recalled the portrait of her mother, proud and regal in the faded paint. She walked to her dressing table, her mind centered on the portrait as though it were right in front of her.

Lifting up her hair, she stood tall and proud, her eyes flashing in the soft candlelight. She imagined the bright green silk against her skin, pulling the rich amber highlights from her dark brown strands. Turning slightly in the glass, she did her best to mimic her mother's pose in the painting, lifting her chin high while staring straight into the mirror with an unbending gaze, a slight smile on her lips.

Next week she would attend her first ball, entering into the society that had once embraced Lord and Lady Caithness. Madeline felt certain she would find Lord Douglas among the guests; he couldn't hide out in his study forever. She must befriend him, apologize for her behavior today, and perhaps he would respond with an invitation to call upon him, to come to tea or an evening of cards at 52 Baker Street.

She smiled. She must return for the diamond, and certainly with the right dress and a little added curl to her long hair she could charm a man. All she needed was a single invitation to his mother's dinner party. *The date has been set for the twenty-first.* Next week. It would be enough time. Madeline caught a flash of candlelight in the mirror and nodded. After all, she had sworn a vow to her Papa to find the French Blue diamond.

And destroy it.

Chapter Four

The women in the room were too damn bright.

Colin stood in the very back corner of the polished ballroom, the scowl on his face deepening further as he watched yet another perfectly curled blonde head bounce her way into the room. This one swathed in white, he thought mutinously, was a slight improvement over the endless pinks.

He had been waiting for hours, ignoring the many acquaintances who anxiously attempted to engage his attention, carefully watching the ornately decorated front door as hundreds of guests flowed in and out, not one of them the fiery figure he sought. One more hour, he told himself, as another feathered creature made her entrance, and he would give up this ridiculous obsession and put the woman out of his mind.

"Lord Douglas, I am simply astounded by your presence tonight." Colin turned, recognizing the amused voice instantly.

"I've just had the most fascinating conversation with Lady Amelia Ravens, truly an enchanting creature, by the way, who was desperate to inform me that the infamous Duke of Douglas was in attendance tonight."

"Edward, I see you've come to witness my torture."

The man continued on as though Colin hadn't spoken. "Of course, I informed the delightful Amelia that, as much as it pained me, I had no choice but to disagree with her. My brother, I declared, no longer attends functions of any kind. He much prefers to lead the life of a boring, angry recluse."

"Has our mother arrived yet? I expected to see her tonight." Colin made no reply to the earlier comments, nor did he attempt to hide his irritation.

"She was delayed. Something to do with an ill servant at Douglas Manor," Edward answered, referring to their family home in the country. Their mother quite detested city life, and Colin had little doubt she took any excuse to delay her trip. Lady Douglas had always been an independent woman and had grown more so since becoming a widow; her sons knew she wouldn't set foot in London until good and ready. "But you will see her soon enough. We are both expected to the dinner party later this week," Edward added cheerfully.

Colin stared hard at his younger brother; he knew perfectly well what was behind this sudden dinner party, at his townhouse of all places. Lady Douglas had obviously decided her eldest son had wallowed enough.

"Two social events in a week," Edward sighed, feigning shock. "Your recovery will be the talk of London."

"Are you finished?" Colin snapped.

Lord Edward Montgomery laughed, handing him one of two glasses filled with a thin liquid that Colin feared to be the watered-down wine making its rounds on the servants' trays.

"For now, though I'm racked with curiosity over this sudden change; I thought you only frequented taverns these days."

Colin ignored the bait. "It's about time you showed up. I had forgotten how painfully late these damn things go." He almost choked; he'd downed half his drink before discovering the sour taste.

"Sorry to disappoint. I was held up at the Stanton affair, found myself entangled with a very persistent young lady and her sister. They were determined I was to dance with both of them before departing, and I, being the gallant gentleman..."

"Couldn't dare refuse." Nearly seven years older, Colin marveled at his brother's ability to withstand the tediousness of society. Even as a boy, Edward had seemed to thrive on the noise and attention, charming young debutantes as easily as their mothers yet still finding time to drop a radical political view in the right ear at White's. *He enjoys it,* Colin realized with surprise, wondering at his own inability to stomach the life he was born to. It would certainly have made things easier.

"Not in the least. They were rather enchanting little things, although a bit too heavy on the chatter. I find I appreciate a woman who values the economy of words."

A group of ladies came into view, hardly more than children, in Colin's opinion, loudly discussing their beaus and flashing glances toward his brother. They were obviously taken with Edward's light hair and easy grin—*Not to mention his immense fortune,* Colin thought cynically—and the scoundrel knew it. Tossing off a wink, Edward ignited an explosion of giggles, the ladies scattering away like excited geese.

"You've come to the wrong event if intelligent conversation is what you're after," Colin said, resuming his scowl. He continued to survey the crowd, unable to capture a glimpse of the bewitching face he sought. This was proving to be a waste of time, but what had he expected? He knew practically nothing about the woman who had burst into his study a week before, other than that she possessed a sharp tongue and terrible fashion sense.

He grinned.

But what of her name? Where did she come from? Colin had exhausted all his usual methods of getting information and come up with nothing. He felt mired in his ignorance, a feeling he detested, and had finally forced himself back into society, hoping to catch a glimpse of her. This first attempt was the immensely popular Farris ball, though after an evening of boredom Colin was beginning to wonder if he had made too much of their brief encounter. After all, he'd found the mysterious woman more insulting and infuriating than most of his enemies. Then he recalled those eyes turning to green fire when he pricked her anger. That mouth, resistant at first, softening just enough to lead him in before taking control. Matching his passion with her own. He unconsciously lifted a finger to his bottom lip, a small reminder of the stinging end to that kiss.

"Who is she?" Edward's voice snapped him to attention.

"She?" Colin kept his eye on the ballroom's entrance, hoping to stave off Edward's question.

"The woman, Colin. The one responsible for you staring at the door with a grin on your face. A definite improvement over your usual expression, by the way."

Colin quickly checked his smile. "It's complicated."

"Undoubtedly. What's her name?"

"I don't know."

His brother gave him a long look. "I see."

Colin glanced down into his empty glass; could they never serve anything stronger at these damn things? He could feel Edward's gaze on him, probably wondering if he was drunk. Colin wasn't used to confiding in anyone, even his family, but he was curious for another opinion.

"I woke up and found her staring over me." He quickly told Edward the story of the woman's sudden appearance in his study, leaving out the details of their kiss.

"And she refused to give her name? What did

41

she want?" Edward clasped his hands together, all seriousness now.

"I cannot begin to say," Colin replied. "She answered all of my inquiries with riddles and then insulted me. At one point she claimed to be lost," he recalled.

"Did you believe her?"

"Not in the least. I should also mention that she stole my keys."

"Your keys?" Edward seemed incredulous. Not that Colin could blame him; he might doubt it himself if he hadn't seen her with his own eyes. "How much brandy did you drink before this woman appeared?"

"They were an old set of house keys; I had forgotten they existed," Colin said, ignoring his brother's implications. "But she was determined to have them; I can't imagine why. And then there was that painting." He trailed off, wondering how he could possibly describe the wrenching look of longing on the beautiful woman's face. "It was as though someone had broken her heart." Later that morning Colin had examined the painting. There was nothing unusual about it, other than the female subject's eerie similarity to his little thief. *Lady Caithness* was engraved at the bottom of the frame, and as he examined the portrait more closely he could begin to see the subtle differences between the two women. Lady Caithness stared out at him with a look of self-satisfied conceit, nothing at all like the innocent green eyes of the woman who had stood before him.

"Colin, do you think this is wise? The woman is obviously a liar or off her head. Either way it would be best to avoid her."

Colin knew his brother spoke the truth; he of all people should be wary of an unstable woman. *I'm barely beginning to recover from Juliana's web of deceit.* He scowled at the thought. But there was something about the cinnamon-haired enchantress who so brazenly stole into his house—a desperate fire in her eyes, such naked honesty—that he could not resist finding her again. *I just want to see her once more. And besides, I have to get my damn keys back.*

"Your advice is sound, Edward," he finally replied. "But I'm rejecting it, all the same." He smiled to take the sting out of his words. "Besides, if she had been sent to do me harm, it was a damn odd way to go about it. She had no weapon, made enough noise to wake the dead—"

"Perhaps she planned to brain you with your keys." Before he could reply, Edward's chin lifted slightly, signaling that they were no longer alone.

"Lord Douglas! So good of you to come, excellent of you to come! You are enjoying yourself? Need a drink?" Colin turned in time to see a red face barreling toward them.

Lifting his glass in answer, he recoiled slightly from the thick scent of brandy wafting from the puffed-up little man. Who in the hell was this?

"Excellent! Good, good, and Lord Montgomery, I see you are looking well, as well. Drink?" The man was actually beginning to sweat, a thin bead of moisture forming on his upper lip.

"Thank you, Farris." Edward nodded his greeting, accepting a second glass of the watered-down wine.

"Well, then! That's splendid! I apologize for not greeting you sooner. I had no idea you would be attending this evening. There I was, listening to Timmons prattle on about some battle or other, when I looked across the room and thought, My God! Is that our own Duke of Douglas? Showing his face in public?"

Colin stood listening to him babble, amazed he could see anything, drunk as he was. Nervous, too, he noted, as the man edged closer and closer, until Colin felt that in another moment he would have little choice but to shove him to the ground.

Edward, sensing the growing agitation, spoke up. "It's good of you to say hello, Farris, but we'd hate to be accused of keeping the host."

Farris's face lit up. "Not at all, gentlemen! Why, there's no one here who could possibly be considered more of a fascination—"

He broke off. The sweat running down his face in waterfalls, Farris quickly sought to patch his mistake. "What I mean is, with your reputation, Lord Douglas, and the gossip over your engagement... We haven't seen much of you in society."

"I've found I prefer less discerning company these days."

"No need to say more!" Farris laughed loudly, slapping him on the back. "No man in your position would feel differently after what you've been through. Who can bear all these women with their endless yammering on about breaking a lady's heart, and who's a cad, and so forth? Nonsense, all of it! Why, I told my wife the other day to hold her gossipy tongue. Not another word about Douglas, I told her, I won't hear of it! Finest man I know, and who's to say Juliana didn't deserve a good jilting?" He snorted with mirth. "I fancy I'd have been better off if I'd done the same thing myself."

With a loud cough Edward motioned his head toward Farris's wife, hovering not far behind her husband like an orange-colored bee.

"Darling, your cravat is crooked! How absurd." Lady Farris pushed her way toward them, her expression as sour as the wine. "You ran off so suddenly and quite neglected to congratulate General Timmons on his latest victory. Unforgivable! You really must go back and speak with him."

She quickly straightened the black tie before finally turning a tight smile toward the other two men, her gaze raking over Colin's simple jacket and shirt. Obviously not the attire, or the presence, she deemed suitable for her ball.

"Lord Douglas, my love!" Farris shouted an introduction. "You should make certain to introduce him to our Aggie. Perhaps she can convince him to dance!"

"How lovely of you to come," she replied, further tightening her lips before turning back to her husband. "Darling, I do believe Aggie will be much too preoccupied for Lord Douglas this evening. Our daughter is much sought after," she reminded him.

"Oh, tosh! All's fair in love, and all that. Look at poor Vickem there." Farris pointed out a wan, glum-faced man draped across one of Lady Farris's chairs. "He's been mooning over Cecilia's girl for ages. Rather pathetic for my taste, but you must admire his resolve."

"Yes, well, we certainly don't wish that kind of attention on our Agnes." Lady Farris sniffed. "Though it would do Cecilia a world of good to lower her standards, really. Everyone knows of their situation." She gave Colin a knowing look, as though he knew, or cared, about these people's lives. "And as if one unmarried daughter wasn't enough, she now has a niece to foster off, as well! And scarcely a farthing to their names! Absurd."

Colin's rude reply was interrupted by Farris's elbow in his side. "You've heard of this niece, haven't you, Douglas? Supposed to be quite a vision for the eyes. That windbag Richards caught a glimpse of her riding in the park and fell in love, said her beauty outshone the Duchess of Devonshire in her day. Lady M...something..." He trailed off, trying to think of the name.

"Lady Madeline Sinclair," his wife icily supplied.

He clapped like an excited child. "That's it! What a coup! Richards will eat his hat when he discovers she's coming here, the bag. He can have old Prinny up to gaze at his gardens all he likes, but it will never outdo my guests."

Colin had not the damnedest clue who Lady Madeline Sinclair was, but he hoped she had a high tolerance for insults.

Lady Farris rolled her eyes. "I wouldn't think too much of yourself. The Sinclair girl is less exciting than we thought." She adjusted her glove. "Turns out she was brought up in some old family place up north—horrid winters, of course—but she lived nothing more than a quiet country life. Lady Reddington spoke to her at the Beasleys' garden affair and claims she's quite of average beauty and, of course, has no fortune to her name."

Colin didn't miss the note of disappointment in Lady Farris's voice. It would seem the *ton* hoped for a more substantial meal to satisfy their endless appetites for gossip, and the realization pricked his anger. "Pity Madeline isn't disfigured in some way. It would certainly make for more interesting conversation."

Edward started coughing, though the inebriated Farris held no such restraint; he burst out in a guffaw, slapping Colin on the arm. "It would give the ladies something to write about!" he wheezed. "They could surely get a month's worth of entertainment from the hideousness of the Sinclair girl!"

Lady Farris shot him a pinched glare, gripping his arm to rather forcefully smooth the wrinkles from his jacket. "Yes. Well. I'm sure the girl is a delight. Let's hope she has managed not to take after her departed mother." She threw her nose in the air, dismissing them. "Darling, I think it's time we made our way back to General Timmons."

"In a moment, dear. I was planning to toast the health of my honored guests!" He swirled his hand in a grand circular motion. "Douglas? May I interest you in anything stronger?"

It was the best idea he'd heard all night, but before he could agree, Lady Farris broke in. "Take caution, darling, or you'll never make it through the evening. Why, it's barely midnight!" she tittered anxiously, and Farris waved her away.

"Just a nip more, my darlingest, and it shall be nothing but wine for the rest of the night!"

His wife's face looked to be near cracking, and she grabbed her skirt in an angry swish.

"Indeed. But I'm afraid I must insist on it." She had his arm in a claw-like hold that caused Farris to emit a faint yelp.

"Gentlemen, it seems I will have to send you without me. The study is down the hall, and I believe you will find a bottle or two of something to your liking. Please don't hesitate," he yelled as he was dragged away.

Lady Farris favored them with one last nod. "So glad to see you, gentlemen," she said, her tone indicating otherwise. "Do enjoy your evening."

Colin watched them go, resisting the urge to laugh. "It seems I've become something of an anomaly. I had no idea."

Edward shrugged. "You refused to speak a word against Juliana, and the story has grown. People only wish to believe the worst, and trust me when I tell you they are quite off the mark."

"How so?"

Edward hesitated. "The latest story has something to do with your falling madly in love with your favorite paramour."

Colin did laugh then, bitterly. "It's better than the truth, I suppose. I'll wager Juliana came up with that one."

"Colin," Edward spoke carefully, still watching Farris tripping away with his wife, "this Lady Madeline Sinclair, do you think it might be the woman you're looking for?"

"Could be." Colin tapped one finger against the glass in his hand, his gaze on the crowd. "What do you know of her?" His faith that Edward would be well informed of society news was not disappointed.

"Only idle gossip. Her father was an earl, and after he died she came to England to live with an aunt. They arrived in London a month ago, and there's been quite a bit of speculation about her. Mostly jealous matrons worrying over the rumors of her beauty, but there is something darker there." Edward sat back on his heels, thinking. "Some scandal over the mother's death. I'll look into it."

Colin nodded his thanks. The last thing he needed in his life was another scandal. Maybe Edward was right; it might be best to put the mysterious woman out of his mind. Extending his arm, he handed his empty glass to a passing waiter.

"You're leaving?" Edward asked, surprised.

"Unfortunately, no, but I will take Farris up on his offer."

"To dance with his daughter?"

"God, no." Colin made a face at the thought. "I'm going to find that bottle."

****

"Are you quite undone by it all, girls? In a few moments we shall arrive at the grand Farris ball!" Aunt Cecilia had been preening about all week, thrilled by the number of invitations pouring into the townhouse. From intimate afternoon teas to lavish dinners, the cream-lined parchments had spurred on Aunt Cecilia's determination to make Madeline and Helena the sensation of the *ton*.

The last week had been a trial for Madeline. Their dire financial circumstances had forced her aunt into a matchmaking frenzy, unwavering in the decision that her daughter and niece must marry, and soon. Trapped in a whirlwind of petticoats, hair ribbons, and lace fans, Madeline and Helena had endured several stern lectures on the best way to walk into a room ("tall as the Queen, darlings!"), respond to a gentleman's jest ("a tiny musical laugh, before quickly hiding the lips behind one's fan"), and even the mundane task of holding a glass ("light and delicate in your fingers, girls; it will speak volumes about your disposition").

With all the activity, Madeline hadn't a spare moment to reflect on her plan for tonight, and now, only moments away from entering the Farris ball, she began to feel the first flutters of panic beneath her stays.

She took a deep breath, her mind recalling the pile of invitations on Lord Douglas's desk. He had certainly been invited to tonight's ball, she knew, but would he dare to attend? In the days since her disastrous meeting with the Duke of Douglas, Madeline had scarcely known a conversation that did not allude to the scandal surrounding his broken engagement.

During an insufferably long tea, Aunt Cecilia had entertained several guests with her own theories on what happened between Lord Douglas and Lady Juliana Reynolds, all to do with the lady's lack of proper etiquette, of course, though Madeline could hardly see how holding a wine glass correctly should keep a lady from being jilted.

Still, finding her way back into Lord Douglas's townhouse wasn't going to be easy. The man had been branded a terrible cad and could easily decide to stay tucked away in his study with one of his bottles. She frowned. Or even more alarming, his injury could have taken a turn for the worse, rendering him seriously ill, even dead.

Enough, Madeline scolded herself; you must try to think in a more positive manner. Undoubtedly Lord Douglas was still alive. He was much too rude and pigheaded to die over a tiny cut, and besides, Helena had told her that absolutely everyone attended the Farris ball.

"Not all young ladies have such luck," Aunt Cecilia continued, keeping her head slightly angled in the cramped carriage, so the enormous purple feather springing out of her turban would not be crushed. "Why, my first season, it was weeks before Father allowed me to attend anything other than those tragic little card parties the Widow Havers used to throw. What horrid sandwiches she insisted on serving, terribly limp watercress."

"That sounds unbearable, Aunt," Madeline replied absently. She sat stiff as a doll in her green silk, scarcely daring to move for fear of falling out of the low-cut gown. Mr. Banbury had certainly fulfilled his promise, she thought with equal parts admiration and irritation, *for there is little doubt I can escape without being noticed.* She marveled over the invention of a dress so soft and flowing at the bottom yet cinching like a vise above her waist, forcing her ample chest to strain against the ribbons like an overflowing pot. She had never sat straighter in her life.

"Oh, it was! I despise limp foods. All proper young ladies do. They must! I will tell you that despite the hardships of my beginnings, I found myself engaged by June, and do you know why, girls?"

It was Helena who answered, stuffed next to her mother in head-to-toe pink. "Because my father wasn't a simpering ingrate?" she replied crossly.

Two additional letters had arrived that week from Lord Vickem. Both declared his love for Helena and asked forgiveness for last year's unfortunate ending; the latter including his promise to meet her at the Farris ball where he would be "honored to dance a waltz or two with you, my dear, though I would rue the very man who dragged you from my arms." This postscript had sent Helena over the edge of panic, and after three arguments with her mother, who absolutely refused to allow her to stay at home, she now sat limply against the plush seats, resigned to her fate.

"Because I was prepared! Never wasted a moment. Every second an opportunity, every man a potential suitor. Determination, girls! Focus."

It will be quite simple. Madeline's mind drifted away from the endless chatter. *I shall merely find Lord Douglas, apologize for attacking him, and then become so charming he will have no choice but to invite me to his mother's dinner. What could possibly go wrong? Though I must make sure to escape Aunt Cecilia's attention for a moment or two. She will not think too kindly of such a conversation with the infamous duke, unless she believes there is a proposal involved.* Madeline thought of Lord Douglas's keys safely tucked away at the bottom of her traveling trunk, wrapped up in her old grey mourning dress. Madeline knew one of those keys would lead her to the French Blue diamond, if only she could get past Lord Douglas and into his house.

"Helena, love, sit up a bit. You'll wrinkle. And Madeline, honestly, child, you're always so pale! Pinch your cheeks for color and very seriously consider how that dour expression affects your face. Are you unwell?"

"I am unwell, Mother!" Helena cried, slouching deeper into the seat.

"Oh, hush! Just forget about your perilous future, and you'll be fine." Aunt Cecilia swiftly turned her eye toward the next agenda. "That's settled. Now, what about our Madeline? We must make the most of your green dress." Her aunt was nodding with approval at the new attire when she suddenly stopped, her smile gone. "Darling, where did you find those horribly old-fashioned gloves? Why, they barely reach the edge of your elbow. What will people say?"

The carriage came to a sudden halt at Aunt Cecelia's question, leaving the small space quiet but for the soft flapping of her fan.

"They were my mother's," Madeline blurted out, resisting the urge to hide her hands. "Papa gave me a few of her things..." She trailed off, unable to explain why she wore them tonight, other than to say the dark silk carried the slightest scent of a long-forgotten perfume.

"Well, it's too late to change them now." Her aunt sighed, clicking her tongue in disapproval. "Though I think it would be best not to mention they belonged to your mother, Madeline. No sense in stirring up talk."

The door sprang open then, and Aunt Cecilia's attention turned to giving the girls a last stream of advice for the night ahead.

"And most certainly do not go off unchaperoned. Oh! I cannot think of a more horrible fate than a lady being discovered alone at such an affair. It could be the end of your season, my dears," she warned.

Slightly stunned, Madeline stepped down from the carriage while trying to remain poised in the tightly swathed green silk. This was the second time her aunt had cautioned her against mentioning her mother. What did she fear?

"This is horrible!" Helena whispered from behind. "Mama will never let me turn down the despicable Lord Vickem now that we are poor."

"You must make the man reject you, Helena. There is nothing else to be done," Madeline whispered back, reminding her of the plan they had adopted earlier.

"I'll do it!" her cousin proclaimed, patting her curls. "I shall make him despise me by talking of nothing but politics. What do you think, Madeline?"

Madeline couldn't believe what she was hearing. "How would that get rid of a suitor?"

"Why not? Mama says no man wishes to spend an evening listening to a lady's opinions, that nothing will make him run away faster." Helena gave a firm nod. "Though I confess I've been having a terrible time coming up with opinions. Do you have any?"

"You must use your own," Madeline interjected. "You dislike Lord Vickem, don't you? That's certainly something. Now, where do you stand on politics?"

"Do you mean, do I agree with them?" Helena looked bewildered. "I suppose they are necessary to the running of one's country."

"Good lord, Helena, which side do you take, Whigs or Tories?"

"I don't know. Perhaps I should find out which side Lord Vickem likes and then choose the opposite?"

Madeline closed her eyes, wondering how anyone could be so utterly oblivious with a war raging on. "Perhaps politics is not the thing. How about literature?"

"Oh, yes, Madeline, how perfect!" Helena cried. "I will speak of nothing but my gothic romances. Mama says men are appalled by any mention of those."

"Backs straight, girls! Do not forget to look like queens!"

Both cousins glanced in the direction of Lady Milburg, in a current struggle to squeeze out of the carriage doors while keeping the enormous purple-feathered turban from falling off. For one harrowing moment, Madeline felt sure both the turban and her aunt were going to plunge straight down into the mud-filled streets, but Aunt Cecilia proved her wrong. With a swish of her skirt and a step so nimble it belied her size, she sailed from the carriage steps and appeared behind them, ushering Helena and Madeline past the large crowd of onlookers, dispensing advice all the way.

As she stepped into the large stone hall Madeline could see the festivities were already at their height. The hallway was filled with lavishly dressed men and women laughing and greeting one another as they made their way into the ballroom. More people spilled out into the reception room, up the winding staircase, and beyond. She had never in her life seen so many people in one space.

And the flowers! Flowers adorned everything: the entryway, the tables spread throughout the rooms, every surface available held tulips, primroses, giant fluffy peonies, and all of them pink. It was as if Lady Farris had brought her entire garden indoors.

Helena, thrilled she had chosen the right color, was beside herself. "Mother! Have you ever seen such a beautifully decorated hall?" she breathed, blue eyes shining. "Why, their curtains are fancier than those in Lady Roberta's country house, and you swore no one in all of London had lovelier curtains."

"Hush, child," her aunt admonished, noticing a few glances from the crowd. "For heaven's sake, do not stand there gaping at the walls." Helena immediately straightened under her mother's hawklike stare. "That's better. Now come along, girls, and try to behave with a bit more decorum tonight."

Aunt Cecilia's brisk, efficient step led the way, and Madeline felt her earlier determination melting away as they moved toward a rather viperous-looking circle of women.

"Lady Milburg! How charming of you to arrive." Madeline found herself introduced to Lady Farris, who greeted her in a pinched sort of way before snapping out the names of her companions. "May I introduce the Duchess of Ravens and her daughter Beatrice."

"It's lovely to meet you." As she spoke, the Duchess's gaze bored into Madeline. Thin to the point of cracking, Lady Ravens stood defensively next to a sullen-faced girl in a yellow gown.

"The honor is mine, Your Grace." Madeline smiled brightly, trying not to look pale. "I've been so looking forward to my first grand affair."

This was met with a cold tilt of the Duchess's head. "Yes, well, there has been much speculation about you. Some of it justified, I suppose."

"A magnificent dress, Lady Farris!" Aunt Cecilia offered, casting an admiring look at the mountains of orange. "I have never seen such a style."

Her ploy worked perfectly; clearly Lady Farris never passed up a compliment. "From France, dear, I would never think to go anywhere else."

Lady Ravens nodded furiously, still staring at Madeline. "You have chosen a very suitable color for your complexion, unlike my ghastly Bea," she muttered, glaring at her silent daughter. "She looks like a dying bird in that dress but insisted on wearing it, just to vex me." Bea made no reply to the harsh attack on her appearance, but Madeline saw the sliver of a smile cross her lips.

"Oh, look, it's my darling Aggie," Lady Farris broke in, eager to cover up the obvious resentment oozing from Lady Ravens.

Lady Farris's daughter made her way toward them, breaking some of the tension. She wasn't a striking beauty but, unlike her mother, had a soft sincerity about her.

"Lady Madeline Sinclair, I meet you at last! May I call you Madeline? I do so wish us to be great friends." Agnes grasped Madeline's hand in hers. "Everyone has been whispering over your beauty, and I see for myself that you are stunning. Don't you think so, Mother?"

Madeline felt her cheeks grow hot as Lady Farris looked her up and down with little favor. "Aggie, dear, have you spoken to Lord Rockford this evening? I'm sure he wishes to have you close by. He is very fond of my Agnes," she informed the circle, as Lady Ravens made a sound not unlike a snort.

"Oh, how exciting, Agnes! What a handsome pair you will make," Aunt Cecilia gushed. "Did you hear that, Helena? And it's only April!"

"It is indeed exciting." Helena managed to say.

"Oh, do not worry, dears. There are plenty of eligible gentlemen left," Lady Farris spoke up. "Why, I do believe I saw Lord Vickem a few moments ago. Isn't he a beau of yours, Helena?"

Helena's murmured reply was gracious enough, though Madeline knew her cousin was seething.

Lady Ravens's loud snicker sealed Madeline's opinion: both Lady Farris and the Duchess were absolutely shallow, horrid people. No wonder Papa left London, she thought. Surely her mother had better manners than this? The conversation continued, thankfully moving away from the cousins and onto the shocking tale regarding the Viscount of Endive most shamefully attending an opera with his mistress.

The evening wore on, and Madeline began to relax, realizing she was not to be given the dreaded cut direct during her first ball, the pinnacle of humiliation, Aunt Cecilia had explained, where one's host would stare at their feet, refusing to acknowledge an unsuitable presence. She found most people reasonably pleasant and she quickly slipped into the art of society conversation: the introduction, a small polite bit of talk, steering away from any mention of her family, then the promise to call sometime in the future, and on to the next. Though it wasn't long before she found herself approached to dance by a string of perfectly polite gentlemen, all of whom had a difficult time keeping their gaze off her dress, she saw not a hint of the coal black curls and arrogant smile of Lord Douglas.

****

"I quite admire the man myself," Sir Walsely said, adjusting the jacket over his enormous belly in order to hide the large wine stain he'd discovered. "Walking about without a care in the world, you'd never think he just tossed off his future wife."

"Undoubtedly, but you must admit the circumstances were rather..." Lord Boddings, slightly thinner though just as drunk, flapped his hand. "I heard Douglas plans to marry his mistress instead."

"Fool!" Walsley exclaimed. "He'll never be allowed in society after that. Douglas would have been better off keeping them both." Both gentlemen broke out into laughter.

"There you are, Madeline! I do hope I'm not intruding." She gratefully turned at the sound of a familiar voice, desperate for anyone who might take her away from more horrible gossip about Lord Douglas.

"Not at all, Agnes." Madeline smiled at the girl, ignoring the booming laughter of the two men behind her.

"Madeline, you must meet Lord Rockford. I've told him all about you. Darling, this is Lady Madeline Sinclair."

Madeline turned to greet the Marquis of Rockford, hiding her surprise at Agnes's much older beau. She knew it was not at all unusual for ladies to marry men as much as twenty years their senior. Nevertheless, Madeline could not help but find it unnerving, noticing how the deep creases made the marquis's face stand out alongside Agnes's unlined one. Despite this, Lord Rockford stood tall and stately before her, a thick head of silver hair adorning his distinguished features. He struck her as a man quite at ease with his own wealth and power, and Agnes hung on his arm soaking up the very presence of him. Madeline executed a perfect curtsey, then looked up and was shocked to see his face had turned the color of fresh cream.

"Sarah," Lord Rockford gasped. Stunned disbelief clouded his eyes, and he grabbed her hand in a stinging grip. Madeline stepped back, confused by such a terrifying reaction. Surely the man was not well! He stared hard at her hands, as though the devil himself adorned her, and Madeline tried unsuccessfully to remove her hand from his painful hold.

"I beg your pardon, your lordship, my name is—"

"Sarah!" he said again, his rasping voice heavy with a desperate passion, and it was then Madeline realized he spoke the name of her mother.

"Darling, really, you must let go of her hand." Agnes laughed nervously. "You shall scare poor Madeline right out of London!" She continued to giggle, but her voice carried an edge of warning to it.

No one paid Agnes the least attention as Madeline and Lord Rockford continued their unspoken struggle. "You knew her?" Madeline asked, unable to stop herself. "You knew my mother?"

Her words seemed to penetrate his haze, breaking the spell between them as Lord Rockford transformed before her eyes. He dropped her hand, the appearance of dread vanishing, replaced by the calm, slightly bored look of a gentleman. "A pleasure to meet you, Lady Madeline Sinclair."

"Darling, Madeline grew up in the most fascinating of places. Did you know she had sheep for pets and even once milked a cow?" Agnes seemed relieved to get back to her original topic. "Imagine milking one's own cow. Could you do such a thing, darling?"

"I could not." Lord Rockford spoke curtly. "You are enjoying your time in London?" he asked Madeline. The tone was detached, but something still burned within him, and she shivered.

"It's lovely here, yes." Why had he called her by her mother's name? There had been terror, and yet a yearning, in his gaze.

"Will you stay long?" he asked, glancing around. "I suppose Sinclair, er...your father is accompanying you." He knows Papa! Her heart beat faster, making it difficult to keep up the polite chatter. Lord Rockford mentioned her father! The first person she'd met in England to actually speak his name aloud instead of in muted whispers.

"I'm afraid he is not. My father died this past winter."

Lord Rockford's gaze settled on her once again. Powerful blue eyes. She was beginning to understand why Agnes clung to him so.

"My condolences. I am sorry to have lost the opportunity to see him again."

She nodded her thanks, racking her brain to see if her father had ever mentioned the Marquis of Rockford. He had so rarely spoken of his former life, plunging into a favorite tale of Odysseus whenever she had inquired.

"Then you've been left all alone in the world, haven't you, Madeline."

"Not at all!" Agnes chirped, nervously. "Why, she lives with Lady Milburg, of course. Such a delightful woman to have for an aunt."

59

"Agnes, I believe I see Lady Boddings. Go and speak to her now." Rockford's gaze didn't bother to graze Agnes as he issued his command, and the young woman very reluctantly did as she was told, leaving Madeline to face Lord Rockford alone.

"I must apologize for my earlier behavior," he began as soon as Agnes was out of earshot. "Your appearance is the exact image of your mother's, and these gloves..." He drew a finger across the delicate pearls. "I remember them well."

He abruptly dropped his hand, moving back to take a glass of Madeira from a tray that had appeared at his side. The small green-liveried servant kept his gaze firmly fixed to the floor. Madeline sipped at her wine, thinking guiltily of Agnes.

"My father never mentioned you," she blurted out, wishing to fill up the sudden silence. "He was rather secretive about his life in London. I'm afraid I know very few of his friends."

"That's a pity, Madeline." Lord Rockford moved a bit closer, and a slight uneasiness began to churn within her, though she did not back away. "I admit I have long regretted the loss of your family. It caused me years of great pain. I do hope you and I can become friends."

She smiled at him, chiding herself for her ridiculous nerves. "I would like that very much, Lord Rockford."

"You needn't be so formal with me," he interrupted, now so close to her they were nearly touching. Madeline tried to take a small step back, to put a bit of distance between them, but the crowd had increased; she could hardly move against the giant swell. "You should call me William."

"Of course, William." Madeline stumbled over his name, unable to shake the feeling that she was doing something terribly wrong. *But surely there can be nothing unseemly in our behavior. Lord Rockford was a cherished friend of my parents! It makes perfect sense that he wishes us to be on more intimate terms.* "I wish Papa could be here to greet you himself," she said.

Lord Rockford took a long drink from his glass. "Yes, it is a terrible pity not to see him again."

"He never stopped grieving over my mother," she continued, all hesitation vanishing at the sudden release of the long pent-up words. "They were very much in love when she died."

His glass shattered. She heard the loud splintering sound, like crackling ice, and then jumped back as the gobletful of wine smashed to the floor. "William!" she cried out, but before she could finish Agnes's voice broke in.

"Darling, what happened?"

Curious glances and mutterings turned in their direction as the guests strained to see what had occurred.

"Do be careful not to cut yourself! Oh, watch for my shoes!" Agnes's flailing only added to the commotion as a flurry of household staff moved in to clear the mess.

Lord Rockford pushed her to the side, waving away her questions. "It matters not. An incompetent servant, is all." He looked up, catching Madeline's eye with a look she could not interpret. "It's gotten quite stuffy in this room tonight." He pulled a handkerchief from his pocket. "Lady Farris always does go a bit heavy on the perfumes. I think I will take in the air before dinner."

He wiped the spilled brandy from his hands, lifting his chin ever so slightly toward the open doors that led to the gardens.

"Perhaps it would benefit you as well, Madeline."

He bowed to her and walked over to a group of

gentlemen, leaving Agnes without so much as a word.

Lord Rockford wished to speak to her alone! Her heart pounded. She glanced around the room, noticing the line of guests, bright and glassy from the festivities, beginning to move into the dining room for a late supper. Did she dare meet him alone? It was a foolish risk, but her heart surged with curiosity. Why had he reacted so violently when she spoke of her mother's death? Madeline glanced down at the pearls winking at her from the black silk gloves. She must find out.

Madeline turned to see Helena, instantly drawn by all the fuss, chatting with a flustered Agnes.

"William? Oh, he must be searching for me. I am always wandering away, such a dolt! Lovely to see you both!"

Madeline watched her scamper away, a plan forming.

"What a strange pair!" Helena said. "She's rather fond of him, I suppose, though I certainly wouldn't marry such an old man, even a handsome one. Shall we go to supper?"

"Helena," Madeline bit her lip, noting her aunt was nowhere in sight. "I must slip outside for a moment. Alone."

Her cousin's mouth dropped. "Madeline! You remember what mother said about going off on your own. She will have my head!"

"I shall be less than a moment, I promise. Please, cousin, it's of urgent importance," she pleaded.

Helena knotted her pale brows together. "This sounds suspiciously like the Lord Douglas fiasco. What if you encounter another madman?"

Madeline knew she had won and backed slowly toward the garden doors, smiling at her cousin's fears. "Don't be ridiculous! I am sure I shall be quite safe."

****

The garden was cool, lush, and quiet, a welcome respite after the heat and noise from inside. Madeline took a deep breath of the fresh air, free of perfumes and spiced foods, and let her thoughts pour over her like a waterfall.

Had she lost her mind? She clearly saw herself, standing alone in the damp grass, foolishly unchaperoned, and waiting to meet an unknown man. Madeline had always believed she had a firm grasp on her sanity, but doubt was creeping in.

She closed her eyes. The hideous nightmare had returned last night, leaving her shaking with terror in the early dawn. It was always the same—her father's hollow eyes seeking forgiveness, the seductive glimmer of the beautiful diamond. Perhaps Lord Rockford could help; he certainly knew her mother well, and his strange reaction to her mother's death still rang in her mind.

But she took a terrible risk meeting him here. Scarcely in London a fortnight, Madeline knew well the consequences of being discovered: disgrace and humiliation. Not to mention the wrath of Aunt Cecilia, she thought with a shudder. Her fearsome lectures on a ruined reputation were enough to keep any lady from running off into the garden. Yet she stayed, shivering in the chilly breeze, as much from apprehension as from the cold.

Was this a mistake? Her father had told her to never mention the diamond to anyone, but surely he would understand! Her hopes of gaining entrance into Lord Douglas's cellar had been fruitless; he was nowhere to be found, leaving Madeline no closer to finding the French Blue diamond than when she arrived in London. She pictured Lord Rockford's eyes when he first greeted her, a cold, commanding blue that held a desperate passion. Could she trust him?

The firm weight of her vow to her father pressed heavily on her chest.

"Lady Madeline Sinclair." The deep voice bolted straight out of the darkness, making her jump. "Or should I refer to you as the innocent young lady I assaulted for no reason?"

She recognized Lord Douglas's voice the moment he spoke—she'd been unable to banish the dangerously seductive tone from her mind, but her heart leaped all the same. She searched the garden's muted corners before spotting him in the darkness, walking toward her.

"It took no small amount of effort to find you, Madeline." He was obviously quite proud of himself for uncovering her name. "My mistake," he continued, setting a half-empty bottle down at her feet, "was looking for a woman in grey serge when, plainly, that is not your normal attire." He finished with a long, heat-filled gaze up the length of her gown, pausing briefly on the nonexistent neckline before ending on her red cheeks. "The color suits you."

If her encounter with the Duke of Douglas had not been seared into her mind like a tattoo on a gypsy, Madeline might not have recognized him at all. A different man than the one she'd met a week earlier stood before her. Tall and handsome in his full dress clothes, he still retained a slightly dangerous, disheveled look that reminded her of their last encounter. His perfectly starched white cravat hung loosely around his neck, the black jacket and waistcoat simple yet with an impeccable cut, one Mr. Banbury would certainly approve, she thought wildly. Gone was any hint of the vulnerability she had seen on his face when he was sleeping, oblivious of her presence. A politely controlled mask of confidence had taken its place, and Madeline found herself more nervous than before.

"How's your eye?" she blurted, desperate to take his attention off her dress. And it couldn't hurt to give him a little reminder, she thought wickedly, of who came out the winner in the last fight.

"Much improved," he replied, brushing aside his unruly curls to show her, "thanks to your remedy."

"My what?" She was having trouble concentrating.

"Garlic and vinegar," he reminded her. "Halbert was convinced you were trying to poison us with the smell."

She smiled, unable to help herself. "It is rather awful, but my intentions were pure."

"That's what I told him. I couldn't imagine such a beauty could be deceitful."

She looked away, suddenly uncomfortable under the intense gaze.

"I promise not to hit you again," she replied, forcing a light tone. "If you promise not to throw me to the ground and—"

"And?" One eyebrow shot up.

"Provoke me."

He laughed then, a full, rich sound that seemed to drop the tension from his face. He was more recognizable now, and Madeline felt her shoulders relax.

"I am sorry," she added. "My behavior that day was unforgivable. I do hope we can start over as friends, Lord Douglas."

She held out her hand, the small warning bell in her head quickly silenced.

"It would be my pleasure." He took the offered fingers, bending slightly to press them against his lips. Not a trace of impropriety, but a sigh caught in her throat all the same, and she held it there, no longer breathing.

In the back of her mind she knew this was not a good idea. She knew perfectly well she should invent some excuse, run straight back into the ballroom and discuss Lady Farris's flowers. She didn't move.

"And since we are already intimately acquainted, I must insist you call me Colin."

"Colin," she said, finally exhaling so the name rushed out in a breathless tone. She wildly searched her mind for something else to say but never managed a word.

Colin pulled her to him, the kiss as much of a surprise as her own response to it. Madeline's body instantly betrayed her, melting against the strong arms that held her until she had lost all sense of her earlier outrage. The world fell away, leaving nothing but Colin's searing lips blistering her own—and the faint smell of lilacs. She gave in to the kiss, responding with equal passion, relishing the low growl of approval from Colin's throat. He shifted against her, sliding his hands down her hips, then lifting her from behind until she was pressed against him more erotically than she'd ever thought possible. The feeling overwhelmed her. Jolts of pleasure made their way through her limbs as Madeline clung to him. He broke free of her mouth, dropping his lips to her neck, circling the white skin until he stumbled onto a most sensitive spot directly below her left ear.

A small, giggling shriek followed the discovery, and Madeline was swept away, all sense of fear vanishing in the newfound feelings.

The garden, swollen with flowers and plants, created a little shelter from the noisy merriment inside, and Colin had long forgotten the ballroom and its inhabitants. He was utterly alone with the green-eyed vixen who haunted his thoughts, this innocently seductive Madeline who clung to him, the thin silk of her dress delivering everything it promised.

Colin knew things were progressing too far, knew he had only moments of gentlemanly control left before tossing her onto the grass, and even as he promised the next kiss would be their last he started pulling off his jacket with the vague idea the heavy material would cushion the ground.

He had paused, yanking his arm from the sleeve before finding her lips again, when the ballroom door burst open, extinguishing the growing passion like a dose of ice water.

Madeline shrieked, and Colin shoved her behind his back, shielding her as he turned to acknowledge the intruder.

"Lord Douglas."

Colin recognized the Marquis of Rockford; the man's humorless smile stared down at them from the open door, music and laughter wafting into the still garden. "I didn't expect to find you here tonight. We seem to have crossed paths once again."

Colin's blood raged with hatred at the sight of Rockford. He took a menacing step forward, but Rockford's next words stopped him cold.

"Terribly sorry to keep you waiting, Madeline," Rockford continued. "Though I see you have found another companion to amuse you. My deepest apologies for the interruption." His stare lingered for a long moment before he turned on his heel and left.

Colin remained rooted to the ground. Rockford knew Madeline's name, had been expecting to meet with her here. Alone.

He swung around, the demeanor of the guilt-ridden, trembling woman in front of him adding to his suspicions. "What are you doing out here, Madeline?" He advanced toward her slowly, demanding an answer.

"I beg your pardon?" Madeline looked desperate for an escape, her gaze darting to the side, her nervousness only increasing her guilt in Colin's mind. He should have listened to his brother; he should never have let down his guard.

Jennifer Ann Coffeen

"I mean, no lady holds court with men in the garden unless she's up to something, so what is it?" He knew he sounded furious, probably terrifying her, but he didn't care. His last moments with Juliana played over and over in his head: hearing her laughter inside his drawing room, opening the door to reveal her skirts hiked above her waist like a common whore... She had played him for a fool, and he would never allow it to happen again.

"What are you suggesting, sir?" she replied, outraged. "That I am some sort of trollop? I won't stand here while you insult me."

She tried to walk away but didn't manage one step before he blocked her. "The man who opened the door, you know him?"

"Lord Rockford."

Colin's jaw clenched. "Is he your lover?"

"Of course not!" Madeline cried.

"But you were meeting him here?"

"Yes—no! Not for what you think. He wants to help me, to answer my questions."

Colin checked himself. He didn't believe that for a moment, but something told him Madeline did. "What questions?"

"I don't remember," she snapped. "And I refuse to answer any more of *your* rude questions."

Despite his anger, Colin instinctively felt Madeline spoke the truth about Rockford. He had spent enough of his youth with women trained in the arts of seduction, and Madeline wasn't one of them. Her passion was timid and new, eagerly exploring newfound feelings in a way Colin found most arousing, and refreshingly honest.

"Perhaps I've jumped to conclusions," he admitted, softening his tone. "But you haven't been entirely honest with me, Madeline. Why did your father send you to me?"

"Send me to you?" She bristled. "Sir, you have

68

an ego as large as the Thames. It may be a shock to discover my duty to my father has nothing to do with you."

"Then why did you break into my home?"

She stared at him aghast.

Colin knew he must sound paranoid, but he felt certain she was in some kind of trouble. He knew well enough what kind of man Lord Rockford was—ruthless, with a gift for preying on one's weakness, finding the one flaw he could fully exploit.

She shook her head, struggling for something to say. "I told you before, it was a simple mistake. My cousin and I—"

"Were lost," he interrupted. "Alone, at six in the morning."

"I must go back now. My aunt will be looking for me."

"Madeline." He pulled her close, the name coming out in a near whisper. "I cannot protect you if you won't tell me the truth."

"Protect me? Why should I need protection?"

"Because Lord Rockford isn't the kind of man you should be meeting alone."

"And you are?" She had him there.

"I must go," she said, stubbornly pushing against his arms.

"Promise me you'll stay away from him." He tightened his grip. "And unless you want the entire ballroom to become aware of your private garden parties, I would advise you to hurry."

Her eyes widened. "You wouldn't dare!"

"I'm waiting." Perhaps he was being a bit hasty in his concerns over Lord Rockford, but Colin didn't care. If she was going to insist on shredding her reputation by sneaking around with strange men, it had better be with him.

"I promise." She sealed her vow by forcefully bringing her foot down upon his boot. "May I go?"

Colin couldn't help himself; he hauled her over for another kiss. This one short and firm, though still rather agreeable, he admitted.

"You may," he said, setting her down. "But this discussion isn't over. I'm still determined to have my keys back, along with an explanation for your thievery."

"I don't know what you're talking about," she began, and he quickly cut her off by placing his hands firmly on her hips and turning her toward the French doors.

"When you get inside, go straight to the dining room. It's bound to be crowded, and no one will notice you've just appeared. I'll come and find you."

Colin thought his advice quite sound, but she turned back to look at him, her mouth open. "You sound as if you've done this sort of thing before, Lord Douglas."

She was back to calling him that, suddenly prim as a dowager after moaning in his arms.

"Would that bother you?"

"Of course not. I should only add it to your list of unsuitable traits," she said, moving toward the door. "I believe 'rake' falls in nicely between 'galling manners' and 'bad tempered,' don't you think?"

She sauntered away, leaving him to watch the sassy sway of her hips, obviously congratulating herself on getting the last word.

Colin grinned, reaching down to the ground. "Madeline," he said, and she turned to see him holding up an ivory slipper in one hand. "You forgot your shoe."

Chapter Five

Once inside, Madeline found Helena waiting anxiously, and together the cousins joined the crush of people in the dining room. Madeline quickly sought out the first person she recognized from her aunt's endless introductions, the cheerfully red-cheeked and slightly rotund figure of Sir Rawlings, who was eagerly waving them over with a daffodil-colored handkerchief. Madeline didn't waste a moment, gripping her cousin's hand and returning the wave, greeting the man as though they had been chatting away with him for hours. This is how Lady Milburg, closely followed by her most intimate friend, the Honorable Miss Lillian, found her niece and daughter moments later, apparently enthralled by Sir Rawlings's lecture on the great English advancements in travel.

"Gracious, girls, have you been here all night? Good evening, Sir Rawlings. I see you are entertaining, as usual."

"Oh, Lady Milburg!" Sir Rawlings pulled himself away from his own voice to acknowledge the newcomers. "Yes, yes, indeed, rather a bluestocking in the making is Madeline. A fine insight on the dangers of the phaeton."

"It is really less the vehicle itself I'm against and more the reckless young gentlemen who insist on driving so frightfully fast." Miss Lillian, a small unmarried woman well past the first bloom of her beauty, was ever anxious to insert her opinions.

"I agree, miss. I cannot tell you how dangerous our roads have become! No decent citizen can make his way across the city these days." Sir Rawlings was in his element, continuing on while Madeline breathed a sigh of relief that her absence had gone unnoticed. *Colin's plan worked perfectly,* she thought grudgingly, still irritated by his high-handed manner. *Colin. The very thought of him makes my heart pound with rage. And with the need to kiss him again,* she admitted, her face heating up. She forced herself to pay attention, still remembering his warnings about Lord Rockford. Madeline didn't know what to believe, but for tonight, at least, she would keep her promise. *Lord knows Colin is enough of a scoundrel to follow through on his threats of humiliation.*

"Madeline, dear, do pay attention. Miss Lillian was just asking if you'd met anyone of interest tonight," her aunt said, interrupting her thoughts.

Madeline looked up to answer and caught a glimpse of silver hair moving through the crowd. Lord Rockford was coming over! Madeline slouched, hoping she hadn't been seen.

"Helena, tell me, is Lord Rockford coming this way?"

Aunt Cecilia's eyes popped open. "Dear girl, he won't do at all! The Marquis of Rockford is courting Agnes."

"Though he is quite dashing," Miss Lillian added, adjusting her glasses to see him better. "If I were but a few years younger, he'd be quite the thing." The sound that followed sounded suspiciously like a low-pitched giggle and lasted a rather long time.

"Don't be ridiculous, Lillian," Aunt Cecilia snapped. "He won't do for my girls at all, not a bit, and I won't hear another word on it."

"I am not interested in Lord Rockford as a suitor," Madeline cried, stunned by her aunt's harsh reproach. Poor Miss Lillian shrank back, obviously crushed that her jest had not been better received. "He was a friend of my mother's."

"Oh, honestly, Madeline, such preoccupation with the past! Do excuse my niece, Sir Rawlings. She's a bit of a maudlin thing." This last was spoken in whisper, though audible enough for everyone to hear.

Madeline's eyes were narrowed when Sir Rawlings jumped in. "Not at all. The past is a wonderful thing to look back on. Why, I myself remember Lady Sinclair quite fondly—rather thought everyone made too much fuss over her behavior." The man trailed off, realizing his blunder, and began madly fumbling about his pockets until he produced a small silver snuff box.

"What I mean to say," he nervously popped the lid, suddenly fascinated by its contents, "is that, of course, the past is rather such a wonderful thing to look back on. One gets a whole new perspective on life."

He paused to snort a fingertip full of the foul-looking powder before mumbling on about his glorious days fighting Napoleon.

Madeline's racing mind couldn't focus on Sir Rawlings's old war stories. She was aghast. *What does he mean, 'her behavior'?* She had lost sight of the silver-haired man and started to crane her neck to look for him again when Helena tugged her arm.

"He's coming toward us!" she yelped, and Madeline immediately sank down, wishing she did not tower so over the other ladies.

"What is it? Has Lord Vickem arrived?" Aunt Cecilia was instantly alert, searching for her daughter's suitor.

"Worse than Vickem," Helena said, to everyone's surprise. "It's your mad duke!"

Madeline's heart dropped to her feet, and without so much as an apology to poor Sir Rawlings she spun to leave.

"He's behind you," Helena added, rather too late. She had been bracing herself for those grey eyes, but instead nearly slammed into a bricklike chin. Colin was mere inches away. In fact, if the man stood any closer her aunt would insist on a proposal. Had he lost his mind?

"Sir Rawlings." Colin greeted the Baron, his gaze still centered directly on Madeline—her mouth, to be exact. Good God, he wasn't going to try to kiss her again, was he? In front of everyone? A shiver slid up her spine.

"I came to beg an introduction." That sealed her suspicions. In her brief, albeit personal, encounters with the Duke of Douglas, she had found him to be the kind of man who didn't beg for anything.

He was up to something, and when she saw Lord Rockford glide past them out of the dining room, his mouth clenched in anger, Colin's intentions became very apparent.

"Lord Douglas! Good to see you looking so fit! I was just having the most refreshing conversation with Lady Madeline Sinclair here. May I have the honor?"

While Sir Rawlings made introductions, Madeline slowly backed a few steps away, putting some much needed distance between herself and Colin. Perhaps he felt they had gotten off on the wrong foot; he did seem to have straightened himself up after the garden. The cravat had been expertly retied, his jacket was back in place and smoothed down, and he was no longer alone. A charming gentleman whom Sir Rawlings introduced as Lord Edward Montgomery stood next to Colin, his height and cynical grin leaving her no doubt they were related.

"Lady Madeline Sinclair." Edward beamed down at her as though he had made some great discovery.

"I have long waited to meet you."

He certainly has a pleasant air about him. Madeline watched his gracious leg to all the ladies.

"I'm flattered, Lord Montgomery, though I can't begin to imagine why," Madeline replied, not a single note of false modesty in her voice. "I'm afraid you will probably find me quite dull."

He smiled at her, the teasing glint in his eyes reminding her of someone. "Oh, I doubt very much anyone could find you dull. My brother certainly doesn't think so."

Good Lord, he's Colin's brother. She blushed fiercely. *What must he have heard about me?* She instantly snatched her hand away, only to find it reclaimed by Colin.

"Lady Madeline Sinclair." Colin lifted the hand to his lips and spoke in a low voice. "I am honored to finally meet you in public."

She nearly fell at his words, catching a brief look at Helena, whose cheeks had gone the color of her mother's turban. Madeline tried to think of a way out of such mortification, until she realized Colin was giving her a slow, teasing wink. Horrible brothers! She wanted to slap both of them with her fan.

"What's that?" Sir Rawlings spoke up. "You've met before, did you say?"

She could feel Helena's panic vibrating from her, but Colin simply shrugged. "Not at all. You were speaking of?"

"The mighty British army's smoldering reign over Old Boney! I had just been reminded of the small part I played in the battle of Trafalgar, under Nelson, of course, and the man is no less a fighter than the rumors imply." Sir Rawlings seemed eager to impress, though Madeline couldn't imagine why. Surely Colin didn't have any experience in the war? He was a duke, with little time for such dangerous activities. Madeline glanced at him from the corner of her eye. He stood patiently as Sir Rawlings listed his soldierly accomplishments, his face relaxed, any trace of his injury vanished beneath the cool exterior of a gentleman.

"You would be more expert than I in French combat, of course, Lord Douglas; it's a shame your military career was ended so young."

Madeline's mouth fell open. "You were fighting in France? You never told me that," she said, forgetting they were supposed to have only just met.

"There are many things you don't know about me, Madeline."

Her attempt to think quickly of a saucy retort was interrupted by a yelp from her cousin.

"Lord Vickem!" Helena hissed, again latching onto Madeline's arm. "He has come after all, Madeline. I am doomed!"

Helena had a naturally sweet voice, the kind that accompanied a pianoforte quite beautifully—and carried a little too well across the room, alerting their entire group to turn and stare at the approach of Lord Vickem.

For a moment, the briefest of moments, as Madeline watched the young Viscount nearly knock over a passing servant and two elderly gentlemen, she thought he did not look so terrible. Perhaps her cousin's judgments were too harsh. Certainly the man looked small and colorless compared to their current companions, and certainly he could have chosen a jacket with less attention to ruffles, but she could see no real harm in the man. His eyes shone with love, the very beacon of devotion to Helena. Surely he could not be all that bad, so eager to come to her, to take her hand...

And then he spoke.

"My mistress's eyes are nothing like the sun!" he cried, holding one hand to his heart. "Coral is far more red than her lips red." Helena squealed, darting out of his reach, leaving his poem to be delivered to Sir Rawlings. "If snow be white, why then her breasts are dun; if hair be wires, black wires grow on her head!" he sang out.

My God, Helena was right! Madeline stared, unable to believe what she was hearing as Sir Rawlings again produced the daffodil handkerchief to wipe his face. Lord Vickem did indeed spit when he talked. She had never witnessed such a thing before. *Could it be his teeth? Perhaps it would help if he spoke a bit more slowly.*

"I have seen roses damasked, red and white, but no such roses in her cheeks."

"Charming." Sir Rawlings sniffed. "I had no idea I could elicit such a greeting from you, Vickem."

"And in some perfumes there is more delight than in the breath that from my mistress reeks."

A loud snicker was heard from Miss Lillian, but Lord Vickem paid no heed, pushing his way into the crowd to corner the wailing Helena.

"I love to hear her speak, yet well I know that music hath a more pleasing sound."

"Is this man known to you?" Edward spoke up from behind, a sharp edge to his voice. While Colin seemed to be finding this all terribly amusing, Edward's amiable expression had darkened to a scowl. "Good God, Colin, the man is off his head."

"I don't know," Colin replied. "The sonnet is well memorized." It was true. Lord Vickem sputtered out line after line of the Shakespearean sonnet, leaving Madeline to fear he would go on forever.

"I grant I never saw a goddess go, my mistress when she walks upon the ground."

"I did no such thing! I am simply attending a ball." Helena tried to wrench her hand away as quietly as possible, but the man had a grip that would hold for days. Her fair skin was beginning to redden, and Madeline wasn't the only one who noticed.

"I would release her, Vickem, if you'd like my advice." Edward spoke first, his hand appearing on the left shoulder of the smaller man, Colin's on the right. "In fact, my advice would be to leave Helena alone entirely."

They loomed over him, two mountains engulfing a stream.

"May I finish my recitation?" Lord Vickem squeaked, shrinking from the two men. "The final couplet is most crucial."

"You may not." Colin spoke this time, steering Lord Vickem away, the little man protesting.

"May I call on you tomorrow, Helena? I do so wish you to hear the final couplet!"

Poor Lord Vickem. Madeline held in her mirth with difficulty. Such a pitiable man, completely unable to grasp how severe his position had become.

Helena, buoyed by Colin and Edward's interception, unwaveringly shook her blonde curls at her tormentor. "I believe I will be very sick tomorrow, a long lingering type of illness."

But Aunt Cecilia's shrill tones quickly interrupted. "Dearest Vickem, we would be delighted to have you call upon us tomorrow! Helena is in perfect health, isn't that so?" Aunt Cecilia smiled sharply at her daughter, fluttering her fan rapidly enough to put a hummingbird to shame.

Before anyone could answer, Lord Vickem was gone, forcefully shuffled off into the crowd by Colin's shove.

"I doubt he will bother you with his poetry again," Edward announced, gallantly winking in Helena's direction.

"I should think not," Madeline said. "Anyone with half a mind could recognize the threat, though I'm not sure that man qualifies."

Helena wasn't listening. She had become too entranced by her rescuer to drag her gaze from Edward's face. "Thank you from the bottom of my heart, kind sir," she whispered, her voice taking on a soft, coy sound Madeline had never heard before. "I don't know what I would have done without your bravery tonight. I should have swooned if he had spoken one more word to me!"

"Think nothing of it, Helena. A beautiful lady such as you will attract all sorts of attention if left alone for too long. Shall I escort you to your carriage?" Helena took Lord Edward's outstretched arm, and they floated off, leaving Madeline staring after them.

"That was certainly easy," she muttered, recalling her advice to Helena about finding another suitor.

Colin shrugged at her, offering his own arm, which Madeline ignored. "Your cousin plays the game. She is only doing what is expected of an unmarried woman. You could take a lesson from her, Madeline, for all I ever see from you is frowns."

She frowned at him. "I have no wish to marry, so it doesn't matter, does it? If certain men do not like my face, they are welcome to turn their gaze elsewhere." She hurried after her love-struck cousin, suddenly desperate to quit the Farris ball.

"Ah, but that's the problem, Madeline. I do like your face." Colin caught up with her, slipping her arm through his in a movement that stole her breath.

"Thank you for helping Helena," she found herself saying. "It was—"

"Brave? See, you're getting better already." Madeline recalled the fan in her right hand and was raising it to his cheek when her aunt bounced into view.

"What a pleasure it's been, Lord Douglas. Such

kindness you've shown us this evening!" Aunt Cecilia artfully bowed her head to Colin while managing to loudly whisper in Madeline's ear. "Do you see the way Lord Montgomery looks at our Helena? I do believe Lord Vickem has a competitor." She swooped her head back up, balancing the turban. "And I must tell you, sir, I will be informing my girls not to believe one word of that nonsense gossip flying around about you. Not a word of it!"

Madeline shut her eyes, wondering how much of the rich wine her aunt had consumed. "Very thoughtful of you, Lady Milburg," she heard Colin reply, a tinge of laughter in his voice.

"Not at all. The least I can do. Now do promise you will call upon us soon, and send my regards to your lovely mother."

"You shall soon have the opportunity of sending them yourself. My mother is due to arrive in London tomorrow morning."

"Oh! I'm sure we will be very glad to see her."

"The twenty-first of April," Madeline said, suddenly recalling the letter she had seen in Colin's study. Lady Douglas was having her dinner party in a few days' time at Colin's townhouse, and there would be many guests and servants about, certainly enough distraction for her to easily slip down to the cellar. "I, too, am most anxious to meet your mother," she hinted. "As soon as possible, really, and I would much prefer a quieter setting, such as an intimate dinner among friends."

"Madeline!" Aunt Cecilia's sharp voice interrupted her, while Colin fixed her with a strangely intense stare. "I do believe all the excitement has clouded your mind. Good evening, Lord Douglas."

Untangling herself from the hordes of people, Madeline soon lost sight of Colin as she made her way toward the entrance. She was relieved to be

going home at last, eager to fall into bed and let the
night's events sweep through her mind. Had she said
enough to prompt an invitation to Lady Douglas's
party? Doubtful, but she held fast to the shred of
hope. Besides, it was impossible to know what Colin
was thinking about anything. The last hour painted
him as the perfect gentleman, but alone in the
garden she had seen something more. He was
insistent, determined to help her, but what would he
say if he knew about the diamond?

Madeline stepped outside, following her aunt
and cousin to the waiting carriage, when a sudden
chill, like an ill wind, blew across her neck.

Jennifer Ann Coffeen

Chapter Six

Her fingers sank into the earth. She was digging again, faster and deeper than before, with her empty, searching hands. The diamond was missing. It had gone from her grasp, vanished into the black soil she had ripped it from. *I must find it!* Already the dark room seemed unbearable without its glow, the warmth of its power. She had to find it...just a little deeper...she would have it soon...

"Madeline."

She froze. The rasping, worm-ridden voice came from below, and her fingers drew back from the dirt.

"Beware, Madeline."

"I cannot hear you," she whispered, thrusting mud-caked hands over her ears. "There is no one here. I am all alone." The earth below her began to move, to rise up, revealing the smooth white outline of bone, her father's hand reaching out for her.

"Beware, Madeline! The curse has you in its eye!"

****

"And the thief Tavernier, refusing to heed the ancient warnings, ripped the blue diamond from the idol's forehead." Brigette raised an egg into the air, her delicate brown eyes shining as she held her listeners enthralled. "It gleamed in his hands like violet fire, burning him with its beauty and its promise of riches." She lowered the egg, cracking it hard against the bowl in front of her. "Men cannot resist such temptations, my lady," she said with a tilt of her head in Sam's direction.

"But surely he didn't escape with the diamond?"

Madeline demanded, ignoring Sam's sputtering defense. "He was being chased by hundreds of natives!"

Brigette, Aunt Cecilia's maid and Sam's newest amour, had turned out to be exactly what Madeline needed for all her questions. She had awakened exhausted from another night of unsettling dreams that left her filled with a growing dread over the diamond's curse. Though all rational sense told her they were nothing more than nightmares, fragments of her fears and memories to be quickly forgotten, Madeline could not shake the horror that filled her nights. Her father's voice was so clear, the images so vivid, that they did not fade away in the light like other dreams but stayed with her, a chronic ache in her mind.

Desperate for help, she was determined to find out all she could of this French Blue diamond. She had little information other than a few ramblings from her father, and so she turned to Brigette, admittedly the only French person she knew, and spent the morning plying her with questions on the diamond's strange past.

"What happened to Mr. Tavernier? Was he captured?" Madeline asked, motioning for the maid to continue.

"Not at all! He escaped India by the skin of his heels and returned to France, but the curse was still upon his back." Her voice took on a dark tone that sent Madeline leaning forward on her stool. "Soon after the French Blue left Tavernier's hands, he was killed, ripped apart by the blood-soaked teeth of wild dogs." Like any true storyteller, Brigette let the words hang free in the air, allowing the audience to savor them like a fine wine.

"I thought the diamond was supposed to be the idol's eye?" Sam spoke up, still bristling from her earlier comment. "What was it doing in the forehead?"

"It belonged in the forehead, *mauvais garçon!*" Brigette snapped over her shoulder. "The idol was a Cyclops, therefore doubling the vengeance upon Tavernier." She turned back to Madeline. "Unfortunately, my lady, the diamond's curse did not end there. It later became the favorite jewel of King Louis XVI before he was..." Brigette made a slicing motion across her throat to signify the King of France's beheading. "And it hasn't been seen since, though I pity the foolish soul who stole it. Anyone who ever had the misfortune of possessing the French Blue diamond perished from a horrible death."

Madeline shuddered, the words from her Papa rushing back. Had the curse of the French Blue claimed her parents? Her mother had died tragically, overcome by a fever so sudden even Madeline's own aunt refused to speak of it. As for Papa, though once very strong, his mind and body had slowly declined into a long, shadowy illness in which he endured months of agony. Could this be the vengeance Brigette spoke of?

"And no one was ever accused of stealing the diamond?" Madeline asked.

"I cannot say for sure, my lady." Brigette looked up in surprise. "I've only heard the stories from *Maman.* She was heavy with me when they fled to London just before the Terror began in Paris. *Maman* has the Sight, you see, and warned everyone it was coming." She cracked another egg, whisking the yolks into a froth. "It could have been common thieves, though some say it was taken to line the pockets of the French revolutionaries."

"Most likely," Sam snorted, and Brigette glared him into silence.

"But there are many who believe the devil himself took it—rose up from hell to reclaim his wicked gem until the time comes to unleash its evil on another powerful man."

"A devil with one eye?"

"*Fermes la bouche,* Sam! You are interrupting my history." She smacked him with her spoon, while he retaliated by giving her a quick playful squeeze that sent Brigette into giggles. Madeline hid her smile. It certainly seemed Greta was forgotten.

"But it is long lost for sure, my lady," Brigette continued, her face filled with a furious blush as she turned from Sam. "Many are still searching for it. It's been said Napoleon would sell his very soul to possess the French Blue's powers, though I can't imagine why. I would be dead terrified to lay eyes on it myself. *C'est un mal très mauvais.*" She crossed herself. "It should stay buried forever."

"Madeline, I have been searching for you everywhere!" Helena burst into the kitchen, sending Brigette and Sam to opposite sides of the table. "This is absolute torture. Mama has arranged for the despicable Lord Vickem to call on me this morning. She says we are only being good neighbors, but I know perfectly well she is forcing me into marriage, and I will be miserable for the rest of my life!"

"Good morning, my lady." Sam tipped his hat, nervously keeping his gaze on the floor and away from the blushing Brigette. His fears were needless; Helena was oblivious to everything but her anxiety.

"And these awful poems! He now insists on comparing me to rodents!"

Madeline glanced at the heavily perfumed parchment in her cousin's hand and read, "What will become of the timid little squirrel? Will she bounce over trees and fill her belly with my nuts?"

"Good Lord," Madeline muttered, rereading that last stanza. "Well it certainly isn't very flattering."

Madeline had hoped Aunt Cecilia would cross Lord Vickem off the suitor list after last night's fiasco, but Helena's problem was not so easily solved. Creditors had a way of changing Aunt Cecilia's mind, but Madeline refused to give up. There must be a way out of forcing Helena into a disastrous marriage, though Madeline knew nothing short of death or humiliation could deter her aunt.

"You must help me, Madeline," Helena begged. "If only that dashing Lord Montgomery were here to help. He and his brother did such a wonderful job saving us yesterday, did they not?"

"I cannot recall," she muttered, refusing to admit Lord Douglas had done anything but irritate her. Despite fighting the attraction, the seductively brooding Colin still plagued her—memories of his hands sliding down her hips, his lips dousing her skin in fire and continuing their journey beneath the soft silk at the top of her gown, the scent of lilacs and sweet grass tickling her nose. Madeline took a deep breath. *Do not even think it,* she told herself stubbornly. *The last person you need help from is Lord Douglas.* But Helena was right; the brothers had managed to get rid of Lord Vickem. Madeline suddenly turned to look at her cousin.

"Helena," she said slowly. "What would you be willing to do to avoid Lord Vickem?"

"Anything! Cut my hair, burn my favorite gown—"

"That won't be necessary," she hastily interrupted. "Sam, will you fetch me a leaf from the very tall vine in the garden? And be sure to wear gloves," she warned, before turning back to her cousin's hopeful face. "Prepare yourself, Helena. You may be rather itchy for awhile."

****

Colin stood in the middle of the small stone cellar, hands fisted on his hips as he glared at the obstinate room that refused to satisfy his curiosity. It had taken several days of prodding the staff, but

86

Halbert had finally received a confession from one of the kitchen maids. Greta had dramatically recounted Lady Madeline Sinclair's sudden entrance through the kitchen door.

"Scarin' the absolute courage out of me when she did so, sir, and I'm ashamed to admit I fainted right dead on the floor."

Despite her faint, Greta was miraculously able to recall a full description of the fine lady's hair and cloak and, more importantly, the crucial detail that Madeline had been in pursuit of something in the cellar. Using Halbert's keys, Colin had dedicated the morning to investigating the dank little room, but so far he had come up empty.

Why the hell was Madeline so desperate to get into his home? She practically tossed herself at his feet last night, begging for an invitation to one of his mother's mind-numbing dinner parties. Why? It certainly wasn't in hopes of impressing the *ton*. Madeline seemed as eager for London society as he was, possessing none of the shallow arts necessary to most women, for which he was thankful. For nearly half an hour Colin convinced himself she was merely desperate to see him again, no matter how many tedious conversations must be endured, but the theory soon disintegrated.

It's something in this room. It explained everything: breaking into his home, last night's behavior, the stolen keys. Madeline was undoubtedly searching for something, but what? *The cellar holds nothing of interest. The dirt floor and damp stone walls should be the farthest thing from a lady's mind, but Madeline took an enormous risk to come here.* He frowned at the silence. There must be a reason, and he wasn't going to rest until he found it.

"My lord," Halbert called through the open door from the hallway. "Did you find anything?"

"Nothing but an unsettling awareness of the

household mice," Colin replied, amused that his butler remained outside the door, unwilling to dirty his impeccable shoes. "You don't think Madeline would be looking for rodents, do you, Halbert?"

"Quite impossible to say, my lord, but if she was I'm sure it would be with good reason."

Colin turned toward his butler, surprised by his confidence. "I see she has already captured your loyalty, then?"

"There is true sincerity there, milord, and we cannot forget it was the young lady who cured you of your...afflictions." Halbert, already stiff as a lance, drew himself up straighter.

"I haven't forgotten." If anything, it only heightened the mystery surrounding Madeline, one with which he was quickly becoming obsessed. "Has my mother arrived yet?" Dusting off his breeches, Colin stepped out of the tiny cellar.

"Just this moment, sir. I informed her you had pressing business with the staff, and she awaits you in the drawing room."

Colin took one last look around the tiny room before heading upstairs to the ground floor, admitting defeat. *Maybe I've been looking at this all wrong.* His brow wrinkled with the puzzle as he made his way to the drawing room. He had tried and failed to get Madeline to trust him, to tell him what he wanted to know, and she had thwarted him at every turn. *Perhaps I should simply give her what she wants.* He smiled at the thought. Madeline's secrets were her own, for now, but he would continue to seek them out.

"Edward has told me all about your young woman." Lady Douglas greeted her son's entrance with an outstretched hand and her usual bluntness. Though much smaller and more delicate, she was a near perfect blend of her two sons, with Edward's easy smile and grace mingling with Colin's dark coloring and intensity. "Don't look so surprised, dear," she continued as he kissed her cheek, ignoring the rest of the greeting. "Your brother does occasionally manage a letter."

"I'm glad to know they are filled with my personal news," he answered wryly. "No doubt in an attempt to mask his own sins. How was your journey, Mother? You're looking well."

"And you are looking better than I've seen you in months." She stood back to survey him with a critical eye. "Edward told me you had a different air about you, and I must say I agree with him."

"I had a slight head wound, but it's healed now."

"No," she shook her head slowly, "you had a vacant, hard look about you for many months before, even before this wretched affair with Juliana. Should I be attributing this miraculous change to the young lady Edward spoke of?"

"If you wish." Colin was purposefully obtuse, unable to miss the real questions behind his mother's curiosity. They were questions he was not yet ready to answer for himself.

"That's going to be it, then?" Lady Douglas settled herself on the sofa, giving him the stern eye that had given him terrors as a child. "I'm not to know anything about this woman?"

"I can honestly say she is the strangest woman I have ever met."

"Colin!" His mother was appalled. "That is no way to speak of a lady. I hope you are keeping these ill opinions to yourself."

"Not at all," he replied cheerfully. "I have told her exactly how strange she is, on several occasions."

Lady Douglas narrowed her eyes at him. "I am going to have to insist on meeting her, Colin, if for no other reason than to make apologies for my son."

Colin laughed and noted his mother's stunned look at the unusual show of gaiety.

"You are in luck, Mother. She is also very anxious to meet you."

****

Toxicodendron, also known as poisonous ivy, a plant Madeline's papa had taught her to spot when she was just a child.

Madeline gingerly held the leaf with her handkerchief. After the merest touch of the poisonous ivy, Helena instantly burst out in red blotchy bumps. They covered her arms and neck and even a large spot in the middle of her forehead, a location the victim herself insisted upon: "Mama can always make me cover up my arms, but this will be impossible to hide!"

"My lady, what have you done! You will be covered for days!" Brigette stared in horror.

"That is the very point!" Helena laughed. "She will never allow Lord Vickem to see me like this!"

When Aunt Cecilia finally dragged herself down for breakfast, she took one look at her daughter's red blotches and started screaming.

"A milk bath and some powder, and do find me the highest-necked gown she has. Hurry, Brigette, we must hide the dreadful spots before Lord Vickem comes!"

But it was all in vain. After nearly an hour, during which Brigette scrubbed her with the milk, powder, and even one of Cook's foul-smelling egg concoctions, the red blotches still remained.

"There is nothing to it," Aunt Cecilia moaned, while Helena sat soaking merrily in her tub of milk. "I absolutely forbid you to set foot in anyone's presence until these splotches clear."

****

Lord Vickem's arrival an hour later was further complicated by the unexpected call of the Marquis of Rockford. Her aunt seemed deeply displeased by Lord Rockford's presence, ordering both men to be placed in the drawing room and forcing Madeline to preside over the odd gathering alone.

"I had the most interesting conversation with Sir Rawlings last night," Madeline began, racking her brain for a suitable topic. She dearly wished Aunt Cecilia would join her. She had gone upstairs, claiming the deepest concerns for her ailing daughter, but Madeline felt certain her aunt's only concern was escaping the present company.

"It was over the evils of England's transportation, fascinating, really, and a subject that affects us all." She smiled encouragingly at the men, fully aware that no one was listening. Lord Rockford silently gazed at her, scrutinizing her every gesture with his icy blue eyes, while Lord Vickem shoved himself deep into the purple cushions, fidgeting in his unreasonably tight pants. "I'm sure you both have very good opinions to share. What say you, Lord Vickem?"

"I am so very worried over my chipmunk," he replied, his voice warring between a whine and a demand. "She is always complaining of her ills. She cannot take rides in the park, will not dance, and even her ears grow too tender to listen to my poetry. I say, Rockford, do you think she might be dying?"

Lord Rockford tore his gaze away from Madeline, startled at the morbid question. "Not at all, man. Why, Lady Milburg informed us she has merely caught a chill, nothing for concern."

"Pity," Lord Vickem muttered. He sank lower in the cushions, sulkily flipping through his notebook. "The very best poetry is done with dying love. Such an inspirational muse."

"I suppose that is true," Madeline said. "Tell me, do you have other interests aside from poetry?"

"Of course not," Lord Vickem answered, not bothering to look up from his notebook. "When one has such a keen talent, what else could one possibly do?" He made a noise indicating her stupidity.

Horrible little fish. Madeline noticed Lord Rockford's gaze settling on her once again. *Where is Aunt Cecilia? Hiding away with Helena?*

She could certainly understand evading Lord Vickem, but truthfully Madeline felt Lord Rockford was the one being avoided. Aunt Cecilia had returned the marquis's formal greeting with a frigid nod when he arrived, dispensing with her usual chatter and dashing upstairs almost immediately. *Strange. I wonder why Aunt Cecilia doesn't like him?* Lord Rockford was nearly engaged to Agnes; perhaps her aunt feared a scandal, though Madeline had her doubts. Why, this morning Aunt Cecilia was sizing up Lord Douglas's fortune, and she had once called him the worst rogue in London!

"I sorrow for myself, I lament like the crows," Lord Vickem said, scribbling in his little book.

"I sorrow for you, as well," Madeline replied, her lips tightening. "May I offer anyone a biscuit?" She held up the small plate, suddenly wishing she had used a few of the ivy leaves on herself.

"I see you've inherited Sarah's grace along with her beauty," Lord Rockford said, accepting a biscuit. He smiled at her startled expression. "I must confess, I have never managed to forget your mother."

"I do wish I knew more about her," Madeline replied, cautiously, hoping he wasn't planning to break another glass. "I'm afraid Papa could be very secretive."

"I'm so sorry we were interrupted last night, Madeline," Lord Rockford continued, glancing over to make sure Lord Vickem remained too wrapped up in crying crows to hear. "I had hoped to finish our conversation."

"As did I!" Madeline busied herself with a napkin, unable to meet his penetrating gaze as she relived the humiliating scene in the garden. "I hope you do not think ill of me. I was rather lost and wandered into the garden by mistake." Good lord, could she never think of another excuse? All of London would think she had no sense of direction at all. "Lord Douglas was offering me directions," she finished lamely, realizing she had somehow made things worse.

"Lord Douglas is a friend?"

"Colin?" She thought for a moment. "We are recent acquaintances, but I would not think to call us friends." Would he agree? Colin did kiss her—several times, in fact—and had whispered some quite amiable things in her ear.

"I don't believe he dislikes me," she continued, before recalling how angry Colin became when she stole his keys. And of course she had no intention of returning them; he wasn't going to take kindly to that. "But our natures do not match well, you see. He is a very bossy man."

"Madeline, would it be too bold of me to offer you a word of advice?" Lord Rockford leaned in, keeping his voice low. "I must caution you against forming an attachment to Lord Douglas. He isn't a man to be trusted."

"How very strange. Colin said the same thing about you." The words leapt from her mouth before she realized her mistake. She started to apologize, but a slim, well-kept hand suddenly gripped her wrist like a vise.

"What exactly did he say?"

Madeline swallowed her gasp, fearful of drawing Lord Vickem's attention. "Or was it Sir Rawlings he was speaking of? Yes, now that I think about it, Lord Douglas was speaking of Sir Rawlings, warning me not to get myself trapped in one of his long war stories." She laughed, mimicking her aunt's breezy tone while gently but decisively pulling her hand away.

"A mistake, then," Lord Rockford said, retrieving his fallen biscuit only to crack it in half between his fingers.

"Gentlemen, I have been neglecting you!" Aunt Cecilia breezed into the room, all smiles and fluttering words, not a trace of her earlier apprehension. "My apologies, of course, and Helena sends hers, as well. Lord Vickem, have you yet managed one of our delectable biscuits? Here, let me find you the largest one."

"Do not bother, I find them disgusting. How is my chipmunk? Very ill and pale? Calling for me?"

Madeline gratefully gave over the rest of the visit to her aunt, scarcely able to speak another word. She was trembling slightly, wondering what could have caused such a reaction. Had Colin been right? Was Lord Rockford not to be trusted?

Lord Rockford said very little himself, politely answering the few questions Aunt Cecilia put toward him. Once or twice he tried to meet Madeline's eye, as if seeking to apologize, but she pretended not to notice. His expression, though no longer twisted by fury, grew colder to her with each passing minute. The line of his chin, rather distinguished in the soft candlelight of the Farris ball, now gave him a menacing air.

A quarter of an hour passed with the customary dull chatter until finally the men stood to take their leave.

"You will tell Helena of my adoration? And do make sure she gets this poem immediately. I have just finished writing it." Lord Vickem's orders to Aunt Cecilia went on incessantly, until Madeline feared he would stay until nightfall.

"Madeline." Lord Rockford's icy tone pierced her, and she reluctantly looked up. "You must forgive me. My reaction today was most ungentlemanly."

"Please don't trouble yourself, Lord Rockford."

"William."

"Yes, of course." Madeline tried to smile as Colin's warnings from last night drifted in and out of her head like the music of the soft violins from Lord Farris's ballroom.

"May I try to make amends? Tomorrow afternoon, perhaps?" Lord Rockford's voice was soft, so as not to be overheard, but Madeline saw her aunt glance back at them several times. "My behavior was beastly, unpardonable, and my only excuse..." He stopped, looking down in sorrow. "One I cannot tell you."

"I don't understand," she replied, drawn by the sadness lining his eyes. He seemed to be fighting a battle within himself, and her fear of him eased slightly.

"When I first saw you, so beautiful and pure, the very image of Sarah, it took my breath away." Clenching his fist, he pressed it to his lips.

"Do pardon us, Lord Rockford, but I must insist we retire now." Aunt Cecilia stepped between them, using her bulk, whether by design or accident, to shield her niece. "You wouldn't wish us all to catch Helena's chill, would you?"

"Of course not, Lady Milburg." He bowed deeply, but not before Madeline witnessed a shocking exchange. While Aunt Cecilia's and Lord Rockford's words remained polite and formal, two pairs of glacial eyes met and gave evidence of a deep-rooted hatred between them. "I look forward to meeting with your beautiful niece again very soon. I have many memories of Sarah, memories I believe she would enjoy."

"I shall also give my regards to Agnes and her family," Aunt Cecilia called after him. "How amused they will be to hear of your visit today." She waved gaily after him and Lord Vickem, smiling until the moment the door clicked shut.

"Madeline!" She whirled on her niece with a prickly frown. "Whatever you have done to call Lord Rockford's attentions on yourself, it must end this very moment. Do you understand?"

"Not at all!" Madeline cried, no longer caring who heard her. "Why do you dislike him so? He was a friend of my mother's..."

"Lord Rockford was no friend to this family." Aunt Cecilia spoke harshly, grasping her handkerchief tightly, as though for support. "And any association with him will bring you nothing but harm."

"Aunt Cecilia, what happened to my mother? Why did my father believe we were all cursed?"

For a moment Aunt Cecilia's upper lip quivered, but then she laughed.

"Cursed? Honestly, where did you get such an outrageous notion? Too much time fretting, that's the cause of this, my dear." Her aunt leaned in closer, peering at her cheeks. "Your face has grown quite a strange reddish color. You aren't feeling itchy, are you?"

"Why, yes, I believe I am." Madeline rubbed at her chin, grasping the sudden opportunity. "It's come on rather quickly. Do you see any bumps on my neck?"

"Brigette!" Aunt Cecilia shrieked, trying to usher her niece upstairs without touching her. "Come, Madeline, right away, up the stairs and into a milk bath. Brigette! Whatever shall we do? It's spreading!"

Chapter Seven

"Watch yerself, fatwit!" Daniel Moore was pulled out of his fog with a jerk as three boys came barreling past him on the wharf, knocking him to the ground in their haste. They laughed as he fell, scraping his knees on the rough dock, only inches from tumbling headfirst into the rotten waters of the Thames.

"Little bastards," he muttered, pulling himself up with a grunt of pain.

Moore considered running after them, teaching them a lesson with a few sharp kicks, but the ragged brats had already vanished into the fading sunlight. Most definitely sideslips, he thought, brushing off his coat. Probably belonging to one of the trollops servicing the next batch of sailors. Moore continued on cautiously. He'd likely be stepping over a dead body or two when he rounded the corner, and, just in case, he deliberately kept a sharp eye on the ground. He didn't want any trouble tonight; he had more than his share already.

As he reached his destination, Moore spotted an elegant covered-top perched outside the tavern, the bright red Rockford crest blazing across the carriage door, a clear signal to anyone passing by that the great marquis himself had ventured into the slums for a drink. It seemed Rockford had grown a bit cocksure. Moore's meetings with Rockford tended toward the more seedy establishments of London, places where a man could stay nameless, conducting his business inside the shadows. Tonight, they would meet here, a dilapidated old tavern known only as

King's, though if anyone of royalty tried to enter the place they would find themselves instantly driven out again by the stench, if not the company. Inside these walls men greeted one another with the sharp point of a knife and the more piercing blade of betrayal, moaned to one another their sad, ale-soaked stories under cover of night, and occasionally sealed their deals in blood.

He spotted Lord Rockford instantly; the man stood out like a lion among scavengers in his rich blue coat and silk shirt. The fancy clothes were a far cry from the tattered breeches and stained weskits the rest of the patrons wore. Such a man should have been ripe for an attack, the ideal target to strike up a conversation with before relieving him of his purse. Bloodshed would be optional, of course, depending on the attacker's mood.

But not one of the fierce-looking drinkers in King's made a move toward the marquis. Even half-blind Harry remained hunched over his watery ale, the one good eye barely flickering in Moore's direction. Rockford's power-wielding tentacles reached deep into the depths of London, and as far as the patrons of King's were concerned, Daniel Moore was about to have a conversation with himself.

"It's good to see you again, Moore."

As he approached the stained table, Lord Rockford's well-groomed silver head turned up to greet him, but Moore's attention stayed fixed on the bald man standing behind the marquis. The man stood motionless against the wall, watching Moore with a bloodthirsty glare and holding one hand stiffly to the inside of his coat. Likely carrying a weapon. Moore suddenly wished the tavern held a larger crowd. The more witnesses he had, the better.

"Don't let Davis intimidate you." Rockford laughed, confident in his power, his place in the world. "May I buy you a drink?"

Moore hesitated for the briefest of moments before his resolve broke. "Gin." One small glass wouldn't hurt.

"You seem nervous, Mr. Moore. Surprised to get my message?"

Moore's gin was quickly placed in front of him, the watery liquid pale and sickly next to Rockford's brandy. "I was suspicious." He took a slow, deep drink, allowing the calm to wash over him. "So what is this all about, milord? All these years of secret meetings, hiding me from the world, and now you're buying me drinks?" He chuckled and lifted up his empty glass toward Johnny the bartender. "Though I must say I appreciate Old Tom." He nodded at the gin.

"Perhaps I'm just interested in the company of an old friend," Rockford said, eyeing him over the rim of his brandy glass.

Moore nearly choked. "Is that right? Well, I am flattered, though you must be worse off than I thought. Your sweet Agnes not amusing you enough these days?" He barked a brief laugh, catching the dark look.

"Agnes is perfectly adequate company."

"Good to hear, excellent! She still friends with your mistress, is she? So pleasant when all the ladies get along." Moore poured another measure of gin down his throat. "How is the beguiling Juliana? She's rather a favorite among the *ton*, is she not? And quite a fresh little thing for you to keep up with, William. But then, you always did like them very young."

Rockford's glass slammed down on the hard wood.

"You dare to insult me." It wasn't a question.

Moore leaned forward. "I'm paying you a compliment," he replied, his voice slowly rising in volume. "Can you not recognize flattery when you hear it? It's been awhile, I imagine." Moore was enjoying himself, aware he was going too far with Rockford, but he almost couldn't stop himself. There was such pleasure in watching the old man swallow his rage.

"You're rather brave tonight." Rockford spoke cautiously. "I see you've obtained your laudanum."

Moore certainly had. He'd wrapped his shaking hands around that sweet green bottle until his miserable existence had faded into a peaceful fog.

"I've known you a long time, Moore, and I've paid more than generously over the years."

Moore shrugged, feeling a splash of wetness on his hand. "When it suits you." Glancing down, he was surprised to find his glass empty.

"I didn't bring you here to dredge up the past," Rockford replied. "I am in need of your services again."

Moore looked down at his glass, then up at Rockford's cold, impassive face. "You'd better buy me another drink." Rockford motioned to Davis, who impassively obeyed.

"How long have you been in my service, Moore?"

Moore lazily stirred his drink with a finger. "Who's to say? Ten years? Time is a blur these days." He caught a glimpse of disgust across Rockford's brow and wondered if there was something wrong with his drink.

"Thinking of replacing me, my lord?" he snickered, knowing Rockford couldn't do so, even if he wanted to. Moore knew a few too many things about the great marquis, certain illegal deeds that would make his fancy friends choke on their beefsteaks.

Rockford shook his head. "I used to be quite like you, Moore. More polished, of course, and I had my father's title, but I too was a reckless fool, willing to overlook caution for greed." He stood up, pacing the room as he continued. "I lost a great deal from my rash behavior. I allowed a man to take something very valuable from me, a mistake I have always regretted."

Moore squirmed low in the sticky chair. How long had he been sitting here? Rockford did blather on lately; perhaps he really did need a mistress, some bit of muslin to listen to his woes.

"You want me to kill him?" Moore said, eyeing the last of the gin before it slid down his throat.

"Nature took care of that for us. Thomas is long dead. It is his daughter I want now." Rockford clenched his glass. "But I believe she is hiding something from me."

This caught Moore's attention. He pulled his head away from his glass, clearly hearing the current of Rockford's rage under that perfectly controlled voice. Rockford loathed anyone who refused to submit to a life under his well-manicured thumb. Moore had grown used to such ways, while making damn sure to take his own secrets to the grave. He rather pitied this wench; she had no idea who she was up against.

"Do you want me to—"

Rockford cut off his question. "I want you to follow her, very closely. I wish to know everything: who's paying her calls, what functions she's attending. See if there's a servant or two you could bribe to find out her schedule. Can you do that, Moore?"

"Following some skirt around? Should be easy enough." Moore stifled a yawn, the damn things this man had him do.

"There's more," Rockford said, his lips curling into a snarl. "The Duke of Douglas, do you know him?"

"I've heard the name." Moore grinned. Who

could have missed a story like that? Got himself cuckolded right before his own wedding.

"Good. I want you to contact me immediately anytime you see him with or around this Lady Madeline Sinclair, is that understood?"

"And in return for my services?" Moore replied. He detested the marquis, right down to the haughty tilt of his head, but Rockford had money, and Moore's vices cost him.

Rockford stood up, pulling a coin from his pocket that instantly caught Moore's eye. A gold sovereign. More than enough for one of those green bottles in the back of Reeves's apothecary shop. Maybe even a little left over for his own bottle of gin. He could run down to Reeves and have the laudanum in his hands in less than half an hour, if only damned Rockford would leave.

"Lie low for now, Moore," Rockford said, absentmindedly flipping the coin. "If I find your services to be satisfactory, you will be taken care of."

The coin nearly slipped from Rockford's fingers, and for a moment Moore prepared himself to dive after it onto the floor. Rockford caught it in his palm, his eyes never looking down, and Moore had to force himself to stay seated.

"But if you fail me..."

The coin hit the table, bouncing once and spinning to a stop, so close Moore could almost touch it, nearly brushing his left thumb. "There will be consequences."

Rockford turned to leave, gesturing with a flick of his hand to the giant, who swooped in behind him, snatching up the gold coin seconds before Moore could reach it.

"Good evening, Moore."

****

"I do not understand why we must spend another dull evening at home."

Lady Milberg threw the lace she had been mending down onto the cherry oak table, the soft fabric swishing aimlessly to the floor. Realizing the delicate cloth was unable to provide the emphasis she had been hoping for, Aunt Cecilia irritably crossed her arms. "Doctor Harwin said it's only a minor skin irritation, and no one is in the slightest danger of death. Well?"

Madeline glanced up from her own needlework, a task she found as maddening as her aunt's complaints, and frowned. Hysterical with fear over the spreading rash and the girls' appearances, Aunt Cecilia had been forced to cancel all their engagements. This unfortunately left her in a terrible temper, with nothing to do but air her objections, loudly and often. "And you, Madeline, hardly look sickly at all! Why, the rash merely puts a little color into your face."

Madeline tossed down her own needlepoint. Irritable and exhausted from another night full of unsettling dreams, she was losing her thin hold on her own temper. "Aunt Cecilia, please. You know we cannot leave Helena. She is very ill! Even Lord Vickem would run screaming."

Madeline glanced over at Helena, humming contentedly over her embroidery. Nearly every exposed inch of her was covered in a thick white salve to ease the itching. At the sound of her name she looked up to smile at them.

Aunt Cecilia took in a sharp breath. "I see your point, dear. She does look ghastly. Don't worry, darling," she called to her daughter. "Cook is making you a special ointment with chicken fat. Swears it will be just the thing!"

"I rather doubt that," Madeline muttered under her breath, as Aunt Cecilia turned back to her original topic.

"But Madeline, dear, why must you and I stay

home? I feel not an itch, and your red spots are nearly gone."

Madeline swallowed her guilt as she pretended to scratch one of the several "spots" she had drawn on herself with rouge.

"Why, Brigette could cover them up with a long shawl and some powder. We can hide you away in a dark corner, and no one will know!"

"Absolutely not," Madeline snapped. "I insist we stay home until we're both completely better." She was in a terrible temper. Not a single word from Colin since the Farris ball, and the dinner party was mere hours away. He had obviously decided not to invite her. Probably found her much too tall and plain-faced for his taste.

But then why kiss me in the garden? Twice?

This is ridiculous! Madeline scolded herself. *Who cares a whit if Colin finds me attractive or not? I simply want my diamond, nothing else.* She pulled Colin's ring of keys from her pocket, staring at them in frustration as her aunt and cousin obliviously argued on.

"It could be days!" Helena said, scratching her nose.

"Perhaps even a week," Madeline agreed, wondering if they had enough of the ivy to last the entire season. She returned to her sewing with her gaze riveted on the tiny pink roses, hoping the firmness in her voice would put an end to the conversation.

"Well, I find this all to be outrageous. A dreadfully dull evening sitting alone! And after you've had such success with the *ton,* Madeline. Everyone is gushing over your beauty, how well you danced, how gracefully you spoke. Why should Helena's bad luck spoil your own good fortune?"

"Perhaps Madeline is happy to stay home, Mama," Helena replied, trying to be helpful.

"So you are hiding from suitors, as well?" Cecilia's neck shot out, like a chicken with her feathers ruffled. "This has become our fate? No one will marry girls who hide away in the drawing room, terrified of men! This will not do. No, indeed, I cannot allow it." She craned her head around to glare at her daughter.

"I am only hiding from one suitor, and I have every right to bury my head until he goes away. Lord Vickem is perfectly awful, Mama," Helena defended herself.

"It's only for tonight, Aunt," Madeline interjected. "And Helena's right. Perhaps it is for the best. Lord Vickem's hot head can cool a bit, and we can be sure to avoid any gossip." She pressed on, hoping to play on her aunt's fear of disgrace. "Really, all his weeping and talk of love, it's bound to look disgraceful if it goes on too long. Let Lord Vickem spend a few nights alone in society, and perhaps he will meet another lady to fall in love with."

"Yes, and he can follow *her* around like a miserable dog," Helena agreed, contentedly returning to the delicate roses she was adding to the bottom of a petticoat.

"And who can tell what will happen?" Madeline rushed on, sensing they finally had her aunt's attention. "There may be another gentleman even more in love with our Helena."

Aunt Cecilia's eyes gleamed with the thought. "You are right, my dear. I'm beginning to think it would be much more prudent to focus on that very handsome Lord Montgomery."

Madeline watched her young cousin's dainty fingers jerk suddenly at the name, snapping the thread in half. *It would seem Helena does have feelings for the dashing Lord Montgomery. Is that a fierce blush under all the white salve? Best not let Aunt Cecilia know, or she will order up the chicken fat.*

"I'm instructing Brigette to give you each another milk bath this evening, and I expect you fresh as daisies by tomorrow. I cannot have it be said that I am secreting my girls away during the season."

"Of course not." Madeline felt relief as the argument died down, the third one today, and went back to her own needlepoint. She let out a yelp as the needle pricked her finger again, the tiny spike falling to her lap. Why would anyone wish to do such tedious work? She could hardly get the thread through the needle's eye, and her picture looked more like a horseshoe than a flower. Madeline's gaze moved around restlessly, the mention of Lord Montgomery sending a whirlwind of thoughts through her mind.

Terribly rude of Colin not to offer an invitation to tonight's dinner. She frowned. But what did she expect? Encounters with such a hot-tempered, disobliging man brought nothing but chaos. They were certainly ill-suited to one another, unable even to hold a civil conversation. Since she'd mistakenly laid eyes on him, they'd done nothing but argue and insult one another. *And kiss,* the treacherous voice in her head reminded her. *Well, that certainly didn't help matters, either. A terrible distraction.* And if his reputation was to be believed, she was not the first woman who found herself alone with the roguish duke in the gardens.

Madeline's back stiffened at the thought of Colin meeting Lady Juliana Reynolds alone in a darkened corner. The man was little more than a rake. Their little tryst likely meant nothing to him, a passing amusement soon forgotten when another skirt caught his fancy. Well, she could forget their encounter, as well! Madeline stabbed the detestable needle into the cloth, ripping the thread so hard it broke off in her hand as the pillow flew onto the floor. She ignored the stares from her aunt and cousin as she scooped up the infernal thing.

Madeline decided to start a list of all the things she disliked about London, the first two being that detestably handsome Colin and, next to him, embroidery.

The door was then opened by Jarvis, his dour face signaling news.

"Pardon, Lady Milburg, but you have a visitor. I told him the household was ill, but he was most insistent." Jarvis drew in his lips, letting them all know what he thought of that rudeness. "Shall I turn him away?"

Madeline's heart went still at the thought of ice-blue eyes, while Helena shrieked, "Yes! Tell Lord Vickem I'm ill!"

"Pardon, my lady, but it is the Duke of Douglas and—"

"Lord Douglas!" Cecilia nearly toppled from her chair as she squeezed herself out of the purple cushions. "I noticed the attraction, of course, but thought it would take much longer than this...of course we will see him! Madeline, do pinch your cheeks."

"Mama, we cannot be seen." Helena lifted a white arm to remind her, as Madeline, without thinking, shoved the ring of keys down the front of her dress.

Aunt Cecilia surveyed her daughter. "Helena, dearest, perhaps you should conceal yourself upstairs. You really aren't fit to be looked at."

"What about Madeline?" Helena asked, quickly gathering her things before her mother could change her mind.

"She has made a miraculous recovery." Aunt Cecilia turned to her niece. "Just snuff out that candle, dear, and no one will see your spots. Go,

Helena! Take the back stairs."

Madeline started to protest but was quickly silenced by her aunt's stubby finger.

"Not another word," she said, watching to see that Helena disappeared. "I suggest you save your breath for making charming conversation with Lord Douglas." She nodded to the butler. "Jarvis, show them in."

The doors opened again, and Jarvis held himself stiff as a pine to announce the visitors.

"The Dowager Duchess and the Duke of Douglas."

"Welcome!" Cecilia gushed, as Madeline's head jerked up. Colin and his...mother?

"I hope we are not disturbing you, lovely Cecilia." Lady Douglas floated into the room. Though tiny in stature, Madeline knew her instantly to be Colin's mother. She shared her son's unusual grey eyes and sharply cut cheekbones. Her hair, cut short in an elegant and youthful bob, had turned an airy white, but Madeline felt positive it had once been dark black, the color of rich earth.

Madeline jumped to her feet, which resulted in a jingling sound from the front of her dress, followed by a loud clatter as her needlework once again tumbled to the floor. She blushed beneath the rouge as everyone turned to her, Aunt Cecilia's slight frown next to Colin's barely hidden grin. *He knows I'm rattled.* The forbidden image of his strong arms circling her flashed through her mind. *Why is he here with his mother?*

Aunt Cecilia fawned over the duchess, introducing Madeline and apologizing for her daughter's untimely illness. "She really is a horrid sight, or I would whisk her right out. Helena will be devastated to miss you!"

Lady Douglas smiled warmly at Madeline, taking her by the hand. "Colin has spoken highly of you, Madeline. When he told me he met you at the Farris ball, I absolutely insisted on meeting you." Her words rang with sincerity, drawing Madeline in.

"Thank you, Your Grace," she replied, trying to look as poised as possible while avoiding Colin's gaze. "I am honored to meet the mother of such a fine gentleman as your son." Madeline congratulated herself; she had managed to get the words out without choking, even with Colin winking at her like an absolute scoundrel.

Madeline's attempts at good manners did not fool Lady Douglas, whose discerning eye moved back and forth between the couple. "Do you find my son to be a gentleman, then? I'm afraid not everyone would describe him as such." Her mouth curled in a teasing smile. "Perhaps he is different with you?" Madeline felt a rising panic at the question. She sensed the duchess wished to know her feelings for Colin, a question she herself was not ready to answer.

"He certainly tries very hard," she replied after a long pause, and Lady Douglas laughed, the sound making her appear quite girlish.

"Cecilia, she's wonderful. Now tell me everything about the season so far." Lady Douglas embraced her friend, and the ladies soon found a similar interest in discussing the newest rage of foreign art. Within moments Aunt Cecilia was gushing wildly, pulling the duchess over to the far corner of the drawing room to proudly display her late husband's collection of snuff boxes.

Grateful to be ignored, Madeline had resumed her seat on the settee when suddenly she was shoved to the side by Colin, who had decided to share the small couch with her, a most ungentlemanly thing to do, in her opinion. "Excuse me, Lord Douglas, wouldn't you be more comfortable sitting elsewhere?" She smiled politely up at him.

"No." At his grin, Madeline quickly dropped her

gaze, the teasing smile confusing her.

"There are other seats available, Colin," she hissed, aware of his hand brushing dangerously close to her knee.

"All various shades of purple, I see," he replied, sounding as if he were truly enjoying himself. "Why are you sitting in the dark?"

"Because Aunt Cecilia doesn't want you to see my face," she snapped, pushing him away. "Perhaps you would be more comfortable standing? Or taking a solitary walk in the garden?"

"You don't have to be nervous, Madeline." Colin wedged himself back onto the couch, so close that their shoulders were touching. "My mother is already quite smitten with you."

Indeed. Her anger mounted. *How her feelings would change if she turns to see me practically sitting on her son's lap!*

"I am not nervous," she replied crossly. "May I offer you a biscuit?" Too late, Madeline realized Jarvis had not yet arrived with their tea, and though Colin shot a meaningful glance at the empty table before them, he said nothing.

Gathering her skirts from underneath his leg, Madeline shoved herself into the corner of the settee, as far away from him as possible.

"Why are you here, Colin?"

"My mother wished to meet you," he said, casually taking up the empty space on the sofa until she was once again pressed up against him. "And I wanted to give you this."

Good Lord, he is going to kiss me, right here in Aunt Cecilia's drawing room! She shrank back, wondering if she should scream.

"I very much doubt it will bite you, Madeline."

The amusement in Colin's voice caught her attention, and she looked down to see he was holding out a small package wrapped in brown paper.

"Open it."

She obeyed, ignoring the small pang of disappointment at not being kissed. *Why should I care? Of course he isn't going to kiss me here, or anywhere, for that matter.* She ripped away the paper revealing, to her shock, the portrait of her mother.

"It seemed to mean a great deal to you," Colin said quietly. "I thought you should have it."

She didn't know what to say. Tears sprang to her eyes as she ran a finger over her mother's cheek, so like her own. "Thank you," she said, looking up to meet his gaze. "Before I saw this, I...I didn't know what she looked like."

Colin watched her for a long moment, his face unreadable as she clutched the portrait to her chest.

"You're welcome." He leaned closer to her. This time she was sure he was going to kiss her, but as he was only a hair's breadth away he abruptly pulled back, moving to the other side of the sofa.

"There is one other thing," he said, his voice sounding rather hoarse. "I have also come to collect my keys."

"What keys?" She panicked, adopting a blank look of innocence onto her face.

"You know perfectly well what keys I'm talking about, Madeline. Are you going to give them back, or shall I have to ravage you for them?"

Madeline gasped. "You are a horrible scoundrel." It dawned on her that Colin had arranged this entire visit to steal her property. *Well, I don't care if he shows up with Queen Charlotte. I'm not giving him anything.*

Her thoughts were jolted when Colin suddenly touched her, brushing a stray curl off her cheek. "I only want to help you, Madeline," he said, his fingers tracing a path to her neck.

"I don't want your help," she whispered back,

111

noticing his eyes were more blue today, less cloudy than before.

He laughed. "I gathered that." His hand moved up to cup the side of her face. "But you're going to get it."

Just then the door flew open, and Jarvis entered with the silver tea tray, tossing a reproachful glance in Colin's direction. Colin moved like lightning, rising and stepping away from her toward the window, before Lady Douglas or Cecilia had time to turn around.

"It's all been decided! Madeline, your future is saved." Aunt Cecilia blew across the room like a strong wind, and for one horrible moment she feared her aunt and Lady Douglas had conducted some sort of marriage arrangement over the snuff boxes.

"Lady Douglas is having a dinner party tonight!" her aunt replied to Madeline's look of terror. "And she has graciously offered her son as an escort."

"With myself to chaperone, of course." The Duchess smiled. "I could not bear the thought of you missing such an affair. My dear friend Sir Lambert shall be in attendance. He is known for his most entertaining conversations. No lady in her first season should be deprived of them."

An invitation! Madeline's heart leapt at the idea that the French Blue diamond could soon be in her hands. She smiled at Lady Douglas but was interrupted before making her reply.

"Madeline suffers from a unique form of shyness, Mother," Colin spoke up from the window. "She has a difficult time conversing with strangers, feels the need to shout at them."

"Oh, tosh! Madeline, you love to speak with strangers! Who else could be more interesting, now, really?" Aunt Cecilia stepped over and stared at Madeline very hard, her head bobbing toward the duchess in a frantic manner. "Isn't it such an honor for Lady Douglas to personally invite you? It would be nothing less than shameful to decline." It wasn't a forced proposal, but Madeline could see her aunt's gleam of matchmaking greed. Aunt Cecilia knew perfectly well what might result from an evening spent alone with Lady Douglas and her son.

"I would be honored to attend with you. Thank you for the kind offer," she said, her mind returning to the keys tucked away in her dress. She must find a way to sneak down into Colin's cellar once she arrived.

"You are positive I cannot persuade you to come along, Cecilia?" Lady Douglas asked. Madeline's head shot up in horror. Her aunt would never let her out of her sight; this would not do at all!

But her aunt shook her head. "Oh, no, I'm sick as a swan, and who will stay behind to care for Helena? Poor child is nearly on death's door. I wouldn't dare think to leave her." Madeline sighed with relief, belatedly realizing Colin's speculative gaze had been on her the entire time.

Their company parted soon after, promising to arrive for Madeline at eight sharp, and Aunt Cecilia instantly shuffled her upstairs to begin dressing. It wasn't until two hours later, as Madeline painfully endured Brigette's attack on her hair, that she realized Colin's keys were gone.

Chapter Eight

"You ladies and your endless romances!" Sir Lambert howled, banging his spoon against the table. "It has become an epidemic, a festering sore on our society. Filling your ringleted heads with such fancy nonsense that any and all decent young chaps become invisible, ignored!"

Madeline could not keep her gaze off Sir Lambert's snow-white brows, fascinated with the furious way they jumped up and down, like two menacing snowdrifts.

"You cannot be bothered to turn your heads unless the man is some downtrodden, brooding prince," Sir Lambert ended, plunging the spoon into his cheese-smothered pheasant tart. "Well?" he called round to his guests. "Does anyone have an intelligent retort? Can't debate myself, now, can I?"

"Don't sell yourself short, Lamby!" Sir Rawlings shouted across the table, followed by a chorus of laughter.

"If anyone could do it, old Lamby could," a red-cheeked earl they called Sterlings added, eliciting more laughter and a few claps.

"My lady, may I offer *lapin au vin?*"

"No, thank you," Madeline replied politely, swallowing her irritation. It was the third time she had been offered the roasted hare in wine sauce, and she could think of nothing less appetizing, except perhaps all the shouting. The intimate evening with Sir "Lamby" had turned out to be more of a lavish dinner with nearly twenty guests, more than enough to set her nerves on edge.

Fortunately there were a few friendly faces: Miss Lillian had greeted her right away, chattering away about Helena's unfortunate illness. Sir Rawlings had also been thrilled to see her, insisting he be seated on her left so she would not miss out on any of his clever quips. "Some are delivered rather speedily. I'd hate for you to miss one."

Lady Farris was also in attendance, dragging a mournful Agnes behind her. Both mother and daughter shared the same tense, unwelcoming smile, and they spared not a glance in Madeline's direction. She pretended not to notice, but it left a very uneasy feeling in the pit of her stomach.

The dinner party progressed into a crowd-pleasing second course of braised veal swimming in cream and a pigeon pie that made even the hare in wine sauce look appetizing. *This evening is turning out to be perfectly dreadful.* Madeline thought enviously of Helena's rash. She held Colin fully responsible for her misery. The man had only spoken two sentences to her the whole evening, both of which she found very dull. And all the while she was seething over her stolen keys. The gall of him! She had no doubt Colin was the thief. He had distracted her with his roguish charms before snatching the key ring right from under her nose. *He's probably quite proud of his own cleverness.* She turned to her left to send him a murderous glare. *Why, he's probably been boasting to his guests all night!* Madeline suddenly grew hot beneath her airy white gown. She watched him slice into his meat, the fork and knife moving with sly, insidious precision. What was he thinking? She knew he must suspect something, but his face remained utterly calm, not a trace of suspicion in the grey eyes, not a hair out of place. *Perhaps he is drawing me out, waiting for me to snap under this awful tension. Well, I'm not going to say one single word, not one! We can spend the evening in absolute silence, for all I care.*

"Is there something you would like off my plate?" Colin spoke suddenly, looking up at her.

"You stole something from me," she hissed.

"I did?"

His voice dripped with innocence, and Madeline wondered how the guests would react if her beefsteak hit Colin in the head.

"You know perfectly well what I'm talking about. The keys you stole from me, right out of my..." She trailed off, unable to speak the words, instead nodding downward to the top of her dress.

"Indeed?" Colin lifted a perfectly roasted potato to his mouth and chewed slowly while he surveyed her. "And do you normally keep your items in such a place? Seems a strange habit, to hide something where a man's gaze is naturally drawn."

Madeline felt her resolve melting with mortification, but she refused to back down. She could certainly spar words with Lord Douglas!

"I would have hoped that a true gentleman's gaze would never venture to such places," she responded, pleased by the haughtiness of her voice. "Much less his *hand.*"

Colin grinned. "I'm not much of a gentleman where you are concerned, Madeline, but I promise the next time my hand strays in that direction, you'll enjoy it."

She had absolutely no response for that.

Colin turned from her, directing his attention across the table to Lady Huntington and his mother.

"If I may intrude for a moment," he asked. "Where would you advise a young lady to hide her personal, private trinkets?" Madeline could no longer restrain herself. She kicked him soundly in the leg, relishing the small grunt of pain that followed.

"What an odd question," Lady Douglas said, giving her son a look of suspicion, but Lady

Huntington seemed intrigued.

"Oh, goodness, let me think! It's been so long since I've had anything worth hiding away, not since my courtship days with Henry." She fluttered her fingers at Lord Huntington, who ignored her in favor of his turtle soup. "But I do recall tucking away a little bracelet in my hair once. Mother had the maids snooping through my room then, and I was very desperate." She smiled over the memory. "Though the hairstyles were much more elaborate in my youth. What about you, Louisa?"

"Perhaps I slipped a note or two into my shoe," Lady Douglas replied, surprising Madeline. "But I will admit to nothing more. What has brought on this subject, Colin?"

Fearing his answer, Madeline edged her foot against his, this time in warning.

"Merely curious," he replied. "Madeline has found herself sadly lacking in a proper hiding place."

Outraged, she delivered another sharp kick to Colin's leg, and was satisfied to see his knife clatter onto the table.

"Gracious, Colin, you seem rather jittery tonight. Is something ailing you?" Lady Douglas asked.

"A bit of cramp is all," he said. "One that will have to be beaten if it doesn't go away on its own."

"Do not threaten me, sir!" Madeline said, the anger in her voice carrying it farther than she intended.

"There, now! That's the kind of talk we need," Lambert interjected with a shout, the spoon now replaced with a chicken leg. "You, there." He pointed the leg at Madeline. "You look like a sensible girl. No strange head feathers or the like. Explain to me what's in the minds of you women today."

Madeline sat dumbfounded as the table quieted, all turning to stare at her, awaiting the answer. "I—

well, I cannot begin to say." She looked up to catch Colin leaning back in his chair.

"Oh, don't ask Madeline," he said in a nonchalant tone. "She isn't planning to marry, so the question doesn't apply."

"Never marry?" Lambert choked. "Well, that's no way to find yourself a husband. No, that won't do at all."

"What I said," Madeline replied, her eyes shooting daggers at Colin, "is that I do not find marrying to be of importance at this time. I have other thoughts to occupy my mind."

"Perhaps she hasn't found the right brooding prince," Lady Huntington interjected, winking at Madeline as though this were all great fun. "Or she is unable to decide between a duke and a marquis?" Madeline suddenly wished Sir Lambert's servant would offer her the roasted hare again, anything to distract her from the horrifying turn of this conversation.

"I, for one, am in perfect disagreement with you all," Lady Farris spoke up, her voice cutting through the chatter. "My darling Agnes is, as you all know, very nearly engaged to a certain man who is neither downtrodden nor a prince."

"So your Aggie hasn't nabbed Prinny, then?" Sir Rawlings's shout was met with a roar of laughter.

Lady Farris responded with a brittle smile. "Not as such. But the real tragedy of young women today is their impertinence, the brazen disrespect for the sanctity of marriage. Isn't that the real tragedy, Lady Ainsley?"

She motioned to her friend, who seemed to be awaiting her cue. "What proper lady would even do such a thing?" she chirped in a suspiciously false voice.

"The guilty name shall not pass from my lips," Lady Farris replied. "Although," she said, pausing to take a single bite of the richly sauced pig, "it may be said that such wanton behavior is hereditary, passed down from mother to daughter." She took another bite, larger this time, as the titters of speculation spilled down the table.

Madeline's heart fell to her stomach as the icy retort hit its mark. Was Lady Farris referring to her? A quick, embarrassed chatter sprang up around her like unsightly weeds, and she had her answer. Madeline's temper flared while Sir Lambert's guests lapped up the new information, savoring the implied insult.

"Surely a person's character is her own, and cannot be accidentally inherited, whether from a novel or otherwise." The words escaped Madeline's mouth, sharper than intended.

Lady Farris set her fork down on the table and turned, the very hairs on her head seeming to rise like those of a disgruntled cat. "Who is speaking there? I do not know this girl." She made quite a show of peering down at Madeline with her spectacles, while Agnes kept her face down in defeat.

"You know perfectly well who she is," Lady Douglas answered back. "I do believe Madeline attended your latest ball."

"I do remember." Lady Farris's spectacles slapped against the table with a rattle. "Agnes, darling, tell everyone about the lovely pearls Lord Rockford sent you last week."

"Mother, that isn't necessary," Agnes whispered.

"Go on, dearest! It might benefit some of our newer guests to know that you have developed a tight bond with Lord Rockford, one that should not be intruded upon." There was no denying it; Lady Farris was speaking directly to her, her hawklike gaze setting Madeline's cheeks on fire.

Madeline nudged Colin's foot again, this time in a silent plea for help as she noticed a hush fall over the room. Why had she not listened to her aunt's warning? Aunt Cecilia had quite firmly advised her to avoid unwanted attention *at all costs*, and now look what she had done! Lady Farris was ready to do battle over her daughter's suitor.

"I meant no insult, Lady Farris," she began, taking a quick gulp of the sweet wine for courage. "I was merely defending my sex. We women are not so easily swayed as some are led to believe."

"I completely agree," Lady Douglas said, coming to her aid. "And I must say I've become confused. We are discussing novels, are we not?"

Madeline shot her a grateful smile. *At least someone in the family has manners.* She glanced at Colin, who looked as though he were enjoying a comfortable evening by the fire rather than watching her drown in humiliation.

"But we are!" Lady Ainsley jumped in. "That's exactly the point. It is these romances that I believe caused the young lady in question to throw off her cloak of decorum and seek a man above herself."

The nail is in the coffin now. Madeline stabbed her asparagus. If there had been any doubt who they spoke of, the viperous chatter of Lady Ainsley wiped it clean. She fumed over this unfounded attack on herself, wondering what could have angered Lady Farris so.

Colin's mother seemed to be feeling the same way, her normally effortless smile cracking around the edges. "Please explain," she turned toward Lady Farris, her manner icy and formidable, "precisely how these novels influenced the matrimonial pursuits of your daughter."

Lady Farris pounced on the question. "I cannot say, for I've never read one myself, but it seems to me our young ladies today have no restraint over their emotions. They cannot think rationally, and therefore should not be expected to make decisions in their own best interests."

"Utter nonsense," Madeline muttered into her glass. She nodded gratefully at the servant poised to refill her wine—such a wonderfully attentive man.

"But this is precisely my point," Sir Lambert said. "Ladies today are finding interests in all sorts of things. No time left for paying us men attention or producing our heirs. What will become of us?"

"Undoubtedly you will perish," Lady Douglas answered dryly.

"Perhaps marriage could be looked upon less as a duty and more as a mutual companionship," Madeline said, stunned that her thoughts had so quickly escaped her mouth. Why could she not cease talking? She took two quick sips of wine to quiet herself.

"Do continue, Madeline," Sir Lambert demanded. "Have you found such radical companionship?" Forks paused in midair as the entire table swelled forward in order to better hear.

"Certainly not," Madeline said, ignoring Lady Farris's pinched glare. "As I said before, I am much too occupied to be searching for such things."

"And how do you fill your time if not on the rituals of courtship?" It was Colin who asked this question, and she turned to smile sweetly at him.

"Embroidery."

"Embroidery!" Lady Huntington gasped. "Dear, that cannot substitute for your duties as a woman. You must set your mind to other tasks."

"I have always enjoyed my music," Miss Lillian called out from the very bottom of the table. "Found it so absorbing I could not be bothered to take a husband." The look on Lady Huntington's face made it perfectly clear what she thought of that choice, but Madeline threw the woman a smile.

"Thank you, Miss Lillian," she called.

"While this is all very amusing," Lady Farris

said, "it still has not answered the question of what is wrong with our young ladies today."

Perhaps it was the overabundance of wine, or the delightful sight of Sir Lambert rolling his eyes at the sound of Lady Farris's shrill voice, but Madeline's inhibitions seemed to vanish.

"There is only one solution!" she exclaimed, beaming directly into Lady Farris's dry, crinkled eyes. "There is nothing whatsoever wrong with us."

The table erupted in noise. Laughter from the ends mixed with shouts of "Good show!" "Well said!" as Lambert banged his fist on the table for silence.

"Preposterous answer!" he cried. "I insist you tell me at whose feet we should lay society's ills. Who is at fault, if not the women?"

"Sir Lambert, there is only one other choice," Madeline replied merrily, forcing the eager crowd to wait while she carefully straightened a wayward curl the same way she'd seen Helena do the night before. Out of the corner of her eye she noticed Colin staring at her, his expression a mixture of admiration and amusement.

"And, pray tell, what would that be?" Lambert choked out, gagging in his excitement.

"Why, the fault lies with the men."

Pandemonium broke out at her reply, and once again Lambert was reduced to banging his fist against the table. "Young lady, I declare you will be wed to a brooding prince by summer's end!"

More laughter, and Madeline smiled sweetly at him. "That is your opinion, sir, and I thank you for it."

****

Directly after dinner, the ladies excused themselves, leaving the men alone to spout wisdom over their brandy. Madeline followed Lady Douglas's small frame out the door, casting a look of longing down the hallway. How maddening to think the

French Blue diamond was right beneath her feet! And here she stood, trapped with Lady Douglas and her guests, unable to sneak away undetected. *And I no longer have the keys.* She realized now this would not be as simple a task as she'd hoped, but there must be a way. She moved slowly into the drawing room, noticing with a sinking stomach how Lady Farris's stern mouth pressed further down than usual. The woman had a habit of shifting her gaze around when planning something malicious, and they darted back and forth now, waiting for the room to fill up. Madeline feared her tirade at dinner had gone too far, and felt a pang of regret at leaving Colin's strong, reassuring presence behind. She was still furious with him for his thievery, an act she certainly planned to blister him about later, but for now she had lost the only ally she could turn to in this strangely woven society.

She sighed, bracing herself for the rude whisperings and angry glares. She had no one but herself to blame. Papa had always claimed she entered the world loudly proclaiming her opinion of it, and procuring Sir Lambert as an admirer had also created a sworn enemy.

"I see you've become quite the charmer tonight. You obviously have your mother's knack for gaining attention." Madeline realized she had sorely underestimated Lady Farris's fury, as the woman marched over to her. "I beg your pardon?" She carefully closed the book of poems she had been pretending to read, resolving to stay cordial.

"Spare us your coy smile. It's apparent you've decided to seduce our men into forgetting any taint that went along with the name Sinclair, but rest assured not everyone is so easily swayed. I for one will always associate your name with the mud it deserves."

"That's enough, Jane." Lady Douglas's voice

cracked from across the room. She stood next to the piano, holding sheet music for a wide-eyed Miss Lillian. "You'll do well to watch your tongue and leave Madeline alone."

"And why should I?" The insolent woman shot back. "Everyone here knows of Sarah's disgrace, how she flaunted her affairs in every ballroom in this city. It is my opinion that Lady Sinclair's daughter should never have been welcomed here, out of respect to decent society." Lady Farris shone her triumphant smirk throughout the room, passing unnoticed by Agnes, who sat hunched and humiliated in the corner.

"I fail to see how another's deeds, committed so long ago, could affect Madeline now." Lady Huntington spoke stiffly from her seat by the fire, where she and three other ladies sat gaping over their game of whist. "Perhaps we should judge the girl on her own merits, which I find impeccable." She gave a firm nod as though signaling an end to the matter before going back to her cards.

"You cannot be so naïve, Lady Huntington. Even her own father had sense enough to flee from his wife's scandal."

"My papa never fled from anything." Madeline's voice fell to a dangerously soft level, her nails digging into the book's thick leather. "He left of his own accord, grief-stricken after losing his wife."

"Cuckolded, you mean," Lady Farris practically spat. "Let us not forget it was your mother's own sins that caused her death."

Lady Huntington gasped, while the heavy, leather-bound book hit the floor with a thud as Madeline started across the room to silence the vicious woman's opinions once and for all. She had hardly taken two steps when the pianoforte erupted, drenching the entire room in noise, and forcing everyone to stare at the tiny Miss Lillian, banging away on the keys as though her hands were on fire.

Through the confusion, Lady Douglas appeared, gently taking Madeline's hand to lead her away.

"It's true," Lady Douglas spoke quietly in her ear. "Though Jane has told you only part of the story, along with a great deal of rumor." Madeline glanced up at Lady Farris, now slowly flapping her fan, satisfied with herself. She had the distinct feeling this would not be the last time she found herself cornered by this woman, but it was the voice at her side that sent her into true despair. *"It's true."*

"I promise I will explain everything later tonight. You must trust me for now." Lady Douglas squeezed her hand tightly.

"That's exactly what Colin would say," Madeline muttered.

The older woman looked surprised for a moment, then smiled. "Well, he is my son, after all. Now stand tall and look as though you are perfectly enthralled by the exquisite music." She raised her voice to be heard over Miss Lillian, still bent over the instrument and frowning in concentration. "You must act as though Jane's words meant nothing to you. It is the worst punishment you can give such a woman."

The doors opened, spilling the men into the room, still immersed in discussion and oblivious to the bitter faces of their wives. Colin entered behind the others, his brain sufficiently numbed from the talk of wheat prices and hunting. How could anyone find interest in such things? Elderburn talked of his methods for shooting grouse with such frightening enthusiasm it was a wonder his wife managed to drag him out of the country for the season. Perhaps marriage did something to a man. Colin himself had inherited the Douglas estate, along with its lands, located five or so miles outside of London. He had fond memories of growing up there, but he had rarely visited the place since boyhood. Upon taking his father's title, his plans changed. He'd planned to bring Juliana there once they married, hoping to raise a family far from the prying eyes of London, but now...

Colin immediately scanned the room for Madeline, eager for the sight of her soft, curving smile, surrounded by the thick pile of dark brown hair bound above her neck. All through dinner he'd had the most ridiculous urge to lean over and pull out the pins, releasing the heavy mass to tumble down past her shoulders, where it would catch the light, letting the red-gold strands shine through. He lifted a hand to his jacket pocket, where the cellar keys lay hidden. Colin felt a twinge of shame for plucking it from the top of her dress in so ungentlemanly a manner but felt his actions had been justified. Truthfully, a small part of him hoped Madeline would confide in him before the night's end. He found his reactions to her confusing. He disliked being away from her, found her absence chilling him like a cold wind the moment she left his side at the table. Yet she was the complete opposite of his former fiancée. Juliana would have reigned at tonight's dinner, remaining perfectly poised and gracious, somehow managing to say all the correct things while seeking connections with everyone she deemed important. When Colin first met Juliana, he'd been intrigued by her confidence, the calm, graceful way she bent everyone to her whims. Colin was immediately drawn to that intoxicating power. Unfortunately, he hadn't been the only one.

He ran a hand through his hair, mentally shaking off the lingering image of Juliana. It was time he let her go, put her in the past.

He spotted Madeline then, her back to him in a corner of the room, her hands delicately gliding over the books on a shelf. As Colin stepped closer, he realized Madeline's motion wasn't quite as delicate as he thought. He watched as she yanked out one book after another, quickly flipping through the pages before violently shoving them back into the wall.

"You've been lying to me, Madeline." Her head jerked up at his voice. "You told me you despised poetry." He nodded toward *Byron's Guide to Poetry* in her hands, a teasing smile on his lips. But Madeline was having none of it. She slammed the book shut so hard a cloud of dust flew up.

"Interesting choice of words, Lord Douglas," she replied tartly. "Though I cannot imagine you of all men could have the audacity to brand anyone else a liar." She thrust the book into his hands. "Even in jest."

She stood rigid, waiting for his response, two bright circles appearing on her cheeks directly below a pair of glaring green eyes. Colin glanced down to see tears shining in those eyes, even as she stubbornly blinked them away.

"Madeline, what has upset you?" She was more than merely irritated; the fiery woman who had sharpened her wit against Sir Lambert's now seemed fragile as glass. It pained him to see her in such distress. He turned to question her, but she was shaking her head.

"Lady Farris," Madeline jerked her head toward the brittle woman hissing away at her daughter, "has very kindly informed me of my family's shame. I'm sure you must have heard the story. It's most entertaining."

Colin began to have a sinking feeling about what must have happened while he was trapped in the dining room. "What did she say?"

"Oh, not much. Only that my mother was a whore who should have been cast out of society, but fortunately her evil transgressions killed her first."

Colin's blood began to churn, and it took all his control not to toss Lady Farris outside into the mud-filled streets. The story had finally reached Madeline's ears. He'd had a feeling it would, sooner or later; the *ton* was not known for its ability to keep secrets. A small sliver of ice dug into his heart as he looked down at Madeline's wounded face. It told him all he needed to know.

"Well, Colin? Is there anything you would like to add to my humiliation?" She crossed her arms, defiantly.

His gaze flicked to Sir Lambert, who had begun to forcefully usher the guests out the door, making no pretense that the dinner party was not over. His mother nodded at him, the slight tilt of her head indicating they would stay behind. Colin looked at Madeline, fully understanding her pain and wishing nothing more than to take her hand in comfort.

"It's high time we called a truce, don't you think?" He handed *Byron's Guide to Poetry* back to her, letting his hand linger slightly over her trembling fingers. "We have been playing games with one another for long enough. I demand the truth from you, Madeline, and I will give you the same in return. What do you say?" He gently squeezed her fingertips. "Honesty?"

Colin stood silent, waiting hopefully for her answer. He watched as she stubbornly blinked back tears, fighting hard against the secret that held her prisoner from him. But he believed in her. Since the moment he'd laid eyes on Madeline, staring so tenderly down at him in his study, Colin had instinctively felt he'd found the person he could trust over all others. It was simply her nature, but one she tried desperately to hide.

"I agree." She finally spoke, wiping an escaped tear from her cheek. "Honesty."

****

Within half an hour only Miss Lillian remained, refusing to be escorted to her waiting carriage until she finished her string of promises to visit the ailing Helena.

"I shall come first thing tomorrow, not a moment after two. I am so terribly concerned. Has your physician been to see her? Such terrible ailments going around these days. My uncle caught the lung fever and was dead within three days!"

"I am sure Helena will be fit as ever when you arrive," Madeline replied, with only the slightest twinge of guilt. "Your visit will be much appreciated." She had little doubt Miss Lillian hoped to arrive at their doorstep with an earful about their evening, likely giving her Aunt Cecilia an illness of her own. *Perhaps that's just what we need. We can all escape to the country house to recuperate from the claws of Lady Farris.*

Miss Lillian vanished into the hallway, chatting away to Sir Lambert about her deceased relations, leaving Madeline alone with Lady Douglas—and Colin, she noted, who stood silently in the corner watching her with the carefully guarded look of a hunter unsure of its prey.

Why am I still here? Madeline's mind swirled between fury and panic. The temperature in the room seemed to drop, and she wrapped the thin shawl around her shoulders, letting the seeds of suspicion grow. Madeline had been sure this outing was nothing more than a bold matchmaking attempt cooked up by her aunt, but throughout the long evening Lady Douglas had made it perfectly clear she did not involve herself in her son's affairs. Was it for no other reason than to make her the target of Lady Farris's well-aimed humiliations?

Sir Lambert suddenly strode back into the room. "Finally got rid of Lillian. Lord, that woman can talk! Rather protective of you, too, Madeline. I had to

129

swear to her I would apologize for Lady Farris's outburst."

Madeline colored at the reminder, but said nothing.

"Louisa, er, Lady Douglas here informed me of what happened, and I must say I'm flabbergasted. No idea Farris's wife had grown into such a harpy. She certainly has a bee in her bonnet about you."

"She believes I am trying to win the affections of Lord Rockford." Madeline sighed, watching Sir Lambert's servant set a tray of brandy and three glasses onto the table. "And, as we all know, Agnes and Lord Rockford are very nearly engaged."

"Are you trying to win his affections?" Colin spoke from the corner.

"Certainly not." Madeline did not appreciate his tone. Why did everyone believe she was interested in Lord Rockford? "I haven't encouraged his attentions at all. His call was quite unexpected."

"Rockford called on you?" Colin broke free of his corner, crossing the room toward her. "Why?"

"I haven't the faintest idea. Perhaps he wished to be polite," she snapped, irritated by all the questions. "He did mention you had a rather suspicious nature, and I must say I agree with him."

"What else did he say about me?" Colin's voice was dangerous now, and he hovered over her, awaiting his answer.

"Nothing of importance," Madeline replied airily. "Though I believe I mentioned what a pity it was you and I were so ill-suited to be friends."

"My thoughts exactly," Colin muttered.

Madeline immediately stiffened, turning her gaze away so Colin could not see how much his words had hurt her. Why should she care if he did not wish to be her friend? After she found her diamond she would never have to speak to him again.

"Nevertheless, an apology is in order," Sir Lambert quickly interjected. "I do not abide anyone insulting young ladies. Except me, of course."

Lady Douglas smiled at her. "Do not take any of George's debates seriously, my dear. It's all rather done for amusement."

"Must amuse the guests, you see! You can spend all your evenings embroidering, for all I care, though it would be a terrible waste of such clever wit." Lambert ended his compliment with a bow worthy of the king. "And I am a mite suspicious of any young lady Colin takes a fancy to. The last one ended badly, you know," he whispered.

"I can hear you, Lambert." Colin's tone was positively surly.

"Good! Might help give you a bit of sense next time." Sir Lambert winked at her. "Though I have more confidence in your latest selection."

"Colin isn't courting me," Madeline stammered, mortified by the implication. "I hardly even know him, and we really don't suit very well at all."

Sir Lambert merely laughed. "May I offer you ladies a drink? Louisa?"

"Thank you, George." She gave him her hand to be kissed, smiling with such obvious affection that it left Madeline curious about Lady Douglas's relationship with their cantankerous dinner host.

"George is a trusted friend," Lady Douglas offered. "Did you know he used to work with my Arthur in the War Department?"

"I did not," Madeline answered, not missing the slight grimace on Colin's face. Even with her limited political knowledge, Madeline was well aware of England's raging war with France and the chaos it had brought to both countries. Her heart sank to the tips of her satin slippers as she thought of the scars puncturing Colin's skin. She turned to him, unable to stop the question at her lips. "Are you involved with the War Department, as well? Is that how you received that scar on your chest?"

Too late, she realized she shouldn't have known such private information. Lady Douglas's glance bounced back and forth between them, amazement lining her brow.

"Madeline happened upon me in a moment of shirtlessness," Colin explained, somehow keeping his expression blank while uttering the outrageous statement. Madeline's face burned, and she eagerly snatched at the glass of ratafia Sir Lambert offered.

"I see." Lady Douglas turned to give her son a stern glower. "Blemishing Madeline's reputation is not my idea of helping her, young man."

The tiny woman looked ready to give her son a blistering setdown, but Colin swiftly changed the subject. "We haven't much time before Madeline will be expected home. It's time to get on with it."

"Yes, of course." Lady Douglas spoke briskly, turning back to her. "I knew your mother many years ago, Madeline, though we were never intimate friends. Sarah was a vibrant woman, terribly young, and I believe she was led astray by the wrong man."

"Then it's true," Madeline spoke up. "What she said about my mother."

"Well, not exactly." Lady Douglas shifted uncomfortably in her chair. "Jane's words were cruel and ill-timed..." She turned to her son for help.

"I don't believe she was a ladybird, if that's what you're asking."

"Colin!" His mother looked ready to throttle him. "That kind of talk is hardly helpful to our situation."

Colin picked up his own drink and shrugged, settling himself in a large blue chair. "I'm sorry to be brusque, but what do you want me to say? It does Madeline little good to be sheltered from the truth."

"Thank you," she replied to him, grateful that someone felt she shouldn't be treated like a child.

She sat with her arms crossed, ignoring the sharp pang of disappointment that Colin didn't wedge himself next to her.

"Sarah was, as many of us were, caught up in the hysteria of the day," Sir Lambert continued, also looking very uncomfortable. "You must appreciate how afraid we all were, what with the aristocrats of France falling by the thousands under the blade of the guillotine."

"Your father went on assignments for England's War Department, as my own Arthur did. These men worked abroad, gone for long periods of time. It was one of the many consequences of such a chaotic time."

"I'm sorry," Madeline said, staring at the uneasy pair. "I'm afraid I don't understand. Did something happen while my father was away?"

Lady Douglas spoke first. "It was well known in certain circles that your mother was having an affair with Lord Rockford."

"Lord Rockford?" Madeline could not believe her words. But Lady Douglas slowly nodded, sympathy etched across her face.

Madeline remembered the stinging grip in her aunt's drawing room. "He said he was an old friend of my mother's," she said softly, suddenly seeing the marquis in a whole new light.

"I'm afraid it was a bit more than that," Sir Lambert said, clearing his throat.

"My mother didn't just die in a carriage accident, did she?" Madeline had long suspected her mother's death had been something terrible. Her father's guilt spread too wide across his face, his anguish rooted in something deeper.

Lady Douglas shook her head, sadness creasing the lines around her mouth. "She was running away from your father...with Lord Rockford."

The news hit Madeline with a jolt. She sat

straight up, knocking the table in front of her so hard the brandy bottle tipped over and would certainly have smashed to the floor if Colin had not snatched it just in time. "Go on," he said quietly, setting the bottle firmly back onto the tray.

Things began to fall into place: Aunt Cecilia's hatred of Lord Rockford, her refusal to talk about her own sister's death. *And Lord Rockford's reaction to meeting me,* Madeline realized with horror. *He didn't just mistake me for a long forgotten acquaintance, he mistook me for his dead lover!*

"Madeline." Colin's voice came from far away, bringing her back to the surface. He sat next to her, a solid, reassuring presence.

"Sir Lambert, fetch Madeline a glass of water," Lady Douglas said, concern etching her features.

"I'm fine now," Madeline managed. She was desperate to leave. Though she had planned for days to get back into Colin's townhouse, she now wished nothing more than to be out of it. Diamond or no.

"Perhaps I should take my leave," Sir Lambert said, placing the untouched water on the table. "Madeline, you have my word nothing spoken here will leave this room."

"I would appreciate that, thank you." She took deep breaths, trying to calm her racing heart.

"Mother, will you give us a moment alone?" Colin asked. Lady Douglas looked highly dubious.

"I really don't think it's such a good idea, Colin." But Sir Lambert took her gently by the elbow.

"A bit of faith, Louisa," he said softly. "Come, see me to my carriage. No harm will be done."

The beautiful drawing room was wrapped in silence for long moments after Colin's mother and Sir Lambert took their leave. The entire evening, the lavish dinner, the missing keys, even Lady Farris's angry words were buried beneath the shattering knowledge of her mother's end. Madeline squeezed her hand into a tight fist. "Is this why you warned me to stay away from Lord Rockford?" she asked suddenly, turning up to catch Colin's gaze. "Because you knew about my mother?"

"No." Colin lifted her chin with his fingertips, brushing away a tear. "I warned you because he slept with my fiancée."

Colin's words were so devastating, so horrifying to her she would have screamed—had he not instantly covered her mouth with his. Madeline gratefully sank into the kiss, letting him hold her tight as tears flowed freely down her cheeks.

"You were trying to protect me," she whispered when he finally pulled away. "I'm sorry I doubted you. I will never speak to that hateful man again." Madeline spoke harshly, her disgust for Lord Rockford spilling out in her words.

"I do want to protect you." Colin pulled away from her, his eyes grey and stormy again. "If you let me, I will do whatever I can to help you."

She shook her head. "I have intruded too much upon your time. My problems shouldn't be your concern."

"Ah, but you are already my concern, Madeline," he said, pulling her closer, until she could barely recall what they were talking about. "And one I take very seriously."

Colin again brought his mouth to hers, leaving Madeline with only the ardent prayer that Lady Douglas would not choose this moment to return. But even that thought soon vanished as she responded to him with a raw urgency that belied her earlier comments. Despite her resolution to distance herself from him, Madeline sank further into Colin's arms, welcoming the intoxicating distraction.

"We should stop," Colin said, practically dragging her arms off him in an attempt to break their kiss. Madeline let out a small whimper of protest as he pulled away, his absence a cold rain. "Though I cannot wait much longer."

"For what?" she asked, confusion shining in the passion pools of her eyes. She shivered as he wound a finger around her disheveled locks.

"For you, Madeline. We've been dancing this waltz together for much too long to suit either of our impatient natures."

"But you don't even wish to be my friend." She blinked up at him, dazed and unable to forget his earlier response.

Colin lifted her chin slowly, and her stomach turned to hot wine. "I want more than that, Madeline. Much more."

She had leaned in for another kiss, eagerly wrapping her arms around his neck, when he stopped her. "But you must tell me the truth."

She sat back, turning away from the soft, coaxing gaze. Could she dare to trust him? Her instincts told her to put her faith in this man, but something held her back.

Greed changes people, Maddie, even those you think you know the best. No matter how well you know someone, you can never tell what hides in his heart.

Papa was speaking of his own wife, she realized. My mother betrayed him, left him for Lord Rockford's arms! A wave of sickness overcame her, and she turned her head away. Papa blamed himself, believed it was he who brought the curse upon his family.

Punishment for stealing a diamond.

"It all makes sense now," she whispered, staring into the fire. A log there cracked in half with vicious finality, like her vow.

"Why did your father send you here?" Colin watched her closely. "This was his home once. Did he leave something behind?"

She took a deep breath. It was no use trying to hide it anymore; she could no longer fight against the feelings she had for Colin. She had promised him honesty, and the truth was that she wanted nothing more than to obey. *Sorry, Papa.*

"What do you know of the French Blue diamond?"

Colin rubbed a hand across his chin, the name striking a chord in his memory. "It was part of the crown jewels of France. I believe it was stolen, along with many other royal gems, in a night raid during the Revolution."

She nodded, her eyes lighting up at his words.

"All the jewels were later recovered," Colin continued, watching the odd, feverish look on Madeline's face. "Except..."

"The French Blue diamond," she finished for him. Their eyes locked together.

He stopped, shaking his head in shock. "It's one of France's royal gems. Men have been searching for it for years. You cannot think... It's buried in my cellar, isn't it?"

She slowly nodded.

****

Madeline's heart pounded a furious rhythm as she followed Colin down the stone steps to the kitchens below. She was grateful for the sudden activity, not wishing to face the heavy sadness that threatened to engulf her once she was alone. The news of Lord Rockford and her mother had numbed her to everything but the task at hand.

It was late. The kitchen staff had long ago retired, leaving the kitchens eerily quiet and cold. She stayed close to Colin, resisting the urge to grasp his hand for reassurance when he halted in front of the door. "You have the key?" she asked.

Colin swiftly nodded, pulling the key ring from his coat pocket and opening the door. Two pairs of eyes scoured the tiny little room.

"It's buried under the eighth stone from the stairs." Madeline spoke the memory seared in her mind.

"He must have meant these stones," Colin said. Pointing to a long row in front of the door, he slid his hand down to the eighth one, probing around it. "It's loose."

Madeline heard the excitement in his voice; it matched her own. She quickly dropped to her knees, helping to pull the heavy stone from the ground. Beneath it sat soft earth, covered for far too many years, and Madeline knew somewhere below lay the French Blue diamond. Colin began to dig, scraping back the dirt with his hands, his sleeves rolled up past his elbows. Madeline sat next to him, their shoulders touching as she peered past him down into the deepening hole.

"Lord Douglas."

Madeline let out a small cry before realizing it was only Halbert who spoke, standing outside the door.

"I beg your pardon, my lady," he said, more concerned with apologizing than with why his employer was digging on the floor. "The Duchess has sent me. She is most concerned over your sudden disappearance and wishes me to return Lady Madeline Sinclair to the drawing room immediately."

"Tell my mother," Colin said, one arm disappearing under the dirt, "we are occupied with digging in the cellar." Madeline jumped up, mortified that Lady Douglas might be thinking the worst.

"Please inform Lady Douglas we would like her to join us." Madeline said with a smile, as if they were all having a little stroll in the park instead of digging in a dank cellar. Halbert bowed, only a small lift of his upper lip revealing his amusement.

"I've found something."

Madeline turned, eager and afraid all at once. Colin held a dark object in his hands, staring in disbelief as he sat in the midst of his large pile of dirt.

"Your lovely shirt is ruined," she said stupidly.

"Look, Madeline." He held up the treasure he'd taken from the ground. A small black velvet bag.

It took all her composure not to scream. She forced herself to peer down into the hole he'd made in the earth, terrified she might see a bone-white hand.

Colin placed the tattered bag in her hand, and she drew it near. It smelled of the earth from which they had ripped it. Raw and rank with years of rotting wood, the dirt had not sheltered it well. She knew exactly what she would find: a diamond, so blue it was nearly purple, glowing brightly as though lit from within, as though the very stone were on fire.

"Madeline?" Colin looked worried, and she realized her expression must be the cause of his alarm. She opened the tattered bag, wincing at the sour, mossy smell that greeted her. Out fell the French Blue diamond. It felt hot, dangerous in her palm. There was no mistake—it was the diamond from her haunting dreams, the thing that cursed her family. The diamond she had been sent to destroy.

"Colin, this is most improper. I had hoped my own son would have better sense than to...gracious, you're both filthy!"

Colin tore his gaze from Madeline to find his mother barreling through the door with Halbert right on her heels. Her look of indignation was slowly giving way to bewilderment as she saw Madeline, kneeling on the ground with a gleaming blue object in her hands.

"What is happening here?"

Colin didn't answer, still watching Madeline with concern. She could not spare a glance from the strange diamond. Her face had grown paler with each passing moment. He had a sudden impulse to toss the thing back into the ground and take Madeline somewhere far away.

"Colin, I must insist you answer me." His mother instructed Halbert to hold up the candle, the light catching the diamond's many facets. "This is most shocking. I knew I shouldn't have sent George away."

"It's all right, Mother," Colin finally replied. "It seems as though I have been harboring the French Blue diamond in my cellar."

His mother gasped, and even Halbert's immovable eyebrows registered surprise. "It couldn't possibly be. Why, no one's seen it for years!"

Colin knew well the story of the stolen French Blue diamond. Anyone who'd spent time fighting for His Majesty was well aware of Napoleon's obsession with finding the valuable gem. England's War Department had launched several private investigations of its own to seek out the gem. It held great monetary and political value these days; to recover the last diamond stolen from the murdered King of France would be a magnificent coup for England, worth more than just the money it could bring. How the hell did it fall into Lord Sinclair's hands? And why would he leave it buried down here for twenty years?

"How did it get here?" his mother asked, coming closer to look for herself.

"Madeline's father buried it," Colin began.

"It's believed to be cursed," Madeline said softly. He jerked his gaze to her, but she said no more. She was lost from him, in her ghostly white dress and dirt-smudged face. Several long strands of hair, forced into curls for the evening, had rebelled and now fell loosely in a thick line down her cheek. She held the diamond cradled as though it were a newborn child, seemingly concerned it might shatter in her hands. There was awe on her face, and fear.

"Well, what are we going to do with it?" His mother placed her hands on her hips, resembling a general preparing for battle. "We must find out more about this diamond as soon as possible. Colin," she barked out, snapping him to attention, "you and Edward speak to someone at the War Department. Perhaps we can find something there to help us."

"No." Madeline finally spoke up, her voice now loud and clear. "I don't think we should involve anyone else in this. I'm taking the diamond with me. I know what to do."

Colin couldn't believe what he was hearing. "You cannot just walk off with a priceless diamond, Madeline. Do you have any idea of its worth?"

"Indeed, my dear," his mother agreed. "Possessing it would be very dangerous."

"I am well aware of its dangers," she said quietly. "But I insist on taking it with me."

"And I insist you will not." Colin stood up, towering over her. He had hoped for a bit of intimidation but was sorely mistaken.

"It belongs to me, Colin. I do not need your permission."

"I believe you have forgotten that 'your' diamond was found in my house." Colin set his jaw as Madeline frowned at him, clutching the diamond more firmly in her hands. He wasn't backing down. There was something strange going on with Madeline. She looked scared and determined, and he wanted to know why.

"Colin." His mother stopped him, placing a hand on his shoulder. "It obviously holds great value to Madeline. I believe she can be trusted to keep it safe."

"Thank you, Lady Douglas."

"And the thieves that will be chasing after her? Can they be trusted, too?" Colin wondered if everyone had gone mad. Did no one but himself realize the dangers of possessing such a sought-after jewel? The London streets were teeming with criminals who would all be clamoring at her door if word got out that Lady Madeline Sinclair possessed the infamous French Blue diamond.

"If you will kindly keep your voice down, no thieves will know about it," Madeline snapped back.

"Perhaps she could take it for the night," his mother suggested, seeing he was about to argue. "Then, first thing tomorrow, we can all decide what is to be done. Would you agree to that, Madeline?"

She nodded eagerly, but Colin still refused. "There is no reason for her to take it out of this house. It will be much safer with me." He continued to protest, determined to have his way, until his mother placed a hand on his arm.

"She has been through quite a shock tonight, Colin. Grant her this one request."

Damn. He was trapped, and despite his grave doubts as to his own sanity, he found himself reluctantly agreeing.

"One night," he said, trying to sound as stern as possible. "First thing tomorrow I will find someone who knows about this diamond, and we will figure out a safe place to store it, understood? One night."

Madeline nodded. "That's all I will need." Colin started to ask what she meant by such a comment, but his mother interrupted him.

"Colin does speak the truth. There are men who would not hesitate to take this diamond—at any cost." She leaned forward, grasping Madeline's hands. "My son will keep his eye on you. In the most proper fashion," she added, turning a stern eye on her son. "But you must be very careful not to speak to anyone of this. Perhaps not even your aunt."

Madeline nodded vigorously. "I will not speak a word to her. Aunt Cecilia would be much too afraid, I think."

Colin frowned as a sudden thought struck him. "Madeline, this curse you spoke of, you don't believe in such nonsense, do you?" She looked up at him, still clasping the diamond like a lifeline, her face wild in the flickering candlelight.

"Of course not."

Chapter Nine

Lady Milburg's townhouse was wrapped in the silence of deep night. All its inhabitants were fast asleep, save one. Madeline's watery green eyes lay open and staring as the day's events raced through her mind like a team of horses in pursuit.

Could she really destroy such a diamond? She felt the hard weight of the jewel under her pillow, strangely comforting. It was worth the fortune of kings, a priceless stone so valuable even a mere portion could give her lifelong independence. And think what it could do for her aunt and cousin! Though Aunt Cecilia kept up a steady patter of frivolous chatter devised to ignore their financial woes, Madeline knew she was terribly worried. Her aunt couldn't hide the tight, strained glances whenever a bill arrived in the post. They lived in fear of the day creditors would arrive to remove the many furnishings and the expensive clothing her aunt had lavished upon them.

The debts were mounting, and under her pillow lay a diamond worth enough to save them all. She would be a fool to destroy it! And she had promised Colin...

Colin.

Tossing off her blankets, Madeline sat up, suddenly feverishly hot under the scratchy wool. Her mind burned with the memory of their final parting that night. Colin had walked beside her to her aunt's door, politely holding her elbow, though she barely registered the light touch. The end of the evening, a short ride through the crisp night air followed by

Lady Douglas's warm words of farewell, lay buried beneath the shattering knowledge of her mother's treacherous past.

As Colin bid her good night, promising to call on her the next day, something happened inside her. Stepping forward, she impulsively flung her arms around Colin's neck, kissing him with a desperate passion she did not know, until that very moment, she possessed. Colin had instantly reciprocated, neither one the least concerned that Lady Douglas might choose to peek out the black velvet curtains of her barouche. The kiss was no longer gentle or teasing but turned impatiently seductive, their lips sealing the promise they had made to one another.

She was trapped. Bound between a vow to her father and the newly formed promise to a man with whom she was rapidly falling in love.

Honesty. The word scalded her, and she quickly pulled the blankets back to her, feeling alone and vulnerable in the darkness of her room. "What should I do?" Madeline whispered her question coaxingly into the inky darkness surrounding her, and the darkness continued to answer back with silence, as it had done all night. Dawn would soon begin making its climb toward the day, and, still with no answer, she fell into a troubled sleep.

****

She was leaving him.

Lady Sarah Caithness squeezed another of her precious hats into the overflowing trunk, determined not to leave her favorite with the blue silk ribbons behind. It was excruciating work, this packing of clothes, but she dared not call any of the servants in to help her. She had told no one of her plans, save Bessie, of course, but that gaping little maid was coming with her. The other ungrateful servants prided themselves on their loyalty and would gladly line up to inform the earl of his wife's sins. But no more! Sarah slammed the lid of the trunk closed. She was running away, leaving behind her boorish husband and his cold, passionless manner.

Sarah paused to smile. The Marquis of Rockford's arousing looks were well known amongst the ladies reigning over London's peak of society. Even the most prim and docile of wives would toss off a stuffy husband for the chance to have Lord Rockford in her bed, but he cared only for her. William offered her the world, and, finally, she had the courage to take it.

A loud wail interrupted her thoughts, and she turned to confront her daughter's nursemaid. "Can you not quiet her, Bessie? The entire household will hear!" She stared down at little Madeline, unable to comprehend the meaning of the flailing fists and red face.

"It's time to leave." Sarah flicked her fingers. "Lord Rockford's carriage has already arrived. A new phaeton," she added with pride. Sarah had nearly swooned at the sight waiting to take her to William: the newest, most fashionable carriage one could buy. "A grand life awaits us, Bessie. We shall want for nothing."

Sarah was certain this would impress the girl, but Bessie just stood there making ridiculous noises at the baby. *Poor simple girl.* She sighed. *I suppose every carriage looks fancy to her.*

"Take Madeline downstairs. Quietly," she added as the child continued to wail. "Tell Lord Rockford's driver I am on my way." Sarah dismissed the maid, her mind flittering back to the pile of gloves in front of her.

A sharp thrill ran through her at the thought of being in her lover's arms again. She laughed, giddy over her luck. Never again would she have to endure an evening of dull conversation and weak wine. She had long noticed the looks from her friends, pity intertwined with shame for being saddled with such a life.

She had just snapped closed the last of her satchels when the door flew open. Sarah's head shot up, a sharp reprimand for Bessie ready on her tongue, but it was stopped cold.

"Thomas!" The word came out in a shriek as Sarah threw herself in front of the large trunk. Her husband had returned early. "You startled me." She laughed, forcing herself under control. "I expected you next week. Did you enjoy your little trip?" Her fingers splayed lightly against her bosom, hoping to provide a distraction from her trembling.

"I left early," he replied, keeping his gaze locked to hers. "Paris is not the place it once was." He spoke with little emotion, his gaze never leaving her face.

Sarah laughed again. Her heart was bursting from her chest, but she gifted him with a soothing, attentive smile. "Well, darling, everyone did warn you. France is terribly fussy these days, but you insisted on going." Swallowing hard, she crossed the room to embrace him, her thoughts running wildly to the awaiting carriage outside. Had he recognized it? "I do hope you've had your fill of adventures."

"I certainly have." He spoke curtly, remaining rigid as a board when she embraced him. "I was longing for the peace and comforts of home, though I see now I was quite mistaken."

Sarah's breath caught in her throat, but she forced herself to speak calmly. "Why, whatever do you mean by that?" she exclaimed.

"I brought you a gift." Ignoring her question, he tossed a small package at her feet, where it landed with a dull thump.

"A present! How delightful. Is it perfume?" Her hands eagerly reached for the strangely wrapped package, ripping it open to reveal the largest jewel she'd ever laid eyes on. "Thomas, it's a diamond!"

Sarah stared, in awe of the gem lying perfectly in her palm as though it belonged there. She ran to the window, letting the light gleam off its many sides as it blazed like a raging fire. "A blue diamond! Where did you find such a jewel?"

"The French Blue diamond." He spoke sharply, a tone she'd never heard before. "It belonged to Louis XVI, before he was imprisoned by his own subjects. So much for loyalty," he added bitterly. "Did you know the diamond is supposedly cursed?"

"Cursed?" she scoffed, wondering how the diamond would look mounted in gold and hung around her neck. Surely she must wear it soon! "Such magnificence cannot bring anything but good fortune." She cast a quick glance at her husband's strangely pale face before returning to her jewel. "Darling, you look rather ill. Why don't you lie down for a bit before dinner?"

"So you can make your escape?" Thomas jerked away from her, closing the door with a thud. "I won't make it that easy for you. What a fool I've been! I heard the whispers, of course, but never paid them any mind."

He was delirious, she decided, a fever perhaps, or something worse. "You must excuse me," she replied, "but I fear I have become rather lost in this conversation." Truthfully she was so mesmerized by the diamond in her hands she could hardly concentrate on anything else.

"Planning a trip, aren't you, my dear?" Thomas's voice was icy as he pointed to the stacks of luggage behind her.

Sarah finally tore her gaze away from the French Blue. "No," she replied, her voice beginning to crack. "What exactly are you implying?"

"I've suddenly been struck with the strangest feeling." He spoke slowly, never taking his gaze from her. "That a certain Lord Rockford is planning to run off with my wife."

Sarah stepped back quickly, knocking into the trunks behind her. "How dare you say such a thing! I will not allow such slander against my name."

"I would hardly call it slander, my darling, seeing as how Rockford's been your lover for several months now."

It was the reek of disdain in his voice that was her undoing, sapping all logic from her mind. Sarah no longer cared what Thomas thought of her.

"Yes, I'm leaving you," she spat out, standing up straight enough to make even her mother proud. "I'm in love with William, and I'm going to be with him. There's nothing you can say to stop me."

"Stop you?" The laugh he uttered was loud and bitter. "I wouldn't dream of it. If the thought of adultery and divorce staining the family name you're so proud of won't deter you, what chance do I have?"

"I don't care!" she screamed, despising the truth of his words. "He's taking me far away, where no one will find us."

Thomas shook his head slowly, as though daring to pity her. "I knew you were a selfish creature when I married you, but this has gone too far. Did Rockford seduce you into this? Is he bringing his other mistresses along, as well? You should all make a very merry party."

"William loves *me!*" She picked up a glass vase from the table and threw it at him, relishing the sound of its shatter against the wall over his head.

"And what about Madeline?" he said. "Have you thought about leaving your child? Deprived of her own mother?"

It was then Sarah made a terrible mistake. Her gaze flickered downward, signaling her guilt.

"No," Thomas said, horror dawning in his eyes. "Leave if you must, but you will not take our child. Madeline!" He threw open the door and ran upstairs, shouting all the way to the nursery.

Sarah nearly choked with relief. This was her chance. Clutching the diamond to her chest, she cast a last regretful look at her trunks before leaving them behind. *William will certainly buy me a new wardrobe,* she told herself. And besides, what did she need with her old clothes? She had a priceless diamond in her hands! With a laugh, she continued down the back stairs, where Bessie stood waiting by the door.

"The earl is here!" Bessie could barely speak, she was so terrified. "We dare not leave now."

"Give me my daughter." She wrenched Madeline from the spineless maid's arms and shoved past her out the door, dashing to the waiting carriage. Thomas's bellows came faintly from the upstairs windows.

"Go! Leave now!" she screamed, and William's man instantly obeyed. They sped off in the open carriage, leaving Bessie staring after them in a cloud of dust. Any moment now Thomas would discover the empty nursery, but it would be too late.

"He's following us, my lady!" The driver yelled his warning over the pounding of hooves. Sarah tried desperately to soothe the screaming baby in her arms, jiggling her around as she'd seen Bessie do, but to no avail. They rode on, the driver pressing the horses to a madman's pace, her husband following at their heels. Sarah shut her eyes in prayer. They were close now, almost to the spot where William awaited her. *He will take care of this,* she whispered over and over again. *William will take care of everything.*

A harsh jerk of the carriage ended her prayer, and with relief she spotted William's rich blond hair just ahead. He looked terrified, his face stricken and pale as they came into view, still going dreadfully fast. Then she lost sight of him as the wheels jolted violently to one side, twisting much too far to the right. Out of the corner of her eye Sarah saw the reins fly from the driver's hands like ribbons in the wind, and she knew. In a final desperate act, Sarah wrapped her body around her tiny daughter, the French Blue diamond clutched tightly in her hand, cutting into her flesh as they met the ground with a sickening crunch.

Madeline sat up in a cold sweat.

The dream was so vivid, so raw; in her heart she knew it hadn't been a dream at all. She had just seen her mother's death.

She felt the hard weight of the diamond beneath her pillow, checking to make sure it had not vanished. She threw off the bedcovers and walked to the window, hoping the night air would help wash away the remnants of her dream. The terror in her mother's face, the fiercely glowing diamond scalding her palm—the images still hovered around the edges of Madeline's mind.

"*Madeline.*" She gasped at the voice, stumbling away from the window as the sound came closer. "*You've seen the truth now.*" The rasping voice, the sharp, worm-filled cough...there was no doubt.

"*Madeline.*" She was on her knees, eyes squeezed shut, too terrified to look any closer. He was here, no longer underground in the dirt but here, in her room, watching her from the window. "*It killed your mother. You must destroy it.*"

"It's only a diamond, Papa. It cannot hurt me." She choked as the words tumbled from her mouth. Colin's words.

"You swore a vow. IT MUST BE DONE!"

She shrieked when the voice swept past her head, ruffling her hair, as the rattling grew closer and closer... "*My daughter...*"

"I'll do it, I'll do it, please don't come any closer!" She shrank down to the floor, screaming now. This

151

wasn't a dream. Someone would come, Helena would hear the screams and run in—

****

Madeline awoke in her bed.

It was still dark outside. She was shaking, gasping, scrambling for the diamond that no longer brought her comfort. After long minutes had passed, her gaze searching every corner of the dim room, she convinced herself it had been only a dream. She pulled the diamond from beneath her pillow and, rolling it up in an old dress, threw it into her trunk. She must end this, the fears, the hiding, these torturous dreams.

Tomorrow. She would destroy it tomorrow.

****

I have recently become aware of the true nature of your relationship with my family. I hope you agree there is little choice but to cease any future engagements between us.

Lady Madeline Sinclair

Lord Rockford crumpled the letter in his shaking fist, rage pulsating through his body.

"Bad news, then?" Moore asked, belching softly as he dropped into a chair across from Lord Rockford.

"Read for yourself." Lord Rockford didn't move, didn't allow one flick of an eye to betray his anger over such an insult. Someone had told her about his past with Sarah. God knows what sordid lies they wove to make Madeline reject him this way.

It must have been Douglas.

Moore tossed a card on the table, leaving a small smudge behind from an unwashed thumb. "Rejection letter from your mistress? I know a few ladies who'd be willing to take her place." He laughed to himself. "Old Betty would be a good match. She's a bit rank, mind."

"It would seem you've been failing in your task."

152

He was displeased to have gotten Moore's attention so easily. He had been planning to smash a fist into his face.

"Now, wait a minute!" Moore jerked up in surprise. "I done all I was supposed to so far. You told me to follow the chit, and I followed her. You told me to come report to you when she was seein' other men, and I left me nice warm bed to report."

William's gaze narrowed on the ale-stained shirt and greasy hair. "I doubt very much you ever made it to your bed."

"Oh, I found me a bed." He snickered.

Rockford's patience broke, and he leaned forward, yanking the glass from Moore's filthy hand. "So, tell me."

Moore gulped like a fish.

"Last night your Lady Madeline Sinclair went to a dinner party at the duke's house. Now, I did manage to chat up the servant. A nice bit of work she was, too. Gracie? Greta? She told me it was given by Lady Douglas, but the duke was indeed attending and..."

Moore stopped, motioning for his drink, but William slid it farther out of reach. "Get on with it."

"I happened to see your lady bein' escorted home by the duke, *very* late." He ended by triumphantly snatching his drink back.

"This will not do," William muttered. It was exactly as he'd suspected. Douglas was behind this; he must have told her. "Stay with her today. Do not let Madeline Sinclair out of your sight."

Moore nodded. "And what about Douglas?"

William's jaw hardened. He threw Madeline's letter into the fire.

****

"Watch out for Mama this morning," Helena warned, as she flounced into her chair at the breakfast table. "I ran into her in the hallway and she is most upset. Apparently Mr. Nevens sent a note refusing any more credit until she pays her bill in full. She has taken it very personally that we cannot purchase any more of his hideous hats."

"Darlings, this is the end!"

As though on cue, Madeline's aunt burst into the room, holding a white hatbox, Brigette trailing behind with two more. "I have never been so insulted. I'm positively sick from Mr. Nevens's treatment of me! But do not fret." She set her box down on the table with a flourish, pausing to smile triumphantly at them both. "Before that horrible money-pinching man could stop my account, I managed to purchase matching feather-and-ermine turbans for the Huntington masquerade ball."

"Good Lord." Madeline dropped her spoon in dismay at the sight Aunt Cecilia displayed. It was indeed covered with feathers of all shades of purple, and lined along the bottom with a revolting brown fur. It was, without doubt, the ugliest thing she'd ever seen.

"And there are three of them!" Helena gasped, as though unable to take it all in. "Mama, what have you done?"

"Aren't they positively darling?" Aunt Cecilia clapped her hands. "I know Huntington is dead set on his god-and-goddess attire for the ball, but I mean, honestly, darlings, what a bore! Everyone knows an Oriental costume ball is the thing these days. But never fear, for we shall stand out amongst the crowd in these." She placed one of the turbans sideways on her head. "Aren't they just the thing? This is the very kind of turban that makes a man fall in love. Just wait and see. You shall both be swooped up instantly tomorrow night, I have no doubt!"

"I scarcely know what to say," Helena began, her eyes wide with horror. "But I must inform you,

154

Mama that those are the most revolt..."

"The turbans are exquisite!" Madeline loudly interrupted, shaking her head at her cousin. "You have outdone yourself, Aunt. They will surely be the...the talk of the ball." Helena stared at her, likely wondering if her older cousin had lost her mind, but Madeline had no patience to argue over hats. Every moment the diamond sat untouched in the pocket of her gown it seemed to pulsate fear through her veins. She needed to get rid of the awful thing, and time was running out.

"Madeline, I'm so pleased to see your fashion sense is improving."

"Indeed it is, under your expert guidance, Aunt." She smiled and handed her aunt a large buttery roll, ignoring what sounded suspiciously like a loud snort from Helena. "And not only that, but I've come to appreciate all the delights and amusements available to me in London. I woke up this very morning with the plan to take a short ride through the beautiful park after breakfast."

She smiled again, trying to look fresh and cheerful despite the horrors of last night.

"Horse riding! At this hour? Why, it's not even noon!" Aunt Cecilia blinked at her niece from across the breakfast table. "I cannot conceive of such timing. No one will be out at all." She nodded to Helena for support while Madeline forced her expression to remain serene. She was determined to go riding as soon as possible, but convincing her aunt was going to require a cunning mind.

"Why not wait until five, when you can mingle with the rest of the *ton*? A much more appropriate hour for riding, if you ask me."

"I do not wish to mingle with the *ton*," Madeline replied, her smile beginning to fade. "I am trying to get a bit of air, is all, and have no desire to be stared at like a doll on display."

"What could be the point of riding in the park if one is not to be looked at?" Aunt Cecilia asked, her incredulous gaze darting back and forth between the two girls. "Why should one bother to own such richly colored riding clothes if not for the purpose of allowing others to gaze enviously upon them in the sunshine?"

Madeline scraped through her mind for a reasonable response but could barely think past blue diamonds and nightmares.

"You must remember, all the eligible men have already seen you by candlelight, and what good has that done? You must use each and every opportunity to show yourself off. Let London see how becoming you look while taking the air."

"Mama, really," Helena muttered, buttering away at her toast. "Madeline can certainly go out again this afternoon. We can take the carriage."

"And, of course, you must take your cousin," Aunt Cecilia barreled on, fully warmed to her topic. "No lady dares to ride alone. It's barbaric."

"I do not think Helena is well enough to go riding," Madeline replied, crossing her arms with her most stubborn glare. She would apologize to Helena later. "And I must insist on going out today."

"Nonsense! Helena is as fit as ever. Why, she doesn't have a red spot on her this morning. It was the chicken fat." Aunt Cecilia nodded. "Just the thing."

Madeline struggled to regain her place in the argument, turning to Helena with a silent plea for help. "Aunt, I do believe—"

"I suppose we should wait until five," Helena sighed casting her gaze down mournfully. "Though it will be such a pity to miss Lord Pentleham and those dashing friends of his. You remember Elbert, don't you, Mama? He's the very wealthy viscount who danced with me last Tuesday and very nearly asked me twice more!"

"Elbert, of course!" Madeline jumped in, racking her brain to remember who this viscount was. "Such a delightful man. Rather doted on you, Helena."

"Will he be riding in the park this afternoon?" Aunt Cecilia's eyes were shining.

"Sadly, no, Elbert runs with a bit of a fast set. No one improper," Helena added hastily, "but several young bucks who enjoy racing their phaetons around the park. I believe Lord Douglas joins them, doesn't he, Madeline? In any case, Elbert tends to ride quite early to avoid the crowds."

Helena's ploy worked to perfection; her mother nearly fell out of her chair at the idea of getting ahead of London's other eligible ladies. "Just think, darlings!" Aunt Cecilia gasped. "All that blood rushing around is bound to make a man fall in love rather quickly! Helena! I insist you wear your green riding dress today, and Madeline the blue. Hurry, darlings. it's getting late!"

Less than an hour later Madeline and Helena, along with two impeccably dressed grooms, set off to Hyde Park, though Madeline's plan hadn't fully come out as she'd hoped. She wasn't alone and was trussed up in the most uncomfortable, impractical riding outfit she'd ever seen, but it would have to do. *Perhaps this is a blessing. Helena has certainly proved herself helpful, and I do need someone to confide in.* Madeline felt the heavy weight of the French Blue diamond tucked inside her pink reticule on its way to a watery grave. *I shall toss it into the Thames. Let it slip far into the deep water where it can never harm another soul.*

"Madeline, I am nearly faint with curiosity. You must tell me what happened at the dinner last night! Did your duke ravish you in the gardens again, or perhaps in his pantry?" Helena began to giggle. "Did Lord Montgomery attend?"

"He is not *my* duke," Madeline replied, coloring at Helena's words. "Colin was most proper the entire evening..." She trailed off, remembering the warm hand on her knee at dinner.

"Mama thinks your duke is desperately in love with you. She said this is the perfect time for you to flirt with other suitors to make Lord Douglas wild with jealousy and therefore ensure the union. I told her such a thing was ridiculous. What do you think, Madeline? If Lord Douglas is already in love with you, would it not be foolish to play games with him? Perhaps you could just ask him to become your husband? I don't see why one can't. I've told Lord Vickem several times I do not wish to be his wife. Surely it works the other way, do you think?"

"Undoubtedly," Madeline answered, her head turned to watch the two grooms behind them. Filbert and Peter were their names. They were amiable but slightly lazy young men on loan from Miss Lillian. *With a bit of luck we can lose them,* Madeline decided, very slightly increasing her horse's pace. It was only a short ride to the docks, though through an ill-advised section of town, and Helena would certainly wonder why they were leaving the park. She sighed. There was no helping it; she would have to admit her plans.

"And Edward looked well? I mean, Lord Montgomery? He seemed to enjoy himself at dinner?"

"Edward was away on business for the evening," Madeline said, turning to face her cousin. "Helena, I have something important to discuss with you."

"Does it have something to do with what's in your reticule?"

Madeline's mouth fell open. "How did you know?"

"You keep glancing at it every few seconds as though it's going to fly away." Helena shrugged. "Not to be rude, but you do seem very nervous today, cousin."

Madeline relaxed her grip on the small bag, forcing herself to speak slowly. She must remain calm or Helena would never believe her. "Do you believe in curses?" She glanced back at the grooms again. They were barely visible now, only a faint outline in the trees.

"Curses? I suppose so. I am quite certain I cursed poor Cook last night when she put that vile chicken fat on my neck."

"No, this is something more." Madeline tried to keep her voice composed. "A curse put on my father and his family, *our* family, for stealing an evil diamond."

"Madeline." Helena jerked her horse to a stop. "What do you have in your reticule?"

With a deep breath, Madeline told her cousin everything, from her father's dying instructions to the news of Lord Rockford's affair with her mother.

"Lord Douglas told you all of this over dinner?" Helena shrieked, nearly unsaddling herself.

"Of course not. It was after dinner. All the other guests had gone, including that most hateful Lady Farris." Madeline swallowed her anger over the memory of that woman's words. "But it's all true. My mother was running away with Lord Rockford when she was killed. She was leaving my father."

"And then your father ran away with you," Helena gasped. "I must say it makes sense. Mama was always a little strange about her own sister. She will hardly speak Aunt Sarah's name! And she does truly hate Lord Rockford." She scrunched up her nose in thought. "Though I am unable to understand the evil curse part. Did Lord Rockford put a curse on your mama? Is that why she fell in love with him?"

"The curse caused her to run away!" Madeline said, desperate to make her cousin understand. "The

159

very day my father laid his hands on that diamond he was struck by its evil. The man he was traveling with, Lord Johnston, was drowned on the voyage to London. Papa then returned home to see my mother betray him and die. Then he fled, leaving the French Blue buried deep in the ground beneath the Baker Street house, but it was too late." Madeline took a deep breath. "The evil followed us, robbing Papa of his health and friends, everything he loved. At first he believed the curse would end with his death, a punishment for his crimes, but then—"

She broke off, unable to tell her cousin of the terrible dreams she had inherited from her father. Would she sound mad? How would anyone believe her?

"My God, Madeline, it does sound rather terrifying when you put it that way. I don't know what to think!"

"We have no choice," Madeline replied firmly. "We must destroy the French Blue diamond."

"Destroy it?"

She nodded. "It was my father's last dying wish. We must destroy it before it can harm another soul."

Helena was beginning to look nervous. "Perhaps you're right, cousin, but how does one destroy a diamond?"

"I must admit I'm not exactly sure." Madeline bit her lower lip. "I thought about throwing it into the Thames. What do you suggest?"

"Fire?" Helena offered. "Or perhaps we could smash it with a rock. Can one smash a diamond?"

"If the rock is hard enough," Madeline said, warming to the idea.

"Perhaps it would be best to seek the advice of a trusted friend," Helena spoke hopefully. "Lord Douglas, perhaps? He and his brother seem rather sensible." But Madeline shook her head.

"Colin will not listen. He is determined to

protect me, or some such ridiculous thing."

Madeline's last words slipped out, surprising even herself. Why had she repeated Colin's words? She had been doing her very best to block him from her mind all morning.

Helena, on the other hand, was thrilled the conversation had turned back to familiar ground. "How terrible and romantic this all is! You are being pursued by an evil curse and a handsome duke all at once! Is your heart absolutely bursting? Mine would be."

"Helena, be serious. Colin merely enjoys ordering me about." She bristled at her cousin's words, her promise to Colin creeping uncomfortably back into her mind.

"Very well, Madeline, we shall talk of other things until you can come to terms with your suitor. I am so glad to be able to help! I promise I shall be very discreet about your curse, and of course we must keep you as far away from that horrid Lord Rockford as possible." Helena threw a furtive glance behind her. "Have we lost Peter and dear Filbert? We've been taking such an odd, twisting route, Madeline. I do believe we should find them right away and go home, perhaps even back to the country for awhile, to keep you safe. Mother may balk, but it's best not to listen to her."

"On the contrary, Helena, I have no wish to hide," Madeline replied stoutly. She kept moving forward, grateful to have lost the grooms at last.

"Madeline, do be sensible!" Helena was growing alarmed. "Lord Rockford mustn't come near you. His attentions already have been most improper."

"I completely agree, which is precisely why I wrote to him this morning."

Helena stopped, refusing to go any further. "Have you gone completely mad?"

"Think about it, Helena. The man is a monster! I

wish him to know that I am aware of who he is. It's only justice."

Helena's pert face screwed up in disbelief. "I do not mean to sound rude, but perhaps you should see a doctor. All this knowledge of your poor mother...I believe it has made you unwell!"

"I am as fit as ever."

"Then why take such an unnecessary risk? I have noticed that men do not much appreciate being reminded of their sins."

Madeline shrugged. "I simply sent Rockford a note informing him that we should never meet again. I was very careful to say as little as possible."

"Madeline, are we lost?" The truth suddenly dawned on Helena as she realized they had ridden out of the park and into a very secluded wooded area.

"Not in the least, but my father's wishes must be carried out in the utmost privacy."

Helena's eyes turned to saucers. "Are we going to destroy the diamond here? Right now?"

"We don't have much time. Come and help me find a good-sized rock." Madeline swung off her horse, already searching amongst the trees.

"How will Filbert and Peter ever find us?" Helena asked worriedly, joining her on the ground.

****

Damn women. Moore wheezed as he ran after the horse tracks, slowing briefly to catch his breath. They were up to something, that he was sure of. They had been whisperin' and gigglin' all over the place after leaving the aunt's house, and now, without any warning, they just took off into the woods.

He would catch them, though. How far could two ladies go? And besides, he knew a shortcut through these woods. Not to mention he had the wrath of Rockford spurring him on.

****

"Gracious, Madeline, it's huge!" Helena held the French Blue diamond in her hand. "It must be worth a fortune. Why, with this diamond you could marry anyone you wished. Or no one at all!" she gasped.

"We are not keeping it, Helena," Madeline said, still scouring the ground for a big enough rock. One with sharp corners, and another flat one to lay the diamond on. "No amount of money is worth the ill luck this diamond has brought."

"But are you absolutely sure the diamond is the cause of such ill fortune? It looks quite harmless to me."

"You sound like Colin," she muttered. "Can you not feel the evil coming off it? It seems to be almost glaring at me."

Helena lifted it up to one eye, peering at it intently. "All I see is a lovely blue, but if you say so, we will of course destroy it." She shook her head. "Though it seems such a waste. Could we save a tiny piece? Maybe to use in a hair jewel?"

"No." Madeline found the perfect rock at last and snatched the diamond back from her enamored cousin's grasp.

"We must end this." She held her breath. Setting the French Blue down on the large flat rock, one hand held it steady while she lifted the sharper rock above her head. "Are you ready?" she whispered, suddenly afraid.

Helena closed her eyes. "Ready!"

Madeline stared hard at the glimmering fire in the middle of the diamond. *Just as I promised Papa,* she thought, and felt the rock hit the diamond with a small vibrating *chink!* like the ringing of a tiny bell.

Helena screamed.

The attack caught Madeline completely by surprise, knocking her to the left and into the large trunk of the twisted oaks. As she struggled to right herself, her first thought was that some small animal had frightened the horses. Then she saw the man. Or smelled him, rather. His tattered coat let off an awful, sour stench that made her eyes water.

He moved quickly, fighting for the diamond that Madeline quickly slipped into her bag. She got only a glimpse of his sunken cheeks and beady eyes before he clawed at her arm, ripping the thin reticule strings from her wrist. She kicked back against him, knocking herself to the ground as she fought to keep hold of the diamond and the ridiculous bag, even as he dragged her along.

"Helena!" Madeline screamed. If only she hadn't run away from Peter and Filbert—but how in the Lord's name was she to have expected this!

"Helena! Madeline! Stay where you are!" Peter's voice! Madeline sobbed with relief.

The thief looked dumbfounded for a moment, holding the pink silk prize in his hands, and then ran, vanishing into the trees while Madeline watched him disappear, too stunned to do more than lie where he'd left her.

"Madeline, what happened?" Helena was by her side in a second. Not waiting for an answer, she yelled for the grooms, who had finally caught up with them, their faces ashen at the sight of their mistress lying in the dirt.

"Madeline has been attacked!" Helena bit out, her voice as sharp as a general's, as Filbert jumped off his horse to inspect the damage.

"Are you hurt, my lady?"

Madeline shook her head, ignoring the painful throbbing in her hand as she scrambled up from the dirt and looked around her, a sick dread filling her stomach. "He took it," she whispered. "My God, Helena, it's gone!"

"A thief, was it?" Filbert examined the ground. "What did he take, my lady?"

"Helena, what will we do? He's taken the dia—"

"Only her reticule," Helena answered loudly. "Of course, my cousin is very upset, Filbert. Help me to take her home, and we shall call for a doctor. And Peter, ride as fast as you can to the Duke of Douglas's home," Helena continued, ignoring Madeline's outraged protest. "Tell Lord Douglas it is most urgent. We need him straightaway!"

Chapter Ten

"You can forego your usual lecture." Edward waltzed through the door of his brother's study sporting a half-cocked grin. "I have already made my apologies to Mother for missing her splendid dinner."

Colin looked up from his desk with a sharp glare. "I'm sure it was a very pretty apology, too. Mind telling me where the hell you were last night?"

"I dropped in to Lord Waveland's ball and lost all sense of time dancing with his daughters." Edward settled himself into a chair with a deep sigh. "Do you know the man has six of them? The lot of them unmarried, though rather sheepish for my taste. Except for the third girl. She's not afraid of a good conversation."

He prattled on, as Colin glimpsed a suspicious pair of bruised knuckles gracing his brother's right hand.

"Mother informed me of all the happenings last night, after soundly reprimanding me for missing her party. I must say, it didn't sound half as boring as I'd expected." Edward casually hid his battered hand from view. "What are you reading?"

"The War Department's reports on the French Blue diamond." Colin closed the large file in front of him before tossing it onto his desk amongst the pile of scattered papers. He'd been up since dawn, poring over hundreds of badly scrawled testimonies, witness accounts, and false evidence relating to the missing diamond. It was tedious work, and his mood was not improved by the sight of his younger brother, who looked like he'd spent half the night carousing in some tavern and the other half fighting his way out.

"If I had known you wanted me to spend hours squinting at old files, I wouldn't have come over. How did you get these, by the way?" Edward leaned over the desk, picking one up. "Aren't they confidential?"

"I stole them," Colin answered, pressing down on his temples to suppress the oncoming headache. "I still have a few friends left in the Department. You should have Halbert take a look at your hand." Edward looked startled for a moment, then glanced down at the dried blood with a shrug.

"Nothing a little brandy won't fix."

It was all he was going to get for today. Edward had turned more and more secretive these past months, reminding Colin of his former self.

"Come, man, don't leave me in suspense! I've heard all about your mysterious diamond in the cellar. Enlighten me on what you've found." Edward leaned forward, helping himself to one of the files from Colin's desk.

Colin reopened the report he'd been reading, pushing past his headache to focus on his task. "I know that England didn't sanction a theft of the royal jewels, which means if Madeline's father was behind the crime he did it on his own."

"Makes sense." Edward nodded. "He was sent over to France on another assignment and saw an opportunity. Paris was a bloody mess then. It would be easy to lose yourself in the mobs."

"He wouldn't be the first," Colin replied grimly. "Many men at the time, French and English, fell victim to the Revolution's greed. The only thing I can't figure out is why he would bury the French Blue for twenty years."

"Fear?" Edward suggested. "My guess is the War

Department was onto his crime, but he planned to retrieve it someday."

"That's precisely what I thought." Colin's headache vanished as he handed his brother a file, yellowed with age. "But I've been through at least twelve of these files, all pertaining to the French Blue diamond, and not one of them mentions the name Sinclair. I'm beginning to doubt they ever suspected him of anything."

"Didn't Sinclair take Madeline and flee the country?" Edward frowned, flipping through the old papers. "That's enough to make anyone suspicious."

"The official statement is that he had a breakdown after his wife's death. He quit the department, left for Scotland, and no one bothered with him again."

"So, England didn't suspect him of the theft, but someone else did. Maybe he was being blackmailed."

"Maybe." Colin couldn't get Madeline's words from the night before out of his head. "Or maybe it's something else entirely. Madeline mentioned her father believed the French Blue diamond was cursed."

"A cursed diamond?" Edward's left eyebrow went up. "That's nonsense."

"I know that," Colin replied. "But I'm just wondering if Sinclair did." *And hence his daughter.* Colin had a very strong feeling this curse had something to do with Madeline's insistence on taking the diamond last night.

But Edward was still skeptical. "If Sinclair was so convinced it was evil, why send Madeline to dig it up?"

"A good question, and one I intend to figure out." Colin stood up, suddenly anxious to leave. He couldn't shake the gnawing feeling that Madeline was in trouble, remembering how she had clutched the diamond, the strange vacant stare in her eyes.

That look had gnawed at him all night.

"It's a bit early for paying a call," Edward informed him, casually propping one boot on the corner of the desk while Colin threw a pile of papers to the floor, searching for his jacket. "People will begin to wonder about your intentions."

"Let them wonder." Any proper gentleman would blanch at the very idea of calling on a lady before two, but Colin had been away from Madeline long enough. The haunted look in her eyes last night removed any concerns for his etiquette. "The *ton*'s gossip does not concern me."

"Does it concern Madeline?"

The question stopped him for a moment. He honestly didn't know how Madeline felt about such things. She did seem terribly concerned over her reputation in Farris's garden, but then again, no one had dragged her out there.

"How well do you really know her?" Edward pressed on, and Colin turned sharply.

"What are you trying to say?" Colin didn't like the look his brother was giving him. Did Edward think he should just toss Madeline alone into London with a priceless diamond and wait for someone to take it from her?

"I am merely suggesting caution. You are under no obligation to continue helping Madeline. Unless, of course, there's another reason for your interest."

"Are you now lecturing me on the ways of the world?" Colin snapped. "I seem to recall last year around this time you were still getting into mischief with your school friends."

"A year can change many things." He grinned. "Perhaps soon I will prove myself to you."

"You can start," Colin said, slamming his hands down on the desk, "by telling me what you were really up to last night. And save the story about dancing with eligible daughters. Unless you got into a brawl with one of them?" He pointed directly to his brother's bloody hand.

Edward shifted in his chair, looking annoyed. "I didn't want to tell you until I'd gotten a bit more steady on my feet, but the truth is, I've joined the fight against Napoleon."

Colin swore. "You've joined the War Department? After everything Father and I went through?"

"There's a war going on, Colin. It's my duty to fight. You know that as much as I."

My little brother has grown rather pompous. Colin's face drew into a deep frown. *I wonder whether a swift punch to the chin might help.*

While certainly more than capable of taking care of himself, Edward's youth was a concern. How would his naïve view of the world hold up when he discovered he was fighting not for England but, rather, to satisfy the power lust of other men? He only hoped Edward's realization came at a lower price than his own.

"I had hoped to have your support," Edward said carefully.

Colin turned to his brother. Below Edward's charming smile he recognized the hard, blank look of a man hoarding too many secrets. He dreaded Edward's idealistic nature, knew how treacherous his path would become, but, despite his fears, Colin knew he had to let his brother choose his own way. It was no less than Colin would desire for himself.

Hoping he wouldn't come to regret his words, Colin gave a hard nod. "You have it."

"Pardon the intrusion, Lord Douglas, but this boy claims to have an urgent message." Halbert's words were interrupted by the shouts of a young man dressed in an oversized livery, his face flushed red as a beet.

"Lord Douglas!" he squeaked. "Lady Helena

Weston sent me to find you right away. You must come to the house, to my mistress's house!" He took a shuddering breath. "The ladies have been violently attacked in the park, sir! Thieves, sir! She is asking for you—you must come!" The message seemed to drain the remainder of the boy's energy, leaving him wheezing at Colin's feet. Alarm broke over Edward's face as he grabbed the boy's shoulder.

"Who attacked them? Was Madeline harmed?"

The young groom babbled out his answer, but Colin didn't wait to hear it. He was already running for the stables, shouting for his horse.

****

The brothers arrived at Lady Milburg's townhouse to discover the servants dashing about like panicked mice. Colin pushed his way into the babbling throng, searching for someone who looked the least bit rational, and finally settled his gaze on a sensible-looking young maid.

"You, there!" he bellowed at her. "Where is Madeline?"

He underestimated the girl's sensibility, for instead of answering she let out two piercing shrieks before slapping her apron over her face. The maid's reaction, coupled with Colin's thunderous expression, sent a new wave of hysteria through the crowd of servants. Colin's patience unraveled as he began to shout his question for a second time, just as Lady Milburg's butler appeared at his side.

"You will find Lady Madeline Sinclair has safely retired to the drawing room, my lord." The butler's cool voice had a calming effect on all those around him. "Doctor Whitman has been brought in to attend to her."

"Was there an injury?" Edward asked, as Colin pushed his way through to the purple-draped drawing room.

He spotted Madeline immediately, standing

defiantly in the middle of a loud, fluttering triangle made up of Lady Milburg, Helena, and an older gentleman in a striped waistcoat, whom Colin could only presume to be Doctor Whitman.

"My lady, please! I must beg you to let me take a look at your delicate wrist."

"No."

"Madeline! Do not be so obstinate! You could have a broken bone, or worse! Influenza!"

"Mother, you cannot get influenza from falling off a horse."

"My lady, please, my examination will take the briefest of moments—"

"I have no wish to be examined, Doctor!"

"How will you be able to wear bracelets?" Lady Milburg inquired, wringing her hands. "Or carry a reticule?"

"Her reticule was stolen, Mother! The pink one! Ripped right off Madeline's arm!"

"You see, Doctor! How could the wrist not be broken?"

The argument raged on, with sharp words and shrieks pinging off the walls. The delicate wrist in question was currently being held over Madeline's head, out of reach of the height-impaired Doctor Whitman, who did not think it beneath him to occasionally jump from the ground in an attempt to catch a glimpse of the injury.

"My lady, please! I must beg you to lower your arm."

Colin strode forward, gingerly stepping into the mayhem until he reached the green-eyed hellcat with her wrist still thrust high in the air.

"Madeline." He held out his hand and waited.

She stared back, deliberating for a long, willful moment between himself, Doctor Whitman, and the door. After a tense moment, in which Lady Milburg had to bite her own fist to keep from speaking,

Madeline made her choice, slowly dropping the wrist into Colin's hand.

"It seems I have come out the victor," he said, unable to keep the arrogance from his voice while carefully turning her palm upward.

"You may call yourself that," Madeline replied, wincing slightly. "I prefer to think of you as the lesser evil."

He gently probed the small wrist. "You fell off your horse?"

"She was pushed!"

Colin looked up to see Madeline's young cousin standing faithfully behind her, hands on her hips in an attempt for authority that was undermined by an expression of guilty fear.

"Helena!" Madeline silenced her cousin with one look. "It was nothing. An accident, no more. I told my cousin not to send for you."

"I am glad she did not heed your advice." He finished his examination, reluctantly releasing her hand. "You can rest easy, Doctor. The wrist is not broken. You won't have to pain yourself with forcing a cast upon your unruly patient. It's only a bruise."

"Excellent!" Doctor Whitman, breathing an obvious sigh of relief, began inching his way toward the door. "Lots of rest, Madeline, and perhaps a bit of goose grease for the swelling."

"Oh, do wait a moment, Doctor Whitman. You must examine Helena, too!" Lady Milburg cried, running after him. "She was attacked by the madman, as well!"

"Don't be absurd, Mother. I was standing on the other side of the rock. He never even touched me."

"I thought you were riding horses?" Edward asked, and Helena stared at the floor, her mouth opening and closing silently.

"Perhaps all the excitement has muddled your memory," he suggested.

"It did, Lord Montgomery! It was quite a terrifying ordeal. I shall take days to recover." Helena flashed him an innocent grin before flouncing into the nearest chair.

"And what about you, Madeline? Will you take days to recover?" Colin's fear and anger seemed to melt away the longer he stood next to her. He would be the first to admit he looked like a besotted fool, but he honestly could not tear his gaze away, struck by the way the dark silky strands had fallen down her back from their usual piled-high mountain. He realized this was the first time he'd seen Madeline without her hair severely pinned and curled. The glints of red were back, pulled out by the morning sun shining through the front windows, and Colin had to resist the urge to wrap his arm around her tiny waist and drag her straight out of Lady Milburg's drawing room to the nearest bed.

"Not at all. Doctor Whitman said it's merely a little swelling." She tucked her wrist back into the sleeve of her dress and out of sight.

"Shall I send someone for garlic and vinegar to add to your grease?" he teased, suddenly wishing to see her blush.

"That's only for infections," she retorted. "And it worked, didn't it? The wound over your eye has completely healed."

"Colin." Edward's voice carried a note of suspicion. "I believe it would be a good idea to find out exactly what happened this morning."

"Yes, Madeline," Helena interjected quickly. "Perhaps *you* should tell them about our terrifying ordeal."

Helena's voice rang out loud and nervous, and Colin found himself intrigued, curious to see if Madeline would turn out a better liar than her cousin. He watched her closely as she gingerly sat next to Helena, adjusted her skirts to hide every inch of splattered mud from her fall, and placed her hands primly in her lap before raising her head to speak.

"Helena and I were riding very near Cumberland Gate," Madeline began. "You know that curvy part where those lovely little rose-colored elderberry bushes sit? Behind the elms?"

Colin didn't have the faintest damn clue what she was talking about, but he nodded to keep her going.

"Well, there we were, just riding along discussing..." Madeline faltered a bit. "This and that..."

"Hats!" Helena said wildly. "And hideous, feather-lined turbans."

"You were discussing hats?" Edward's tone was disbelieving.

"It was a very particular hat, Lord Montgomery." Madeline tossed him a stern look before continuing. "So then, we were riding along, and I just mentioned to Helena that perhaps I had seen a small snake, as I do know how she detests them."

"Snakes are horrid!" Helena agreed.

"And so I told Helena to hide herself behind the bushes while I sought out the vile thing and killed it."

"On or off her horse?" Colin interrupted.

"I beg your pardon?"

He sat on the edge of the sofa, leaning so close he was practically whispering in her ear. "Did Helena get off her horse to hide in the bushes, or did she try to hide herself and the horse behind the bushes?"

Madeline looked like she wanted to hit him. "I hardly think a little detail like that matters. The important thing is Helena went to hide behind the elderberry bushes. They are so lovely and thick, exactly the kind my aunt keeps in her gardens at Norfolk, do you remember, Helena? Perhaps that's why you chose them. They reminded you of home."

"I must disagree, Madeline. I believe it is very important," Edward said. "It can make all the difference in discovering—"

"She was off the horse," Madeline snapped. "Isn't that right, cousin?"

"Yes," Helena whispered.

Madeline shot Edward a glare. "Just then, as I was dismounting to kill the snake, I heard a strange, grunting noise and felt something knock me onto the ground. I quickly got up—I was afraid of falling on the snake, of course—and that's when I saw the man running away and realized my lovely bag was gone."

"Did he touch you?" Colin felt his anger rising at the thought of some bastard putting his filthy hands on her...his Madeline...

"Well, only his arm, when he knocked me down." She thought. "Oh, and I suppose his hand, when we fought over my reticule. Colin, why is your eye twitching like that?"

"Did you recognize this man?" Edward quickly asked.

"No, I was too busy trying to hold onto my—" Madeline stopped herself. "My reticule, of course. I only caught a glimpse of his back. He was slightly taller than normal, with a dark hat."

"It was more a cap, really, but this man had it pushed down over his face, probably to disguise it."

The entire room turned to gape at Helena, struck by her avid description. "Then you were unable to see his face?" Edward asked.

"Oh, I didn't say that! The hat flew off, you see, while he was running away, and I saw him quite clearly as he passed by. He had light-colored hair, but dirtyish—not a lovely wheat color like yours, Edward—and a triangular-shaped face with sunken-in cheeks that certainly needed a good shave. His eyes were quite tiny and round, with a scar over one eyebrow, and he was wearing a dirty shirt and a tattered blue coat—ouch!"

"So sorry, Helena." Madeline's voice interrupted her cousin. "Did I step on your foot?"

Colin stared down at Helena, her pert little face scrunched up as she rubbed her foot. "Which eyebrow?"

"His right."

"It was only a silly bag, nothing to fuss over," Madeline whispered, clenching her fists in her lap.

Colin didn't believe a word. "What was inside?"

She went pale. "A few hairpins, I think."

Another lie. Whatever the cousins had been up to in the park, Madeline was going to great lengths to hide it. "And why were you unchaperoned?" Colin pressed, determined to get some sense from their story.

"An excellent question, Lord Douglas. Oh, heavens, no, you cannot sit in such a way. Think of the servants!"

Lady Milburg had swept back into the room, waving Colin off the edge of her sofa and settling him into one of the yellow chairs.

"There! Isn't that more proper and comfortable? I must say, I'm going to have a firm talk with Filbert and Peter. What were they thinking, dallying so far behind you like that?"

"It was my fault," Helena cried out. "I wished to speak privately with Madeline and insisted the grooms keep their distance."

"Why would you take such a risk?" Lady Milburg was horrified, and Colin was gratified to see both cousins rather shamefaced. Now perhaps he would hear something of the truth.

"The blame is entirely mine, Aunt," Madeline spoke up. "It was I who ordered Filbert and Peter to

177

remain a good distance behind. And even then they were extremely reluctant," she added. "It was a terrible mistake."

"That is for certain," Colin muttered. "I think we can safely conclude Filbert and Peter are no match for the two of you." Madeline and Helena both stared at the floor.

"But what I insist on knowing is why you *deliberately* rode through the park unescorted. And don't tell me it was to discuss hats." He gave them both his firmest glare, his patience at an end.

"We wanted to discuss our suitors!" Helena practically shouted out.

"A most crucial discussion, Aunt, you must agree," Madeline chimed in.

"Well, of course, it is," Lady Milburg said crossly. "But why would you sneak away to do that? How on earth could you talk of such things without my advice?"

Colin's interrogation came to a crashing end as Lady Milburg's loud indignations continued to fill the room. She went on and on, voicing her displeasure over being left out of any discussion of suitors.

Edward made his way across the room, edging around the heated debate Lady Milburg was having with her charges. "I believe Helena is telling the truth." He spoke quietly. "About the man who attacked them, anyway. The rest of it I can't begin to make out."

Colin mulled over the outrageous story, tuning out Lady Milburg's piercing voice. The two cousins might not have been skilled liars, but each had a natural-born gift for tying a conversation into knots. He agreed with Edward. Someone had certainly attacked them, but why the ridiculous lies? Unless...the idea struck him like a blow to the stomach. The thief had been attracted by more than just a pink reticule.

"It's that damned diamond." Colin stood up, blood pounding in his ears. He should have known right away, but their outrageous story and his concern over her injury had distracted him.

"Madeline!" he barked, startling Lady Milburg from her lecture. "I would like a private word with you. Now."

"Lord Douglas, I must protest! I fully understand your irritation at my niece, but it is most improper to shout across one's music room."

"I'm waiting, Madeline."

She turned to glare at the giver of such a rude demand, refusing to budge.

"Lord Douglas is quite upset with us," Helena hissed to her cousin in a failed whisper. "He looks angry enough to toss you out the window!"

Madeline straightened her back to the snapping point. "I would rather toss myself from the roof than endure any more of his boorish questions," she replied loudly. "I beg your pardon, Lord Douglas, but I am presently engaged in a conversation with my aunt."

"I don't give a damn."

"Shall I assist in the conversation, Lady Milburg?" Edward swiftly interjected. "It might help to have a gentleman's perspective."

"Oh, yes, Lord Montgomery, how kind!" Aunt Cecilia tittered. "Do speak to my daughter. Perhaps she will listen to you." Lady Milburg beamed and fluttered her eyelashes.

Madeline, for her part, wished to give Edward a good kick right in his amiable smile. She was in a most terrible mood, her wrist ached, her head felt full of sand, and now she had no choice but to face the wrath of Colin. She did so as slowly as possible, dragging herself toward where he stood with arms crossed, ready to do battle. Well, she was having none of his brutish intimidations.

"Where is the diamond?" he demanded, cutting her off before she could even reply. "And I vow to God, Madeline, I will not tolerate any more of your confounded misleading answers."

"You have a horrible temper, Colin. Has anyone ever told you that?"

"No one."

Then, in the most outrageously rude action she had ever endured, Colin leaned over her, peering straight down the front of her dress.

"What are you doing!" she hissed, clutching her chest.

"If you refuse to answer me, I have no choice but to search for myself." He started toward her again, and she quickly slapped at his arm.

"The diamond isn't in *there*, you horrible man." She kept her hands fastened to the front of her dress, biting her lip nervously as he leaned toward her, his lips almost brushing against her forehead.

"Then where is it?"

She hesitated while several plausible lies flittered through her head, but the murderous look on his face changed her mind. "With my pink reticule."

Colin tilted his head as though he hadn't heard her correctly. "The stolen one?"

"Yes!" she snapped, remembering a pair of greedy hands knocking her to the ground. "And do spare me the lecture. I am well aware of my failure."

It had all happened so quickly. One moment she had held the rock in her hand, moments away from fulfilling her promise to her father, and the next she had been thrown to the ground, fighting for her life. She had barely gotten a glimpse of the thief; her attacker seemed to have emerged from the bark of the trees.

"Failure?" Colin's voice rose again. "What the

hell does that mean? What the devil were you doing, taking something like that into the woods?"

"Such blasphemes!" Aunt Cecilia cried, before Edward turned her attention with compliments on Helena's pink ribbons.

"I thought it would be safer with me." Madeline spoke quietly, hoping to avoid her aunt's attention. The excuse sounded pathetic, even to her, but how could she tell him the truth? She expected another outburst, but he said nothing, instead stepping back from her, as though seeking distance.

"Colin?" His eyes had turned cloudy again, foretelling the storm. "Why are you looking at me like that?"

A bitter gaze swept over her. "You promised me honesty last night," he said, no longer meeting her gaze. "Does your word mean so little to you?"

She drew back as though he had struck her. "You dare to question my word," she hissed, dangerously close to tears. "I have done nothing but try to keep my word since I arrived in London! Can I help it if I swore to my father first? How do you expect me to choose, Colin?"

"Lord Douglas, if I may intrude." Jarvis had suddenly appeared, dragging a terrified Filbert in his wake. "Lady Milburg's footman has returned with most pressing news of the attacker."

"It's true, sir," Filbert managed to squeak out, looking almost faint beneath Colin's deep frown. "I took it upon myself to run in the direction the ladies said the man had gone, and I believe I may have caught up with him. Though he escaped me again." Filbert looked deeply embarrassed at this admission. "He was short, with a tattered blue coat."

"That's him!" Madeline said, ignoring Colin's sharp gaze. "Where did he go, Filbert?"

"He took off, my lady, running something mad into the streets, and that's what gave me my first suspicion. Only a guilty man would run away like that."

"Very astute," Colin said. "Then what happened?"

Filbert answered quickly. "I followed him to a nearby apothecary shop, where he vanished inside. I waited, but he must have gone out the back way, for he never did come out again. I went inside and spoke to the owner. He told me the man's name was Moore."

"Moore," Colin repeated.

"Yes, your Grace, and he patrons a seedy little place called King's Crown Tavern, near the docks. That's all the owner would say, and I ran back here to tell you."

"Excellent work, Filbert." The footman beamed.

"Lady Milburg." Colin's voice did not rise, but the force behind it quelled the patter of voices instantly. "Edward will stay with you until I return. You are all to stay inside until I know it's safe."

Her aunt staggered and nearly fell down. "Why, that's all a bit highhanded, Lord Douglas! Could we not keep a few appointments?"

"No."

"Lord Douglas!" Aunt Cecilia looked at her companions for help. "I do not begin to understand."

But the rest of her complaint fell flat, as Colin had already left the drawing room.

"Colin!" Madeline ran after him into the hallway, barring his path. "Where are you going?"

He took a small step forward, matching her insolence with his own. They stood toe to toe with identical stares, and Madeline put her hands on her shapely hips before drawing herself up to her full height. Tall as she was, compared to most of the dainty women of the *ton*, Madeline still had to perch on the tips of her satin shoes to meet his eye. She did so now in hopes of forcing an answer.

"It doesn't concern you, Madeline."

She pushed herself even taller. "It does. Answer me."

"I'm going to find the man who attacked you."

"And get my diamond back?" Relief washed over her. Perhaps she hadn't failed her father, perhaps there was still a chance...

His face turned dark. "Among other things."

"What kind of answer is that?"

"The very kind you have been giving me since we met," he snapped. "If you would like to hear the truth, you might try offering it up sometimes."

Her eyes flashed. "And what is that supposed to mean? Haven't I explained why I couldn't keep my promise to you?"

"You call that an explanation?" He looked incredulous. "I must go." With a sharp turn on his heel, Colin stalked toward the front door.

"Wait!" Madeline's hand clamped down on his arm like a vise. "What are you going to do to this man?" He kept walking, dragging her behind him down the hallway, but she refused to loosen her grip.

"What I have to do to keep you safe."

"Colin!" She yanked hard on his arm, finally stopping him. "What are you saying?"

"He hurt you, Madeline." He turned to look down at her, sliding a hand across her cheek.

"He pushed me to the ground! It was nothing!"

"Not to me." His hand rested above her chin, a single finger brushing featherlight across her lower lip. "I cannot allow anyone to touch you, Madeline."

"But..." She trailed off, confused at this sudden show of tenderness. "You're so angry with me. You called me a liar. I don't understand."

Colin leaned down and kissed her, hard and fast, and then he was gone.

****

Lady Waverly and her mother, the Baroness of

Amber, happened to be passing by Lady Milburg's residence on their way to Pall Mall for a visit to the linen drapers.

"And that is Lady Milburg's house, Mother. You remember dear Cecilia? We had tea with her a week ago Tuesday." Lady Waverly shouted this information, sure that her ailing mother would recall the event if only the words were a bit louder.

"Tuesday?" the Baroness gasped. "Is it here already? We must hurry home then, before Charlie arrives from school! I shall have an apple tart made up for him, I will indeed. He always loved apple tart, since he was a boy."

Lady Waverly rolled her eyes. Ignoring the fact that her brother Charles had not seen the inside of Oxford for over twenty years, she flapped her hand for the coachman to stop. "No, Mother. This is LADY MILBURG'S house. You had tea with her on TUESDAY. Remember the house, Mother? You commented on the lovely tulips. Remember the TULIPS, MOTHER?"

The Baroness shook her delicate grey curls, frowning at her daughter. "Why on earth would Charlie want tulips in his apple tart? What a ridiculous notion! Honestly, I have never heard such a thing. Is that one of Bitsy's strange French recipes?"

"No, Mother." Lady Waverly had just taken a deep breath, determined to try again, when she heard a loud crack. She quickly turned toward Lady Milburg's house in time to see the bright red door flung open and a tall man emerge to stalk fiercely across the lawn.

"Good Lord, Mother, it's the Duke of Douglas," Lady Waverly gasped. "He's coming from Lady Milburg's house, and it's barely noon!" She leaned out of the carriage, peering at the scene. "How very cross he looks! His scowl could knock me straight from my seat. Don't you think so, Mother?"

"Who is cross with my Charlie?" the Baroness demanded in a loud shout that sent her daughter frantically signaling to the coachman to drive on. "I will not have that, at all! He is a darling boy and so loves his apple tart."

****

"Well!" Aunt Cecilia huffed when Madeline reentered the music room. "I must say I do not know what to say! I have always been very fond of Lord Douglas, but such conduct today! I do not know!"

"He was very angry, Mother. Surely he didn't mean it." Helena spoke from the window, where she stood peeping out to see what Colin was doing. "He's leaving!" she said, pressing her face against the glass. "Sam just brought Colin his horse. Poor Sam, he does look terribly afraid, and...gracious! Is that Lady Waverly's carriage?"

Madeline made no reply, barely lifting her head at the news. She stood alone by the door, carefully winding and rewinding the torn silk handle of her pink reticule around her finger, all she had left of it from the morning's adventure.

"Yes, I do agree Lord Douglas had good reason to be angry," Aunt Cecilia continued. "How shocking to hear of you girls going off alone in the woods. One can hardly blame him for yelling at you, Madeline, but his treatment of me, well!"

"He's leaving, Madeline!" Helena shouted. "Colin's riding off toward the north, or is it east? Anyway, he's heading in the direction of the church!"

"Best place for him, I'd say." Edward spoke as he turned to Aunt Cecilia. "Allow me to make my brother's apologies for him, Lady Milburg. I'm sure he would never forgive himself for any rudeness against you."

"Well." Aunt Cecilia faltered under the smile. "Then of course I shall forget all about it. We are a

185

forgiving family, Edward dear. May I call you Edward?" She laughed girlishly before turning to her daughter. "Helena! Stop gawking out the window and come play the piano for Edward."

****

The door to King's Tavern slammed open like a crack of thunder, startling the half dozen patrons inside, who'd been drinking since breakfast. Colin strode up to the bar, shoved past the rather disreputable man with one eye, and demanded the bartender's attention.

"I'm looking for a man called Moore," Colin called loudly, making damn sure every drunk in the tavern heard him. He'd already scoured the room for light-colored hair and a tattered blue coat, but no one matched Helena's description. "I was told he frequents your establishment. Have you seen him?"

The bartender merely shrugged, casually pulling out a smudged glass. "I don't remember much past a man's height, sir. It's what's kept me alive all these years."

Colin slammed one fist on the scarred wood in front of him. "Then tell me his height, damn you! Was Moore here today? Did you serve him?"

The one-eyed man next to him grunted, holding his glass up to keep the liquid from spilling out as Colin leaned menacingly across the bar. The bartender's face had gone sour, and he took a step back. "Moore was here about an hour ago, but he didn't stay for more than one drink. Said he had important business to attend to and ran off."

"Did he say who this business was with?" But the bartender had finished handing out information. He turned his back, quietly refilling a glass while the man next to Colin stared hard at the newcomer with a cold, empty socket.

Frustrated, Colin briefly toyed with the idea of jumping over the bar and beating the information

186

out of the man and everyone else in this filthy bar. It would likely prove effective, and certainly make him feel better, but it would be a real irritation to clean up. With a sigh, he reluctantly changed tactics. "Any idea when Moore will be back for another drink?" He dropped a gold sovereign on the bar. "It's a matter of utmost importance to me."

The new strategy worked, and the bartender's eyes lit up with greed.

"I'll tell you..." He leaned forward, his fingers inching closer to the coin. "I don't much like to talk about my patrons, it's bad for business. But I can say that Moore is the type to enjoy a drink or two in the evening, and he never leaves until I kick him out at dawn."

Dropping another coin on the table, Colin nodded his thanks. So Moore was a drinker. It was almost too easy. After a long night at his favorite tavern, he would be obliviously drunk, and what better time to force the truth out of him? Colin knew damn well Moore didn't work alone. Someone had hired him to rob Madeline, undoubtedly whoever he had "business" with today.

He wanted that name.

Upon leaving King's Tavern, Colin headed his steed for the location in the park where Madeline and Helena claimed to have been attacked. He had little hope of finding anything but welcomed a hard ride to clear his head.

Had Madeline simply used him to gain access to her diamond? It wouldn't be the first time. All his life women had sought him out for their own interests. They threw themselves at him. And now Edward, too, he realized. All of them eager to get their hands on a title, money, or both.

"But Madeline doesn't want your money," he muttered with a sharp jerk of the reins. "She doesn't even want you." Beneath him, Phinneus gave a harsh snort, voicing his disapproval of the rough treatment. Slowing to a stop, Colin eased up on the reins, gently patting behind Phinneus's ears to soothe the animal.

He was wasting his time wandering out here in the woods. What he wanted to know only Madeline could tell him, and she had made it perfectly clear she wasn't talking. He'd been so sure she was different from other women! Frustrated, he turned the horse toward home, chastising himself for being so gullible. When she looked at him last night, her eyes full of unshed tears, he had felt a bond form between them. It was more than simply wanting her. For the briefest of moments Colin had allowed himself to envision the rest of his life with her.

****

Daniel Moore stood silently across the street as Lady Farris and her damp-looking daughter quickly exited Lord Rockford's home. He remembered the family well. Rockford had paid him a tidy little sum to dig into old Farris's finances before bothering to court the homely girl. Moore watched nervously as Lady Farris grappled her way into the large open barouche, speaking sharply to the footman when her pink parasol shifted away for the briefest of moments, exposing her pale face to the weak spring sun. After several minutes of shuffling, the woman managed to right herself into a haughty pose intended to catch the eye of the many other ladies and gentlemen beginning their rides through the city to mark the start of the season. Moore permitted himself a small laugh as the coachman rode off wincing under the shrill orders of his mistress. It didn't look like Rockford was planning to propose anytime soon.

Moore approached the entrance to the Marquis of Rockford's stylish townhouse, stiff and uncomfortable in his borrowed coat and gloves, taking care that the high dark collar covered his face from view. He was greeted at the door by Davis, whose round features were blank today except for a menacing twitch of the right cheek as he silently led Moore down the elegant hall. They stopped in front of the library, the door already open in invitation, a large fire blazing in the hearth. Moore pushed his way forward, only to be stopped by Davis's hand on his shoulder.

"Open your coat."

Moore hesitated, staring at the thick, heavy hand now gripping him. For all its brutishness, the hand was not an unsightly one. It had a rather surprisingly graceful shape to it, smooth and cool, a hand that could be counted upon to serve Lord Rockford's guests their teacakes just as easily as it could choke the very life out of a man.

Moore opened his coat.

Seeing no weapon, the servant nodded, motioning him into the library, where Lord Rockford waited alone. No servants, save Davis, were anywhere in sight, leaving no chance for any gossip being retold over those piping hot teacakes. Rockford was too cautious for that. He'd always been a very careful man.

Davis closed the door as Moore stepped cautiously inside, his gaze moving swiftly over the dark wood bookcases filled with rich volumes, the leather seats positioned carefully in front of the fireplace. The setting was cozy, warm and inviting, a place where a man could feel comfortable enough to let down his guard. Moore spotted the great Lord Rockford himself affecting a relaxed, non-threatening stance near the window.

"I assume this is a matter of extreme importance," Rockford's voice held a note of amused arrogance, "since you dare to show yourself at my residence."

Moore kept one eye on Davis, wrapping his coat tighter around him. "I've found something I think you'll be interested in, sir."

"Found?" Rockford's expression didn't change, though the amused tone had vanished.

"Well, I've stolen something, that is." Moore dug in the back pocket of his trousers, where he'd hidden his prize. "I snatched it from the Sinclair chit just this morning. Who knew she had such riches on her? Besides the obvious." He snorted at his own jest, triumphantly producing a small pink reticule.

"A lady's handbag?" Rockford said. "I hadn't realized I hired you for petty thievery."

"It's what's in the handbag." Moore stressed, tossing it across the table with a loud thud. "Look for yourself."

Davis took a step forward, but Rockford raised a hand to stop him. Obviously intrigued about what his lovely was carrying around with her, Rockford peered inside the small bag—and nearly choked.

"Madeline had this?" Rockford sputtered, ripping the pink fabric away to get a closer look at the enormous rock. "You actually saw her with it?"

"Snatched it right out of her little hands," Moore replied, leaning back in the chair like a proud rooster. "It's a real diamond, ain't it? Must be worth a bloody fortune." The stunned look on Rockford's face could only mean one thing. He would pay big for Moore's little gift. Very big.

"Sarah's diamond," Rockford whispered, gently caressing the deep blue jewel. "I haven't seen this since that day..."

He abruptly stopped speaking, jerking up to meet Moore's curious gaze, as though remembering he was still in the room. "Well done, Moore," he said, wrapping the blue diamond in a snow-white handkerchief.

Moore's hand shook with anticipation of his

money. He greedily licked his lips.

"Davis will see you out."

Moore jumped to his feet. "You're not paying me?" Too late he realized his mistake, as the giant stepped forward and, with one menacing look, put Moore back in his chair.

"The job isn't finished yet. Though I do appreciate this little treasure you've brought me, the Duke of Douglas is still in my way."

"You want me to go back there?" Moore gulped with fear at the thought. "Your lady Madeline, she saw my face! She'll scream for help the moment she sees me."

"I imagine Douglas is already looking for you. I don't imagine it will take him long to track you down, do you?"

Moore's stomach twisted at the words. "He's going to kill me."

"Not right away," Rockford said, shaking his head sadly. "Lord Douglas is much too wise to kill you before you tell him the information he wants, and you aren't going to tell him anything, are you?"

"No!" Moore gulped, squeezing his hands together and watching Davis out of the corner of his eye. "I haven't told a single soul about this diamond! Not a soul!"

"Yes, yes," Lord Rockford cut him off. "The diamond you found is an added bonus. It may prove very useful in the future." He smiled. "But what's important now is that we get to Douglas before he finds us. I imagine he's quite enraged."

Moore tried to calm his shaking hands. He'd run low on his dose of laudanum, been dry for two days now, and the shakes were getting worse. His head was filled with cotton and his body with a gnawing, craving hunger for the sickly sweet medicine, the welcome oblivion, the intoxicating numbness. He grabbed the glass of ale Davis handed him and drained it in one gulp, the liquid sloshing down his chin. "I'll take care of it, the first opportunity. I just need a little something to tide me over."

"Stop blubbering, Moore," Rockford said, his expression lined with disgust as he reached for a gold sovereign. "You'll get your precious laudanum. Now pay attention, I have a plan."

Chapter Eleven

Colin returned to his townhouse in a foul mood.

If possible, his afternoon ride had only increased his temper to the point where nothing but a good stiff drink would help. Calling for Halbert, he threw his jacket and riding gloves onto the nearest table before striding into the drawing room to find the surprise of his life.

"Colin! How wonderful to see you again. Halbert feared you wouldn't be back until tonight, but I insisted on waiting. Did you miss me, darling?"

There, draped comfortably across his imperial burgundy-and-gold chair like a spoiled cat, was none other than his former fiancée.

Juliana had returned.

Graceful and haughty, all too aware of her own beauty, she offered him her tiny hand to kiss. And Juliana *was* beautiful in her white gown, Colin admitted, perfectly made up, hair artfully curled to highlight her soft pink cheeks. She looked happy and well rested from her trip abroad, the exact opposite of himself.

"Well? Aren't you going to give me a proper greeting? It's very bad manners to simply stare, you know." She smiled, waving to Halbert to place the tray of tea and cakes on the table as though she were mistress of the house.

"I didn't realize you had returned so soon." Colin approached her slowly, ignoring the outstretched hand. "Did you enjoy your trip?" Halbert shot him a look of pure distress, as though wondering if he'd be forced to toss Juliana out on her ear.

Her dainty shoulders rose ever so slightly. "A bit boring, to be honest. Mother was simply hideous to travel with and would barely let me out of her sight. I can't imagine why." She sent him a wicked look. "But I am finally free. Mother is off visiting her sister and won't be back until nightfall."

"Tea, my lady?" Halbert offered.

"No, thank you," Juliana replied, her gaze never leaving Colin's face. "I'm not here for tea."

"I didn't think you were," Colin remarked.

She laughed. "We are of the same mind, Colin. It's why we get along so splendidly well."

Reluctantly, he let himself relax, deciding to welcome the sudden distraction from his dark mood. He sat down, stretching himself out on the sofa while indulging in another look at the woman he'd almost married. Juliana was precisely the same, bright and fearless, with a smile that made every man feel alone in the room with her.

"May I get you anything else, milord?"

Colin suddenly realized Halbert stood over him, the wrinkled face carrying an unmistakable expression of warning.

"No, thank you, Halbert. You may go. I'll be fine." He stressed the last part, slightly amused at his butler's concerns. Why shouldn't he have a chat with Juliana? They had been engaged, after all, and Madeline had made it very clear he had no claims on her. She wished to be wholly independent, to remain alone and bound up in her secrets. Well, he would let her.

"One last thing, milord." Halbert, obviously reluctant to leave his employer alone, scrambled in his pocket to produce a familiar ring of keys. "I have discovered your misplaced keys. Shall I place them back inside your study?"

The keys to his cellar. Misplaced was a rather kind description of Madeline's thievery, and Colin scowled at the sight and the memory they produced. "Leave the keys. I'll take care of them later."

"Of course." With a low bow, Halbert dropped the keys on the table next to him with a loud clatter and left the room.

"You have all new furniture in here, Colin. It's beautiful," Juliana recaptured his attention. "I do so love red and gold." She ran a smooth, white hand along the arm of her chair.

"I know," he replied. "I purchased it as a wedding present for you."

His comment was met with a soft look of surprise. "I never thanked you for your gallantry in regard to the end of our relationship. All of London believes you simply left me brokenhearted. You could have told a much different story."

"I could have," he replied, keeping his voice light. "But you needn't owe me any gratitude. I didn't do it for you."

"Oh?"

"I have no desire to be known as a man who cannot keep a woman faithful."

She rolled her eyes. "Honestly, Colin, you take things too seriously. You always did." Gliding to her feet, Juliana joined him on the sofa, sitting precariously close. "I enjoyed every moment of our nights together."

Colin drew back. Juliana was more than just a beautiful woman. She knew how to please a man, and the power of that knowledge oozed from her, filling the air like a heady perfume.

"William and I are finished now," she continued softly. "It was a childish mistake."

Colin's anger returned with the mention of Rockford, shattering her spell like glass. "So that's it? And now you expect me to welcome you back?" He stood up, pulling her hand from his arm. "The *ton* may not know that truth, but I will never forget it. I could never marry you now."

To his surprise, the words affected her, and Juliana sat back against the cushions, her skin burning with shame. "I suppose I deserve that," she admitted. "But let's not fool ourselves. Every married couple we know is unfaithful. Our marriage plans were not about love. It was an arrangement that suited us both and had the added benefit that we were very attracted to one another. Is that so terrible?"

Once their relationship had been enough for him, but now? He had not thought past his lust for Juliana, mistaking it for something more, something he had never really felt before, until a stubborn green-eyed hellcat bit him on the lip.

"I understand where I failed," she continued. "I was spoiled and impetuous." She took his hand, pulling him back down to her on the sofa. "Discretion was not a word I yet understood."

"And you do now?" he asked, his voice laced with doubt.

"I've grown up quickly since our last encounter. I was a vain, spoiled child, but I've learned my lesson. There will be nothing but the truth between us now, Colin." She leaned in closer, and he could smell the light scent of lilacs on her neck.

"And the truth is, I still want you," she said, with a dark seductive smile. "Very much."

Though well versed in her games, it took all of Colin's force of will to quell his body's natural response. He kept still as a statue as she brushed her lips briefly against his, and her mouth opened, drawing him expertly toward her.

"No, Juliana," he said, holding up a hand to push her away. But she refused to let go. Plunging her nails into his palm, she yanked him back.

"Kiss me again."

And he did. He let his body take over. Blocking

his mind, he curved one hand around her neck to roughly return the kiss. All the anger and frustration he'd felt since finding her with Rockford burst forth, and the kiss was much harsher than he intended.

She didn't seem to mind.

"You've grown bolder since our last encounter," she said, turning to give him better access to her neck. "I knew you would return to me." She let her hand slide down his cheek, to his chest, and farther down.

Colin pushed Juliana onto her back, following her with another torturous kiss. She fought with the buttons of his shirt, tearing at them while he yanked the pins loose from her blonde ringlets.

The passion quickly turned punishing as Colin struggled to keep his thoughts from intruding. Juliana's constant chatter certainly wasn't helping the situation.

"We are one and the same, my darling," she moaned. "I knew you couldn't stay angry for long, not when there is such fire between us." Colin suddenly froze as Juliana continued her journey downward, kneeling on the floor between his legs. Was this how she truly saw him? As a man who cared only for his own lusts? If so, then he was no better than the woman he presently held in his arms.

"We cannot do this," he said aloud, pulling Juliana's hands off him and gently taking her hands in his own. She laughed, misunderstanding.

"You're right, darling. We wouldn't want the servants to walk in, would we? Let me just lock the door."

The moment she left him his senses returned like a brutal slap. What the hell was he doing? This was the very same woman who had betrayed him with another man, a woman he'd sworn never to see again. Colin sat up on the sofa, suddenly angry with himself. Was he willing to throw away everything with Madeline? His gaze settled on the ring of keys with a sharp memory. The diamond. When she held the French Blue in her hands there was no mistaking the terror in her face. She didn't want the diamond to satisfy her own greed—she didn't want it anywhere near her! *So what was she doing with it in the middle of the woods? What in God's name did her father ask her to do?*

Madeline's mysterious vow. What would he do in such a situation? Honor his word, of course, and Madeline was doing no less. And yet he condemned her for it, even after she had warned him she must fulfill her promise.

"Damn," he muttered, reaching for the buttons on his shirt. He was instantly filled with self loathing for his actions this afternoon. He had allowed himself to become so jaded, so angry, that he dared to compare Madeline's deeds with Juliana's betrayal.

"Darling, what are you doing?" Juliana's hand reached out, running her fingers over his chest. "Colin, love, did you wish for me to take it off again?"

"I have to go," he replied. Redressing as quickly as possible, he turned from her, not missing the shocked look on her face.

"Have you forgotten something? An important appointment? Surely it can wait." She sauntered over to him, slipping one expert hand downward.

"I can't, Juliana." He pulled back with a jerk. "You shouldn't have come here."

"I don't understand." She dropped the seductions and stood glaring at him, arms crossed. "Are you still angry over William?"

"There's someone else." Once he said the words aloud, he knew them to be true. Madeline. He wanted her, more than any woman, any thing, he'd ever wanted before. And he would do whatever was necessary to beg her forgiveness.

"It's that Sinclair woman, isn't it?"

He started in surprise.

"Don't think I haven't heard her name," Juliana hissed, a look of pure jealousy marring the features he'd once admired. "She's really dangling after you, isn't she? Pathetic."

"Good bye, Juliana." And with that he turned and walked out, leaving the infuriated woman behind him.

Chapter Twelve

Madeline stood impatiently in her aunt's too cheerful music room, twisting her hands together while she watched the sunlight fade into darkness outside. Colin had been gone for hours, each passing moment drenching her more in fear that his revenge would consume him and she would lose him forever. A lengthy absence could mean many things: perhaps Colin was unable to find the thief Moore; perhaps he was lying in a pool of blood; or perhaps he never wanted to see her again...

Madeline shoved away from the front window. She could not think of it, could not bear to torture herself with images of Colin hurt, or worse, and instead resumed her pacing through the room, wishing it contained a dark corner or two. Aunt Cecilia's front music room was a lively one, normally used for greeting guests or entertaining after a long dinner. It was the brightest room in the house, decorated to give the guests a relaxed, jovial feel, but this evening it made Madeline's skin prickle with anxiety. The very walls seemed at war with her emotions, the light yellow wallpaper mocking her with its forced joy, a bowl full of roses on the table failing to entice her with its soft beauty. Madeline kept moving, hoping the lively contents would fade into the background, but Helena's peal of laughter caught her attention.

Edward had been left with the task of distracting the women until Colin's return and was certainly giving it his best. He tried to engage them all in a proper game of whist, fanning the cards out enticingly on the table, but when Cecilia excused herself and Madeline refused, he was left with only Helena for a partner.

Enthusiasm not dampened in the slightest, he immediately set out to teach his eager student faro, the rather scandalous French game that had been making its way around London. Madeline recalled her aunt referring to the game as "vulgar amusement" and did not doubt Cecilia would be less than amused to hear the indecent giggles in the music room, but it was too late.

Helena took to faro instantly, reveling in the forbidden game along with Edward's attentions. Her small whispers penetrated the room, hovering below her teacher's teasing voice, leaving Madeline with the distinct feeling that the charming Edward was instructing her cousin on how to gamble. *She's falling for him.* Madeline watched Helena's ivy-colored eyes crinkle in mischief as she tried to slip an ace into the sleeve of her walking gown. Edward caught on to her before Helena could successfully hide her prize and, calling out, "Foul! Villainous cheat!" before charging after the card, slid his hand up into the thin muslin.

Madeline turned away from the playful scene, suddenly fearful for her cousin. She knew Edward's heart was as unavailable as Colin's, making Helena's flirtation a dangerous one. It was all too much. She gave up any pretense at diverting herself and settled on pacing the carpets—wearing them thin, as her father used to say when she worked her way back and forth through his study. It was an old habit from girlhood that Madeline indulged now, as she relived Colin's angry words in her mind. "Stubborn, insolent man," she muttered, stamping her feet.

Edward abruptly looked up from his cards. "Did you say something, Madeline?" While his gaze was

201

turned toward her, Helena reached out and stole a card from the pile.

"Just voicing my opinions on your infuriating brother," Madeline replied, her pace quickening around the bright yellow chair, "and his insistence on risking his life to vex me. I do hope I'm not interrupting your game."

"Not at all." Edward threw down a second ace, winning the game and drawing a shriek of protest from Helena, who still held her stolen card. "While Colin is exceptionally skilled at causing irritation, he also has a knack for taking care of himself. He'll return soon enough."

Madeline stopped, whirling around to face him. "How can you be so glib about this? Colin has been gone for hours. It's almost nightfall!" She angrily searched Edward's face for a speck of concern. "Your brother could be wandering about out there, lost and cold. My God, what if he was hurt? His eye has only just healed, you know."

Edward's face turned red, and he began rather aggressively clearing his throat.

"Are you daring to laugh at this, sir?" Madeline demanded.

"Not at all!" He coughed. "I too am...deeply concerned that Colin may have become lost, and he was only wearing his light riding jacket." Edward choked on his suppressed laughter, quickly turning his head away from Madeline's glower.

"Edward! This is not at all the time for such mirth!" Helena whispered, pointing out her cousin's darkening frown. "Madeline is very upset, you know, and Lord Douglas has been gone a rather long time."

"Indeed he has," Edward said, making a massive attempt to control himself. "Though if he heard your opinions on him, Colin might never return. You must take care not to insult a gentleman's ego, my dear ladies!"

Madeline couldn't believe what she was hearing. "What does that have to do with the subject? We are discussing Colin's life, not his ego. Something terrible must have happened to him or he would have returned by now."

"Not necessarily," Edward insisted. "There are several other tasks that could delay him."

"Such as?"

"Perhaps he is disposing of a body."

"Edward!" Helena shrieked, jumping to her feet. "Honestly! What a thing to say. He's only jesting, Madeline. Pay him no heed."

But she stared hard at Edward and wondered if he did indeed speak something of the truth. Colin had been terribly angry when he left. Maybe his vengeance reached deeper than she had imagined. "Perhaps he isn't coming back at all," she said quietly, staring at the door.

Edward looked up, surprise creasing his eyes. "Now that I can positively refute. Colin could no more stay away from you than he could cease breathing. The man is obviously in love."

A stillness drifted through the bright yellow music room, absorbing any response Madeline might have had to Edward's words. She could do nothing but stare at him, watching as he urgently sought another topic.

"Is Lady Milburg well, do you think?" Edward asked loudly. "She's been gone quite awhile."

"Mother?" Helena rushed to help him. "She is likely off bothering poor Brigette somewhere. Shall we send for her?"

Even more likely, Aunt Cecilia was making herself scarce in the hopes of kindling the tiny flame that had sprouted up between Edward and Helena, Madeline thought, breathing deeply. She suddenly felt as though the walls were closing in.

"I'm going outside," Madeline announced, to the

203

surprise of Edward and her cousin. "Alone."

Outside, in her aunt's tiny forgotten garden, Madeline felt she could catch her breath again. She settled herself onto the hard stone bench, trying to diffuse the cloud of dread that had settled in her mind. What could be keeping Colin? And why would Edward say his brother was in love with her?

"Surely he's dead by now," she whispered aloud, letting the words pierce the evening air. "Left alone to bleed in the street. That horrible cursed diamond has either turned him into a murderer or killed him!"

"I did not murder anyone," a voice said from behind a nearby bush, plunging her heart to her toes. Colin appeared out of the darkness, as though formed from the shadows, and stared at her a long moment before skirting around the giant topiary to face her. "For God's sake, Madeline, do you not have the smallest amount of faith in me?"

She stared up at him. He stood tall and dangerous in his well fitted breeches, the top button undone from his shirt, giving her the barest hint of the beautiful chest she remembered from their first meeting, and her pulse quickened. He was still wearing his light brown riding jacket, a little dirtier now and with a rip in one sleeve, but he was alive. Before she even knew what she was doing, Madeline flung herself into his arms. "You're back," she whispered, burying her face in his chest.

All the tension in Colin's body melted away with her embrace. He had been unsure of Madeline's reaction when he returned, and inhaled her sweet, light scent in relief. He knew he had spoken out of anger and frustration. His fear that something could have happened to her, alone and defenseless in the woods, had made him lose his senses. But all that was forgotten now. He lifted Madeline's chin with both hands and kissed her, long and sweet, seeking forgiveness with his mouth.

The moon was bright in the sky when he finally broke away, regretfully brushing one hand across her cheek, smiling over the glazed look in her eyes.

He peeled off his jacket, tossing it aside on the bench, and sat down, his guilt over what had almost happened with Juliana like a pain in his chest. His hands encircled Madeline's waist, pulling her onto his lap.

"Colin!" she protested with a small squeal. "This is a most undignified way to sit."

"Is that so?" he teased. "I find most young ladies think perching on a man's lap to be all the rage."

He felt the firm thud of her elbow directly below his ribs. "I am not amused, Colin. Now tell me, did you find this Moore thief or not?"

"I did not."

"What!" She would have fallen to the ground if he hadn't been holding onto her. "What happened? Where is my diamond?" Madeline squirmed on his lap to face him.

"I'm getting to that part. Stop fidgeting, Madeline, or I'm going to ravish you right here on this bench, and you'll never hear the end of the story."

She went absolutely still.

"Moore had already left the tavern when I got there," he began, wondering if she was still breathing. "But I think I've got a good idea when he'll be back. I'll find him, but finding the French Blue might prove more difficult."

"I don't understand," she answered, holding herself still as a pine. "Why wouldn't this Moore have the diamond with him?"

"Because I believe there's a good chance he's already given it away."

"Gave it away!" She jerked around in his lap. "To whom? Where is it?"

"Someone hired Moore to follow you." His jaw tightened as she stared at him, confusion and fear mixing with her lovely features. "I'm sure of it. Do you remember ever seeing him before?"

She shook her head, still stunned at his news. "The only man I've noticed following me is you. And Vickem, of course, when I'm with Helena. My God, he was following me all this time?" She anxiously peered into the dark.

"Someone must have known you would have possession of the diamond," he continued. "Moore is our only link to this person." She shivered in Colin's arms, and he tightened his hold on her. "He won't bother you again. I promise you that."

She whipped her head around. "You won't..." She let the words fade, as though afraid to continue.

Colin sighed in irritation. Where did she get these ideas of him? One moment he couldn't defend himself against a drunken thief, the next he was a murderer. "If I do ever kill for you, Madeline, I promise to keep you informed."

"I would never ask you to do such a thing." Her words disappeared in the cooling night air, making Colin very aware of how alone they were. "Then you've never killed anyone?" she inquired hopefully.

Colin shifted on the cold bench, reluctant to talk about such things. "I was in a war, Madeline. I cannot tell you I've never had to defend myself, but..." He trailed off, staring up at the dark sky. "I am no murderer, not for revenge, not for my country, not for anyone."

Her shoulders fell in relief at his words, but before she could speak further Colin pressed on. "My hands are not clean, Madeline," he warned. "For five long years I blindly followed the orders of other men, convincing myself those actions were justified, and I must learn to live with that." He looked over her shoulder, his voice strangely distant. He was surprised to be talking about his past; he rarely did, and never before to a woman.

"How did you become involved in the War Department?" she asked quietly, and he found himself wanting to answer.

"My inheritance, you could call it," he said. "My father served under Sir Bradley when I was a boy, though he kept this part of his life a secret from us. After graduating Oxford, I was restless and eager, so I joined, hoping to mold myself into a legend." He laughed bitterly. "Though my father was vehemently against my decision. Our last words to one another were in heated exchange over my choice. It was a mistake to go to France, I realize that now, but there was no convincing me. I was just as mule-headed as my brother is and our father before us."

"Edward? He cannot go to France, too. He will be in terrible danger!"

Colin shook his head at her outraged expression. "Edward has decided he will be a hero, and I cannot persuade him otherwise. To be honest, I believe it's the adventure he really wants. It's made him reckless. He leaves for his first assignment at the end of the month."

"Then we must stop him!" Madeline insisted. "Helena will be devastated by the news. Why, she's become quite attached to your brother."

"Edward is a grown man. His decisions are his own." Madeline opened her mouth to argue, but Colin stopped her with a squeeze of his hand. "I doubt he would take kindly to our interference in his life. *You* certainly don't appreciate taking anyone's advice."

"I never meant to step on your gentleman's ego," she apologized, crossly. "It's only that I was worried Moore wouldn't fight fairly."

"I see." He cocked an eyebrow at her. "And it's your belief that I always fight fairly?"

"Well, you are a gentleman," she replied. "But now that you mention it, probably not. Then you do plan to kill him?"

"No," he nearly shouted. "Didn't I just say as much?" The woman could make him insane. There she was, wriggling around on his lap like he was made of stone and trampling all over his—what did she call it? *Gentleman's ego.* Where in God's name did she come up with that?

"If I do seem confused, you have no one to blame but yourself," Madeline snapped back with a toss of her head. "There are wild rumors going on about you, did you know that? Wild, indeed. How should I know what is true?"

"What are these rumors?" he demanded.

"You must have heard them," she said, lifting her head to the moon. He couldn't read her expression. "It's just idle gossip, really, about you and...Juliana."

Unfortunately, Colin understood perfectly. He was aware of some of the ridiculous stories circulating about him and his former fiancée, and could only imagine what Madeline had heard. "Let's start over," he said, sensing her embarrassment. "You tell me the truth. The real truth, this time," he added sternly, "about what in God's name you were doing with the French Blue diamond in the woods this morning, and I'll answer any personal questions you wish. Agreed?"

Madeline pondered his offer, biting her lip in a way he found a little too enticing. "You won't question what I tell you, no matter how strange?" she asked.

He grasped her hand, bringing it to his lips. "You have my word."

"I agree," she finally said. "I guess there's really no point in hiding it now, is there?" She took a deep breath. "My father sent me to find the diamond and destroy it. It was his last request before he died, and I swore to honor it."

Colin shook his head in disbelief. "He asked you to find the diamond and then smash it with a stone?"

"No, smashing it was Helena's idea."

"But of course," he muttered, not doubting Helena's part for a moment. A sudden thought occurred to him. "Madeline, you said your father had been ill for many years?"

"Yes, for most of my life Papa wasn't in good health. Why do you ask?" she said, staring at him suspiciously. "Are you implying he was mad?"

"Not at all," he said quickly. "I am merely curious. Did he tell you why he wished for such a valuable diamond to be destroyed?"

She straightened her shoulders. "He had a very sound reason indeed. My Papa believed the French Blue diamond was haunting him."

"Because of the curse nonsense?"

Colin instantly regretted his outburst, as Madeline, looking both crushed and furious, immediately tried to remove herself from his lap. "You don't believe me, do you? You still think I'm little more than a liar. I never should have spoken a word to you of my vow."

"Madeline," Colin pulled her back onto his lap despite her struggles. "Listen to me! Whatever you tell me I'll believe."

She remained still, watching him warily. "Even if what I have to say sounds rather...unusual?"

Colin nodded, then tucked her head under his chin and took a deep breath. "Tell me from the beginning."

And she did. Her story hesitant at first and then tumbling out in a torrent of sadness and fear, she told him everything she had been through since coming to London.

"And last night my father came to me in another

nightmare. It was horrible," she said, leaning back against him, desperate for his strength as she revisited the awful dreams. "He showed me how my mother died. I saw the whole terrible crash as if it were happening right in front of my eyes! Papa had given her the French Blue as a gift, not believing the stories of a curse and…she died with the diamond in her hand. It killed her. That's why Papa buried it for all these years." When she finished, she lay back in his arms, terrified of his reaction. She half expected him to laugh, or simply get up and walk away.

"So the diamond is cursed," he began, his expression unreadable in the dim moonlight. "And smashing it to pieces will end this evil curse? Do I have this correct?"

"Something must be done!" she fired back. "The French Blue has brought nothing but suffering to all who've been in its possession. And it's already begun! My attack this afternoon was no coincidence."

"Now there's something we agree on," he said. "But I believe whoever sent Moore was motivated by greed, not an ancient curse."

"Don't you see!" she pleaded, desperate to make him understand. "My mother died the very day he brought the diamond into their home. Can you not see how it all fits together?"

"I can see you have convinced yourself it has," Colin replied with a long sigh. "All right, I've heard enough. I'll help you get your diamond back, and then *we*," he stressed with a tight squeeze around her middle, "will decide what's to be done."

Grateful to be relieved of her burden, Madeline agreed, shifting her weight more comfortably on Colin's lap.

"It's your turn," he said, rather forcefully holding her still.

"My turn for what?"

"Questions, Madeline." He rubbed his chin on

top of her head. "I'll tell you whatever you wish to know about my past."

She bit her lip, wondering where to begin. "Was Juliana really..." She didn't quite know how to phrase such a thing, but finally continued, "in a dalliance with Lord Rockford?"

Colin sighed but kept his promise to answer. "I found them together. It was fairly obvious what was going on. Rockford has a rather colorful history with women."

"And you ended the engagement, of course. But why does everyone blame you?"

She felt him shrug. "No details were given, and so the *ton* made up their own version of the events. It was much more thrilling to make me the villain."

Madeline's heart ached for him. She reached out her hand and gently placed it on top of Colin's, wrapping her fingers around the clenched fist. "I'm so sorry," she whispered. "She must have hurt you very much."

"I was angry, yes, but not hurt. Truthfully, I was never in love with Juliana." That stopped Madeline cold, and she pulled out of his arms, staring up at him.

"Then why was she going to marry you?" she asked.

He shrugged. "To become a duchess, I suppose. Love isn't considered a reason for marriage, Madeline. You know that as well as I do." He shifted as though uncomfortable, suddenly taking her hand in his.

"There's something else I need to tell you about Juliana."

"It can wait," she whispered, no longer wishing to hear about his past. She placed her fingertips against his lips to silence him, enjoying the newfound power as his words died in his throat at her touch. Madeline's heart thumped so hard against

211

her chest she felt dizzy. There it was again, that smoldering look, seductive and intoxicating, beckoning to her with dark promises hidden inside the deep smoky-grey depths. They moved toward one another at the same time, Colin reaching her first, flattening her back against the tiny bench before bringing his lips down to meet hers, his hot mouth a sharp contrast to the cold stones that held her up, and she pressed against him, letting him nip at her neck with deadly precision.

"I find I am always alone with you in gardens," Colin said. "For the best, really. If ever I had so much as a decent sofa nearby, you'd be on it."

"What would I be doing on the sofa?" she asked breathlessly, trying to bite him back.

"Waiting for me to make love to you."

"Oh." That certainly got her attention, and her eyes shot open, making Colin laugh again as he pulled her closer to him.

"I'm serious, Madeline. I cannot wait any longer. Do you want me in your bed?"

"I..." Madeline's mind conspired against her, removing all words from her head save a single conversation from earlier. "Edward says you are in love with me," she blurted out, cringing in his arms even as the words flew from her lips. "Was he...is that true?"

Colin went silent as a monk in prayer. A heart-wrenching moment went by while Madeline's stomach dropped to her knees and she cursed herself for speaking. Finally Colin moved, the stunned look draining from his handsome face as he wrapped his arms around her. "Edward has always been very astute."

Then he was kissing her without restraint, exploring her with his flaming hands until she moaned. "Colin!"

"Say it," he whispered. "Tell me you want me."

"I do, please!"

His reply was to slip one hand beneath her cloak and inside the bodice of her dress, while the other hand amused itself beneath her skirt, sliding up to cup her backside. Madeline could not help but respond. Wrapping her leg around Colin's, she focused on pulling open his shirt, eager to place her mouth on his neck.

"Madeline." She dimly heard Colin talking but ignored it, engrossed in her task, reveling in the wicked pleasure of his skin against her hands. "We cannot do this out here, Madeline. Someone will see us." His words finally penetrated when he pulled away, her bare skin slapped with the cold air.

"Of course." The disappointment sat like a lump in her throat, strangling her words, and Colin met her eyes in sympathy.

"Look at me." He lifted her chin. "I will come to you tonight, after midnight. Which bedroom window is yours?" He asked the scandalous question with no hint of embarrassment, and Madeline answered without thinking.

"Upstairs, the third room on the right. What are you planning to do?"

"Leave the window unlatched," he answered her, expertly sliding her dress back into its proper place.

****

Ushering Madeline back inside Lady Milburg's music room, Colin took one look at Helena, bemused and rumpled, barely propping herself up on the pianoforte, and suddenly wanted to pummel his brother.

"Edward." Colin greeted him with a deep frown, wondering where the hell Lady Milburg had vanished to, while his gaze took in the scene. His brother remained seated at the game table, grinning like a rogue with several cards scattered at his feet.

"Good evening, Colin. All is well, I assume?"

"No thanks to you," he snapped. "I found Madeline wandering alone in the garden." He was furious with his brother and didn't bother to hide it. Fortunately, Madeline herself wasn't up for noticing anything. She slipped into the room pale and dreamy. Colin actually had to steer her into a chair. *Likely for the best.* He didn't know how Madeline's temper would fare if she discovered his brother had been seducing her cousin.

Edward just smiled at him, not the least bit ruffled. "You underestimate me, Colin. Helena and I had a perfect view of Lady Milburg's lovely stone bench from the back window. After you arrived," he continued, seeing Madeline's head jerk up with horror, "it was decided we should respect your privacy and find another way to occupy ourselves."

"We've been reading!" Helena spoke a little louder than necessary. "Out loud to one another."

"A delightful pastime," Edward agreed.

"And a dangerous one," Colin said, shooting his brother a warning look.

"Ah! Lord Douglas!" Lady Milburg suddenly appeared at the door with her maid. "You do make unusual entrances, do you not?" She spread a stern glower across the entire room, not waiting for an answer. "Shall we be making a party for supper, then, or do you feel we ladies will be safe alone now?" Her gaze narrowed sharply, moving back and forth between him and Edward, now no longer grinning in his chair. "Or perhaps you and Lord Montgomery plan to spend the night and completely destroy my girls' reputations?"

A clear setdown, and Colin felt Madeline's aunt was more shrewd than he realized. "We are leaving, Lady Milburg, and I do apologize for the inconvenience." He bowed stiffly to her, motioning to Edward with a flick of his head. "Though I will beg your indulgence once more. I must insist on your permission to escort Madeline for the next few days, just as a precaution."

"Are you planning to attend Lord Huntington's masquerade ball tomorrow evening?" she asked, her voice rising slightly.

Huntington is throwing a masquerade? What the hell for? He must be desperate to impress his new, much younger wife. Colin shuddered slightly. *I can't imagine anything less appealing than spending an evening running about in costume.* He smiled, all the same. "Of course. I wouldn't dare miss such an event."

Lady Milburg turned to look at her niece, sitting motionless and pale in the corner. "Then we shall see you tomorrow, Lord Douglas."

He bowed to her again, a worthy adversary when she wished to be, and threw Madeline a brief, heat-filled glance over his shoulder.

"Until tomorrow."

Madeline thanked the heavens she was already sitting down, for surely her knees would have buckled from the scorching, absolutely sinful gaze Colin gave her. She barely managed a nod of farewell, and was too preoccupied with watching his slow stride disappear from the room.

"Well! I certainly set them both to rights. We must use a bit more caution, girls, for though it is perfectly lovely to flirt most shamelessly, one must gently remind gentlemen of their proper duties."

Madeline tore her gaze from the now empty doorway. "What are you speaking of, Aunt? What duties?"

"To propose, of course!" Aunt Cecilia sighed helplessly over her niece's ignorance. "I am certain it shan't be long. Lord Douglas and Lord Montgomery were positively enchanted this evening. Well done, darlings."

"But Papa said I am not supposed to marry!"

Madeline cried out, jumping to her feet in alarm. She regretted the words the instant she spoke them, but it was too late.

"Why in the name of King George would Thomas tell you that?" her aunt demanded.

Trapped, she turned to her cousin, who shrugged helplessly. Madeline sat back down, too exhausted to think of any more lies. "Papa feared I was too much like my mother, that my marriage would end as tragically as his."

Aunt Cecilia cursed sharply, stunning the room into silence. "Now listen here, Madeline. Your father was an absolute idiot. I have no doubt he was a good father," she continued, interrupting her niece's protest, "but he was an idiot, nonetheless. Other than looks, you are not a bit like Sarah! In fact, you possess all the very qualities my sister was lacking. You are generous, caring, truthful, well, mostly truthful..."

"Then why did you forbid me to speak of her?" Madeline insisted, trying to take in this new knowledge. "And warn me to stay away from Lord Rockford?"

"Oh, dearest, for your own protection! I feared the *ton* would not see past your face. They can be quite superficial, you know. But I never felt you would follow the same path as my sister, and I cannot conceive how Thomas could, either. Your father underestimated you, my darling."

Chapter Thirteen

Midnight approached.

Madeline's lone candle flickered; time had passed quickly, according to its dripping state. She could tell by the deepening black outside that the appointed hour crept near. The house was silent as an ancient crypt, and in a moment of sheer boldness Madeline cautiously tiptoed from her bed, gripping a shawl around her shoulders as she unlocked the latch to her bedroom window. The sharp, pinging click of the metal pierced the tomblike stillness, forcing her back to the safety of her blankets, where she sat utterly still after arranging them in a perfect folded square around her legs. She wasn't sure how punctual Colin planned to be, but the passage of time was unnerving, ridiculously so.

She felt a sudden need to throw off the bedcovers and resume her earlier pacing. In truth, she had been in a haze of panic since emerging from the garden. The garden. Her cheeks burned at the memory, and she pressed both palms against their tender skin. After the shocking conversation with her aunt, she had instantly fled to her room, fearful her thoughts would spill onto the very floor and give her secrets away.

I will not think of that tonight, she told herself firmly, and her thoughts gratefully returned to her impending visitor. Colin had said he couldn't wait any longer. For what? She had stupidly agreed with him but had little idea what she was unwilling to wait for. She was woefully ignorant of the arts between a man and a woman. Her father would

217

never have dreamed of discussing such a thing, though he certainly encouraged her to read his beloved Greek mythology, the consequence being that Madeline had many colorful examples of intimate encounters from stories of Zeus and his cohorts, though she doubted very much Colin planned to turn himself into a bull.

But the honest truth was Madeline had no idea what to expect. In the end, she recalled the brief and rather horrifying marital advice she had received from her aunt during a cozy winter night in Norfolk.

"There are two ways to go about it, my dears," Aunt Cecilia had informed them, pausing only to signal Brigette for more wine. "A lady can be little more than a body to her husband, a pretty thing for him to admire and respect in her laces and jewels, and that's all very well." She took a long drink, watching them both out of one unsteady eye. "But, a real lady, a *real* lady can become a *real* companion to him, if you understand my meaning. Do you understand my meaning, girls? She can be a willing participant in his desire. Do you know what I mean by desire, girls?"

"Mother." Helena had barely managed to get the words out through lips pressed together in mortification. "If you speak another word on this subject, I shall hang myself with the curtains."

Unfortunately, that signaled an end to the conversation, though Madeline dearly regretted not asking a question or two. What did her aunt mean by *desire*? Colin seemed rather desirous of her already, but was Madeline doing enough to make herself a companion? A real companion? She certainly didn't feel very friendly at the moment, stiff and exhausted from the long wait, along with a growing suspicion she was expected to be unclothed. After hours of deliberation she had finally come to the conclusion that she was not quite ready to be a willing participant in a man's desire, feeling it would be safer to become a pretty thing for Colin to respect—from a distance, of course. Later she could work her way up to willing participant, after a year or two, perhaps. Buoyed by her decision, Madeline carefully smoothed a hand across her tightly pinned curls, enhanced by a gold silk band, and hoped she had done an adequate job of making herself an object to admire.

A rattle at the window made her sit straight up, shoving her hands into her lap as she peered into the dark room.

"Madeline?" It was Colin, his face outlined in the window, bathed in the glow of candlelight and the moon. She was in awe of him. Madeline recalled her first glimpse of this man, how she had imagined him from another world, part man, part god. Overwhelmed with emotion, she held out her hand in reply.

Colin slipped effortlessly through the window, closing it behind him before stealing across the room to the edge of her bed to stare down at her, a hint of a grin tugging at his lips.

"Madeline," he began again, his whisper weaving her name through the room like a leaf in the wind.

"Yes?" she managed to reply, lifting her head up to be kissed.

"Why are you wearing all those clothes?"

The spell shattered like glass. Madeline glanced down to see she was, indeed, wearing one of her most elaborate ball gowns, a white satin with delicate pearl-and-lace embroidery around the sleeves, and had even gone so far as to don a matching pair of slippers and an ermine-lined shawl.

"No reason at all," she replied flippantly, tossing off the covers. "I was merely cold." She knew she must look utterly ridiculous and was grateful to

Colin for keeping his composure.

"How thoughtless of me. You are right, of course. The night air is carrying quite a chill. Would you care to borrow my jacket?" he teased, whipping it off and placing it around her shoulders.

Madeline laughed, his light smile a caress to her nerves. "I didn't know what to wear," she admitted. "You are the first man to ever come through my window."

"Thank God for that." He slipped the jacket and the fur off her shoulders, replacing them with his warm hands. "Are you afraid of me?" She shook her head, tilting her neck to one side to graze the tops of his fingers with her cheek.

"Then shall we remove some of these clothes?" He didn't wait for an answer, but peeled a silk glove off her arm, sliding a hand across her bare skin. Madeline closed her eyes, allowing the exotic waves to lap against her, the seductive heat of him, the hard coils of muscle on the back of his neck as she slipped her hands into his hair and pulled herself up to his mouth. Colin took his time. Ignoring her demanding pleas, he teased the inside of her mouth with his tongue, sliding it in and out, deepening the kiss until she feared her legs would no longer hold her.

"I've been dreaming of your bedroom," he whispered, "since the very first moment I laid eyes on you."

"Is it what you imagined?" she asked, marveling at the way he knew exactly the right spot to kiss on her neck.

"Almost." She felt the top of her gown sliding down to her waist and the exploding sensation of his fingers moving to brush against her breasts. "Though in my version you were much more naked."

Madeline froze. Wrenching herself from his arms she quickly moved back to force a bit of space between them, while frantically pulling up her dress. "I'm—I must apologize. With everything happening so quickly, I couldn't breathe." She shook her head, knowing she was making a mess of things, but how could she explain that the very idea of being naked in front of him sent her into near-hysterics? Although Madeline's knowledge of men was limited, she did guess he would find that rather insulting. In the end, desperation overcame humiliation, and she went with the truth. "I cannot take my clothes off in front of you," she informed him, her face practically steaming from embarrassment. "I have decided it is much too terrifying, and better left to other ladies." Madeline finished her speech with a hard nod, positive he would laugh or, worse, storm out of the room to leave her feeling like a fool.

But Colin merely stood staring at her, tenderness lining his expression. "I completely understand. Would there be any objection to the removal of *my* clothes?"

She narrowed her eyes at him. "I beg your pardon?"

"I would be happy to make the sacrifice and dispense of my clothes first. You may do with me what you will, and later, if you find your fears have lessened, you can join me."

A giggle escaped Madeline's lips. Both relieved and delighted by the outrageous notion, she nodded her consent, placing a hand to her mouth as she watched him pull off his boots.

"There is one condition, of course," he suddenly added, looking utterly adorable in his bare feet. "Something you must do for me in return."

"Yes?" she asked, anticipating some indecent request.

"Unpin your hair."

Madeline's breath caught in her throat, and she obeyed, lifting her hand to release the heavy pins, her eyes shining. And it was in those few moments of silence, with the room bathed in a soft glow from the gentle flickering of candles, Madeline's hair falling in unbound drifts around her shoulders, Colin's gaze seeking hers while he slipped his fingers through button after button of his white shirt—it was then Madeline learned the meaning of desire.

Her final hairpin removed, Madeline gently dropped it to the floor with the others. She had not a care for anything but Colin's golden skin flashing in the dim light and the warm swirling sensation gliding through her. Standing only a few feet away, she could see how well formed he was, the muscular chest larger and more inviting without the clothes, his coal black hair blending into the dark corners of her room, intensifying the grey-blue eyes, now pools of desire causing her to draw long breaths in anticipation.

"I see your breathing has improved." Colin spoke in a lightly teasing voice before quickly sliding off the remainder of his clothes, his fawn-colored breeches joining her hairpins on the floor. A sudden cloud passed over the soft moonlight, plunging the room into a deeper shade of black, and Madeline thanked God for His mercy. She had caught a full, healthy view of Colin without his pants on, and, despite the throbbing beat of longing now prickling beneath her skin, she almost screamed. *If I live through this night,* she swore, *I will never again ignore Aunt Cecilia when she drinks.*

"Madeline." The voice came from the shadows, or perhaps the cloud had shifted. She could not tell with her eyes squeezed shut.

"Yes?"

"Nothing will happen here tonight that you don't want. I promise you that." And she believed him. Heart and soul, her body cried out for him. Madeline opened her eyes, focusing on the mass of red scars on his shoulder, his only flaw, that somehow made him more beautiful to her. She suddenly wanted to run to him, throw herself into his arms and kiss his shoulder, erase the injury with her mouth. Naked and vulnerable he had come to her this night, offering everything, offering himself. Madeline was no longer afraid. She wanted this night. She wanted him.

"I know," she whispered, moving toward him. She slipped off her white dress, leaving only the thin lace chemise that scarcely covered the tops of her breasts, and went to him, finding her place in his arms. "I trust you, Colin." The words struck lightning between them, and he bent down, taking lace and breast together in his mouth for an agonizingly wonderful moment before releasing her, bringing her lips to his with a ferocity that stole the last of Madeline's air.

"What should I do?" The tiny whisper brought Colin back to his senses, and he looked down at the passionate woman in his arms. Her mouth was pink and swollen from his kisses, her pale cheeks blooming with a rosy glow of desire, and she bit him softly on the chin, suddenly eager to learn everything she could, everything he had to offer. Colin's hands shook as he pulled her arms above her head and slipped the thin material off, letting the lace and silk float down her back as they both shivered in response. Cupping her smooth bottom in his hands, he pressed her against his arousal, letting her feel how much he wanted her. He smiled at her ragged gasp. Ever an attentive student, Madeline discovered almost immediately how sinfully glorious his skin felt against hers, and she pushed against him again, several times, until he finally stopped her with a moan.

"If you keep that up, it will be a very short night," he rasped in her ear, pulling away from her slightly to regain control of himself.

She ignored his warning, recklessly following after him. "I wish for this to be a very long night, Colin."

"So do I."

He lifted her then, stepping over the pile of clothes to place her in the middle of the bed, spreading her long hair out on the pillows like a dark fan. "You're beautiful, Madeline." He knelt next to her on the bed, crossing the tips of his fingers up and down the length of her body, unable to stop touching her. His hand glided from her long smooth neck down to her breasts, round and heavy, and he paused to take a nipple into his mouth, suckling hard until she was writhing beneath him, uttering little whimpers in his ear. He continued on, sliding past her flat stomach with a small kiss at her navel, and then farther down, until he reached the very heat of her and slipped his finger inside.

"Oh, my." She sounded shocked and amazed at the same time, repeating her words twice more, and he might have smiled had he not been concentrating so hard to slow her down. Madeline was obviously determined to drive him mad, bucking against him, pushing his hand further inside her for more of the sweet torture.

"Hold me," he whispered, placing her hand around him. She readily agreed, closing her hand so tightly, so perfectly around him Colin's control almost snapped. She squeezed him again, and he knew he should tell her to stop, but couldn't bring himself to end it, instead plunging another finger inside her, finding the one spot he knew would send her over the brink.

"Colin!" She arched against him, lost to everything now but her own fulfillment, and Colin pulsed gently, then faster, against the most sensitive part of her, loving the feel of his hand pressed between her thighs as she thrust harder against him. He knew the moment when her pleasure exploded and put his hand over her mouth to muffle the scream.

"Open your legs for me," he said, and she obeyed, running her tongue over his fingers, nibbling on the thumb while he settled between her wet thighs, spreading himself out along the length of her body with a deep sigh of satisfaction.

"Please, don't move," she whispered, holding him tight in her arms, "and please do that thing again. I liked it very much."

"I know you did, love." He kissed her, long and passionately, letting his tongue slide in and out until she was feverish with desire. "Look at me." He raised her head until their eyes met, and he had to stop himself from forgetting his words and kissing her again. "After tonight we will belong to each other, do you understand?" She nodded at him. "There is no going back."

"I do not wish to go back," she replied softly, kissing his neck, and that was all Colin needed to hear. He leaned back to steady himself on top of her. Colin grasped her hips between his hands and slowly began easing inside, hoping to cause as little discomfort as possible. She sighed and placed one hand to her mouth in a gesture Colin found to be utterly innocent and seductive at the same time, and his body throbbed to be inside her, to make her his own. Poised at the tip of her maidenhead, he paused to offer her one last hot kiss filled with the promise of what was to come, and, taking a deep breath, he plunged into her, breaking past her virginity in one swift motion.

Madeline shrieked. Stunned by the sudden invasion that ripped through her body, she jerked against Colin but was unable to move him. "Release me!" she cried, slapping the massive chest. "You're doing something wrong! Get off me!" She struggled against him harder, unable to stop her tears.

"Hold on, my love. I know there's a little pain..." *A little pain? The man must be joking.* Madeline felt positive her body had been ripped completely apart and was not at all shy about telling him so, ending with her prediction that she would never again be able to walk. "We've made a horrible mistake, Colin," she moaned through her sobs. "Perhaps we are ill-suited to one another. We should never have done this."

The words caught in her throat when, without any warning, Colin wrapped his arms around her and flipped them both over, settling her on top of him, still holding her tightly by the hips. He lifted her up, the power of his arms amazing her, and settled her down precisely on top of his hardness. "Colin, what—" She couldn't decide if her body welcomed or rejected the intrusion of something so large, and she pulled back, fearful of the discomfort.

"It's okay, love. Ease into it."

Startled by the new sensations of sitting in such an intimate way, all Madeline's fears faded from her mind. She felt freer without Colin's weight pushing her down into the bed. The pangs inside her began to ease and, when she lifted herself up, the horrible ache vanished completely.

"Is it better now?" Colin asked, concern lining his brow as he reached up to wipe the tears from her cheeks. She nodded. Relieved by the sudden change, she allowed his fingers to find her again, pushing her back against his knees, until Madeline cared for nothing but his touch. She melted into him, easing her body back down, and was surprised to feel pleasure behind the throbbing. There, she felt it again, stronger this time, and moved her hips faster, until Colin let out a low groan.

"Am I hurting you?" she asked, jerking against

him in horror.

He groaned again. "There is nothing you could do that I wouldn't like, believe me." He pulled her down for another searing kiss, and Madeline was suddenly seized with the impulse to slide her tongue in his mouth, holding his chest down with her hands until he was shaking beneath her.

"Did you like that?" she whispered, not waiting for an answer but lowering her mouth, sinking down inside him.

The very last of Colin's control broke, snapping in half like a thin thread, and he grabbed Madeline by the waist, hoisting himself up until they were face to face. He slid his hands around the soft smooth skin of her beautiful back and drove into her. Hard.

She gasped, arching into his hands, begging for more. "Colin!"

"Did you like that?" he replied, pulling out ever so slightly before plunging back inside, squeezing his eyes shut in ecstasy. "My God, Madeline."

Colin lost all sense of time, mesmerized by the taste of her skin, the thin line of sweat in the valley of her breasts, the panting sounds that would forever be burned into his memory. He didn't know how long he made love to her, stupefied with pleasure and a feeling he could not describe, when he realized she was yanking on his hair. "Colin!"

"Love, am I hurting you?" he pulled back, starting to end it, ashamed at himself. He had been too rough with her, too forceful for her first time—

"Keep moving!"

Her nails dug into his skin, and he didn't dare argue. He wanted to tell her he'd known from the moment he laid eyes on her that she would be a fiery vixen in his arms, that climbing in her window was the best thing he'd ever done, but their bodies had caught a rhythm, moving rapturously together as one, and Colin could not spare the time to speak. He pushed harder and harder into her, slipping a finger down between them again to send her into bursts of fire that made her cry out. He was nearing his finish and desperately wanted to bring her to fulfillment first. She gasped, low and animalistic, when he touched her, and he knew she was very close.

"Madeline, don't let go of me, just hold on."

"Yes," she breathed.

Colin drove into her once, twice, mimicking the movements with his hand until he felt her tighten around him, squeezing him with all her strength, and then he was lost, overcome by the wave of his own release.

Madeline pressed her face against Colin's chest, her eyes shut tight against him as the last of the overwhelming ripples of pleasure shuddered through her. Madeline had never known she could feel something so beautiful, had never realized such a bond between two people could exist. Is this what Colin had meant? She would never have believed him.

She slid off his chest, landing, with a deep sigh, in strong, protective arms surrounded by a pile of blankets. A delicious exhaustion nagged at her, but she fought against it, wanting this night to never end.

"How did I do?" he asked into her hair, and Madeline smiled.

"Very well, Lord Douglas, though your timing was a little off at the end. We shall have to try it again sometime."

He crushed her to him, muffling his laughter in her hair, and Madeline thought she had never before been so happy. She thought of Lady Douglas's wistful voice when she spoke of her husband and wondered if this was what marriage was like, warm and secure in someone's arms, sharing laughter under the blankets. *Though they could probably make much more noise if they were married.*

"You look as if you are thinking wicked thoughts, Madeline. Care to enlighten me?" He couldn't seem to keep his hands off her body, idly stroking every surface of it. From the tips of her hair to her elbow, all of it had been graced by his light touch. Madeline's entire being vibrated with a gentle hum.

"I was thinking how I never knew, never realized, how lovely this could be." She waved her hand, suddenly too shy to name it. "All of this between a man and a woman."

Colin grew serious then. "Neither did I."

He pulled himself up on his elbows, leaning over her so they were eye to eye. "Madeline, everything has changed between us now. Do you realize what I'm saying to you? There's no going back after tonight."

"I understand." She didn't want to talk about that now and instead concentrated on kissing him, a long possessive kiss that resulted in a growing awareness of his arousal against her leg. "Can we—be together again? So soon?"

He shook his head slowly. "I don't want to hurt you, love."

Madeline's stomach flipped over at his words. He had been calling her that all night.

"Oh," she replied, trying not to look disappointed. Would they ever get a chance to be together like this again? She couldn't imagine Colin sneaking in through her window every night.

As though sensing her frustration, he kissed her. "But that doesn't mean we have to go to sleep just yet. There are other things we can do."

"Such as?" She was instantly intrigued.

"I can have my way with you. And later," he whispered, sealing the dark promise with another long kiss, "I'll teach you to do the same to me." And then he was gone, his dark head vanishing under the blankets, leaving her to wonder what he could possibly be doing, until she felt the hot rough scalding of his tongue in her most intimate place, and she nearly gave them away by screaming. Madeline put her hand between her teeth, biting hard to muffle any sound, and gave in to being absolutely entranced by her first lesson.

****

The walls surrounding her were damp and crumbling, so black she could scarcely make out the pale skin of her own trembling hand. "Hello?" she called out, noticing a sliver of light from above. Her gaze sought out movement, a figure above her. "Help!" She yelled to the dark shadow, her voice louder this time, on the edge of panic. "I'm trapped down here. Can you help me?"

"I warned you, Maddie."

She shrieked as a dark, crumbling mass fell from above, showering her head and outstretched hands.

"You did not destroy the diamond. I warned you of its evil."

"Papa!" She screamed toward the fading light as piles of dirt dropped onto her, spilling into her mouth and nose. She wiped frantically at her face, trying to see. "Papa, is that you? Help me, let me out!"

"Beware, Maddie. You have unleashed its power."

"No!"

****

"Wake up, love. Open your eyes!"

Madeline struggled to obey the strong, steady voice at her side, choking and gasping as she clawed at her eyes.

"Madeline, wake up!" She did, her eyes widening

with surprise and relief as she realized she was safe in her bedroom, alone...with a rather naked Colin.

She bolted up in the bed, holding the sheets to her chest. Oh, Lord, she was dreaming again. Did she scream? Did the servants hear? The thought of being discovered in bed with Colin was almost as horrifying as her nightmare.

"You were crying in your sleep," Colin said, gently pulling her back down onto her pillow. He leaned over her, gently wiping a tear from her eye. "And your face had the most horrible expression. You looked terrified."

"A dream," she whispered, shaking off the last of her terror. Colin's arms felt warm and solid around her, and she snuggled in closer, eager to forget the terrible nightmare.

"About the diamond?" He was watching her closely, and even in the dim moonlight she could see the faint lines of concern etched across his beautiful face. Distracted, she reached up to trace a path along his jaw.

"I don't remember now," she lied, kissing the trail she made with her fingers. "Make love to me again." She shivered, the nightmare still hovering around her like a cold mist.

"Are you sure?" He was already slipping his hand beneath the blankets, his swift fingers easing between her thighs.

She bit his ear in reply, pressing against him as the last of her nightmare melted under the heat of his hands.

Hours later, before the sun could spill its revealing light onto the bed, Colin reluctantly slid out from beneath a sleeping Madeline, pausing to untangle his arm from hers. His body protested at the move, questioning the good sense of abandoning a warm, contented woman, sprawled so seductively across her bed, for the damp chilled air that awaited him outside. He gave in to the temptation, burying his face in Madeline's hair, intoxicated by her scent, by the feel of her soft, honeyed skin. He had watched over her most of the night. She slept badly, tossing restlessly about, muttering strange broken sentences about her father. *Whatever is haunting her dreams is damned disturbing.* Colin noted the dark smudges beneath her eyes. *And no doubt it has something to do with that bloody diamond.*

She stirred beneath his hand, and Colin abruptly sat back, smiling down at her.

"Good morning." He spoke casually, trying to erase any trace of his earlier thoughts. "I didn't mean to wake you."

She sat up, obviously disoriented when she first awoke, a trait that made Colin smile. "What time is it?" She yawned, pushing her hair from her eyes.

"A few hours before dawn." He stood up. "I have to leave." Colin spoke the words cautiously, suddenly feeling like a cad. No decent gentleman would simply abandon a lady after lovemaking. At least not one he wished to see again, Colin thought with a twinge of regret for his past.

"Of course you do," she mumbled sleepily, flopping back onto her pillow. "If Aunt Cecilia were to find you here, the very walls would crack open from her screams."

Colin grinned at the image. "I don't doubt it for a moment. She's more than suspicious of me already." *And with good reason,* he thought, pulling on his shirt. In the grey dawn he found himself slightly ashamed of his actions. Not that he regretted making love to Madeline. He wouldn't change a single moment of their night together, but he had allowed his lust to overtake his mind, leaving him to crawl out of her bedroom like a dishonorable rake. There was time enough to make things right, he reasoned. He would obtain Lady Milburg's permission for marriage tonight.

Still reluctant to leave her without an explanation, Colin sat down on the edge of the bed, pulling Madeline close. "As intimidating as your aunt is, I have other pressing business to attend to before dawn." He leaned in to kiss her but was too late.

"You're going to look for Moore?" she asked, struggling to sit up and push an unruly mass of hair out of her eyes. "Where is he? Do you think he still has my diamond?"

"If he doesn't have it, he damn well knows where it is," Colin replied, turning serious at the thought of the man who had dared to touch his Madeline. "I was told he spends most of his nights drinking in King's Tavern. With any luck, I'll find him there, and he'll lead me to the diamond." *And the bastard who hired him to follow you.* He stole a quick glance outside Madeline's window, deciding there was still time for a last embrace.

"Promise me you'll be careful," she insisted, once again interrupting his amorous attempts. "And don't think of doing anything foolish with this man. You must remember he is a dangerous criminal."

Colin had his doubts about how dangerous Moore really was, but he agreed, finally capturing Madeline's lips in the long-anticipated kiss.

"I want you to promise me you and Helena will stay inside today," he instructed when he finally dragged himself from Madeline.

"Why?"

"Because I don't trust anyone," he said simply, both amused and exasperated by her need to question everything he said. "I don't want to worry that you've enticed your cousin into any more schemes while I'm away."

"Very well." She yawned. "Though I certainly disagree with your notion that I enticed Helena into anything. I suppose I can work on my infernal needlepoint today." She smiled sweetly up at him, and he couldn't resist kissing her one more time.

"I'll be back this evening to escort you to Huntington's ball." He did his best not to grimace at the thought. He would much rather spend the evening alone with Madeline...in her bedroom.

"Be sure to wear a costume!" she said. "Helena is going as Aphrodite—my aunt's choice, of course."

"And you?"

"A secret." She grinned at him. "We shall see if you can guess tonight." She placed a chaste little peck on his lips while one of her hands snaked downward to capture his arousal. "I should like a last kiss before you go."

The woman was outrageous, and Colin fought hard between his need to leave before destroying her reputation and his flaming desire to make her scream for mercy. "You shouldn't do that," he whispered darkly, pulling her hand away.

"Why?" she asked, innocently slipping her hand downward again, and Colin decided he quite admired her inquisitiveness after all.

"Because when you look at me like that, with your sexy little mouth questioning everything I say, it makes me so hard." He pushed her back onto the bed. "So hard I forget all about your aunt, the servants, or anyone else discovering us, and all I can think about is ravishing every part of your body while you beg me for more." He abruptly stopped talking when her treacherous fingers surrounded him again.

"Then we shall have to be rather quick."

Chapter Fourteen

Daniel Moore stepped into King's, his cracked boots contributing a smear of mud to the tavern's filthy floor. His mood was a good one, relaxed from a recent trip to the apothecary, and he congratulated himself again on a job well done. Even Rockford hadn't been able to hide his pleasure. The old bastard had beamed like the moon at the sight of the dark blue diamond dangling from Moore's fingers.

Rockford's greed was pathetic, Moore thought with a snicker, almost as pathetic as seeing the great marquis fawning over his dead lover. Still, Rockford was satisfied, and Moore had finally got the money he was owed. That and a glass or two of gin was enough for his simple tastes. Stealing the diamond had been easy; all he'd had to do was bide his time, wait for the right moment, and the diamond was his. He should steal from women every day.

Moore sauntered up to the bar, shoving past old Half Blind, who'd been sitting on the same filthy stool so long it likely was stuck to him, and nodded to the bartender already eyeing him suspiciously. He patted his side pocket, relishing the feel of Rockford's coins, a down payment for the shining blue diamond he'd stolen from Rockford's pretty little wench. And there would be plenty more coming his way, Moore told himself. That diamond was worth a bloody fortune, and it would all be his for the taking. Moore laughed. Fitting that Rockford should have fallen for a daft chit. He still couldn't believe he had seen the Sinclair woman try to smash her diamond with a rock. Lucky he'd been there to stop her! And now...he slipped two fingers inside the pocket, unable to stop himself from caressing the coins...it was time to celebrate.

He slapped one hand down on the bar. "Tell you what I'm gonna have, Johnny. I want a glass of your finest brandy, the kind the marquis himself drinks."

"You can't afford a glass of grog," Johnny snorted, while Half Blind Harry grunted his agreement.

"Want me to give him a taste of my boot?"

"Excuse me, gentlemen," Moore slapped down a sovereign directly between the men, relishing the shock on their ugly faces. "I'll take my brandy now."

Johnny's eyebrow rose to the heavens, but he was never one to turn down so much as a farthing. He scooped up the coin, pocketing it before turning to get Moore's drink, while Harry merely grunted again and voiced regret at missing the chance to pummel someone. Moore smiled. He could get used to this.

"That's a lot of money, Moore. You onto something?" Johnny asked the question, setting the brandy down in front of Moore's twitching fingers. He took a long, thirsty gulp before answering, letting the sweet liquor glide down his throat like he was a real gentleman. Maybe he'd pick up a woman later, after he finished his work, of course. Some pretty thing, small and plump like Rockford's maid. He rubbed his hands together in anticipation. That'd be just the thing to start off his new life.

"You've not been stealing from your Lord Rockford, have you? He'll not take kindly to that."

Moore slammed down his half-empty glass, laughing right in Johnny's face. "This?" he said, pulling out a second gold coin. "This is nothing, barely scratching the surface." He turned, still chuckling to himself, and noticed he had gained an audience. The men at the table next to him suddenly found him more fascinating than their game of dice.

"Where'd ya get the blunt, Moore?" one of the men yelled, a blubbery bastard called Mel.

"Yeah, how much more's in your pocket?"

"Plenty," he answered back, the brandy only adding to his feeling of power. "Not that you'll be seeing any more of it. After tonight, I'll be drinking in better swills than this."

"Watch your mouth." Harry's one icy eye glared over the rim of his glass.

"I'll say what I want. If you or anyone else gives me trouble, they'll pay the price with their heads." He sat back, enjoying the look of fear on Harry's face.

"So tell us, then." Johnny traded another glass of brandy for a coin. "What's the marquis got you doing for him now?"

"I'm onto something bigger than old Rockford," Moore replied. "No more beating up vagrants and hiding in bushes. I'm in business for myself now." He downed his next drink in one swallow. "Isn't it a lovely afternoon, Johnny?" Moore slapped another shiny coin down and grinned. He was nearly out of the money Rockford had paid him, but so what? There was plenty more to be had, once the job was done, plenty more.

Johnny snorted. "It's evenin' now, Mr. Moore, but time probably means little to a fancy man like you." Another brandy slid across the bar. "You had yourself a visitor here today, Mr. Moore," he added casually, and Harry's eye flicked in their direction.

"What kind of visitor?"

The bartender shrugged. "Man came in here looking for you, asking some questions. Course, I didn't tell him nothin', did I, Harry?"

Half Blind grunted in response.

"But he was a mighty persistent one. I'd watch

myself, if I were you."

Moore's hands shook so badly he could hardly hold the brandy. "What did he look like?"

Johnny smiled. "You know me, Mr. Moore, I don't remember much past a man's height. It's what's kept me alive all these years."

"Was he a big man? Dark hair?"

"He was a gentleman, very clean-lookin', and a real dark scowl. That's all I remember, that scowl."

It was enough for Moore. He knew exactly who had been hanging around, hoping to get his hands on him this afternoon. The Sinclair bitch must have recognized him and called in Douglas to find her diamond.

"Did he say he was coming back?" But Johnny had turned his back. Moore shuddered, downing the remains of his glass in one desperate gulp. He needed to find Rockford, get himself a new hiding place. He stood up from the stool with one last longing glance at the empty glass.

"Well?" Mel called out, crossing his arms together. Moore knew he had the attention of the room and reveled in it. All of Lord Rockford's warnings about keeping quiet, the threat of Lord Douglas, vanished in favor of the men's anticipatory looks. One more couldn't hurt. One more drink and he'd go straight to Rockford.

****

After Colin slipped away in the cold dark, Madeline lay awake, unable to sleep. Instead, she let her mind float freely over her night with Colin, allowing the memory of his hands and mouth to ignite her flesh until she was in a fever. Madeline sat up in the middle of the disheveled bed, letting the morning air cool her skin while the night of lovemaking continued to flash through her mind. There would be consequences for her decision, she knew, but for all the world she would not change it.

Colin had come to her, awoken her body and spirit to something she had never known, feelings she could never regret. Unfortunately, these same feelings left her racked with uncertainty. Colin said things had changed between them; she couldn't agree more. She had been wholly truthful with him, telling him everything of her past, even the terrifying nightmares. *And he believed you.* She hugged herself tight. *He didn't think you were mad.*

So, what next? She couldn't imagine Colin would keep sneaking through her window at night, unless... He didn't wish to marry her, did he? Madeline clearly recalled what marriage had done to Papa, the loss of his beloved Sarah destroying any future happiness. She feared becoming swept up in such overwhelming passions, yet she had little desire to entrap herself in a convenient society marriage filled with deception and greed. Those women found themselves to be little more than chattel to their husbands, and her time spent in the throes of London's marriage mart had only reinforced this view.

Absolutely not, Madeline decided. *I will inform Colin that marriage is not to be an option for me, and that will likely relieve him, as well. The idea does seem to terrify most men.* Her conclusion gained strength in her mind. She gingerly pulled herself out of bed, uncomfortably aware of a dull tenderness between her legs. She was a ruined lady, after all. What was to become of her? Perhaps Colin would suggest they continue their situation, give her *carte blanche*? Her instincts certainly bristled at the idea of becoming anyone's mistress, not to mention that Aunt Cecilia would keel over at such a fate for her niece.

A sudden image sprang to Madeline's mind. She remembered seeing the grand duke's beautiful mistress riding through the park, her fiery head held high, pointedly ignoring the dreadful whispers that surrounded her carriage. Madeline shuddered. She would never wish for such a public display of her shame.

Could it be possible for her to live as an unmarried woman while keeping her relationship with Colin a secret? It wasn't a ridiculous notion; she planned to discuss it with Colin as soon as they could be alone again.

Feeling infinitely better, Madeline quickly washed and dressed before heading downstairs. Ravenous for the first time in days, she felt as though the mist surrounding her had finally cleared. It had been over a week since she'd slept the night through, but the usual exhaustion had vanished. She felt bright and elated, and very much hoped Cook would be serving her delicious sweet rolls this morning. Stepping into the hallway, she jumped when Helena's door popped open.

"Madeline!" she hissed, opening the door a slight crack. "Come in quickly. I must speak with you." Helena's arm snaked out to pull her inside before slamming the door behind her. Her cousin was in quite a state, wringing her hands and fluttering about the room like a wounded butterfly.

"Whatever is the matter?" Madeline had a moment of panic that Helena had somehow discovered her nocturnal guest, but her cousin's next words erased that fear.

"I must confess to someone! It's most horrible." Helena flopped down on the edge of the bed, still wringing her hands and sniffing.

"It cannot be so terrible, Helena. What has happened?" Helena seemed reluctant to speak, very unusual for one who normally couldn't wait to spill her deepest secrets.

"You must never tell Mama," she begged, grasping Madeline's arm.

Madeline promised, extracting her arm. "I shall never breathe a word of it. Now, tell me what happened, and we will find a solution together."

The words seemed to have a calming effect on Helena. "You are most loyal, Madeline, and such a good person. I promise I will understand if you never again wish to be acquainted with me and my sinful ways."

"Helena." Madeline stopped the new flow of tears with a firm look as a sudden thought occurred to her. "Is it the despicable Vickem? Has he done something to upset you?"

Helena's curls shook in denial. "Not at all. In fact, I hadn't realized until just now, but I haven't heard from him in days!"

"It's not important," Madeline replied hastily. "If it's not a lovesick suitor, then what?"

"I didn't say it wasn't about love!" Helena burst into tears after making this statement, plunging headfirst into loud, unladylike sobs that took Madeline nearly a quarter of an hour to subdue. By the time she did manage to quiet her cousin down to a reasonable bout of sniffles, her dreams of fresh sweet rolls had melted away.

"Now," Madeline said, after wiping a rather large amount of moisture from Helena's face, "do not think about crying again until you've given me some kind of answer."

The tone of Madeline's voice must have signaled the end of her patience, for Helena sat up straight, gaining control of herself. "It's Lord Montgomery," she confessed, her voice barely audible.

"Edward?"

Helena nodded with a hiccup. "He, I mean we..." She took a deep shuddering breath. "I've allowed him to take liberties with me." Madeline's gaze immediately went to her cousin's square-shaped window encircled by pale gold curtains.

"What liberties?"

"Last evening, when you went into the garden, Edward wanted to follow you, but I," she blushed, "I told him it wasn't necessary, that we could see you perfectly well from the back window. Oh, I am so ashamed, Madeline! I was only thinking of myself, and I so selfishly wanted to keep playing cards!"

"Never mind that. Then what happened?" Madeline prompted her.

"Edward—I mean, Lord Montgomery—and I continued to play until he won the next hand and declared that I owed him fifty pounds! Fifty pounds, Madeline! Can you believe such a sum? Of course I had not realized we were playing for money and immediately informed him I had only two pounds and was most dreadfully sorry, and...and he said he would allow for a trade." A sinking feeling settled in Madeline's stomach, and she wondered how Colin would react when she murdered his brother.

"And what was this trade?"

"One kiss for fifty pounds," Helena announced. "And so...I kissed him." She burst into sobs.

"Just the once?" Madeline felt a sense of relief and uncurled her fist.

"Twice! And the second time wasn't even part of the trade! Madeline, does this make me a painted woman? A harlot?"

"Helena, you are not a harlot." Madeline had a very clear picture of Edward's little game and planned to blister his ears at the first opportunity. "It was wrong of Edward to flirt so shamelessly with you, but no real harm has come of it. Though perhaps it would be best not to be alone with him in the future."

"But that is the truly horrible thing. I do not wish to stay away from Edward. In fact, I believe that I am in love with him!"

"Helena," Madeline's voice turned serious. She

had not forgotten her conversation with Colin the night before. "You scarcely know the man, and though he is indeed very charming, let us not lose our heads." Helena's eyes were red and raw from crying, and Madeline could already see that this was no passing flirtation for her sensitive cousin. "Listen to me. Edward is not the kind of man who is seeking to settle down in a marriage. Do you understand?" She knew the words stung, and Helena wept bitterly against her shoulder. "I do think it would be best not to continue this."

"Do you think he is a rogue?" she whispered, her blue eyes wide.

Madeline thought for a moment, then shook her head. "No, I believe Edward is simply a young man."

"But he is older than both of us!"

"It is different for men," Madeline informed her. "They are more reckless than we are, and much less sensible." She took Helena's arm, pulling her to her feet. "Now come, let's go downstairs before Aunt Cecilia wakes up. We can do something about those horrible ermine turbans. In fact," she said, grinning wickedly, "I have just thought of the most wonderful place to get rid of them."

Helena brightened instantly. "I knew you couldn't love such an ugly thing! I was quite sure you must be pulling one over on Mama. Really, how humiliating to make us all wear them together!" Madeline nodded, dragging her cousin toward the door. "I do hate those turbans," Helena continued. "How did you become so knowledgeable about men, Madeline? It is most helpful."

"I believe it comes with age," Madeline said. And she led her cousin to the hallway, keeping her gaze firmly away from the window.

Chapter Fifteen

"Now today, girls," Aunt Cecilia began, entering the drawing room where Madeline and Helena both sat with books in their laps. She was dressed in a richly embroidered pelisse that made Madeline wonder the precise amount of the bill to Mr. Banbury.

"Today, we are going to have a proper afternoon at home, under my watchful eye." She gave them both a good stare before continuing. "I don't want any mishaps today. We have a very important ball to attend tonight and must rest our minds in preparation."

"Why is tonight's ball so very important?" Madeline asked, closing her novel. For once, she welcomed her aunt's distractions. She had been reading the same sentence for the last half hour.

"Why, indeed! I would never have expected such modesty from you, Madeline." She laughed, settling herself into her purple chair. "And after such marvelous efforts from you and Helena! Who would have thought the two of you would have managed such handsome, wealthy men, and brothers, no less!"

Madeline quickly turned to Helena, hoping the mention of Edward would not send her into tears. After a full morning of brooding and endless discussion, Madeline had managed to revive Helena's spirit, but it was precarious, at best.

"Mama." Helena snapped her own book shut with a long, shuddering breath. "What are you talking about?"

"Your lovely suitors! Now listen, darlings, I

must pay a call upon Miss Lillian. She was most insistent on seeing me this afternoon, but I shan't be an hour, and I expect you both to indulge in restful behavior." She smiled gaily at them, but Madeline saw the strain around her lips as her hands pulled nervously at her gloves. Her aunt looked terribly worried. Something was wrong.

"Is everything all right?" Madeline asked, concerned.

"Such a question!" Aunt Cecilia laughed, quickly turning away. "Now I will just dash off to Miss Lillian's and be back in time for tea. Don't read too much, girls, or you'll get a headache!" And, in a flutter of feathers, she was gone.

Madeline stared after her aunt, fearing the anxiety over their finances was taking a toll on her health. "Do you think your mother is acting oddly?" she asked Helena.

"Mama?" Helena shrugged, and Madeline was glad to see she looked more annoyed than tearful. "She is likely in a fuss over money again. Perhaps she is asking Miss Lillian to lend her some."

Madeline had her answer, as painful as it was. She stood up, too restless to resume her reading, and instead wandered over to the window to see if she could spot the direction her aunt's carriage had gone. But her aunt was nowhere to be seen. Instead, she noticed a phaeton, carrying two women, as it came flying up the street.

"Helena," Madeline said, fastening her gaze on the impeccably dressed blonde woman stepping down from the overly large carriage, "are we expecting any visitors this afternoon?"

"I'm not aware of any," she replied, running over to join her cousin at the window. "Why? Is anyone—dear God!" She shrieked as the two women approached the house.

"What is it, Helena? What's the matter? Do you

know that woman?"

"Not exactly. I mean, I know of her. I have seen her, of course, but we have never spoken. Oh, why on earth would she call on us?"

"Who?" Madeline grabbed her cousin's arm to stop her rambling. "Who is calling on us?" Helena opened her mouth to reply, but it was Jarvis's cool, unruffled tones that broke the news.

"Pardon the intrusion, Helena, Madeline." He nodded to them both, showing no reaction to the sight of two ladies peering anxiously out the front window. "Lady Juliana Reynolds is here to see you."

"It's Juliana, Madeline! Oh, why has she come here?"

True to his nature, Jarvis waited patiently while Helena finished her hysterics before turning his attention to Madeline. "Shall I show her in, my lady?"

Juliana had come to see her, without any kind of warning or introduction! What could Juliana possibly wish to speak with her about? The thought of discussing Colin with his former fiancée filled Madeline with dread.

"Of course you must show her in," Madeline said with a confident smile. "Thank you, Jarvis."

"Mildred, wait for me in the hall," Juliana commanded, her long locks still coiled perfectly despite the open carriage. She turned a sculpted smile upon the two cousins, and Madeline sincerely wished she had allowed Brigette to attend to her own hair this morning.

"Good afternoon," said the visitor, nodding to Helena who was still standing by the window, looking terrified. "You look rather more grown up this year. Is Lord Vickem still chasing after you?"

"He is most persistent," Helena replied, trying to gain control of herself. "Would you like to sit down, Juli—"

246

"And this must be Lady Madeline Sinclair." Juliana turned a pair of large, honey-colored eyes on Madeline. "I have heard a great deal about you. In fact," she continued, "the moment I set foot in London, yours was the first name I heard. Isn't that amusing?"

"I cannot think why I should be given such attentions."

"Can you not?"

Juliana smiled knowingly, and Madeline quickly looked away, suddenly aware that the proof of her night with Colin must be splashed across her face.

"I do believe I will sit, Helena. Thank you for the offer." Juliana placed herself gracefully on the couch and motioned for Madeline to join her. "Will you sit next to me, Madeline? I believe we have much to discuss."

Madeline went toward the poised woman but at the last minute chose to sit in her aunt's chair across from the couch. "I understand you have recently been abroad," Madeline said with a challenging tilt of her head. "Did you enjoy your trip?"

"Oh, yes, that," Juliana replied, as though they were speaking of a new bonnet. "Tiresome thing, traveling is. One must feign interest all the time. It's extremely exhausting." She sighed. "But I do hope for more excitement now that I am back in London, though Mother insists I spend most of my evenings at home." She looked highly irritated at this. "I am practically a prisoner."

"That must be difficult," Madeline agreed, beginning to wonder if Juliana had merely come here to complain. She struck Madeline as a typical lady of the *ton*: spoiled and selfish, able to slip on a charming persona as easily as she could don the most fashionable dress. "May I offer you a refreshment?" She turned to Helena, who had not yet moved from the window. "Shall I ring for tea?"

"You needn't bother, Madeline. I cannot stay long," Juliana said. "The truth is, I have come to discuss a very important matter with you."

Madeline dug her nails into the plush arm of Aunt Cecilia's purple chair. "Since we met only a moment ago, I cannot imagine what we have to talk about."

Juliana's laugh was like a warning bell. "Come now, we are women. We have nothing to hide from one another! I have heard that you and my Colin have become quite good friends. He's rather your champion, of sorts."

Helena let out a small squeak, but Madeline didn't dare take her gaze off Juliana's expression of nonchalance. Madeline had no idea her relationship with Colin was under such scrutiny from the *ton*. What else had Juliana heard?

"Please, don't take offense," Juliana added. "I find it all very sweet. In fact, I'm happy that he found someone to amuse him while I was away." She stood up, wandering over to the shelf of snuff boxes. "What lovely little pieces! Such exquisite taste."

"I beg your pardon," Madeline said, her patience with this game at an end. "You said you had something to discuss with me? Perhaps we should discuss it." She didn't miss the flash of annoyance across Juliana's mouth, though it was quickly replaced with another soft smile.

"Of course. Let me be blunt. I thought it best to inform you that your friendship is no longer required." She gave a triumphant look. "Now that I have returned, Colin will wish to resume *our* relationship right away."

Madeline couldn't believe what she was hearing. Had she only assumed Colin had cut all ties to Juliana after she betrayed him? Hadn't he said so?

"But you're no longer engaged," Helena blurted out from the window seat, and Juliana abruptly turned toward her; obviously she'd forgotten Helena was still in the room.

"I hardly see how that should matter," she replied tartly.

"Helena is merely making an assumption," Madeline said, crossing the room to stand next to her cousin, "that Colin would not welcome you back after your prior behavior." Madeline was pleased to see her words had succeeded in erasing the false smile.

"Colin has told you about our little mishap." Juliana stood absolutely still, sizing her up. "I had presumed he was more of a gentleman, but it seems I was mistaken. How much do you know?"

Madeline's temper flared at the command. "Enough to conclude that Colin acted as the perfect gentleman, despite your shameful behavior. And more than enough to know," she continued, her voice rising, "that Colin would never allow himself to be betrayed by you again."

"My God," Juliana said, her eyes widening in wonder. "You are in love with him, aren't you?"

Instantly speechless, Madeline took a step back, shaking her head.

"But it's true." Juliana clapped her hands together, eyes alight with the victory. "I cannot believe it. Has he taken you to his bed?"

"How dare you ask Madeline such a question!" Helena cried. "My cousin is a respectable lady, and has never done anything improper with Lord Douglas."

Madeline looked toward the ceiling, wishing to God she would be struck by lightning, or that Vickem would pay a call, anything to end this tortuous afternoon.

Juliana laughed. "You may keep your little secret, Madeline, but let me leave you with a word of caution." She walked toward the door, retying her bonnet on the way. "You are not the first lady Colin has seduced, including myself, and you will not be the last. Ask him yourself, if you don't believe me. I'm sure he will be happy to tell you of my visit to his home yesterday afternoon."

Madeline felt sick. Try as she might, she could think of no reply. Her mind was consumed with the dreadful doubt that Juliana had planted. Was it true? Had Colin seduced other women? She felt a sharp pain at the memory of his words in the garden. Had he said the same things to Juliana? Taken her to his bed?

"Colin and I have a very special bond," Juliana continued. "He will always return to me. Do you understand?"

Madeline understood perfectly. What she didn't understand was how Colin had ever become engaged to such a venomous, hateful creature as Lady Juliana Reynolds.

"Good day, Juliana," Helena replied, ushering their unwanted guest to the door with an icy glare. "Please do not feel obligated to call on us again."

****

Daniel Moore stumbled out the door of King's Tavern, hoots of laughter and raucous insults drifting behind him like a foul wind.

"Grimy bastards!" Moore shouted into the morning air. Slobbering their fat lips over their glasses of ale, pretending to listen and cheering him on until the money ran out. He stumbled again, this time falling to his knees, while his stomach lurched in protest at the violent movement. How dare they laugh at him! He was better than all of the stinking...

Moore let out a sharp curse seconds before vomiting expensive brandy onto the cold muddy earth. He sat still for a moment, dizzy but better otherwise, then shook his head hard to clear it. He needed to focus, pull himself together, and...why the hell did he leave King's?

He shrugged, scooping his hat out of the mud. After today things were going to get easy. No more begging Rockford for scraps or drinking watered-down ale with slavering idiots. He was finally going to get the money he deserved, and who knew? Maybe he'd even end up a gentleman himself.

He got to his feet, confidence returning. He was going to make them all pay, starting, he thought with a sneer, with the great Lord Rockford himself. Moore opened and closed his fists in anticipation, his hands still steady despite the drink. He was good at what he did, the best, and he deserved every bit of the fortune that diamond would bring. It was time he stopped taking orders from Rockford. He took a deep breath, forcing away the fogs of his brandy, and stumbled around the corner, only to feel a jerk, his shirt nearly pulled from his body before his back slammed against the wall.

"I've been waiting for you, Moore."

Colin held the struggling body an inch or so off the ground, one arm slung across the filthy, sweat-soaked chest. Mr. Moore obviously felt bathing was beneath him, and Colin's nostrils burned from the stench, though his grip held steady as he forced the smaller man against the bricks. It was nearly noon, and Colin's mood was not improved by the many hours spent waiting for Moore to finish his night of drinking.

"It's you," Moore gasped, his mouth working like a gaping fish. He didn't waste time asking questions, but went straight into peddling his lies. "You've got the wrong man..."

"Don't insult me," Colin snapped. "I came here to ask you some questions. And I'm warning you, Moore," he shoved him further up the wall, "if I'm not satisfied with the answers, I'll leave your dead carcass out here for the harbor boys."

Satisfied to see his threat gaining proper cooperation, Colin watched the man nod and gulp his agreement, his sallow skin whitening with terror as Colin lowered him to meet his eye.

"Where's the diamond?"

"Diamond? I'm not sure what you mean, milord, I think you have the—"

"Wrong man? Then you've got a twin running around the city attacking women. Rather bad luck, I'd say." He lifted Moore off the ground again, effortlessly slamming one fist into his midsection. "Let's see if I can aid your memory a bit, shall I? I am interested in the diamond you stole yesterday afternoon, in Hyde Park. You do recall that, don't you? Knocking Lady Madeline Sinclair to the ground and robbing her? You made a terrible mistake, Moore." Colin tightened his grip. "Madeline belongs to me."

Moore's eyes widened in fear at these words. "I don't have it! I swear to you! I took the diamond to the marquis. I never even meant to steal anything!" Moore was bleating out his story like a cornered sheep. "He was only paying me to follow your lady, but then she pulls out this diamond and tries to smash it. How could I help myself, I ask you? Take pity on me, my lord!"

"The marquis?" Colin released his hold, letting Moore drop to the dirt like a sack of wheat as his guts churned with a sudden rage. He knew it had been more than just a robbery. But had a gentleman of the *ton* actually hired this little bastard to follow Madeline?

"Who's behind this?" The deadly serious tone caused Moore's head to jerk up. "Who else knows about the French Blue diamond?"

"The French what?" Moore squeaked. "All I was supposed to do was lay low, keep my distance, so the

Lady Madeline—your lady, of course—doesn't get suspicious. How was I to know she was gonna smash up her diamond? I couldn't let a thing like that happen, my lord. It goes against my nature. So I grabbed her, maybe roughed her up just a bit..."

Too late Moore realized the error of his words as Colin knocked him back to the ground, roughly shoving one mud-splattered Hessian boot onto Moore's greasy neck.

"Shut your mouth," Colin replied to the barely audible pleas for mercy. He turned his attention toward the dirty, deserted area behind the tavern. There wasn't another soul in sight. No one had seen him arrive, and even if someone did catch a glimpse of a well dressed gentleman in the shadows, it wouldn't be the type of person who would care. Colin let his anger wash through him, placing a little extra pressure in the right place. "Who hired you?" he whispered. "Who's the man behind this?"

Moore began gurgling for air, his face turning the color of a rare steak, and Colin pressed his foot down harder as he imagined those filthy hands touching Madeline's white skin. He knew all too well what kind of man Moore was, a hired villain, likely a murderer for the right price, and his blood raged. Colin's gaze swept past Moore's face and down his coat until they centered on a pair of empty hands clawing the air. Moore's hands, void of any threat, any weapon to fight back with.

The boot lifted off Moore's neck, hovering above the gasping man as he sobbed his thanks for sparing his life.

"Thank you, my lord, I promise—"

"If you touch Madeline again, I'm going to kill you," Colin said, pulling the choking man onto his feet. "Now, for the last time, I want the name of the man who hired you—"

The sound of a gunshot spit from behind him,

cracking into the stone above their heads. Moore screamed as Colin dropped him, ducking instinctively as he turned to see who the hell was shooting at him.

"Run, man!" Another shot screeched past Colin's ear, and he slammed himself onto the ground, struggling to make out the murderous figure in the deep shadows. A friend of Moore's, no doubt. He heard the little bastard wheezing as he scrambled to his feet, heard pistol shots ringing out. Colin rolled to his side, barely escaping another wound, and the shots finally ceased. He jumped to his feet, his hand already thrust out for a fight, but it was too late.

Whirling around, Colin was just in time to see the glint as the bright noon rays of the spring sun bounced off the knife before it plunged into his chest.

Chapter Sixteen

You are not the first lady Colin has seduced.
Madeline repeated Juliana's words in her mind
while Brigette scraped back another piece of hair,
mercilessly twisting it around a pair of scalding
tongs. *Including myself...* The tiny maid was
determined to fit the entire mass into another
terrifying bun of curls, but her mistress no longer
had the strength to put up her usual protests. All of
Madeline's energy was focused on tending the
burning coals of her rage against a most villainous
scoundrel named Lord Douglas. It had been several
hours since her encounter with the viperous Lady
Juliana Reynolds, and since then her emotions had
run from confusion to fear to humiliation—until they
had settled quite comfortably on anger, a place she
felt certain they would stay for quite awhile.

"Honestly, my lady, such long hair!" Brigette
painfully dragged her from her thoughts, wrenching
another wayward piece back into place. "It's
beautiful to be sure, but impossible to curl with all
this weight. Maybe you could cut it short like your
cousin's?" she suggested hopefully. "It's very much
the fashion nowadays."

"No."

Madeline had no patience for anything as trivial
as her hair. Dressed for the Huntington affair in the
white silk ball gown adorned with clusters of pearls
and slightly wrinkled from spending the night on
her floor, she couldn't care less what she looked like.
What did it matter? Juliana had made it very clear
she was little more than a conquest, and the

memories of her midnight encounter with Colin now made her cheeks burn with shame.

But I do not regret it, she firmly reminded herself, forcing her shoulders back with pride. She ignored Brigette's shriek of protest at the sudden move, concentrating on her anger.

She had no intention of marrying, so why should she care if she was ruined? Why, look at her Aunt Cecilia! She seemed perfectly happy since her husband died, answering to no one and free to do as she chose. Who would trade all of that to spend their life with some insipid man?

"Certainly not me," Madeline muttered. But as quickly as her anger flared, it vanished, leaving her in despair. Did Juliana really pay a visit to Colin yesterday afternoon? Why didn't he tell her about it? "After going on and on about his bloody honesty," she said aloud, causing Brigette to jump with fright.

"I beg your pardon, my lady?" Brigette began, no doubt scandalized by her language. Not wishing her thoughts to be disturbed, Madeline shook her head at the maid, sending a cascade of hairpins scattering to the floor.

My first mistake, Madeline reflected, drumming her fingers together, *was becoming preoccupied by this ridiculous infatuation with Colin. How distracting he has been!* She should be relieved that it was over, allowing her to concentrate on her true purpose in coming to London. The second mistake, she continued, warming to the new ideas, was putting all of her trust in Colin. Why, look how quickly she accepted the word of a mere stranger, naïvely believing he would help. She had been in London for several weeks now and was no closer to destroying the French Blue diamond than when she arrived. She must start fresh, find the stolen diamond for herself, and push aside any feelings she might have had for Colin.

Madeline nodded hard, already feeling immensely better. "I must find this Mr. Moore," she muttered quietly. "I cannot allow anything else to distract me from my task."

"Did you say something, my lady?" Brigette said, rummaging through the pile of ribbons on Madeline's vanity table. "If you don't mind me saying so, you have a queer look about you today. Should I have Cook fetch one of her remedies?"

"I am perfectly well, thank you," Madeline replied, smiling determinedly. "And I promise to sit still now while you finish yanking on my hair." With a dainty shrug, the maid selected a pair of combs and continued with her work.

Unfortunately, searching for Mr. Moore on her own would not be easy. Where would she begin? *The tavern.* Colin went looking for Mr. Moore at some tavern near the wharf...*What was the name?* She wracked her mind but came up empty.

"Lady Milburg is requesting your presence downstairs." Jarvis's voice boomed from the hall, and this time Madeline was unable to restrain herself. She shot straight out of her chair, nearly destroying all of Brigette's hard work.

"My lady!" Brigette cried. "We will be here all night if you do not let me finish."

Madeline allowed Brigette to coax her back into the chair, trying not to panic. It was almost time to leave for the ball, and her stomach tightened at the idea of facing Colin. He would be arriving at any moment, expecting to find her smiling and happy. What would he say when she told him about Juliana?

"Perfect!" Brigette announced finally, holding the mirror up to Madeline with a look of relief and triumph. "I had my doubts, but it came out beautifully in the end. Just like the Empress Josephine."

Madeline glanced at herself in the glass. She had chosen Persephone for her costume, the beautiful maiden of spring whose forced exile in the underworld caused her mother to turn the earth into an ice-covered desert.

"Angry with grief," she whispered, her heart softening for Persephone's tragic mother. In the mirror, Madeline's large round eyes looked terrified, and her pale skin, surrounded by a cluster of curls held up with pearl-encrusted combs, gave her a vulnerable, sad look.

"Don't you feel lovely?" Brigette sighed, but Madeline pushed the mirror away.

****

"I shall hardly speak to Edward at all," Helena announced, adjusting her long coquelicot-colored gloves ("Most certainly the color of Aphrodite!" Aunt Cecilia had earlier insisted.) as she descended the stairs. "Nothing more than is strictly necessary. I shouldn't like him to think me impolite. What do you think, Madeline?"

"I think we are both going to tumble down the steps if you do not hold on to your train," Madeline replied. Her cousin gasped, quickly reaching down to swoop up the trailing lace attached to her own white gown, richly trimmed with the same bright poppy color as her gloves.

With Colin's arrival approaching, Madeline was unable to concentrate on anything else. Would he recognize her dress from last night? Her cheeks began to burn as a smoldering scene from the night before sprang into her mind. *Of course he won't.* She forced the image away. *He probably has taken off so many dresses he cannot remember them all.*

She blinked hard, surprised and angered by the sudden sting of tears. *Horrible man! He will not make me cry. I will follow Helena's lead and speak not one single word to the rakish Lord Douglas, and I hope he finds me impolite indeed.*

"I believe it's for the best, really. We certainly would not suit one another, anyone can see that, don't you think, Madeline?" Helena didn't wait for an answer, but immediately dropped her voice to a whisper when she spotted her mother. "Oh, Lord, I believe Mama is still looking for those awful turbans."

"I do not understand where they have gone!" Aunt Cecilia exclaimed, her hands carefully caressing the spotted ermine tippet draping her shoulders. "How will anyone know I am dressed as Hera, without a feathered turban? Helena, drop that lace this instant! It is meant to trail behind you on the floor like Aphrodite's seafoam."

"I believe my costume is most complete without the hat, Mama, and do not forget we also have our masks." Helena smiled innocently.

"Well, I am stunned! Brigette, whatever could have happened to our beautiful turbans?"

"I could fetch one from your collection, Lady Milburg," Brigette offered, casting a suspicious glance at Madeline and Helena.

"Of course! What excellent thinking. Bring the striped turban, if you please. But what about the girls? They shall have no head ornaments at all."

"We will be perfectly fine," Madeline said quickly, fearing what the maid might produce. "Brigette has done such an excellent work with our hair that it would be a shame to put anything on top of it."

Her aunt looked unconvinced. "Well, there's little I can do for your heads, but you shall certainly smell like goddesses. Stand still, girls, I have a new perfume, Eau d'Orange."

"Don't you find it rather strong?" Madeline jumped back, wrinkling her nose at the sharp-smelling citrus mist.

"Madeline, honestly! Persephone would never have such a dour look on her face, even during her stay in Hades." Aunt Cecilia laughed over her own wit. "And why are your spring leaves sagging? You must keep them right in the center or everyone will see how shockingly low your dress is cut."

"Lord Montgomery has arrived," Jarvis announced.

Madeline's heart dropped as she desperately pulled up the vine of silk leaves surrounding her chest. What would Colin say when he first saw her? Would he notice how angry she was? Would he take her into his arms and explain everything?

"Be strong!" she whispered, giving her cousin's hand a squeeze, though the words were for herself, as well.

"Such stunning attire! I shall be fighting the suitors off all night." Edward entered, wearing a dark blue dress coat and white mask.

"Lord Montgomery, how dashing you look!" Aunt Cecilia exclaimed. "Though I must admit I cannot make out your costume."

"Lord Poseidon, at your service, my lady." He bowed beautifully to Helena.

"Excellent costume!" Aunt Cecilia answered for her daughter, who remained stone-faced. "Though perhaps a more elaborate mask would help?"

"Thank you, Lady Milburg, but I shall not attempt to compete with all of you. Helena, you cannot be anyone but Aphrodite, goddess of love."

Madeline vaguely heard her cousin mumble something in reply, though the words escaped her. Her gaze was still fixed expectantly on the door. No one accompanied Edward? Where was Colin?

"Madeline! Lord Montgomery is speaking to you." Madeline winced as she felt a sharp pinch in her side. "I do hope you will someday grow out of all this endless daydreaming," her aunt admonished. "I cannot see what good it does you."

"It is a very becoming expression for her, Lady Milburg," Edward said with a wink at Madeline. "Lends an air of mystery, though I am quite sure I need no clues to tell me she is looking for my brother."

"Colin isn't with you?" Madeline grabbed Edward's arm, forgetting her promise to ignore Colin completely. "Where is he?"

In that brief moment before Aunt Cecilia's loud warning cough reached her ears, Madeline noted Edward looking slightly confused.

Edward hastily found his smile. "I do recall him saying something about a late appointment. I believe he plans to meet us at Huntington's."

"Well, then!" Aunt Cecilia clapped her hands together. "That's all settled. Shall we go?"

He's lying, Madeline thought, strangling the dark green fan between her fingers. *He doesn't know where Colin is.*

"Helena, may I have the honor?"

"You may not!" Helena shrieked, backing away from Edward's outstretched arm.

"Helena!" Aunt Cecilia was shocked. "What a thing to say to Lord Montgomery's generous offer." She emphasized the last words, sending Helena into a furious blush.

"What I meant to say is..." Helena looked miserable, and Madeline's heart went out to her cousin. "I would much prefer to walk alone." She hurried toward the doorway, refusing to meet Edward's confused gaze.

"You must excuse our manners, Lord Montgomery," her mother apologized. "My poor girls are most upset over our lost turbans. We had them made especially for this evening, you know. It's a terrible loss."

"A tragedy," Edward agreed, "and one you need

not apologize for."

"We are not to go anywhere without Lord Douglas," Madeline insisted, wondering why no one else seemed the least concerned Colin was missing. "Remember, Aunt? We promised him last night. You recall it, surely." She frowned at Edward, who was busy trying to catch Helena's eye.

"Oh, tosh!" Aunt Cecilia replied, ushering Helena out the door. "His dashing brother is here. He will do, of course! And I must admit, though I kept my opinions to myself last night, as I do so hate to argue with men, it vexes them so, don't you agree, Helena? But in truth, I cannot abide all this nonsense about needing escorts. I, of course, am here to serve as your most attentive chaperone!"

She flew out the door in a chatter of words, leaving Madeline with little choice but to follow or be left behind.

"Come, Madeline, my brother has not abandoned you. I'm sure there is a sound reason for his lateness."

Abandon her? Why would Edward use such a strange phrase? Was Colin unable to face her? Did he decide to flee like a coward after realizing what a terrible mistake he had made? She felt alone and ashamed, utterly ruined beneath all her finery.

"Though I do believe your cousin is ignoring me." Edward approached her, offering his rejected arm.

"I hadn't noticed a thing," Madeline replied absently, all thoughts now centered on his brother's whereabouts. Had he truly left her for Juliana, or was it something worse? She had been so swept up in Juliana's visit, its repercussions resounding in her brain, that it never occurred to her that something terrible could have happened to Colin...

"Perhaps he had an appointment this afternoon," Edward suggested. "He must have been delayed."

"He went looking for Moore!" A flood of relief washed through her as she remembered Colin's plans to find the thief. Madeline sagged a bit against Edward's arm. Perhaps she was not to be discarded after all. "At a tavern called King's. He was planning to wait for him there."

"He told you this last night?" Edward quickly lost his look of banal good humor. "And you haven't heard from him since?"

Her sense of relief instantly vanished. "I—ah, I believe he said he was planning on going early this morning," she improvised, not wishing to divulge Colin's late night visit to his brother. "But certainly he should have been back hours ago."

Edward's expression had turned serious, making him all at once less boyish. "Don't worry yourself, Madeline. I wager he is simply awaiting us at Huntington's."

"Then he isn't in any danger?" *Or with Juliana.* She no longer knew what to think, only that she desperately needed to see Colin again. Whether she would kiss him or call him a dastardly rake, she didn't quite know.

"What a question! Colin is perfectly fine," Edward replied with a quick glance at her plunging neckline. "Though he will be absolutely livid when he sees you in this dress."

Chapter Seventeen

Madeline began searching for Colin the moment she entered Huntington's masquerade ball. Lord and Lady Huntington, reigning over the room as Zeus and Hera, had spared no expense for the festivities, drenching the entire bottom floor in gold, laurels, and ivy leaves to perfect their god-and-goddess theme. The guests followed suit, bursting in with costumes so elaborate Madeline found it nearly impossible to tell the men from the women, servants from lords. Her gaze scoured the bright Grecian costumes and glittering masks, determined to find a tall, dark figure moving amongst the crowd with an arrogant grace.

Unfortunately, all she found was Vickem.

"Hatched from the very bowels of the world egg, I stand before you! Hunter, lover, archery master of the heart."

"Good God, I think he's dressed as Eros." Madeline moved to shield her cousin from sight but was too late.

"Chipmunk, do not fear. It is still I, your loving Vickem, masked for one brief night as the great god Eros, the greatest, most passionate god of them all."

"Oh, excellent costume, Vickem!" Aunt Cecilia clapped her hands. "Miss Lillian, come and see Vickem's wonderful costume." She waved to her friend, who had just arrived as Athena in a high-necked jonquil gown. "I daresay he looks just like a painting."

Helena peeped over Madeline's shoulder, letting out a small gasp at the sight of the Viscount dressed in puce-colored tights and golden wings.

"Even his bow and arrow are gold!" Helena whispered. "What on earth is he doing with it, Madeline?"

Oblivious to the growing stares, Vickem knelt down on one knee, placing the bow against his shoulder. "And now my sweetest treasure, I will perform the ceremony as old as time itself, the final act that will seal our love so that no one can ever again come between us..."

"Vickem, if you toss a single arrow at Helena, I promise I will strangle you with it." It was Edward who spoke, quietly enough to not alert the large crowd of onlookers, but menacingly enough to send Vickem to his feet.

"Oh, Lord Montgomery, you are too vile!" Miss Lillian screeched with pleasure. *At least someone is enjoying this.* Madeline kept a polite smile despite her dark thoughts.

"It is you," Vickem sputtered, backing away. "Foul villain! Destroyer of love! My golden arrows are little match for your despicable threats, Lord Montgomery." With a final glare, he darted away into the crowd.

"That man is a blight on decent society," Edward muttered, watching Vickem disappear. "I cannot imagine what you did to attract him, Helena."

"You and I are of the same mind, Lord Montgomery!" Aunt Cecilia responded. "I wonder what my daughter does to entice any young man."

"Edward, how good to find you at last." Lady Douglas appeared with Sir Lambert trailing behind her. "I do hope you are behaving yourself."

"Lady Douglas and Sir Lambert. What a surprise to find you both together this evening," Aunt Cecilia called out in an absurdly loud voice. "And how well you look, Lady Douglas. Let me guess—Zeus and Hera?"

"Acis and Galleta," Lady Douglas corrected, with a smile, before greeting Madeline warmly.

"Though I have steadfastly refused to be turned into a fountain." Sir Lambert laughed. "Good evening, Madeline." His eyes narrowed at her plain white gown, now decorated with little more than her aunt's pearl brooch. "May I guess...Aphrodite?"

"She is Persephone," Aunt Cecilia answered, "Maiden of spring, but her vine leaves were trampled in the carriage."

"How terribly awkward," Miss Lillian intoned.

"Well, I find you to be stunning, my dear." Lady Douglas smiled, sending Madeline's gaze to the ground. She could not imagine how she was supposed to look the duchess in the eye after spending the night with her son. Madeline's humiliation was complete. She hoped to God Colin appeared safe and unharmed, so she could murder him.

"Though I'm sure my Colin has already told you so," Lady Douglas continued.

"I'm afraid I cannot say, madam. Colin has not yet arrived."

"Hasn't arrived?" Lady Douglas turned sharply to Edward, who made a show of looking completely unconcerned.

"You know how my brother detests any social function. He'll be here soon."

"Oh, I'm sure Lord Douglas is just nervous," Miss Lillian said, eager to help. "Who wouldn't drag their feet a bit when they're likely to see the woman who—"

"Late, is he?" Sir Lambert boomed, dropping the hand that had previously lain upon Lady Douglas's shoulder. "One cannot keep up with young men these days, always racing about to one thing or another. Do not fret, Madeline, he'll be here presently. And for now, you can entertain me," he added with a teasing gleam in his eye.

"I'm afraid I'm not very amusing tonight," Madeline apologized.

It wasn't her imagination. Sir Lambert had most definitely stopped Miss Lillian from finishing her sentence. Why? What could the older woman possibly know that would make Lady Douglas look so terribly uncomfortable? *Perhaps Colin isn't coming at all.* A sick feeling washed over her. *What if he really is with Juliana?*

"Do you agree, Madeline?"

Too late she realized Sir Lambert had continued talking to her, and she hadn't heard a single word. "How fortunate you managed to stay dry in all this rain," she quickly blurted out. When all else fails, comment on the weather, Aunt Cecilia had advised.

"Er, yes, of course." Now Sir Lambert seemed to be at a loss for words. "Though I'm afraid I cannot take the credit myself, it must go to the skies, which have been clear as a bell all day."

She noticed her aunt, grimly shaking her head back and forth as if tolling a death knell. She supposed if a lady were to use the weather for conversation, she should look out the window once in awhile.

"You must excuse my niece, Sir Lambert. She is most upset over several new turbans that have gone missing. We were supposed to wear them tonight, you know."

"A tragedy," Sir Lambert said, turning toward the furtive whispering behind him just in time to see Helena repeatedly slap Edward's hand with her fan. "This evening is beginning to look positively fascinating."

He beamed at the small group before offering his arm with a flourish. "Perhaps a dance will cheer you up, my dear?"

"Sir Lambert!" Helena practically lunged at him.

"I must be unforgivably rude and ask that you dance the next with me. I have," she hastily improvised, "a most pressing desire to dance."

Sir Lambert could hardly refuse such a request, and, tucking Helena's small hand under his, he sallied through the door to the ballroom, casting a sympathetic shrug over his shoulder to Edward.

Lady Douglas turned an inquiring eye on her youngest son. "I am not sure what is ailing poor Helena's nerves tonight, Edward, but you are obviously to blame. What have you done to the girl?"

"I have been nothing but the most perfect of gentlemen!" Edward protested, beginning to look extremely vexed. "Yesterday I had no difficulty at all in pleasing Helena—"

"Never mind," Lady Douglas cut him off. "I would like to have a private word with you. Please excuse us, ladies." She grabbed her son's arm, pulling him forcibly away as she said quietly, "Come, fetch me a glass of wine. It will help conceal your humiliation."

Edward in tow following his mother, suddenly turned back. "Madeline, stay with your aunt," he ordered in the same high-handed voice of his brother. "I will be back in a moment."

"Of course," Madeline murmured, turning quickly so he would not see the flash of anger in her eyes. Stay with her aunt, indeed! She was not a child. If Colin felt protecting her from diamond thieves was so important, he should have had the courtesy to do it himself, she fumed.

Madeline gave what she hoped to be a compliant wave to Edward as he disappeared into the crowd before quickly turning to Miss Lillian.

"There is poor Agnes again. How ill she looks!" Aunt Cecilia said, as though surprised the last hour of festivities had not brought bloom into her cheeks.

"Well, she certainly should be," Miss Lillian

sniffed. "She's only just had her heart broken, and in a rather humiliating fashion, too, I should say."

"What do you mean?" Madeline asked, for once intrigued by the gossip.

"Lord Rockford broke off their courtship," Miss Lillian whispered with delight. "He is refusing to marry her after all. Can you imagine?"

"No," Aunt Cecilia breathed. "Why on earth?"

"No one can say, but..." Miss Lillian's voice dropped to a whisper. "My finest source tells me Lord Rockford is in love with another."

"I don't believe it," Madeline said, shocked that Lord Rockford would be so careless.

"There can be no other explanation," Miss Lillian replied vehemently, leaving Madeline questioning the existence of her source.

Aunt Cecilia moved off, calling for wine, with Miss Lillian in her wake, chaperone duties forgotten as she faded into the crush of costumes.

Madeline picked up her own skirt, her fury with Colin growing with every moment she stood alone in the middle of this ridiculous affair. She did not need his permission to walk about! She could certainly go anywhere she pleased. Who was to stop her? And with a final glare in Edward's direction, she slipped on her mask and disappeared.

****

"Colin, my darling! Are you hurt? Oh, stop the carriage, it's my Colin! We must help him."

Colin awoke to the sound of Juliana's hysterics as she ordered her footman to lift him off the ground.

"What the hell is going on?" Colin demanded, unable to make out why exactly Juliana was standing over him, tugging at his arm.

"You are awake!" she gasped, kissing his cheek. "Thank God for that. Now just lie still, and James shall have you up in no time." She snapped her fingers at the boy holding Colin's other arm, who looked terrified at the prospect of lifting the larger man.

"What is it, Julie?" another woman called loudly from the carriage, her voice like a wasp's sting. "Is it a vagrant? Get James to toss him out of the way."

"It isn't a vagrant at all, Mother. It's Colin!" Through dazed eyes, Colin caught a glimpse of the countess, her lips turned downward in obvious dissatisfaction at the whole event. She peered skeptically at him through a pair of spectacles.

"For the love of heaven, what is Lord Douglas doing lying in the street like a dirty commoner?"

"Hold fast, sir, we'll get you right up," the boy wheezed.

"James, I demand you let go of me this instant before you kill yourself." Colin forced himself to sit up, shaking off the footman as he rubbed a strange, dull throb in the center of his chest. Then the memory hit him. He'd been stabbed. By Moore.

He made the mistake of repeating this aloud, instantly setting Juliana off into a frenzy.

"Stabbed! Who would commit such a heinous crime! Are you bleeding? Let me get a look at it."

"There isn't a trace of blood," Colin said, standing up to keep Juliana from unbuttoning his riding jacket to get a better look. "I know I saw a knife, I threw up my hands to stop it, but someone must have hit me from behind." He rubbed his hand against the painful knot just above the base of his neck. The blow was very well aimed, one that meant to kill him if the knife failed.

"Hit you, sir!" James was appalled.

"I could have sworn the knife went in," Colin began, clearly recalling the sharp glint of the blade coming toward him.

"Julie! Get back in the carriage before he spills mud on your gown!"

Everyone ignored the countess as Colin

investigated the deep tear in his jacket. There was something hard beneath. "It was my pocket watch," he said, both stunned and gratified by the discovery.

"Your watch, sir?"

"It stopped the knife." He held the small golden circle, a gift from his father when he'd graduated Oxford. "See? There's a hole in the front of my jacket, right where the watch was kept, but it doesn't go any farther."

"They were aiming for your heart, sir." The footman looked grave. "We'd best call a doctor to look at you."

Colin shook his head, still rubbing away the sharp sting. The men obviously hadn't bothered to check whether their murderous work was done. They had left him there, merely unconscious, and without the name of the man who had hired them to follow Madeline...

Madeline! Panic set in his heart as he looked frantically around for Phinneus. It was nearly dark now. Hours must have gone by while he was lying in the mud, and Madeline was at Huntington's ball, helpless and alone.

"What unbelievable luck that we came upon you at such a time!" Juliana said, clinging to his arm with a coy smile. "It truly must have been fate, Colin, don't you think? A chance to be together again."

But Colin was no longer listening, his mind filled with the terrible things that could be happening to his Madeline. He couldn't bear to lose her now; he'd only just realized how empty his life was without her, how meaningless. There was no time to lose.

"Juliana, where were you headed?" he asked, his gaze taking in her shockingly low-cut ice blue evening gown.

"Why, to the Huntington ball! I am already a bit

late, but Mother insisted on having the most awful row with me over this dress." She leaned in closer, and Colin wondered how any woman could have let her daughter outside in such attire. "She is a beastly woman to live with, Colin. I fear not marrying you has been a horrible mistake."

As if on cue, a high-pitched shout rang out again. "Is anyone listening to me? I insist we leave this instant. I will not be seen aiding common men in the streets!"

"Juliana," he interrupted, taking a firm step away from her. "I couldn't care a whit about your mistakes. I am in love with someone else, and I need you to take me to her. Now."

****

Finding her way about in such a crush was proving to be a nightmare task.

The same chaos and confusion that had aided her escape from Edward's watchful eye now became a barrier. Aunt Cecilia was nowhere to be seen, and Madeline despaired ever finding her way amongst the churning colors and glittering masks.

Two garish figures, dressed as what she assumed to be Eurydice and Orpheus, judging from the handmade stringed instrument in the man's arms, passed her by. Orpheus managed to slide one hand down Madeline's hip before she slapped it. "A feisty little Aphrodite, eh?" he hooted, sailing away, leaving Madeline fuming and a little desperate. She knew she could not remain alone for long. Edward was likely already searching for her, preparing another lecture.

And this time, Madeline thought, brushing at the sticky handprint on her dress, *I cannot disagree with him.*

Darting around an enormous circle of Heras, Madeline headed to the side of the ballroom, hoping to find it less crowded. She was wrong. The crowd grew thicker, and Madeline felt herself pushed toward the back corner of the room, where candles seemed to have burned lower, for it was rather dark and more ominous, tossing dark shadows across the wall and making it harder to distinguish the figures behind their masks. She suddenly tripped over the trailing train of an Aphrodite and pitched forward into the arms of a tall figure in a black-and-silver mask.

"Persephone," the man said, slowly taking in her costume, and Madeline wished to God she had not lost her leaves. "Queen of the Underworld."

Trembling, Madeline untangled herself. She needed no extra candlelight to recognize him. Lord Rockford gave her a long smile, like a tiger opening its jaws.

"Even your mask looks fearful, Madeline. Do I make you nervous?"

"Not at all," she lied, grateful he could not fully read her expression behind the mask. She took a deep breath to calm herself. "You are the first to guess my costume correctly," she said, rather impressed. "Everyone else believes I am simply another Aphrodite."

"Ah, but they don't have the advantage I do." Lord Rockford adjusted his golden hat, which Madeline now saw was more of a helmet, and bowed to her. "May I introduce myself as Hades, Lord of the Underworld, and your husband, Persephone."

"A strange coincidence." Madeline swallowed hard, feeling a bit faint.

"Perhaps, or perhaps we were meant to make such a choice." Lord Rockford looked deadly serious, lifting his mask to see her better. "Your mother also had a particular fondness for Persephone. 'I heard the footfall of the flower spring,'" he quoted.

"I am not my mother," Madeline said, her eyes knowingly meeting his. "I would never make the

273

choices she did, that you made together."

Lord Rockford's lips drew tight around his mouth.

"I haven't forgotten. It pains me to see our friendship extinguished so quickly over mistakes of the past."

"It had to be done," Madeline explained. "Under such circumstances, it is the best for everyone."

"Is it?" He turned away from her, idly surveying the crowd. "I am surprised to find you all alone. Has Lord Douglas abandoned you for the delectable Juliana?"

"Why would you ask that?" she demanded, her back stiffening.

"I was merely curious." He shrugged. "And they did just arrive together."

Madeline whirled to look toward the entrance to the ballroom, and her heart dropped. It was true. Though she had feared it all night, she still couldn't believe her own eyes. Colin was walking through the crowd, his dark head several inches above the other guests, and there, hanging on his arm as though she belonged there, was Juliana.

Lord Rockford was the first to speak. "I do hope I haven't distressed you, Madeline."

She shook her head, barely able to hear him. "Papa was right," she whispered. Colin had betrayed her, humiliated her. "I never should have come to London." She watched as Juliana paused to speak softly in Colin's ear, her eyes gazing lovingly into his.

Lord Rockford took her gently by the elbow, turning her away from the sickening scene. "I believe you should sit down, Madeline. Let me find you a glass of wine."

"How could he?" Madeline cried softly. Coming to London had been such a terrible mistake! She didn't belong amongst the glittering intrigue and casual betrayals of this soulless city. There had been a moment, in Colin's arms, when she thought perhaps she could stay, build a life in London society, but now...

"I must leave. I will fulfill my promise and return home immediately." She spoke aloud, no longer caring who heard her. What did it matter now? Her heart was shattered, her future meaningless.

"Please, let me find you a chair, Madeline. You've gone quite pale."

"I don't want to sit down, thank you." Madeline turned to the man who had betrayed her father, had tried to run away with her mother. He had once offered to help her. Did she dare trust him? Did she have a choice? "Tell me, if I were to ask you the name of a tavern, would you know it?"

"That depends. There are a great many taverns in London, nearly one on every street corner."

"Yes, but this one is very particular, a terribly seedy place by the docks. King's something..."

"King's Crown."

"That's the one!" She tore off her mask, earlier fears gone in her excitement. "Do you know it?"

"I have heard of it, yes." He smiled ruefully. "Enough to know it is not at all a proper establishment for a lady. What could you possibly want there?"

"I'm looking for a man who frequents this place. He..." She hesitated. How much should she tell him? "He stole something that belonged to me."

"And this item he stole, it is important to you?"

"Very important," Madeline stressed, thinking of the blue diamond. "I must find it. I cannot leave London until I do."

Lord Rockford seemed lost in thought for a moment, running his hand along his chin. "And you wish to leave London then?"

"Immediately."

He smiled, his mouth relaxing as if he had finally solved a great dilemma. "Then I will help you."

****

"Where the hell is Madeline?"

Colin barked the question at his brother, not bothering to listen for the reply as he scanned the room for her dark shining tresses. He was in a foul mood, a fighting mood, and his fists curled in anticipation of a good brawl. The ride here had been agony, his imagination torturing him with thoughts of what could have happened to his Madeline, alone and unprotected, while Juliana did her damnedest to seduce him.

"I told you never to let her out of your sight," he continued, seriously considering punching some sense into his brother. "Why would you bring her to such a damned crowded place?" His lecture was interrupted by the sight of London's most respectable lords and ladies running around like errant children. What the hell was going on at this ball? He still saw no sign of Madeline, but he did manage to spot General Timmons dashing by, dressed in what looked to be peacock feathers. He stared at the bizarre costume. *Perhaps my own sanity is slipping.*

"And what in God's name are you wearing?" Colin shouted again, for the first time noticing Edward's mask, which he now regarded with extreme suspicion. Had everyone gone mad?

"It's a masquerade ball," Edward snapped, matching Colin's tone. "And if you could control your discourteous bellows, you would see Madeline is directly behind you, perfectly sound."

Colin spun around, spotting Madeline only a few feet away, standing next to Lady Milburg, who was staring in horror at the two shouting brothers.

She was safe.

Colin found he could breathe again, slowly allowing the tension to drain from his chest as he drank in the sight of her. She was dressed as a goddess, tall and majestic in a bone-white Grecian gown, the long waves of hair spilling down her back held by pearls above her ear. She was truly magnificent, and nearly naked. "Where the hell are her clothes?" he bellowed, his eyes narrowing at the immodestly low-cut bodice.

"She decided not to wear any," Edward replied, crossing his arms. "I agreed to keep her safe in your absence, not keep her dressed. Believe me, the first part was trying enough."

"What do you mean?"

"Everyone in the room saw you enter the ball with Juliana," Edward replied. "You should have worn a mask and used some discretion. What the hell were you doing?"

"It's not what you think," Colin muttered, annoyed that his brother thought so little of him. "It's taken me half an hour to get her off my arm. The woman is a viper. She isn't nearby, is she?" They both turned in unison to look behind them, but saw only a group of women dressed as Aphrodite.

Colin felt his shoulders tense. He had been hoping Juliana's trip would be a permanent one, but he should have known she wouldn't stay out of London for long, scandal or no.

Edward shook his head. "She's been dragged off by her mother."

"That won't last," Colin replied. It amazed him how little feeling he had for Juliana. It seemed another lifetime when he had planned to marry her. She so completely paled in comparison to Madeline, Colin couldn't recall why he ever proposed to the woman in the first place.

"If you see Juliana, keep her away from me. I'm

going to talk to Madeline." He started off, but Edward stopped him.

"There's something else you should know," he began sheepishly. "When I was talking with mother, Madeline disappeared and..."

"For God sake, Edward, what is it?"

"I found her talking with Lord Rockford."

"Damn." She had promised him, had sworn she would stay away from Rockford. Why wouldn't the stubborn woman listen?

"And she is perfectly furious at you," Edward said, his amiable tone returning. "Believes you have abandoned her, or some outrageous notion."

"She told you this?"

"I heard her talking to Helena. I tried to intervene, but you cannot talk any sense into those women. I nearly had to drag Madeline away from Lord Rockford. She threatened to kick me! And earlier, in the carriage, Helena called me a black-hearted eel. Can you imagine? I don't even know what that means."

Despite everything, Colin suddenly wanted to laugh, his brother looked so perplexed. "I take it you have fallen from Helena's graces, as well?"

"I don't understand it, Colin. Helena and I have always gotten on. She used to be so...inviting toward me, but now whenever I step into the room, she either runs away or insults me."

Colin slapped Edward's arm in sympathy. "Perhaps your charm has worn thin."

"I'm glad you find this so amusing," his brother muttered back. "You will need your sense of humor when Madeline gets hold of you."

Colin lost his grin. He stole another glance at Madeline, rigid as a queen while Lady Milburg related another of her animated stories. She had certainly seen him but stubbornly refused to meet his gaze. Instead, she very deliberately turned away, pushing a lock of hair from her shoulder while pretending to listen to her aunt.

Even rigid with anger she was still the most beautiful woman he'd ever seen. He couldn't keep his gaze off her, could see every curve of her shape under the flimsy fabric. *And apparently I'm not the only one*, he realized with a start and proceeded to glare several passing men into submission.

"I'm sure after you finish groveling at her feet she will forgive you." Edward had noted where his sibling's attention lay. "Now, tell me where the hell you've been."

"I'll fill you in later," Colin said, already leaving his brother behind. "It's a long story, and I need to speak with Madeline."

Colin made his way toward Madeline's icy back and was immediately besieged by her aunt.

"Lord Douglas, we had given you up for lost! Miss Lillian thought a centaur must have carried you away." A chorus of laughter broke out at her aunt's statement, which Colin ignored, trying in vain to catch Madeline's eye.

"But honestly, sir, where is your costume?" she sputtered, clearly mortified for him. "Did you not realize this is Huntington's masquerade ball?"

"Terribly embarrassing," Colin said, not the least bit bothered. "I had mistaken this house for the Grand Palace." A brief pause followed, in which Lady Milburg seemed to be weighing his sanity, and then she and Miss Lillian broke into laughter.

"You are too terrible, sir!" she chuckled, beaming at him. "Imagine showing up at court this way! Very amusing, indeed." He nodded his thanks, noticing Miss Lillian still eying him suspiciously from inside her enormous yellow hat.

"I do apologize," he explained. "I had a slight mishap on my way here and was unable to change." This sentence he addressed directly to Madeline, but she deliberately turned her head away, Helena's small white glove placed protectively on her arm.

"Do not fret, Lord Douglas. We shall not abandon you to your humiliation." Miss Lillian smiled coyly at him, smoothing down the top of the dress where she had put a bit too much of herself on display. "I'm sure one of the servants can stir up something for you to wear."

"A cape, at least!" Lady Milburg chimed in. "It won't do to have everyone laughing at you."

"I am in your debt," Colin murmured, refusing to take advice from anyone who would don a striped turban with a fake bird protruding from the side. "Thank you for thinking of me."

"Well, you certainly could use a proper lady to see to these things. I suppose you wish to speak to my niece." Lady Milburg raised her voice to be sure Madeline heard her. "She is incredibly cross this evening, something I attribute to you, Lord Douglas. I do hope you plan to be charming."

Lady Milburg slid off before he could reply, presumably in a hurry to find him a glittering mask or some tights. Colin sighed. He wished to God he could forego all this nonsense, drag Madeline off into a dark corner somewhere, and kiss her senseless.

"Edward claims you are ignoring him."

Colin's voice sent a jolt of desire through Madeline's veins, which she instantly quelled. *So, he has finally come to beg for an apology. Well, I am not as easily persuaded as my aunt.*

"Don't be ridiculous." She turned, flipping her fan coldly. "Helena and I have tolerated your obtuse brother with our most charming manners, isn't that right, cousin?"

Poor Helena looked like a doe caught in a trap. Her pixie-like face was scrunched up in a rare look of defiance, all directed at Colin, of course, yet she struggled to subdue the tears that suddenly sparkled in her eyes.

"Earlier this evening, when he commented on the fine music, I replied, 'Do be quiet, Edward, no one cares,' in a most respectful tone."

"There!" Madeline smiled triumphantly. "You see? Edward should have nothing to complain about. In fact," she continued, enjoying the stupefied look on Colin's face, "I would say Helena and I should be doing the complaining. After all, we were the ones being held prisoner and bossed about for no reason."

"Interesting," Colin mused, glancing back and forth between her and Helena. "This certainly explains Edward's theory."

"And what is that?" she asked haughtily.

"That the two of you together defy any notion of logic."

She wanted to slap the smile right off Colin's face, but Helena's sudden sobbing interrupted her violent thoughts, and she was forced to scramble for a handkerchief.

"And you are mistaken about my brother. He did have a good reason."

Madeline wiped at Helena's face, unexpectedly finding herself trapped in Colin's heated gaze. Her heart immediately began beating its treacherous thump, conjuring up several memories of his hard, demanding mouth. "What reason is that?" she snapped.

"I told him to protect you."

"Please excuse me," Helena choked out, grasping the lacy handkerchief. "I should go and find my mother."

"What in God's name is wrong with Helena?" Colin asked, staring after her.

"She is in the throes of an inconvenient love," Madeline replied impatiently. "And how dare you presume I need your protection, without even consulting me! You are a horribly arrogant man."

Colin let out a long breath as though praying for patience. "Madeline, I have already apologized for being late. How difficult are you going to make this?"

"Very difficult," she snapped. "If my conversation bothers you, why don't you go and find your Juliana? I'm sure she has much more pleasant things to say."

"She is not *my* Juliana," he nearly shouted. "How the hell could I have known that she would drive up—"

"I don't want to hear another word," she interrupted. "I have listened to enough of your lies. Tell me," she added, all the worry and anguish of the last hours bubbling to the surface, "is this a usual occurrence for you, sir? Do you make a habit of climbing into ladies' windows, or do they normally just open their doors?"

"What do you mean by that?" He was plainly startled by the question. "I was not climbing in anyone's windows, Madeline. I was being assaulted in the street."

Madeline's fan fell to the floor. "Someone assaulted you? What happened?"

"It was Moore," he replied, looking grim. "And he wasn't alone. Someone else was waiting for me. I was set up."

Madeline gasped. She had been right! He had been in danger! And all this time she'd allowed her jealousy to overcome her...

"So you haven't...abandoned me for Juliana?" Her gaze went searching over his body for any sign of injury. How could she ever forgive herself for believing Juliana's lies? She had been so blindly furious, only thinking of her anger, when all this time Colin was wounded and alone.

"I wasn't hurt," Colin said softly, reading her thoughts. "A slight bump on the head, nothing more. And I swear, on my very life, there is nothing between Juliana and me."

Despite the roomful of overeager eyes, he quickly reached out and squeezed her hand, the pad of his thumb pressed warmly against the thin silk of her glove. Madeline swallowed hard. The raw tenderness etched on his face nearly sent her into a flood of tears worse than Helena's. She could have stayed there forever, rooted to Lord Huntington's marble floor, her hand in Colin's, focused only on the sparks of desire between them.

"Lord Douglas, aren't we having the most marvelous time? Look what I have found! Lady Huntington has given me the most splendid mask for you to wear."

Aunt Cecilia's voice sliced between them like a blade, causing Madeline to drop Colin's hand with a guilty smile.

"How kind of you to bring a mask for Colin. I'm sure he's very grateful," she said, trying not to laugh at Colin's outraged expression.

"It's pink," he aptly pointed out.

"Now I do believe the correct name of the color is coquelicot. Isn't it lovely? We didn't want you to feel left out of the festivities."

Unable to stop herself, Madeline envisioned Colin wearing the frilly pink mask and began to giggle.

"Ah! A pleasant expression at last from you, Madeline. It must have been the wine." Her aunt smiled knowingly at Miss Lillian, who had just popped up and was utterly scandalized.

"Madeline and Lord Douglas are standing much too close!" Miss Lillian hissed from beneath her hat. "People are beginning to whisper, Cecilia."

Aunt Cecilia took a drink out of her own glass and patted her feathers. "Such a damp rag you are tonight, Lillian! But you are probably right. Lord Douglas, do be so kind as to take a few steps back.

We don't want to cause any gossip, do we?"

Madeline couldn't decide what was more humiliating, creating a scene with Colin, or her aunt's obvious descent into drunkenness. She shot Colin a look of apology, but he merely bowed to her aunt and Miss Lillian.

"I have been swept up in the excitement of the evening. I do apologize." He smiled, accepting the pink mask with a gracious air. "Perhaps I may beg the next dance with Madeline?"

"Of course, of course." Her aunt's glass of Madeira sloshed dangerously about. "It's exactly what I told Miss Lillian: they are only having a bit of fun. Didn't I say that, Miss Lillian? But she did insist I come over and exercise my chaperone duties. Miss Lillian's a bit of a damp rag," she whispered.

"Oh, do be quiet, Cecilia. You're making as much fuss as the young people." Miss Lillian sternly took hold of Madeline's arm, pulling her farther from Colin. "Do not forget you have already promised the next dance to Sir Rawlings. He is approaching right now."

Sir Rawlings! Madeline had completely forgotten her promise to dance with him. She turned to Colin with a silent plea for help. Her aunt was painfully foxed from too much wine, and they had already attracted too much attention for one night. But she must speak to Colin alone! Relieved that he had not been rekindling his romance with Juliana, she felt weak. But what had happened with Moore? And where was the French Blue?

"Oh, look, it is Sir Rawlings! Madeline, didn't you promise to dance with him?" Her aunt turned to greet the man, spilling a few droplets of Madeira on Miss Lillian's dress and thereby causing the elder woman to emit a piercing shriek.

"Behind the front stairs is another hallway," Colin murmured softly in her ear, taking full advantage of the sudden chaos. "I will wait for you there." And he slipped away, vanishing at the very moment of Sir Rawlings's arrival.

"Douglas," Sir Rawlings began in a loud, jovial voice, handing Miss Lillian a peacock-colored handkerchief. "Where did he go?" he asked, dumbfounded.

"Good evening," Madeline said, paying little attention to his sputters. She sighed softly, still feeling the slight tingling of Colin's fingers on her skin. To the surrounding crowd, Lord Douglas had done nothing more than touch her faintly on the elbow, but to Madeline it had been as intimate as a kiss.

"Ah, yes...good evening," Sir Rawlings replied, pulling himself together. "I had thought...it looked like you were all rather in distress."

"In distress?" She wasn't sure if she'd heard correctly; her mind was suddenly wrapped in a dreamy fog.

"You're trembling, Madeline. Has Douglas said something to offend you?"

"Of course not." She barely looked at him as she spoke, her gaze still following Colin's dark head through the crowd. "What would make you think such a thing?"

Chapter Eighteen

Aunt Cecilia must be looking for me. Madeline knew full well her aunt was likely measuring the hours by cups of wine. The ball had moved into utter chaos, sending anyone with a decent chaperone home long ago. She pulled her mask off, grateful for the blast of cool air that hit her forehead. Her gaze flickered past the streams of dresses and feathers and she marveled at how advantageous the crowd could be to young ladies who wished for secrecy.

Madeline slipped quickly down the staircase, pausing briefly at the bottom to hide behind a large green silk screen. She carefully peeked out, searching the immense entrance hall for any sign of a wayward servant or late-arriving guest. Finally satisfied she was alone, Madeline crept around to the back of the staircase as Colin had instructed. There she did indeed find another hallway that led farther inside Huntington Manor and away from the bright cheery background of the masquerade ball.

The hallway was quiet, dimly lit by a few forgotten candles, and Madeline watched the shadows bounce off the walls before her like spirits bobbing in the dark. The sharp click of her shoes on the cold marble floor screamed her presence with every step, heightening her already mounting anxiety.

Resisting the urge to turn and run, Madeline continued toward a flicker of light ahead. A tall candelabra awaited her, burning fiercely in its twisted iron, the sickly yellow wax forming a small puddle at her feet. She quickly stepped back, turned toward the wall, and let out a shriek of horror. The light from the candelabra revealed rows of pale, bodiless faces all staring down at her with grave foreboding. Their colorless, empty eyes gave her a chill reminder of her father's face the night he died, piercing her heart with pain. Just as Madeline cried out again and turned to flee, she heard her name. Soft as a feather it floated through the hall, and, frozen, she squeezed her eyes tight to keep out the ghosts.

Silence. A moment passed, and she heard nothing more.

Enough of this, Madeline finally reprimanded herself. *I will not indulge these childish fears.* Brushing a hand over her eyes, she forced them open and drew a deep breath, grateful to find the faces were nothing more than marble statues of Greek warriors, their glares of mistrust quite fitting for such vengeful men.

Madeline sighed with relief. They were just statues, nothing more than Lord Huntington's homage to his love of Greek art. It was little wonder Lady Huntington kept them hidden back here, Madeline thought with a smile. She could imagine what her aunt would think of such garish creatures. Released from her fright, she started to laugh, but a hand shot out from the darkness, cutting off the sound. Madeline's fear returned like a bolt of lightning through her veins, and she went numb. Before she could react, her attacker's arm had encircled her waist and abruptly pulled her backward, forcing them both into the tiny alcove behind one of Lord Huntington's foreboding heads. Madeline began to struggle when a familiar deep voice rasped in her ear.

"Be silent, Madeline." The hand then reached up to douse the candelabra, plunging them into darkness.

"Charles, love, are you quite sure no one will see us?" A peal of laughter made her freeze, and Madeline gripped her skirt in one hand to keep the silk from rustling.

"I would simply perish if someone discovered us together," a female voice squealed. "Could you imagine?"

The woman certainly wasn't worried about anyone hearing her, Madeline thought crossly. She could barely make out the two figures coming toward them in the weak light. A young woman in a dark gold gown with a plunging neckline stumbled by, holding on for dear life to the arm of her suitor, whose disheveled appearance showed he was in much the same state of drunkenness.

"Don't worry yourself, my darling Aphrodite. No one even knows about these rooms." Charles hiccupped so violently he nearly lost his balance. "We'll be back upstairs before your beauty has a chance to be missed." They were both flushed, giggling like naughty children as he swung open one of the doors and ushered the woman inside.

"Charles, it's so dark—oh!"

Madeline heard the door slam shut, sweeping the silence back over the hallway.

"Seems I wasn't the only one with this idea." Colin dropped his hand from her mouth.

Madeline whirled around, furious. "What are you doing?" she hissed, so relieved to see it was Colin that she smacked him on the shoulder. "I thought you were an evil spirit!"

"Of course you did," Colin sighed, pulling her into his arms. "Despite my calling out your name three times before Wakefield descended upon us with his guest."

"You called my name?" Madeline shivered, grateful for the feel of his warm, solid hands on her back. "It sounded so ghostly."

"You were making enough noise to wake the dead," he replied, wryly, leaning down to nibble her neck. "Not that I mind your screams, but still, I'd rather they were directed at me than at unsightly statues."

"Colin!"

Ignoring her protest, Colin kissed her, his mouth sweeping away the last of her fears, reminding her of the passion she had been yearning for ever since he'd left her that morning. His tongue swept inside to taste her, and she didn't make him wait. Grabbing him by the lapels of his dark jacket, Madeline kissed him back, eager to rekindle the fire between them, biting his lower lip in response.

"I missed you," he whispered huskily in her ear, and before she could reply, the door across from them opened, revealing the bulky shadow of Charles peering into the hallway. Madeline and Colin froze, their lips still pressed together, not daring to move.

"There you are!" Charles called out drunkenly, and Madeline tensed, positive they had been discovered.

"Found your shoe, Urina." He leaned down to scoop up a white slipper, tossing it triumphantly behind him. Urina's shrill voice answered him with a string of compliments on his manhood, before Charles once again disappeared behind the door.

"And you obviously missed me." Colin's voice emerged from the dark. She couldn't make out his face but had a feeling it was plastered with an arrogant grin.

"I am still angry with you," she replied, trying to concentrate on something other than his mouth. "Why are we here?"

He shrugged and pulled her closer. "Privacy."

After a long moment they parted, both of them shaking. "We should go," Madeline said, trying to push him away but unable to remove her hand from his chest. "Someone will see us."

"They won't," Colin reassured her, letting his hand glide idly down the side of her neck, making her dizzy. "Anyone coming down this hallway tonight has their own reasons to keep quiet, as I'm sure you've noticed. You recognized the Marquis of Wakefield, I presume?"

Her mouth dropped open. "The duke's son?"

He nodded, enjoying her outrage. "And believe me when I tell you that was not his wife."

Colin took her hand and pulled her farther down the hall and into another of the closed rooms, shutting the door firmly behind them. They were pitched into darkness, the only light a faint glow from the moon outside, and Madeline's heart thumped wildly in anticipation.

"Do you think they saw us?" she asked. She felt oddly safe with Colin tonight, the tension she'd carried the last week draining away, leaving her reckless. He shook his head with a wicked grin and lit a single candle, revealing a roomful of books and a stone fireplace. Could this be Lord Huntington's library?

"I think they are fully occupied with one another." He lifted his hand to her cheek, painting the skin with his fingertips.

"Are there others who sneak down here?" she asked, fascinated. "Looking for 'privacy'?" She repeated his word, blushing a bit.

"You'd be surprised at the lords and ladies who hide away during a ball."

Her jaw dropped, making him laugh.

"What on earth are they all doing?" Madeline couldn't help but ask. She wondered if her Aunt Cecilia knew about such things. The lectures about going off alone began to make more sense.

"This."

Colin pulled her to him. His mouth captured

hers, crushing her against him. There was no teasing this time, no soft nibbling. Colin's fervor had reached a new intensity, and she embraced it, matching it with her own. This time Madeline felt no fear or embarrassment at the force of his passion, only a rich excitement that left her desperate for more. She pressed back against him, the fire that had built throughout the night exploding in one kiss.

She protested as he broke away, then sighed with pleasure when he swirled the tip of his tongue on her ear, where he proceeded to whisper what he planned to do to her. It was the most inappropriate list of things she'd ever heard, and Madeline's knees nearly buckled before he slid down her neck to resume his attack. Her hands finally were able to rid him of his jacket, tossing it to the floor. She slid her hands into his shirt, moaning at the feel of his skin, like hot metal. She wound her hands around his neck and held on as he knelt down to press his lips against the soft silk between her legs. She would have certainly fallen to the floor if he hadn't been holding her up, his hands firmly on her backside, while he pressed against the sheer fabric with his mouth. *A pity my dress is in the way*, Madeline thought before floating into a passionate oblivion.

A deliciously long time passed before Colin stood up again, pulling her to him like a man dying of thirst. "I cannot wait," he whispered. Running his hands up her legs, he lifted her, holding her inside the flimsy dress. Madeline moaned. She'd never known such an erotic feeling as this and prayed it would go on forever, while he laid her beneath him on the large couch, his hands already pulling away her chemise.

"I've dreamed about making love to you like this," he rasped in her ear. "So sweet and groaning in my arms."

She shook her head, his words turning her to

jelly. "You make it sound inevitable."

Colin smiled down at her, the grey-blue eyes smoky with something she could not read. "It is, Madeline."

She pulled him down for another kiss, ravenous for the taste of him. She loved when he spoke her name, slow and leisurely with a hint of male pride as though she belonged only to him. She writhed beneath him until he held her hip with the one hand that had worked its way up the inside of her skirt while the other freed her breasts from the thin fabric.

Pleased with his handiwork, Colin trailed his tongue down her pale skin, taking one bright nipple between his teeth. She was gasping now, unable to hold onto any thoughts, all her concentration fixed on not crying out at what he was doing to her.

When his hand slid onto her thigh, she grew bolder, moving toward the waistband of his pants. His groan told her he liked what she was doing, and Madeline plunged her hand inside to explore until she found what she sought and caressed it gently between her fingers.

Colin jolted as though hit by lightning, and she pushed against him harder, seeking to touch him as he was touching her, loving the hard feel of him in her hand. It was a long moment before she heard him calling her name, dragging her back to the surface.

"Madeline, love, open your eyes and look at me." After a short struggle she obeyed, blinking up to find him both amused and strained. Had she done something wrong?

"Did I hurt you?" She brushed back a lock of his hair that had fallen into his eyes, and Colin laughed.

"I wouldn't care if you did, but Madeline, you don't have to..." He broke off as she touched him with her tongue, desperate to resubmerge herself in the wondrous abyss she had just discovered.

"God, your mouth is so incredibly hot." His groan broke through her haze. Why did the man insist on talking so much? She tried to pay attention, but it was very difficult. Half her clothes had been removed, Colin was lying on top of her naked to the waist, and she had been doing her damnedest to take off his pants.

"You should stop," he whispered harshly.

"I don't want to stop." She grabbed him by the hair, pulling him down to her again. "Will you show me what to do? I wish to know everything you do, Colin."

He stared at her for a long moment before giving in, smiling at her enthusiasm. "You're impossible to argue with, my love. I'll show you anything you'd like, though you're doing quite well on your own."

She didn't speak anymore; she couldn't, really, for Colin had relieved her of the remains of her dress, flipped her over, and dipped his head between her naked legs.

"Colin!" She bit her hand to keep from screaming, from alerting the entire household that Colin was performing the most erotically delicious sensation she had ever known.

He stretched himself on top of her, and Madeline gasped loudly at the sheer pleasure of the contact of his body on top of hers. He kissed her most intimate place, his tongue sweeping inside to fulfill all the sinful promises he'd whispered so erotically in her ear. Madeline would have begged for more if she'd had any breath left in her body. Instead, her eyes widened when he delved into her once again.

A long time later, when every last nerve in her body was screaming for release, Colin lifted her hips, easing in. "I'll go slow," he whispered.

"Don't you dare," Madeline answered back, and it was all the permission he needed. Colin's response was explosive. He drove into her, mimicking the action with his tongue as he held her against him, pressing her further back with his passion until they both fell off the couch and onto the floor.

"Are you hurt?"

She surfaced from the watery haze of their intimacy and realized he was looking down at her with the most intense gaze. Tenderness and lust shone in his eyes, and she whimpered when he slid his thumb across her bottom lip. Slowly.

"Shall we go on?" she replied.

****

With a deep sigh of contentment, Colin pulled Madeline closer to him, adjusting their bodies slightly until the top of her thigh fit perfectly against his hip. His passion fully and satisfyingly spent, he was able to focus once more, to take the time to notice the curve of her hip, her smooth creamy skin. Colin wrapped his arms around her tiny waist, inhaling the scent of her neck. Like honey, he thought, with a vague undercurrent of...citrus.

"Have you been eating oranges?" he wondered aloud.

"Why were you with Juliana tonight?" She spoke quietly, asking her dark question directly into the center of his chest. At the sound of her voice, with its heart-wrenching sadness, Colin forgot all about the oranges and lifted the palm of his hand to cradle her head.

"Have you so little faith in me?" he asked softly, gently stroking the silky strands of her hair. He remembered well the searing glare of betrayal in her eyes, a look he would not soon forget.

But the answer never came. Instead she pressed her face harder against him, her only reply the sudden flood of tears staining his skin. Colin dropped his hand from the top of her head. "Madeline, look at me." He dragged her chin up until their faces were almost touching, determined to set her straight. "I gave you my word I would return. Does that mean anything to you?"

"Of course," she cried, welling up again as he slipped the edge of his thumb under her lower lip. "But..."

"Then you should have nothing to worry over," he interrupted softly, sliding his thumb to the side before leaning up to bite the full, lush lip that beckoned him. "If you trust me, that is," he added with a stern nod before fully capturing her mouth for a proper kiss.

"You make it sound so simple," she finally replied, breathless now from the long kiss. Colin was already aching with renewed desire and had to hold himself back from making love to her again. Determined to regain some control over himself, he took a deep breath and moved his hands away from her breasts to her back, where he began to chastely massage her shoulders.

"It is that simple," he replied, coaxing her muscles to loosen beneath his fingers. "A man's word is sacred." She finally relaxed against him, allowing him to soothe her. Colin felt confident she had seen the error in her ways.

"But a lady who tosses away her virtue cannot expect a man to honor his word." Madeline's voice rang out with such conviction that Colin was struck dumb.

"Who the hell told you that?" He didn't mean to shout, but truly Madeline was the most exasperating woman he'd ever come across. How could she even consider such an idea? His outburst was soon regretted, for Madeline's expression immediately hardened into indignation.

"No one had to tell me anything; it is common knowledge." She slammed her hands against him, attempting to roll away, but Colin was having none of it. His hold tightened on her shoulders, refusing to let go.

A small struggle ensued, during which the stubborn woman tried several times to knee him in the groin. He would have beem a eunuch if she'd had her way about it, but Colin did finally manage to subdue her, hauling his tigress back to his chest where she belonged.

"Perhaps I was a little irrational," Madeline reluctantly admitted after a long silence. "But what was I supposed to think? Edward was most secretive, changing the subject if anyone so much as mentioned your name, refusing to answer my questions." Her face turned pink. "I thought he must be trying to spare my feelings. That he couldn't bring himself to tell me..." She trailed off, refusing to meet his gaze.

Colin suddenly felt as low as a black-hearted eel, whatever that was. Of course Madeline had doubted him. He had seduced her in the middle of the night, taken her virginity, and then left her all alone to fend for herself. And the moment he returned, what did he do? He was disgusted with himself. Instead of proposing like a gentleman, he'd dragged her off into a stranger's study and taken her right on the floor. She had every right to expect more, Colin realized. There was no excuse for how he had behaved.

"Would it help to know I was in agony these last hours, thinking of you?" He stood up, cradling her in his arms as he lifted her off Lord Huntington's Persian rug. Colin knew he could not erase his actions, but he was determined to make it up to her.

"You were?" She wound her arms around his neck and squeezed tight, resting her head against his shoulder like a kitten. "Were you so worried about me?"

"Part of the time," he answered, startled by how gruff his voice had become. "But I was in agony for other reasons."

"Like what?" Madeline peered up at him, her eyes like two round orbs.

"I was burning for you, Madeline."

He laid her on Huntington's green sofa, planning to put a little distance between them so he could have a proper discussion.

"What were you thinking about?" she asked with that irresistible combination of seduction and timidity that drove him mad with desire.

"Your mouth," he said, all his good intentions vanishing. "The feel of your body writhing beneath mine, and..." He leaned down to whisper into her ear.

"Oh," she gasped, all at once shocked and delighted. "You can really do that?"

"Would you like me to show you?"

"Yes, please." She pulled him down, sealing her mouth onto his, and Colin's last thought was that the sofa was indeed an improvement.

****

"Do you really believe I am in danger?" Madeline threw out the question rather casually while slipping on the last of her clothes. She had a feeling most women would fall into hysterics at the merest hint of peril. Helena would likely cry for days, but Madeline was perfectly calm. She found herself much more occupied with refastening the infernal pearl brooch that Aunt Cecilia had slapped on to keep her gown from plummeting scandalously. The brooch had somehow become crushed in her fall to the floor.

"I do," Colin said, still trying to shake dust and debris from the back of his black evening jacket. It had been tossed, during a particularly passionate moment, beneath Huntington's ancient wine bar, which obviously needed a good cleaning.

"Why do you think Edward followed you around?

Certainly not for his own enjoyment." Fed up, Colin took a firm hold of the jacket and gave it a good smack against his knee, instantly releasing a black plume into the air. "Good God, this is soot! When was the last time Huntington used his own library?"

Colin was so clearly appalled Madeline couldn't help but giggle. *Such a beautiful man.* She watched him pull the sooty jacket over his shoulders. She loved looking at him like this, getting dressed in the soft flicker of the candlelight, though she missed the sight of his nakedness already. He suddenly turned, caught her staring, and grinned.

"I'm glad you find this all so amusing. I must say you're rather disheveled yourself." He nodded toward her dress, which she was still holding closed with one hand.

"It's this infernal brooch. Helena fastened it for me, and I cannot see how she did it." Madeline's face turned a bit red, embarrassed that she could no longer manage to dress herself. She had been perfectly capable of taking care of herself at home. What had happened to her these last few months?

"Here, let me help." Colin swiftly pulled it from her hand. "We cannot have you returning to the ballroom half dressed. There would be no denying our rendezvous, then." He finished fastening her dress and checked to make sure the brooch would hold before he turned his grey-blue eyes to hers. "Not that I would ever deny anything I do with you, Madeline."

She melted against him, captured once again by his words, and the kiss that followed left them in danger of never leaving Huntington's library at all.

"Poor Edward. I have been giving him a terrible time," she said, steering the conversation back to a safer topic.

Colin shrugged in reply. "He probably deserves most of it, but I wouldn't worry. Besides, I'm back now, and until I know it's safe, I'm not taking my eyes off you. Or my hands, for that matter."

He grabbed for her waist, and Madeline slapped his hand away. She was determined to find her shoes before he could coax her out of her dress again.

"I should at least apologize," she continued on, her remorse gaining momentum. "I truly like Edward. It was just that I was so very upset after Juliana's visit, and he has been most shamefully flirting with Helena. Now that I think about it, Colin," Madeline's remorse quickly turned to indignation for her poor lovesick cousin, "you must really speak to him about his behavior. He cannot continue to be so charming when he is planning to run away to war. Why, Helena believed he was courting her!" She finally found her slippers, lying forgotten in the corner, and scooped them up.

"Well, don't you agree?" Madeline turned to see Colin's reaction to her cousin's plight, and found him staring at her, his face strangely pale under the faint glow of the candlelight.

"Juliana came to see you?" His voice sounded different to her, oddly strained, as though he... Was Colin afraid?

"This afternoon," she answered, trying to ignore her own twinge of fear. "She said the most dreadful things, all of it ridiculous, of course, and I am ashamed to say I believed her." Colin made no response. In fact, he stood frozen in place, not a single muscle moving to dispel the sick feeling creeping through Madeline's heart. "Juliana was very blunt," Madeline rambled on. "She still has very set plans to marry you, and will stop at nothing to get what she wants. She even claimed you had recently seduced her." She laughed and desperately grabbed Colin's hand for reassurance. "I was a fool to believe anything she said. Can you ever forgive me?"

"I'm afraid," he replied, his hand lying cold and

motionless in hers, "it is I who need to beg your forgiveness."

She didn't understand. No, that wasn't true— she didn't *want* to understand.

Stepping toward her, Colin placed both his hands firmly on her shoulders. "Madeline," he began, "what Juliana told you, and God knows what she said, but it may not have been strictly a lie."

"It wasn't?" She could scarcely breathe past the cold, hard lump that had formed in her throat. "You seduced her?" Colin had betrayed her, just like her mother had betrayed Papa.

"I rather think it was the other way around," he said dryly, and Madeline felt her tolerance snap like a dry twig. She had heard enough.

"So it's all true," she cried, shoving his hands off her shoulders, wishing to get as far from him as possible. "You took Juliana to your bed. How could you, Colin? Of all the disgusting..."

"I ended it," he insisted, refusing to let her move away. "I was so angry with you for lying to me, and Juliana suddenly appeared. But still, I couldn't go through with it. How could I, when the only one I wanted was you?"

"You expect me to believe that?" she shot back.

"Yes!" Colin's face showed an anguish that threatened to melt her anger, but she fought against it. "I have made love to no other woman but you since we've met, I swear on my life, Madeline."

"But you kissed her," she continued, unable to get the image out of her mind. "You allowed her to..."

"Madeline, stop." His voice was harsh with regret as he gathered her into his arms. He held her tightly against his chest until her struggles ceased. "It was a terrible mistake. I tried to tell you, that night in your aunt's garden. I so wanted to tell you the truth, to seek your forgiveness."

"But you didn't," she spat out, refusing to be

lulled by Colin's strong embrace, his light masculine scent that made her all too aware of their recent lovemaking. "You kept silent and let me believe you were an honorable man."

"I am an honorable man."

"You lied to me!" she screamed, wrenching herself from his arms. "After all your lectures, all your talk of honesty, it is you who is the liar!"

Madeline sank against the wall, holding her arms against her chest for protection while Juliana's warning burned in her mind. *You are not the first lady Colin has seduced, including myself, and you will not be the last. He will always return to me.* It all made sense now. Juliana's words had not been mere threats. She had seen Colin the day before, rekindled her romance with the man she had betrayed.

"I am a fool," she whispered, hugging herself tightly to ward off the horrible chill invading her bones. Why hadn't she listened to Papa's warnings? She was indeed cursed, doomed to such a fate. If only she had fulfilled her vow, destroyed the French Blue diamond and left London forever, none of this would have happened.

"For God's sake, Madeline, sit down before you faint."

"Stay away!" she hissed, as he took a step toward her. "If you wish to comfort someone, go find your beautiful Juliana."

Colin's hand dropped to his side. "Is that what this is about?" he asked incredulously. "Jealousy? You needn't bother, Madeline. You have twice the beauty of Juliana, and yours doesn't hide a black heart."

"I am certainly not jealous!" she shot back, offended by the idea. "I am simply shocked that after everything she has done you would wish to see her again. I can only imagine it's more gossip for the *ton*

301

to feed upon." Madeline knew she sounded absurd, but she could not bear to tell him the truth: she was in love with him and he had broken her heart with his confessions. She might cry, then, and that was something she could not allow.

"Well, let them talk," he snapped. "Juliana means nothing to me, and she and the damned *ton* will have their answer as soon as I announce our engagement."

"Whose engagement?" Madeline asked, choking on the words. Colin couldn't still mean to marry that woman, could he?

"My engagement to you," he bellowed. "For God's sake, Madeline!" Colin seemed to catch himself, forcing a deep breath. "Hopefully your aunt will consent without too much bother, and we can get it over and done with by the end of next week."

"Next week?" Madeline suddenly felt the room had gotten much smaller, and she desperately wished for an open window.

"I know it's a bit rushed, but we cannot keep chasing each other into libraries and gardens, not without a ceremony, at least." Colin's attempted smile came out more like a grimace. "I can arrange for a special license."

My God, he has really thought this through. "Have you spoken to my aunt?" She took a deep breath. And then three more.

"No." He was staring hard, his smile fading. "I planned to speak to her first thing tomorrow. You should really try and exhale, Madeline, your face is turning purple."

"Perhaps you should wait." The words tumbled out in a gasp as she finally released her mouthfuls of air, clutching the back of a chair for support.

"Why would I do that?"

She closed her eyes, trying to think of something rational, something that would release her from this conversation, and this room. "Aunt Cecilia has a breakfast party scheduled for tomorrow."

"Madeline, what are you saying to me?" Colin's voice had turned rigid.

"I don't ever remember accepting a marriage proposal." There. He couldn't argue with that, could he? Now perhaps he would drop this farce and let her leave with whatever remained of her pride.

"Lady Madeline Sinclair, will you marry me?" Her eyes flew open with horror. What could he be thinking? Had he lost his mind?

"No."

"Why the hell not?"

Colin was angry. His ear-splitting reply left little doubt of that. He stood in front of her now, the fierce stance again reminding her of Adonis striking out to battle. *Even to the lock of hair in his eyes.* It was a momentary distraction. But there was something more this time in Colin's expression. He looked astonished, completely taken aback by her refusal.

"Answer me, Madeline."

"Keep your voice down," she said, fearful that at any moment her aunt would burst through the doors with a priest. "I have already explained my thoughts on marriage."

"Which is what, exactly?"

"That I do not wish to marry. Ever."

His eyes narrowed to tiny pinpricks, and she rushed on before losing her nerve.

"I'm sorry if it upsets you, but I was very clear."

"I see." She was thankful he lowered his voice then, but its strange, deadly-soft tone somehow managed to strike more fear into her heart. "Then perhaps I was not clear enough. My proposal was merely a formality, Madeline. You have already consented to marriage."

"When did I do such a thing?" she gasped.

He stepped closer to her, backing her against the wall. "Last night, when you allowed me into your bedroom, and again just now." He raised his voice, holding up one hand when she tried to interrupt. "When you followed me into this room and let me make love to you. You did consent to that, didn't you, Madeline? Do you deny it?"

"I deny nothing, but marriage and making love are not the same thing." She thought the veins would pop out of his head.

"Maybe not in your mind, which we've established is broken. What will you do if you're with child? Have you thought of that?" Colin was back to shouting, his outrage echoing off the walls.

"I—I didn't, but I am perfectly sure I am not." The idea of pregnancy was a shocking one, she admitted, but it didn't matter. She would not marry a man who didn't love her, who would be unfaithful to her, child or no.

"And I'm perfectly sure that by the time you do know it will be too late to salvage your reputation or a life for yourself." He crossed his arms, looking rather satisfied by his ominous prediction, and Madeline's blood boiled over.

"I don't care," she said defiantly. "I shall raise it on my own."

"What kind of man do you take me for?" he roared. In his anger, he slammed one hand directly above her head, rattling the wall so hard it sent a bottle of Huntington's brandy crashing to the floor, and they both jumped from the loud noise. Madeline seized her chance. Snatching her shoes from the floor as the brandy bottle rolled away, she didn't stop to put them on but quickly darted past him and ran out the door.

She heard him calling her name again but didn't dare slow down, ignoring the searing cold of the marble under her naked feet. The hallway was deserted. Madeline didn't know what she would do if forced to encounter Charles and Urina now. She quickened her pace, dashing past the silent, voiceless statues whose stone eyes seemed to denounce with harsh judgments, until she found her way to the ballroom entrance and ran inside.

"Splendid! Another Aphrodite ripe for the plucking!" A man dressed as Dionysus sailed by her, nearly knocking her to her knees, and Madeline shoved past him, desperate to be absorbed into the crowd.

Consumed with her worry, she looked back to see if Colin followed her, but her glance was greeted only by an endless sea of masks. Perhaps he had decided not to pursue her after all. *Good riddance.* She forced back hot tears. Whirling quickly toward the crowd again, she slammed into the back of a large looming figure.

"Madeline?"

It was Lord Rockford, looking absolutely shocked to see her in front of him holding her shoes.

"What happened to your gown?" His expression regrettably reminded her of Lord Huntington's statues.

"My gown?" She looked down to see the damned brooch had once again popped free. With a gasp, she grabbed at the fabric before it plunged her further into humiliation as a peal of laughter captured her attention.

"Really, darling, isn't it obvious what happened? A gown doesn't come off by itself, you know. Usually one has a bit of help."

Madeline realized with horror that Lord Rockford wasn't alone. Next to him, filled to the brim with a satisfied contempt, stood Juliana.

"And who has been helping you with your dress, Madeline?"

Colin was right. Madeline felt a surge of hatred

for Juliana's delicate smile. Her beauty truly did hide a black heart. Oh, how could he ever think of betraying her with such a woman?

"A faulty clasp is all," she replied, refusing to be intimidated. "I'm going to have a very serious talk with Mr. Banbury about his ball gown attire. I don't care if it is a costume!" She whirled around, searching for a friendly face to help her. "Have you seen my aunt? The hour is growing terribly late, and I would like to go home now."

"You've been with Douglas, haven't you?" Lord Rockford's voice was so cold and accusing she drew back. Huntington's contemptuous statues had indeed come to life.

"Lord Rockford, William, I—" She didn't know what to say, could think of nothing to defend herself. It was as though he could see right through her. His normally warm blue eyes raked over her. "Please don't look at me that way."

"You should get used to it," Juliana sang out. "You've ruined yourself in public! No decent man will touch you now."

"Juliana told me." Lord Rockford shook his head at her. "She warned me he had some kind of hold over you, that you were in love with him, and I didn't believe her. But it's true, isn't it, Madeline?"

"No!" Madeline cried, unable to explain, but Lord Rockford turned a deaf ear to her pleas.

"Do you know what kind of man Douglas is? He has no manners. No society would accept him if not for his title."

"And my money," Colin spoke from behind her. "You cannot forget my massive fortune, Rockford. I imagine that helps, as well."

Madeline turned to find Colin, perfectly calm and at ease with his hands folded behind his back. His expression was mildly interested, as though they were discussing the fine music and not her impending fall from grace.

She despised him.

"Colin, darling, I'm so glad you could join us! Your little Madeline seems to have been skulking about in darkened corners. I fear she may have compromised herself." Juliana's voice was growing steadily louder, capturing the curious attention of a widening circle of party guests.

Colin simply shrugged. "Surely what a woman does with her husband is of little interest to anyone else."

Juliana nearly choked. "Madeline is not your wife," she replied, the skin around her lips hardening into a sneer. "She should never have been alone with you."

"But she is my betrothed," Colin said, smiling in victory. "We haven't officially announced our engagement, but you can be the first to congratulate us."

Ignoring Colin, Lord Rockford stepped forward, his lip curled in rage. "Is this true, Madeline?" His eyes flashed with an intensity that overwhelmed her, and he grasped her arm, leaning in shamefully close. "Have you accepted an engagement from Lord Douglas?"

"I…" Stunned by the sudden intimacy, Madeline was slow to react, until she realized Colin had pulled her away.

"It is unwise to touch what belongs to me," Colin replied, his tone now a dangerous one. "You have forgotten yourself, Lord Rockford."

"I do not belong to you!" Madeline shrieked, furiously regretting ever laying eyes on the Duke of Douglas, much less following him down into the library. "And I most certainly did not accept any engage—"

"Of course, I must speak to Lady Milburg first," Colin carried on, paying her little heed. "It is a most recent engagement, you understand."

"Of course," Lord Rockford replied, backing away with a tight smile. "I didn't mean to overstep myself. I do apologize and wish you all the best. Good evening."

"I, too, wish you all the best, Lord Douglas," Juliana managed to spit out while furiously gathering up her skirts. "Though I fear it will be in vain." And before Madeline could make any reply, they were gone.

"I don't know which of us she insulted more," Colin said, watching her stalk off.

"You bastard," Madeline spoke slowly, carefully cradling her anger to keep it from exploding.

"Madeline." The curse seemed to remind Colin of her presence. He reached out to soothe her, but she shrank away.

"Do not touch me! How dare you tell William that we are engaged!"

"So now it's 'William,' is it? I had no idea you were on such intimate terms." He ignored her protests and clamped down on her arm, pulling her closer. "I think it's time we finished our talk." Keeping a firm grip on her arm, he dragged her out to the balcony, but it was too late for any hope of privacy. The outrageous entertainment had been discovered by the crowd and proved too enticing to ignore.

"Let go of me," she yelled the moment the balcony door shut behind them. She pulled hard against his hand to free herself. "Everyone is watching us."

Colin smirked at her. "I didn't realize you'd become so concerned with impressing the *ton*," he snapped. "Or is it just your William you're so worried about? He's very possessive of you, I see."

"Lord Rockford is my friend," she said. *Or was.* He would probably never speak to her again after tonight. As though he could read her mind, Colin's eyes narrowed in jealousy.

"I warn you, Madeline, I doubt he would think so highly of you if he knew how you spent the last hour."

Her head jerked up, taken aback by his viciousness. "You disgust me."

"Is that so? And how do you think I feel about a woman who gives herself to one man while planning to marry another?"

Tears burned Madeline's eyes. Is that what Colin thought of her? That she rejected him to marry Lord Rockford? He couldn't have been more wrong, but she wasn't going to tell him that. If he wanted to think the worst of her, so be it. "You have no right to tell anyone we are engaged. I have never accepted your hand, and I never will, not ever. It is my choice, not yours."

"And what is your choice? To become a whore?"

She slapped him. Hard. Directly across the face, and the moment she finished, his words flashed through her head and she slapped him again.

"I deserved that," he said quietly, making no move to stop her.

"You deserve to be horsewhipped in the streets, Lord Douglas. I am thoroughly ashamed—ashamed I was ever foolish enough to believe myself in love with you. You have humiliated me, bullied me, and broken my heart. I never want to see you again."

And she turned, freeing herself from his grasp, and ran from him, her fingers wound tight around the now destroyed neckline of her white dress. She heard him call after her, the words wrenching through her heart, but she paid them no mind and flew from the balcony straight into Helena's arms.

"Madeline, you must come with me now! Everyone is talking, and Mama is in a fit! What were you thinking, to go off alone with Lord Douglas?"

Dazed with her pain, Madeline mutely obeyed, following her cousin blindly through the eagerly condemning crowd with its open-mouthed stares and loud whispers.

"My God, she was alone with him on the balcony."

"Scandalous... Shocking, to be sure... She has ruined herself!"

And above it all the tinny, shrill tones of Lady Farris, pleased to have her revenge at last. "A disgrace! Just like her mother. The Sinclair curse lives on. Did I not predict such an ending? It was written in her blood."

Even the malicious brand could not pierce through Madeline's anguish enough to gain a reaction, and she continued on, Helena's hand grasping hers tightly.

"Pay no attention to that horrible woman." But the damage had already been done. Everyone was talking, gasping, falling over themselves to get a glimpse of the ruined Lady Madeline Sinclair.

Chapter Nineteen

"It will soon be forgotten. Too silly and trivial for anyone to recall." Aunt Cecilia tapped her hands nervously together, desperate to reassure herself. "A lover's quarrel is all. Everyone has them! Why, Lady Isley's daughter did exactly the same thing last week. Had a tiff with her new husband at Vauxhall Gardens and cried like an infant in front of everyone until her father dragged her home. Rather romantic, don't you think?" She reached out to place an awkward pat on Madeline's shoulder. "And it all turned out perfectly fine, just as this will." Aunt Cecilia gave a solid nod of reassurance, but her pale, drawn expression told the real truth.

Madeline was brutally aware of the damage she had done. In one fateful evening she had disgraced her family, disappointed her aunt, and destroyed any chance she had of making a life for herself in London. Her future spread before her like the bleak, sullied weather they rode through. A rain-soaked melancholy beat down on the carriage, filling Madeline with grief for the loneliness that would soon follow.

"I do think it would be wise to stay away from Lord Douglas for a few days, dear, at least until we have this little muddle sorted."

Her aunt cautiously voiced the suggestion, plunging Madeline back into despair. *Colin.* Try as she might, she could not erase his last words from her mind. She had left him, devastated by his cruel words and the fresh pain of her broken heart.

She shook her head, trying to clear the jumbled

thoughts spinning through her. Nothing made sense to her anymore, but most of all she couldn't understand how she could still love the very man who had hurt her so.

Madeline finally looked up at her aunt and cousin, both staring at her, the two identical pairs of blue eyes bright with concern.

"I will never see him again."

****

Less than an hour later, Helena was gently leading her upstairs to her darkened bedroom, refusing even Brigette's assistance. Madeline sat unspeaking as her cousin fluttered around the room, readying the bed and finding a nightdress.

"Not that one," Madeline said softly, as Helena picked up her soft blue nightdress. It was the one Colin had found the morning after their first night together. Madeline squeezed her eyes shut against the memory of his hands slipping the silky fabric over her, his lips kissing her goodbye as he left her lying in bed, no longer a virgin. "Please find something else."

Helena gave her a strange look but obeyed.

"Lord Douglas hurt you."

"Yes, very much."

Helena nodded, pulling the pins out of Madeline's hair. "Can you ever forgive him?"

Madeline's head jerked back in surprise. "Why would I?" she asked, incensed at the thought.

"It will be easier for you, Madeline, if you marry." Helena suddenly looked terribly uncomfortable. "Not that I would ever tell anyone to marry against their wishes, but people can be so cruel, and I would hate to see you..." She stopped, unable to go on.

"Ruined and humiliated?" Madeline finished for her. "I'm afraid it's too late for that." She jumped to her feet, hair spilling behind her as she paced the

312

room. "And believe me, Helena, I would rather live the rest of my life in disgrace than be bound to a disloyal, traitorous husband." She now understood her father's shame, the real reason he never returned to London.

Helena stared at her in surprise. "Colin was disloyal to you?"

"He has resumed his affair with Juliana! After everything that evil woman has done to him, he refuses to let her go. He is still in love with her."

"He confessed this?" Her cousin looked stunned. "I cannot believe it."

"It's the truth. He admitted that Juliana came to see him, that they were alone together." Madeline walked faster, ignoring the twinge of pain that followed her words. "And the rest we both heard straight from Juliana's own lips. How could Colin deny it?"

Madeline turned her head away, impatiently brushing away the tears while Helena looked on in horror.

"Oh, Madeline," she said, both hands covering her mouth. "I believe there must have been a terrible misunderstanding. Just this evening Edward swore to me his brother had no intentions of going back to that wretched Juliana."

"You spoke to Edward tonight?"

Helena slapped her hands over her mouth. "Oh, heavens! I forgot I wasn't going to tell anyone that part."

If she hadn't been so distraught, Madeline would have laughed. So much for her cousin's resolve to never speak to Lord Montgomery again. It would seem Madeline was not the only one of the family to sneak into corners tonight.

"It was only a kiss!" Helena cried. "I know I shouldn't have let him, and I did call him a cad afterward, but he's so very handsome—"

"There's no need to explain." Madeline stopped her with a wave of her hand. "I am quite aware of how easily a lady can be swept off her feet."

In fact, Madeline thought, she herself was the perfect example of how foolish a woman could be.

"But Madeline, you have it all wrong! Edward said Lord Douglas isn't heartbroken over Juliana at all, and he told her that very thing on the way to the Huntington ball. He said it had been a mistake to ask for her hand, and it was better for both of them that they had never married!"

Madeline's pacing came to an abrupt halt. "He said that?"

"And when Juliana tried to hint that they could still be together, then..." Helena blushed. "Edward really shouldn't have told me this. It is quite shocking."

"Helena! What did he say?"

Her face was on fire, but she managed to choke it out. "He said that he now understood the difference between lust and love. That he had met someone," she swallowed, unable to meet Madeline's gaze, "he had met someone who had shown him there was a difference."

Madeline sat down on the bed, her legs no longer able to hold her as the horrible things she had said to Colin flashed through her mind. She'd lied first, broken her promise of honesty for the sake of a diamond. But still—he admitted to kissing Juliana! Madeline clenched her eyes shut, unable to stand the idea of Colin's lips on another woman. The very thought could send her running for the chamber pot.

"That evil woman!" Helena continued, her outrage growing. "Juliana has been after Lord Douglas all this time! Madeline, can you ever forgive him?"

"It's too late now," she said, dropping her head into her hands. "Everything is ruined after tonight. I wouldn't be surprised if your mother sends me away first thing tomorrow."

Helena shook her head vehemently. "Mama would never send you away. I wouldn't let her," she stated, pulling back the quilts. "Now try and sleep. Brigette will be sitting right outside. If you need anything, just call out and she'll fetch me right away." Helena smiled at her, tucking the blankets in tight. "We'll figure something out in the morning. We can always leave London altogether. I must admit I don't care much for a husband, either."

****

Madeline lay heavy on her quilts, mercifully left alone with her thoughts. She rolled into a ball, finally, succumbing to the hot tears pressing into the backs of her eyes. Exhausted from the day, her last thought before falling into an uneasy slumber was the warning her father had given her the night he died. *Destroy the diamond. You must get rid of it. To possess it for too long is a curse. The misfortunes it brings will rob you of everything you love.* Her father's words had come true.

****

Night descended further into dark gloom, the spattering rain long obscuring any dim glow the moon could offer, and a cold, menacing blackness surrounded the Duke of Douglas's townhouse. The only light for miles came from inside, a struggling fire in the study where Colin now paced back and forth before his brother.

"I'm going to see Madeline," Colin announced, unwilling to endure this excruciating wait for another moment.

"For God's sake, Colin, it's the middle of the night. What are you planning to do? Pound on Lady Milburg's door like a madman?" Edward sat comfortably across from him, his jacket and mask tossed onto the floor and a stiff glass of brandy in each hand. "Here, drink one of these. It might restore your good sense."

Colin waved away the brandy and continued his pacing. "I have to talk to her, immediately." He was in no mood to argue. His instincts told him to go to her, and he expected his brother's full cooperation.

"That sounds like a splendid idea," Edward said, draining his own glass before starting on Colin's. "Make sure to wake up all the servants while you're there, so you can finish destroying what little is left of Madeline's reputation."

Colin glared at the harsh words, but Edward continued on.

"You're going to have to marry her, you know. There's been talk of the two of you going off alone together, and once the *ton* gets hold of that..." He didn't finish, letting Colin fill it in for himself. "It's the only way to quiet down all this nonsense."

Colin's jaw clenched, remembering well the uproar that had followed Madeline from Huntington's ballroom that evening. Damn Juliana! He was going to break her neck for spreading all this gossip. But Colin knew he also had himself to blame. Seducing Madeline in Huntington's library had been his first mistake. He should have stopped there, but when she rejected him and then went running to Rockford, Colin had lost his mind in a fit of jealousy. He would have chased Madeline out to her aunt's carriage if it had not been for Edward's firm interference.

"I'm going to see her," Colin said. He picked up his jacket from the back of the settee, leaving a faint black residue behind. "Now. I'll climb through the window again and be gone before sunrise."

"Again?" The word caught Edward's attention, and he sat up. "Are you telling me you've climbed through Madeline's window before?"

When Colin didn't answer, Edward raised his

voice, suspicion knitting his light brows.

"You *do* intend to marry her after all this, don't you? Madeline doesn't deserve to be treated like a common ladybird."

Colin bristled at the censorious tone from his younger brother. "I am fully prepared to marry her. How can you even ask such a question?"

"Good." Edward settled back in the chair, not bothering to apologize. "Then it's settled. Sit down and have your drink. You can beg for her hand first thing in the morning. What the hell happened to your jacket?" He held up Colin's half-finished brandy, swirling it enticingly.

"She has already refused me," Colin said quietly, feeling a sharp sting of pride at the confession.

"Refused you?"

"Twice." Colin grabbed the brandy glass from Edward's outstretched hand and drained it in one swallow. "Madeline is being completely unreasonable. She is going to marry me. There is no other way." Colin neglected to admit the raw ache in his heart at the thought of losing her, of spending one more night away from his Madeline.

"I'm sure with a little prodding she'll come around," Edward tossed out, attempting to help. "Women are like that. She's probably fast asleep, dreaming about wringing your neck on the wedding day."

"You don't understand." Colin's voice was strained to its breaking point. He wasn't making sense, but was too anguished to care. "The things I said to her. She despises me. I have to make it right."

Edward stood staring at him for a long time, seeing his brother with new eyes. Finally, he sighed, setting his empty glass down on the table before getting to his feet. "Let's ride, then. But you'd better wear my jacket."

Chapter Twenty

The Earl of Sinclair's breaths grew sharp and painful, each one a clear indication of the unavoidable. His paper-thin hands, once resolute in their strength, now blindly sought her out for the relief she could not give. A stale, piercing smell surrounded the helpless figure, the scent of flesh too long encased in illness, already beginning its decay.

Madeline and the servants had created a makeshift bedchamber in the dining room when her father could no longer manage the stairs. The illness wasted no time overtaking the once grand room. Mrs. Whitmore's herbs and tonics toppled onto the tarnished silver, limp flowers slumped passively in the corner, great-grandmother's linens lay stained with the sweat from a fevered brow.

She kept count by her father's side every night. It was her ritual. One breath every four seconds, then every six. She strained to hear it as it wound down—eight seconds, then ten.

The hoarse gasping had once bothered her. Madeline would try to breathe for him, inhaling strong and deep as if in encouragement. Now she sat quietly, counting, waiting.

She smoothed his wrinkled sheet, clean and white from the last time she had changed it, before leaning forward to whisper something comforting in his ear. Her gaze no longer searched for recognition; her father was fully occupied in these last shuddering breaths. She had just bent over him with a soft smile of pity, when the withered hand shot out and grabbed her by the throat. Madeline pulled back, stunned by the sudden strength. The icy fingers choked her, burned into her skin. Horrified, she saw that his eyes were open, black pools glaring from a white skull, and soundlessly she screamed. He was stealing her air.

"I'm sorry," he mouthed, dark flecks of spittle at the sides of his lips. "I'm sorry, Madeline..."

Large, merciless hands gripped her neck, forcing it back as she fought against them, her nails ripping at the long, well-manicured fingers.

This is not your father! screamed the panicked voice inside her head.

"These are not my hands!" Papa yelled.

****

She woke up fighting, clawing at the remains of the nightmare, and hit something solid with a crash. Fully awake and gasping for air, Madeline realized she was all alone.

The nightmares were growing worse, more vivid, more terrifying. Her neck still ached as though she had truly felt those mysterious fingers digging into her flesh.

Wiping the moisture from her eyes, Madeline knelt down to retrieve the scattered items on the floor. Her lone candle had broken in half from its fall, and she tossed it aside, along with her reticule and the pearl brooch. "Much good that did me," she muttered darkly.

It was then she noticed the small white paper. A note. It must have fallen from her reticule. Madeline stopped breathing. Could it possibly be from Colin? She snatched it up, her heart beating frantically as she ran over to the window to read by moonlight.

Madeline,

The man you seek will be at King's Crown Tavern tonight. If you still wish to find him, I offer my services as your escort. My carriage will be in front of your townhouse at half past midnight. I will

wait for one hour.
William

Madeline swallowed her disappointment, leaning her head against the cold glass of the window. She was a fool to have thought the note was from Colin. Why should he write her? After all, she had firmly rejected him. There was no changing that now.

The diamond. She could have the French Blue in her hands tonight, destroy it, and end her family's curse. Glancing quickly at the clock in her room, she saw it was nearly a quarter past one. Would Lord Rockford still be waiting?

Madeline whirled, tightly clutching the note as she searched for something dark and suitable to wear. She would have to hurry to make it to Lord Rockford's carriage; time was running out. And if she failed? What if she did not return home by morning and was discovered gone, missing from her bed?

It would no longer matter, she determined. Her reputation was already in tatters, beyond repair. She had only one chance to salvage it, a chance she must take. Straightening her shoulders, Madeline reached for her grey serge dress.

Chapter Twenty-One

The sound of the carriage reached him first.

A crunch of the wheels upon the rough ground awoke the quiet night, and Colin was instantly alert, craning his neck to see into the darkness. The black carriage stood in the shadows like a great dark beast lying in wait. Straining to see under the weak light of the moon, Colin could just make out the red crest of the Marquis of Rockford.

The marquis.

Moore's words scalded him like fire. *I took the diamond to the marquis.* The man had been in front of his eyes the whole time. How could he have been so blind? It was Rockford, all along. He was the bastard who hired Moore!

Then he saw the figure of a woman running quickly toward Rockford's carriage. Fingers digging into the reins, Colin nudged his mount closer, his heart beating in denial. She paused at the window, speaking intently to the passenger inside for a long, wrenching moment. Colin's gaze never left the woman. Tightly wrapped against the chill, he could not see her face, could just barely see her small gloved hand reach for the opening carriage door.

"No!" he shouted, unable to stop himself. But his words were lost in a strong gust of wind that blew at the folds of the woman's cloak, wrenching them aside to reveal a glimpse of an all-too-familiar grey dress.

"Madeline!" The anguished cry ripped from his throat as he watched the woman he loved run away with Lord Rockford.

She whipped her head around, the hood of her cloak falling onto her shoulders, unveiling the long, boundless waves, black in the night.

"Colin?" she called, peering into the darkness. "Are you here?"

Damn this infernal wind. Colin's repeated shouts were snatched away by the blustery air, and he raised one hand to signal her, still calling her name.

And then she was gone. Two arms from inside the carriage grasped her gloved hands and pulled her inside. The door slammed with a harsh click, and before Colin could reach her Rockford's horses were running, pulling Madeline and the carriage into the night.

In a burst of fury, Colin was after them. Ignoring Edward's bewildered voice behind him, he nudged his horse hard, forcing them both to the limit in a mad pursuit for Madeline. There had been a catch in her voice, enough to tell Colin she still cared for him, and he would go to the ends of the earth to reach her.

****

"Wait!" Madeline cried, trying to steady herself against the rocking seat as the carriage picked up speed. She flung herself to the window, peering desperately out into the night, but saw only darkness. Had it merely been her imagination? She could have sworn—

"Did I startle you?"

She turned to find herself seated across from an impeccably dressed Lord Rockford, watching her intently.

"I apologize for my hastiness, but the hour grows late, and we have little time now to recover your diamond."

Madeline reluctantly forced herself to turn and face her companion, her gaze still anxiously darting toward the window. "Of course," she replied, politely. "I didn't mean to delay us. It's only that I thought I heard someone shouting my name."

"Someone?" He lifted a silver brow.

"Colin." She spoke the name like a grave confession. "It sounds silly, I know. It must have been the wind." It couldn't have been Colin, she scolded herself. She had told him she despised him, that she never wanted to see him again. Why would he come to her now?

"Undoubtedly it was the wind." Lord Rockford gave her an indulgent smile, and she nodded at him, not trusting herself to speak.

"Do make yourself comfortable, Madeline. The journey won't be long. You've abandoned your Persephone costume, I see."

"I thought it much too inappropriate for such an outing."

"Such a shame," he sighed. "Sarah would have loved the ball this evening. She simply adored costumes."

It occurred to Madeline that Lord Rockford was still dressed in his formal ball attire, the dark red Hades mask lying next to him. His eyes grazed over her as though she still wore the too-revealing gown of earlier in the evening, while an uneasy suspicion crawled up her spine.

"It really was the strangest thing!" she said, a bit too loudly. "I was positive I heard my name, and I even thought I saw a man waving to me. Do you suppose my eyes and ears could be playing tricks?" Madeline turned her attention back to the window, unable to stand another moment of Lord Rockford's scrutiny. And then she saw the horse.

"Colin!" she cried, wrenching back the curtain. Though their carriage rode at a breakneck pace, Madeline could clearly see the unmistakable figure, tall and muscular, riding beside them. He shouted to her, but his words were once again swept away.

She whirled around. "Lord Rockford, you must tell your man to stop the carriage. We've left Colin behind!"

"A pity," Lord Rockford said, seemingly undisturbed by her plea. "Douglas has proved endlessly difficult to do away with." He leaned back against his own seat, settling comfortably despite the hard jolting of the horses.

Madeline stared at him, aghast, as he casually removed his hat and gloves. "I don't understand. Why would you wish to do away with Colin?" She stopped as his left hand, now freed from its leather glove, caught her full attention.

"My God, it was you," she whispered, unable to take her gaze from the sickeningly familiar long, sleek fingers. "You were the man in my dream. The hands that were choking me—they were yours!"

"What dream?" Lord Rockford asked. "Do calm yourself, Madeline. You look quite hysterical." But Madeline paid him no attention. The dream consumed her mind with full force, the choking hands vivid in her mind as everything fell into place.

It wasn't Colin her papa had been warning her against; it was Lord Rockford.

"You hired Moore to follow me." She finally spoke, turning to him with eyes blazing green fire. "It was you who stole the French Blue diamond from me and sent your men after Colin. *You* are behind all of this!"

"I'm afraid I can take only half the credit, my darling." He smiled at her, and Madeline shrank back at the endearment. "I did indeed send Moore to follow you, but my possession of the French Blue was a complete accident. I'd heard of it, of course, but I could never have guessed Thomas would have the nerve to steal such a diamond." And to her shock he pulled the French Blue from his jacket pocket.

She held her breath at the sight of it.

"If you didn't know about the diamond, then why did you have me followed? What did you want?"

"You, Madeline."

"My God," she whispered.

"From the moment I laid eyes on you, it was as though my Sarah had returned, after all these years, unchanged by time."

She shrank back, forcing as much distance as possible between them in the cramped space.

"Douglas's ill-timed interference nearly ruined everything. You were much too enamored of him for my taste." He smiled. "But Juliana took care of that, didn't she? I always knew the girl would turn out to be useful."

Madeline covered her ears as the horrible truth dawned on her. Colin had asked her to trust him, and she couldn't do it. Instead, she had let jealousy rule her, had put her faith in this madman. "There will never be anything between us," she hissed at him, her temper flaring up. "I didn't know my mother. She may have loved you, but I never will."

"All we need is time, my Persephone." He placed the red mask over his head with a dark laugh. "You will see we were meant to be together."

"Don't call me that." She shrieked as the carriage rocked harder, swerving dangerously to the side. "We are going to crash. Tell your man to slow down!"

"All the arrangements have been made," Lord Rockford continued, unfazed by the violent jerking of the carriage. "We must outrun your impatient suitor. It's a shame Douglas would not die when expected. We have an appointment that must be kept. The *Seafarer* sets sail at first light, and we will be on that voyage, Madeline." He smiled at her. "It will give us plenty of time to get to know each other."

"You're insane," Madeline lashed at him and

325

then, in absolute desperation, pounded on the top of the carriage. "Let me out!" she screamed. "Stop, driver! Let me out of this carriage!"

Her captor merely laughed again. "It is useless, of course, though my driver is an old acquaintance of yours."

She shrank back. "Moore," she said. And then reached up and with one gloved hand punched Lord Rockford right in the eye.

It was with the sickening jerk of the carriage that Madeline remembered the curse. She glanced at the diamond in Lord Rockford's hand, glinting brightly despite its dark surroundings, and realized it had come for her.

"It was you I wanted, my Sarah, I have waited for so long."

The French Blue diamond. Her mother.

Madeline was jolted from her stupor into the terrifying present. It was happening again; her mother's tragedy loomed over her. Madeline had inherited more than her mother's face—they shared the same fate.

"No!" she screamed, reaching up and grabbing Lord Rockford by the arm so violently the diamond was knocked out of his hand and fell to the floor, where it rolled beneath her seat. "Tell Moore he must stop! Don't you see? The curse is after us both. We will crash, just as my mother did!"

And then it happened. Strangely, Madeline felt the carriage slow a bit, as if perhaps in an attempt to turn, but it went deadly wrong. She felt the wheels crack beneath them, and then a brutal swerve jerked her across the seat into Lord Rockford's arms, which immediately closed around her.

"I'm sorry, Colin," she sobbed, her face pressed against Lord Rockford's chest. She would never see him again, never feel his arms around her, his lips pressed against hers. She knew Colin was following her, chasing her just as Papa had chased her mother twenty years ago. *But the difference is that I so very much want to be caught.*

"My Sarah..."

Lord Rockford shouted as the carriage fell to its side, and Madeline clawed at him, desperate to get away, fighting with all her strength, a strength born from sheer terror.

She was in the water. The carriage was sinking, and Madeline, finally free from Lord Rockford's odious grasp, concentrated on kicking the door that held her prisoner, already blocked by the rushing water. When it wedged open, she knew they were in the Thames. There was no escape but to swim, and she must get out before the water reached her head. Choking back her panic, she dove into the relentless, churning waters, Lord Rockford's screams echoing behind her.

****

"I've got you, Madeline."

The voice was strong and steady, and she gratefully reached toward it. She was shivering with cold, but there was a warm weight around her, keeping her from falling. She felt weightless and heavy at the same time, and she kept her eyes tightly shut. *I must be dreaming.*

"Put your arms around me, Madeline! Keep your head out of the water. We're almost to shore."

Water. She was still in the water.

Madeline's eyes popped open, her suspicions immediately confirmed with a slap of icy cold water. She saw the weight around her shoulders was Colin, his mouth set in grim determination as he pulled them both out of the Thames.

"You came for me," she whispered quietly against his neck. She was safe now. She knew this with an utter conviction she had never felt before.

327

She trusted Colin, with her life, her heart, all her secrets. He loved her.

Colin dropped to his knees the moment they were both free from the water, Madeline held tightly against him. He didn't speak, instead forcing himself to take deep breaths in an attempt to convince himself that Madeline was alive. Colin would never describe himself as a fearful man. He'd faced down several terrifying moments in his life with a cool calm that kept him from fatal harm. But when he saw Rockford's carriage spin off the road and crash into the Thames...

He buried his face in her wet hair, inhaling the scent of her beneath the filth of the river. It had been the worst fright of his life, one he doubted he would ever recover from even if he kept her locked in a room for the next twenty years.

Madeline broke the silence as they both watched the top of the carriage sink into the dark waters. "Lord Rockford, he...he didn't get out."

"The diamond." She spoke again through chattering teeth. "The French Blue. Lord Rockford had it all this time. He was the one who hired Moore to follow me, and he sent men to attack you." She broke off, clinging to him as her tears fell.

"I know," Colin said, anger deepening his voice. "When Rockford pulled you into the carriage, I saw Moore driving. That's when I knew you were in terrible danger. I knew Rockford was the man we were looking for."

"And you followed me," she said, lifting herself up until they were eye to eye. "I said such horrible things to you. I told you I never wished to see you again."

He gently brushed the tears from her cheek. "I was coming to beg for your forgiveness." He paused, trying to recall how Edward had put it. "To profess my love at your feet. But when I saw you with

Rockford..." He stopped, the anguish of those brief moments still fresh in his mind. "I knew then what it was to lose all sense of hope."

"You thought I was running away with him!" she exclaimed. "That I had betrayed you, just like Juliana."

He shrugged, no longer wishing to dwell on the past.

"And you followed me anyway," she continued, staring at him in confusion. "Even though you thought I had run off with another man, you still came after me. Why?"

"There was a glimpse of something in your face when you saw me. You looked happy, relieved." He struggled to describe it. "I followed that look, praying I wasn't too late."

And I nearly was. He glanced toward the wrecked carriage. Not a soul had stirred from it. Both Moore and Rockford appeared to be forever trapped beneath the water.

Madeline followed his gaze. "The French Blue!" she suddenly exclaimed, urgently grasping his hand. "Lord Rockford had it when we crashed. It must still be there!"

"Good," Colin said, pulling her closer. "You finally managed to get rid of the damn thing."

They stayed quiet, watching until the carriage was no longer visible in the night, feeling a warm sense of peace despite the bone-curdling chill of the wind on their damp clothes.

"It's done," Madeline said, softly. "I have fulfilled Papa's wishes at last."

She was shaking, and Colin knew he must get her home quickly. He started to stand with her still in his arms when she suddenly jerked against him.

"You said you were in love with me," she nearly shouted. "Did you mean it?"

"Every word," he said, grinning down at her. "I

would have gone into hell for you, Madeline." He kissed her then. Despite their wet clothes and her violent shivering, he could not help but pull her to him, crushing her lips against his own to tell her what was in his heart. She returned his embrace with fervor, startling him with the new passion that had emerged from his vow.

****

"It was me he wanted." Madeline whispered her dark confession into Colin's chest as he gingerly lifted her to the ground.

Colin didn't reply; he only stopped outside the door to Aunt Cecilia's townhouse and waited.

"Moore stole the French Blue, but Lord Rockford didn't know anything about it until then. It was me he really wanted. He was obsessed." She spoke rapidly, the sudden torrent of words falling from her lips, drenching them both. "It was my mother...he loved her, Colin, truly loved her, and since he could not have her again..."

"He took you," Colin finished softly, his voice shaking in anger. "Try not to talk now."

But Madeline ignored him, babbling on uncontrollably, utterly unable to cease. Was this what it was to be hysterical? She certainly felt strange, numb and overwrought at the same time, practically shredding Colin's lovely white shirt between her fingers. She had never been one to fall prey to hysterics. Papa always said his daughter had been blessed with too stout a mind for such nonsense. No, she certainly was not hysterical in the least. She told Colin all of this and more, certain he would understand.

"And I asked Lord Rockford for help, but only to get my diamond back. I was desperate to find it, to destroy the curse, you see. I felt it was the only way." She paused abruptly.

He looked blank. "For what?"

"For us to be together."

Madeline spoke simply, all the hurt and anger from earlier melting away under Colin's tender gaze.

"I love you," she whispered, tracing the line of his strong, beautiful cheekbones with her finger. *My Adonis*, she remembered, smiling to herself.

"And I love you," he replied, capturing her with a smoldering gaze. "Curse or no curse, I will never let you go again."

A loud, splintering sound separated them with a jolt. Madeline turned to the door in time to see it ripped open, and she and Colin jumped back like scurrying mice.

"I've found them!" It was Edward, his boyish features marred by concern and relief.

And then Madeline spotted the figures behind him.

"Mama, you must calm yourself! I'm sure Madeline has a good explanation."

"How can one possibly explain spending the entire night out with a man? There will never be a suitable explanation! And look! She is utterly drenched, and it's not even raining out!"

Helena and Aunt Cecilia both stormed toward her like angry plums in their matching purple robes. It was all too much—Aunt Cecilia's stern disappointed frown, Helena's pale mouth twisted in shock—even stout-minded ladies had their limits. Before anyone could utter another word, not even the smallest question or reproach, Madeline finally gave in to her hysteria by fainting dead away.

Chapter Twenty-Two

"It's my fault, Mama, I am to blame! Madeline told me all about her father's diamond, and now I've killed her!"

Colin held Madeline in his arms, cradling her like glass while patiently waiting for her to finish her faint. She looked terribly young and vulnerable, her bare feet peeking out from beneath the ugly grey serge dress. He smoothed the dark strands of hair spilling over her left shoulder, wishing for nothing more than to whisk her away somewhere safe...and quiet.

"It's all my fault!" Helena sobbed. "It was my idea to steal Mama's carriage and ride to Lord Douglas's townhouse, and it was I who told Madeline she should smash her diamond instead of tossing it into the Thames."

"Helena, what are you talking about? What diamond?" Lady Milburg asked, overcome with confusion, but her daughter was too deeply embroiled in her confessions to respond.

"And the turbans!" Helena cried out. "It was Madeline's idea to throw the turbans into the fire, but she was only trying to cheer me up after Lord Montgomery broke my heart, and honestly I was happy she did it!"

"At what time was I responsible for breaking your heart?" Edward demanded.

"Madeline threw our turbans into the fire?" Lady Milburg gasped. "Our lovely purple turbans I had made especially for Huntington's masquerade ball?"

Staring at the still unconscious woman in his arms, Colin wondered what else she had been up to.

"They were truly hideous, Mama. We had no choice," Helena sniffed.

"I've heard enough." Lady Milburg marched past her daughter, pulling a bottle of smelling salts from her pocket and proceeding to shove it under Madeline's nose. "Lord Douglas, kindly remove your hands from my niece. She is not properly attired for your comforts."

Colin ignored the order, stroking his thumb across Madeline's cheek as her eyelids slowly fluttered open.

"I will not be ignored this time, Helena," he heard Edward persisting. "What the devil do you mean, to say I broke your heart?"

Madeline was fully awake now. She opened one eye, recalled where she was, and promptly shut it again.

"You're going to have to wake up sometime," Colin informed her, and she managed to frown at him, even with her eyes closed.

"Do something about Helena and Edward," she whispered, barely moving her lips.

"I meant nothing, Lord Montgomery," Helena snapped. "I am very upset and have no time to discuss your sins."

"What sins?" Edward cried out defensively. "I demand to be told of my own sins."

"Colin!" Madeline hissed louder, opening one eye to glare at him, but he merely shook his head.

"You have no cause for your censure of me. I have been nothing but charming since the moment I met you, Helena!"

"That is precisely the problem, Edward." Madeline finally acknowledged her awakened status by sitting up and slapping Colin's hands away. "You have charmed Helena so well she has fallen in love with you. And since you will be leaving soon, you can understand her pain, can you not?"

With a cry of joy, Helena threw herself into her cousin's arms, sobbing apologies against her shoulder.

Colin stood up, placing one hand possessively on Madeline's elbow, the only place her cousin was not crying upon, it seemed. "I believe an explanation is due."

"I completely agree," Lady Milburg announced in reply. "And I must say this explanation of yours had better include an *immediate* marriage." Her gaze moved over their wet, clinging clothes to narrow in on Colin's hand possessively clutching her niece. "Or I have no wish to hear it."

Chapter Twenty-Three

"Go in peace." Madeline whispered the words to the warm afternoon winds, opening her palm to release a handful of rose petals in honor of her Papa and the mother she never knew.

She lifted her cheek to the sun and smiled, thinking it was a lovely day to be a bride. Spring had finally arrived in London, lifting Madeline's spirits with a freedom she had not felt since her father's illness began. Even her nightmares had ceased, and she knew her father was finally at rest.

Oh, Lord, she was a bride.

Madeline dropped the rest of the petals to the ground, jolted by the realization. In all her daydreaming she had nearly forgotten that less than an hour ago she had quietly married Colin right here in Aunt Cecilia's garden.

Soon to be her former garden, Madeline reminded herself, running an idle finger across the stone bench where her new husband had once kissed her senseless. Colin had generously settled all her aunt's debts, though they both declined returning to the Baker Street townhouse.

"Too many ghosts reside in that residence," Aunt Cecilia had informed Colin when he made the offer. "And I believe I will require something a bit larger than that old townhouse. After all, I still have Helena to provide for. Honestly! I believe she may live with me forever!"

Madeline laughed over her aunt's words, hoping in time the delicate attachment between her cousin and Edward might bloom into something more.

"So beautiful."

"What?" Madeline turned to see Colin, tall and unapologetically handsome as he approached her.

"I was commenting on you," he said with a grin. "Staring majestically into the clouds while destroying a flower." Colin laughed and pulled her to him. "What are you doing out here all alone?"

"Just thinking," she replied, nestling against him. "I was wondering if Helena and your brother will ever be as happy as we are."

Colin thoughtfully rubbed his chin against the top of her head. "It's difficult to say what the future holds for them. Edward has gone; his ship leaves at the morning's first tide."

"Did he say goodbye to Helena?" Madeline was stunned and saddened that he had gone so quickly.

"He said his farewells," Colin answered wryly. "So many times, in fact, that I had to drag him away before my mother insisted on a second wedding."

Madeline couldn't help but laugh. "Oh, that's terrible. I do hope Helena isn't very upset."

"I wouldn't worry," Colin said, gathering her closer into his arms. "Helena is not the only one who has fallen under a spell. I believe my brother will be returning for her sooner than you think."

Madeline pondered over this, but was soon distracted by the sudden urgency of Colin's kiss.

"And how did my wife enjoy her wedding?" he asked, releasing her breathless and dazed.

"She didn't," Madeline answered, continuing to kiss him. "I was terribly nervous. I couldn't remember what to say." She kissed him again, longer this time. "I much prefer the after-the-wedding part."

"As do I."

He took over then, swiftly settling them both on the stone bench out of view of the windows. "Do you think anyone will miss us if we dash upstairs?"

"Colin!" She was shocked, though desperately eager. "My aunt has prepared a very elegant wedding feast for us. We cannot disappear now."

He groaned, tossing a glance behind them at the house where Aunt Cecilia, in a high-necked lavender gown, was loudly encouraging her guests to drink more wine.

"I suppose not, but I'm warning you, Madeline, one more hour and I'm taking you home, wedding breakfast or not."

"Where exactly is our home?" she asked.

He drew a thumb across her cheek. "We can live wherever you wish, my love. I am fully prepared to leave my current townhouse. I know it holds too many memories for you."

Madeline shook her head. "The curse has lifted now. Can't you feel it?" She couldn't explain it, but she knew whatever evil had been following her, had been looming over them, was gone.

"I feel it, too," Colin admitted, wrapping his arms tightly around her shoulders. And they fell silent, each thinking their unspoken thoughts. Though her aunt and Colin's mother had insisted on obtaining a special marriage license as quickly as possible, it had still taken nearly a week. During that time the news of Lord Rockford's accident had quickly spread, and his body had been found, washed ashore and lifeless, to the horror of the London *ton*. Madeline shuddered at the memory.

But the rest was a mystery. Though an extensive search was done, headed up by Sir Bradley, not a trace of Moore or the French Blue diamond had been found. Madeline had felt nothing but relief at the news. The diamond was finally gone, buried deep beneath the waters where it could never harm another soul.

"It's over," she whispered, tracing the line of Colin's chin with her fingertips until he turned to her. Lord Colin, Duke of Douglas, her love, her husband at last.

He smiled down at her, the blue-grey eyes mesmerizing in the bright sun. "I beg to differ Madeline, my love. It has only begun."

Epilogue

The bell tingled softly, announcing the arrival of a new customer, and the man shrank from the sound, wishing no eyes upon him. Despite the early summer heat, he was dressed in a dark heavy coat with the collar turned up, hiding his face. As far as London was concerned, he was long dead at the bottom of that filthy river, and he wanted to keep it that way.

"May I be of assistance, sir?"

The clerk was not without suspicion, as he glanced at the strange attire, but was wise enough to observe that the coat and hat were of excellent quality, something only a well-to-do gentleman could afford.

The customer approached the jeweler, a small, neat little man with black hair and wire-rimmed glasses that he glared over from time to time. He nervously cleared his throat. "I have something I'd like to sell. A diamond."

"A diamond?" The jeweler had gotten a glimpse beneath the finely cut coat to the customer's dirty shirt.

"It's not just any diamond, mind you; a lot of people would like to get their hands on what's in my pocket." He leaned forward expectantly, patting the bulge near his arm to show he was serious.

"I'm not interested," the jeweler said, his friendly face now turning to a sneer. "I don't purchase stolen goods. Take your business elsewhere."

"I think you might change your mind," the

customer interrupted, opening the coat to reveal his prize, "when you see what I have to sell."

The jeweler stepped back. "My God," he breathed, unable to take his gaze away. "Where did you get this?" Gone was the thin-lipped suspicion, the distaste for the low-class customer. His eyes drank in the vision, greed removing everything in its path.

Daniel Moore smiled. "They call it the French Blue diamond."

A word about the author...

Jennifer is a writer and performer currently residing in Chicago IL with her husband and son.

Her short story *LOVER'S GAMBLE* is also available from The Wild Rose Press.

For more information on Jennifer's upcoming works, visit her at:
JenniferAnnCoffeen.com

Thank you for purchasing
this Wild Rose Press publication.
For other wonderful stories of romance,
please visit our on-line bookstore at
www.thewildrosepress.com

For questions or more information,
contact us at
info@thewildrosepress.com

The Wild Rose Press
www.TheWildRosePress.com

To visit with authors of The Wild Rose Press
join our yahoo loop at
http://groups.yahoo.com/group/thewildrosepress/

CPSIA information can be obtained at www.ICGtesting.com
Printed in the USA
LVOW122022010412

275410LV00001B/1/P